About the author

A. O'Connor is the bestselling author of nine previous novels including *The House*, *The Secrets of Armstrong House* and *The Left-Handed Marriage*, and is a graduate of NUI Maynooth and Trinity College Dublin.

Also by A. O'Connor

Acknowledgements

A big thank-you to the team at Poolbeg, especially Paula, Kieran and David. Thank you, Paula, for the inspirational cover. And thank you, Gaye Shortland, for the diligent edit.

For Phyllis

PROLOGUE

England 1988

CHAPTER 1

The murder trial was drawing to an end. The prosecution barrister Joseph Grady approached the accused. He was a man in his sixties whose commanding presence captivated the courtroom. Tall, with brown hair peppered with grey, his eyes were alert and challenging, set in a determined, distinguished face.

"Mrs. Thompson, to summarise the events of your husband's death. You say that on the morning of the day your husband died you left to stay with your sister for a week's holiday in Winchester?"

"That is correct."

"You say you left him on that morning, Monday the 8th of June 1987, and he was in a morose mood. Is that correct?"

"Well, he was always in a morose mood, but he was in a particularly morose mood that day."

"The next day, Tuesday the 9th, you received a phone call from your husband's brother to say he had received a suicide note from your husband in that morning's post."

"That's what happened," confirmed Mrs. Thompson and she turned to address the jury. "He explained that he could no longer live his life due to his depression and wanted to end it!"

"We are already aware of the contents of the suicide note, Mrs. Thompson. The jury has already read and examined it – the *typed* suicide note – and there is no need for you to tell them its contents."

"It's ridiculous that I can be charged with his murder. My sister confirmed I was in Winchester, the suicide note shows my husband took the poison himself and meant to –"

"All very well, Mrs. Thompson, and all very plausible." Joe walked up and down the courtroom. "You claim you never saw the suicide note or saw him typing it?"

"Of course I didn't. He typed it after I'd left for Winchester. I wouldn't have left him if I thought he was going to commit suicide, would I?"

"One would hope that you wouldn't, Mrs. Thompson. Now, it has been confirmed from the ribbon on the typewriter in your home that the suicide note was typed on it. It has also been confirmed that only you and your deceased husband had keys to access your home."

"That is correct."

"So let me ask you: did your husband ask you to post anything on your way to the train station?"

"I've already told you –"

"Just answer the question, Mrs. Thompson. I repeat: did your husband ask you to post anything on your way to the train station?"

"No."

"So you can absolutely state you never saw the suicide note, or the envelope it was posted in, prior to the start of this trial?"

"Of course I didn't."

"You did not type it or post it?"

Mrs. Thompson became annoyed. "I've already said it's nothing to do with me! The envelope has been checked for my fingerprints, and mine aren't on it!"

"As we've already heard, indeed they are not," said Joe and turned to address the judge. "My lord, Mrs. Thompson's fingerprints are not on the envelope, the prosecution confirms. However, using the most up-to-date scientific methods, we have done a DNA test on the saliva on the back of the stamp on the envelope and the flap. It matches Mrs. Thompson's and not her husband's!"

"I-I-" Mrs. Thompson began to stutter.

Joe swung around and looked straight at Mrs. Thompson. "Mrs. Thompson, why is your DNA on the back of the stamp of the envelope you claim you never touched or saw? Why is it on the flap of the envelope you claim your husband closed?" Joe's voice rose as he spoke.

"I don't know anything about such things," said Mrs. Thompson.

"Obviously not."

The courtroom began to erupt in talk.

"Silence!" demanded the judge.

"I put it to you, Mrs. Thompson, that you poisoned your husband on the morning of June the 8th, then typed the false suicide note, and the address on the envelope, making sure to use gloves so that no evidence of your fingerprints would be on it. You then went to your local post office, purchased a stamp, and posted the letter before setting off to your sister's in Winchester. And that is why your DNA is on the stamp and the flap!"

"That's not true!" shouted Mrs. Thompson.

"It's quite true, Mrs. Thompson. And the jury has already heard that your intention was to claim on the insurance policy you had taken out on your husband last year!"

"No!"

"I urge the jury to return a guilty verdict without wasting any more time," said Joe.

After the jury delivered a unanimous guilty verdict on Mrs. Thompson, Joe pushed the door of the courtroom open and quickly made his way down the hallway outside, followed by several members of the press.

"Mr. Grady, did you always believe Mrs. Thompson to be guilty?" questioned a journalist.

"Certainly – the DNA test just confirmed my belief," said Joe.

"This is one of the first cases to be tried using DNA – do you think it will alter the way criminal investigations are done in the future?" asked another journalist.

"I think we have just witnessed that it has and it will," said Joe.

"Have you any sympathy for Mrs. Thompson?"

"I never have sympathy for the guilty," said Joe, realising no matter how quickly he walked the press would keep pace with him.

He saw a Gents' toilet and decided to go in to escape the pack. He paused at the door and faced them.

"Ladies and Gentlemen, I thank you as always for your interest and now I bid you good day." Then he entered the Gents' and closed the door behind him.

He quickly went into a cubicle in case he was followed. Once he had locked the door he managed to start breathing properly again. He put his face into his hands and sighed with relief.

He heard the door outside open and two men walk in, talking.

"Well, what do you make of that?" asked the first man.

"Typical of Grady – always likes to pull a rabbit out of a hat – and usually at the last minute."

"If it wasn't for the DNA test, she was about to get off."

"Oh, I imagine The Footman would have tripped her up anyway over some minute but damning detail – he always does."

"Why do they call him The Footman?" asked the first man. "I've heard him being called that before."

"Well, it's because rumour has it he was a footman."

"What? An actual footman, as in a butler?"

"Yes – the rumours have circulated about him for years."

The first man burst out laughing. "Can't imagine him polishing silver and taking orders!"

"Well, you can never tell whether these stories are true or not. I remember, when I was at Cambridge, we had an English lecturer and rumours were rampant he was the son of a bus conductor – turns out it was completely untrue. Gave the rest of us a laugh though."

"Next time I see Grady I'm going to have to stifle my laughter. A footman!"

Joe's face creased in concern as he heard the men continue to dissect him.

A taxi dropped Joe off outside the building his chambers were in. He quickly made his way inside, took the lift up to the top floor and entered his offices.

"Congratulations, Mr. Grady – we heard the verdict on the Thompson case," said his secretary Sally Johnson.

"Thank you, Sally. Any messages?"

"Yes, several from your wife. You're to call her as soon as you arrive here."

Joe nodded and continued past her desk into his large wood-panelled office. No sooner had he put his briefcase on his desk and sat down than his phone rang.

"Yes?" he said, picking it up.

"Joseph, I've been ringing all day," said his wife Ann.

"I'm just back from court now, dear."

"I'm sure. Joe, you need to leave immediately or you won't be here in time for the engagement party."

"Yes, I know – I just need to make a couple of calls."

"*Now*, Joe! As Pamela's father, you have to give the speech!"

"Yes, dear."

"I checked the timetable for you, and there's a train leaving Kings Cross in half an hour. If you leave now, you'll just make it."

"I'm on my way."

"Don't be late." Ann put down the phone.

Sally came into the office with paperwork as he put down the phone.

"I just need you to sign these papers, Mr. Grady."

"Certainly, Sally. Order me a taxi for Kings Cross station, will you?"

"It's your daughter's engagement party tonight, isn't it?"

"That's right."

"Well, I hope you have a lovely evening."

"So do I," said Joe, looking dubious.

The taxi pulled up at Kings Cross station. Joseph paid the driver and quickly made his way up the steps. He glanced at his watch. It was ten to six and he was just in time for the train to Cambridge.

He sighed irritably as he joined the queue at the ticket counter. He quickly moved up the queue and then waited with barely controlled impatience as the woman in front of him made a fuss about the price of the fare to Scunthorpe.

Finally his patience snapped and he leaned forward. "My dear lady, the price of a ticket to Scunthorpe is as it is. It will not change. It will neither decrease nor increase between now and the time when you buy your ticket. Now either accept the price and purchase the ticket or kindly stand aside and let the rest of us purchase ours!"

The woman looked at him, startled. "How rude!"

"Indeed you are! Now is it to be a ticket to Scunthorpe or not for you?"

The woman pursed her lips and bought the ticket.

Joe quickly stepped forward, bought his ticket to Cambridge and made his way quickly across the station to the trains. He stopped suddenly when he saw the news stand for *The Evening Standard*. He stared at the headline on the news board: CASSANDRA FULLERTON ARRESTED. He went to the stand and picked up a copy of the paper whose front page was dominated by a photo of Cassandra. He started to read the accompanying article.

"Are you buying that, sir?" asked the newspaper seller, jolting Joe back to reality.

"Eh, yes, of course." Joe started searching his pockets for change but couldn't find any. He opened his wallet and handed the seller a large note.

"Nothing smaller?"

"I'm afraid not."

Tutting, the man started looking through his bag for change.

"Could you hurry, please? I'm rushing for my train," said Joe.

"I've only got two hands," said the seller.

"Perhaps then if you could use them a little more quickly?" suggested Joe.

The seller handed Joe his change and Joe tucked the paper under his arm and raced across to the train platforms. Just as he reached the platform for Cambridge, to his horror the train pulled out.

"Bugger! Bugger! Bugger!" shouted Joe as a railway attendant gaped at him.

CHAPTER 2

As the train ran through the English countryside, Joe picked up his newspaper and stared at the photo of Cassandra on the front page. He remembered when he saw her first so many years ago in the drawing room at Cliffenden. She had been wearing a gold cocktail dress. He had stood stock still, staring at her. Her back was turned to him as she looked out a tall window. Then she had turned around and smiled at him, saying, "Hello there! Are you new here?"

He was jolted back to the present as the woman across from him leant forward and pointed to Cassandra's photo.

"I hope they hang her!" she said spitefully.

Joe quickly folded the newspaper away. "Quite a misguided hope," he said, "as hanging is no longer an option."

"Well, I'd wish they'd bring it back for her!" declared the woman.

"Indeed, and you could be like one of the old crows who sat knitting, watching the guillotine come down on the French aristocracy," he said.

"I'd pull the lever myself!" said the woman, oblivious to the fact she had been insulted.

"It always amazes me the bloodthirstiness of people who otherwise look completely unexceptional and ordinary."

The woman frowned as if she didn't really understand what he had said but had at last registered that he was insulting her.

Joe opened the newspaper again and held it up, blocking her

from his view and cutting off further conversation.

Shortly afterwards, the train slowed down and came to a halt. Joe looked out the window and couldn't see a train station. They seemed to be in the middle of the countryside.

"*Ping ping ping!*"

The train's intercom suddenly sounded and the announcer coughed loudly. "*This is an announcement from British Rail. Due to an incident on the line we are experiencing a short delay. British Rail apologises for any inconvenience caused and we hope to continue our journey shortly. This ends this announcement from British Rail.*"

"Bugger!" said Joe loudly.

"Oh dear!" said the woman opposite him, smiling smugly. "I do hope you haven't anywhere important to go."

The 'short delay' the British Rail announcer promised ended up lasting nearly two hours. Joe frantically ran from the train station at Cambridge to a taxi rank and jumped into the first one available.

"Quick as you can!" he ordered once he had given the address. He looked at his watch in despair.

The taxi drove down a long tree-lined avenue. The houses on either side were large gothic Edwardian and Victorian houses on large grounds. The further the taxi travelled down the road the larger the houses became.

"The next one on the left," said Joe and the taxi pulled in through a large gateway and continued up a long driveway to a grand Edwardian house. The lights were on in all the windows and there were numerous large cars parked outside.

"Thank you," said Joe as he paid the driver.

He hurried up the steps of his home and braced himself as he let himself in.

Inside, the doors to the drawing room and sitting room were open and filled with smartly dressed people. He searched the crowd for his wife but saw only his daughter Pamela with her newly declared fiancé John.

"Darling, I'm so sorry! I missed the train," he said, kissing Pamela's cheek.

Pamela didn't look happy. "I said you would."

"Then the train I took was delayed two hours out in the middle of nowhere!"

Pamela looked sceptical. "John's father had to make the speech instead of you."

"I'm so sorry," said Joe. He turned and smiled. "Congratulations, John."

"Thank you, Mr. Grady."

"You're really too much, Daddy."

"I know, I have no excuse."

"Mummy is furious."

"I'm sure she is. Where is she?"

"Upstairs. Distraught!"

Joe nodded, looking ashamed. "I'd better go and make amends."

"You'd better!"

Joe walked through the crowd, smiling at the guests as they shook his hand and offered congratulations. He walked up the large staircase to the first floor and made his way down the corridor to the bedroom at the end of the house where the music and chatter from downstairs became faint.

The door to their bedroom was ajar and he went to push it open then stopped short.

Through the crack he could see his wife Ann in an embrace with a man, kissing passionately.

He peered closely and saw the man was Timothy Mason, a close friend of theirs.

"Oh, Ann," sighed Timothy, pulling back and looking at her. "Why do you put up with it? With him?"

"For the children, Timothy. I've told you before."

"But that's no excuse now. Pamela is getting married and George is off in California. They don't need you anymore. It's no reason to stay married to him."

"I couldn't put them through a divorce, Timothy. They would be devastated. And he is their father. Besides, there would be the scandal. I couldn't possible put any of us through the scandal. We'd be the talk of the place."

"So we just put up with the situation?"

She smiled at him and stroked his face. "It's not such a bad situation, is it? Joseph is away in London half the time with his work. He doesn't interfere with us. He certainly doesn't make any demands on my time."

"I just want you all to myself," said Timothy.

"But you have me, Timothy, any time, any place, anywhere. You know how much I love you." She reached forward and began to kiss him again.

Joe shrank back and rested against the wall. He then gathered his senses, and crept back down the corridor to the top of the stairs. Then he turned and began walking back down the corridor, calling loudly, "Ann! Ann!"

He entered the bedroom, smiling broadly. Ann was sitting at her dressing table.

"Hello, dear, I'm so sorry I'm late. I missed the train! And then the train stalled as there was an incident on the line." He glanced around the room and wondered where Timothy was hiding.

Ann looked at his reflection in the mirror as she combed her hair.

"You missed giving the speech!"

"Unforgivable of me, I know. But I believe John's father did a wonderful job in my place."

She turned around and looked at him accusingly. "It's your job to make the speech at your daughter's engagement party! Not John's father!"

"I know. I hang my head in shame!"

"I'd like to hang your head in a noose!" she said.

"I'm a bad husband and father."

"The worst!"

He came over to her and kissed her neck. "And you look radiant tonight."

"I look radiant every night, Joe!"

"Indeed you do."

"Anyway, let's go and join the party before everyone has left."

She quickly stood up and Joe thought he saw her eyes flick nervously towards the bathroom.

"Yes, dear," he said. "I just want to freshen up first." He walked towards the bathroom.

"No!"

"No what?"

"No, you don't need to freshen up. You've wasted enough time. You need to get down there and talk to our guests." She grabbed his arm and began to pull him to the door.

"But of course I need to freshen up, dear. I've had a long journey from London." He shook off her hand and headed towards the bathroom again.

"The toilet is blocked – you'll have to use the one down the corridor," she announced.

"Blocked?"

"Yes, blocked!"

"I must take a look at it and see what the matter is. Besides, all I want is a splash of my favourite aftershave." He put his hand on the door handle and began to twist it.

She rushed over and grabbed the hand on the door handle.

"You smell divine! You have no need of a splash of anything."

"Well, just a light spray then."

"Nor a spray!"

Ann and Joe's hands fought over the handle.

Joe stood back and looked at her. "My dear, whatever is the matter with you?"

"You! That's what's the matter with me!" she said and burst out crying.

"There, there, dear," he said, leading her over to the bed and sitting her down. He grabbed a tissue and handed it to her.

"You arrive in late, hours late, to your own daughter's engagement party," she sobbed. "Without so much as an apology."

"I said sorry!" He looked at her in mock sorrow.

"You left me with everything to do on my own – and now – and now – you are delaying instead of making your way straight downstairs and entertaining our guests!"

He smiled at her as his eyes twinkled. "Well then, we shall make our way down to our guests without further ado."

"It's the least you can do," said Ann and she stood up.

He offered her his arm. She took it and quickly led him out of the room and down to the party.

The next morning Joe and Ann were eating breakfast when the maid brought them in two newspapers: a tabloid for Ann, a broadsheet for Joe.

Joe began reading the front page which was full of the Cassandra Fullerton story.

"Well, I think last night went off alright, considering the minimal input from you!" said Ann. "John is such a nice boy. She's made a wonderful match. His family are among the largest landowners around."

"A nice boy, I agree with you . . . but I would have hoped for a little more for Pamela than just staying here and marrying her first boyfriend."

"Like what?"

"I'd have liked for her to have moved to London and experienced life there," said Joe.

"If it was up to you we would have all moved to London years ago!" said Ann. "But I'll never move to London. All our friends are here. I could never leave them."

He glanced up at her. "Indeed!"

"I hope George is alright. He never sent a message to his sister for her engagement."

"Perhaps he's joined one of those cults in California?"

"Don't, Joe! You know how I worry."

"Relax, dear. George is perfectly alright and will make contact when he needs his next instalment of money."

"You know there is more to being a good husband and father than just giving money!" snapped Ann.

"I know, but it does compensate for everything else that I do badly, doesn't it?"

"The worst thing about being married to a barrister is it is impossible to have a normal argument with you!"

"And the best thing is the money?" he said, smiling at her.

"Point proven!" she snapped in despair.

She opened the newspaper and started leafing through it as Joe concentrated on reading the Cassandra Fullerton article.

"I see you won your case yesterday," she said as she stopped at an article about the case Joe had just fought.

"Yes," said Joe, hoping she would be quiet so he could continue reading in peace.

"What an extraordinary woman! She laced his coffee with rat poison – imagine such a thing!" said Ann.

He looked up at her irritably. "I am aware of the details of the case already." He picked up his cup of coffee and took a sip.

Ann went to the front page and began to read the headline story.

"Have you seen all the fuss about this Cassandra Fullerton being arrested?" she asked.

"Yes, I'm trying to read it."

"About time they caught up with her," Ann said as she read on. "It's disgraceful what these aristocrats get up to. They should try working for a living like the rest of us."

Joe raised his eyes to heaven as he thought of his wife's life of cocktail parties and tennis matches.

"*Tut, tut, tut,*" said Ann as she read on. "Well, I for one hope they throw the book at her! She seems to be the most appalling woman. Handed every opportunity in life, and what does she do with it? Lock her up and throw away the –"

"*Will you be quiet!*" Joe shouted across the table, causing Ann to jump.

"Whatever is the matter with you?" said a shocked Ann.

"Can't you see I'm trying to read the damned article for myself? I do not need a running commentary and a character assassination from you about a woman that you've never met!"

"Well, I'm entitled to my opinion like everyone else."

"Not when it's based on some tabloid journalist's salacious gossip."

"I really don't know what is the matter with you. You're so . . . testy!"

"Well, you won't have to put up with me for much longer. I have to get the train back to London tonight," said Joe, standing up and folding the newspaper under his arm.

"Tonight!"

"Yes, urgent business with work."

"But you've only just arrived!" Ann was aghast.

"Can't be helped," said Joe as he walked out.

"And we have the Sykes' bridge party tomorrow night!" she called after him.

Joe made his way down the hallway and into his office, trying to put the thought of his wife in Timothy Mason's arms out of his head. He sat down at his desk, spread the newspaper out and studied the photo of Cassandra Fullerton. Getting up, he walked over to a locked drawer and, choosing a key on his key-ring, opened it. He began riffling through what was stored away there. Finding the photograph he had been looking for, he took it and went back and sat down. He placed the photo of the beautiful young woman beside the photo on the front of the newspaper.

"Cassandra," he whispered. "Cassie."

PART 1

Ireland 1937-1938

CHAPTER 3

Florrie Grady came rushing down the street of the village of Dunmore which wrapped itself around a bay on the south coast of Ireland. It was two days after Christmas and it looked like snow as she reached her home on the coast road.

"Joe! Joe!" she called excitedly as she raced into the cottage.

She found her seventeen-year-old son sitting at the fire, trying to keep himself warm. Joe had left school the previous summer but had been unable to find permanent work since. Florrie feared it might be the emigrant ship for her only child, which would have broken her heart.

"What's the matter, Mam?" he asked as he looked up at her, startled.

"Nothing at all, son! I've got wonderful news," she said, smiling broadly. "Dr. Kelly has told me that there is a position for you up at Cliffenden, starting tomorrow. Eight sharp."

"What?" Joe's head was in a spin at the news. His mother had been the housekeeper at Dr. Kelly's house for years.

Florrie sat down beside him and grabbed his hands.

"Doing what? In the gardens?" said Joe.

"Not the gardens. Inside the house, as a footman," she said, nodding enthusiastically.

He pulled his hands back and started to laugh. "But sure I'm no footman!"

"Never mind that. Now listen to me. Dr. Kelly was up tending to Lady Dorothy over some ailment and she said they were short of a footman as the last one had been caught stealing and had to be dismissed on the spot. She said they were in a terrible – eh, 'pickle' was the word she used . . . as it is in between Christmas and New Year and the agency in Dublin wouldn't be able to send them a new footman until January, and what were they going to do between now and then, and them having loads of guests at New Year? And so Dr. Kelly said he knew an 'exceptional' – that was the word he used – young man who could fill in for them. You!"

"But, Mam, I know nothing about being a footman, or working in a house like that." Joe looked petrified.

"Dr. Kelly explained all that and Lady Dorothy said as long as you looked the part and didn't show them up totally, you'll do!"

"But, Mam, I wouldn't know what to say around those people." Joe was terrified and excited all at the same time.

"You say nothing, son! You do as you're told, look handsome, and smile a lot. Smiling can get you through life when you've nothing to say, you know."

"And how long is the job for?" asked Joe.

"Dr. Kelly said just for a few days until they get a proper footman in January. But, son, if you impress them and they like you, they might keep you on in the gardens or stables or something. Oh, son, it's a great chance for you!" She smiled delightedly.

He stood up and looked at himself in the mirror.

"I'd better scrub myself up," he said.

"You at Cliffenden, Joe! I'd never have dreamed it!"

The next morning Joe made his way from the village and up the road along the coast that led to Cliffenden. It had begun to snow and there was a light dusting beginning to gather on the ground as he reached the gates, and began walking up the long avenue. As he continued to walk the imposing house came into view. It was a stately home that was situated near the cliff's edge overlooking the sea. He had passed the gateway too many times to mention during his seventeen years of living in the village. Sometimes he had crept into the grounds and stared up at the palatial building, imagining the lifestyle that existed in there, fuelled by overhearing the gossip that buzzed through the village about the place. He never thought he would step into the gardens, let alone into the house. As the snow began to pelt down heavier, he fought the overwhelming desire to turn and head to the safety of his small cosy home. The only thing stopping him was the look of disappointment that would be on his mother's face. He breathed in deeply, pulled his overcoat tight around him and walked on.

As he approached the house, it loomed even bigger before him.

He hadn't a clue what to do. His mother had told him he was to ask for a Mr. Bruton. But where could he find this Mr. Bruton in a house so large?

He spotted a man tying up a fir tree with rope, into a cone shape, to stop the branches being laden with the falling snow and breaking from the load. Joe had seen the gardener in the village but had never spoken to him before.

He carefully walked towards him.

"Excuse me, sir," said Joe. "I'm looking for Mr. Bruton."

The gardener stopped and looked him up and down.

"What for?"

"I'm to start work here today – as a footman."

"You're Florrie Grady's boy, aren't you?"

"Yes, sir."

"And what do you know about being a footman?"

Joe felt himself go bright red as the gardener looked incredulously at him.

"Go up to the back of the house. You'll find the door to the kitchen there. Go in and ask one of the women to get Mr. Bruton."

"Thank you," said Joe.

He hurried past the gardener and towards the back of the house.

As he walked along the side of the house, he gaped through the tall windows into the large rooms filled with beautiful furniture. At the back of the house he saw women working in the kitchen and, steadying himself, went to the door. He knocked lightly, opened the door and stepped into the warm kitchen which was filled with delicious cooking smells.

The four girls who were working away at a large table stopped and stared at him. Although Joe had seen a couple of the girls in the village, he knew they weren't local. He had heard that all the household staff at Cliffenden were hired through an agency in Dublin.

"What do you want?" asked a woman in her fifties who was seated beside the stove in an armchair.

"I'm – I'm –" Joe stuttered.

"Well, out with it, lad!" snapped the woman.

"I'm Joe Grady – I was told to ask for Mr. Bruton," Joe managed.

The four girls at the table burst into giggles, making Joe go bright red.

"Well, why didn't you say?" snapped the woman. "Kathy, ring the bell for Mr. Bruton – and, the rest of you, get on with your work!"

"Yes, Mrs. Crowther," they all said in unison.

As Kathy rang the bell, Mrs. Crowther sat back in her armchair and took a sip from a glass that seemed to contain sherry.

Joe looked around the giant kitchen as he waited. It was decked out with dressers, some laden with crockery and others with all sorts of pans and brass utensils hanging from them.

The girls seemed to be doing everything from making pastries to plucking pheasants, while Mrs. Crowther looked on.

Finally a tall, thin, bespectacled man in his sixties arrived in, impeccably dressed, with a cross look on his face.

"Yes, Mrs. Crowther?" he asked.

"Your new footman has arrived, Mr. Bruton," Mrs. Crowther informed him with a smirk.

Bruton looked over at Joe and his cross features became even crosser.

"I see!" He sighed as he looked Joe up and down. "Well, I don't know, I really don't. They send me a boy with no experience and no cop-on by the look of him."

"It's only for a week," Mrs. Crowther reminded him.

"But what a week to thrust this on me!" snapped Bruton. "What's your name?"

"Joe."

"Joe what?"

"Joe Grady."

"*No!* Joe – *sir*!"

Joe felt himself go even redder as all the kitchen girls burst into giggles again.

"I don't know, Mrs. Crowther, I really don't. How am I to turn this into a footman in time for the New Year's Eve do? They send me up a lad as raw as a cabbage in the field, and I'm expected to scrape the muck off him!"

"Sorry, sir – but I did have a bath this morning," said Joe, causing the girls to erupt in laughter once more.

"I'm speaking metaphorically, boy, metaphorically!" Bruton roared, causing Joe to jump. "Follow me!"

Joe quickly followed the butler past the giggling girls and down a corridor. Bruton opened a door and held it open for him to enter.

Inside was a small office. Joe spotted a black footman's suit hanging from a press. Bruton took the suit down and held it up against Joe.

"Well, at least you're the same size as the last footman. Put that suit on and come and meet me in my office, two doors down. You can leave your own clothes in that press for the moment."

Bruton left. Joe closed over the door and inspected the suit. He had never seen such a suit before and was frightened to handle it, but realising Bruton would be waiting he quickly changed into it. As he went to leave the room he caught a glimpse of himself in a mirror and hardly recognised himself. The suit seemed to have transformed him. His mother would cry if she saw him. He quickly patted down his brown hair. Opening the door, he walked down to the office and saw Bruton working on papers at his desk.

"Sir," said Joe as he hovered at the door.

Bruton came from behind his desk and looked at him.

"Well, that's an improvement at least. Follow me."

He beckoned and Joe walked quickly to keep up with him as they went down by the kitchens and up a large flight of steps.

"Now, as you know, you're only here for a short while," said

Bruton, "so I am only going to show you the bare essentials of being a footman. Just enough to get us by."

"Yes, sir."

"The Fullerton family are of course one of the most respected families in the country. You do not speak to the family, you do not look at them, you do not stare at them, you do not even glance at them, you do not even breathe in front of them if it can be helped. Understood?"

"Yes, sir."

"The last footman stole gin from the cellars and then had the audacity to proceed and get drunk on it. If you steal anything I will throw you to the police and you will never see the light of day again. Understood?"

Joe glanced at him, trying not to let tears sting his eyes. "I've never stolen a thing in my life, sir."

"That is what they all say. And the likes of you have never been put in a place where there is so much temptation to steal," snapped Bruton.

"I don't steal," muttered Joe under his breath.

They reached the top of the stairs and Joe's breath was taken away as he stared at a gigantic hallway with rich carpets, furnished lavishly. A huge chandelier hung from the ceiling.

"As I said, you've never been in a place where there is so much temptation," said Bruton. "But I'll be watching your every move."

Joe quickly followed him across the hallway into the dining room and again the spectacle of luxury that greeted him stunned him.

"Now the normal duties of a footman, as well as household duties, would be to see to the eldest son's needs when he is in residence, as I, the butler, see to the master of the house. But you won't be here long enough to take on that role and so there is no point in me wasting my time training you in those duties! Mr. Teddy will have to do without! If I can just get you to be able to serve drinks without spilling, and open the front door and take coats without falling over, I shall consider I have done a wonderful job. Have you a steady hand?"

"Yes, sir."

"Hold both hands out," demanded Bruton.

Joe did as he was told and held his hands out. Bruton inspected them and seemed satisfied that they didn't overly quiver.

"It is also the footman's duty to lay the table – breakfast, lunch and dinner – but I shall be doing that and you can assist me," said Bruton.

"Yes, sir."

"Now, follow me to the drinks cabinet and I will explain –"

"Bruton!" came a woman's voice from the hallway.

"My lady!" answered Bruton.

A woman and man in their late fifties entered. Joe immediately recognised them as Howard Fullerton, the master of Cliffenden, and his wife Lady Dorothy. He had often seen them passing through the village in their car. He had stared at them as if they had come from another world, and now he was here in the same room as them.

"Ah! This is the boy that Dr. Kelly recommended to me, is it?" Lady Dorothy said.

"The very one, my lady."

"I was just about to enquire about the footman situation," Lady Dorothy said as she walked up to them, followed by her husband.

Joe stood stock still as Lady Dorothy walked around him, inspecting him, looking him up and down.

"Hmm – tall, well built, neat brown hair, dark eyes, strong jawline – yes, he does look quite well, doesn't he?" said Lady Dorothy.

"Passable, my lady," said Bruton.

"I think he's far more handsome than the last footman," she said as she peered at his face.

"Has he any experience at all, Bruton?" asked Howard.

"None, I'm afraid. The words 'sow's ear' and 'silk purse' are ringing in my ears," said Bruton.

"Well, look, it's short term, and Dr. Kelly has come up trumps," said Lady Dorothy. "As long as he stands there and we are seen to have a footman, that's all that matters. So many houses have had to get rid of their footman as a luxury they can no longer afford."

"You make him sound like a mannequin in a shop window," chuckled Howard Fullerton.

"Well, in a way, that's all he needs to be!" said Lady Dorothy.

"What is your name, boy?" asked Howard.

Joe stood still, staring ahead, too frightened to say anything.

Howard looked at Bruton, alarmed. "Can he not speak, Bruton?"

"Joe, sir, his name is Joe," said Bruton.

"I see," said Howard, bemused.

"Anyway, we shall leave you to it," said Dorothy as she led Howard out of the room with the parting words: "I daresay, Bruton, that if Cliffenden survived the War of Independence then we can survive a few days with a half-simple footman."

When they were gone Bruton turned on Joe. "Why didn't you answer when the master spoke to you?" he demanded.

"You told me not to speak to the Fullertons!"

"Except when you're asked to speak by them!" said Bruton loudly.

"Yes, sir, sorry, sir."

Bruton raised his eyes to heaven and headed towards the drinks cabinet. "Follow me!"

Joe's mind was whirling as Bruton swept him through a drilling of instructions all morning. Bruton's training was so fast and brutal that it was nearly impossible to keep up with it. Only Joe's quick mind and his fear of being roared at enabled him to take in at least half of what was being taught.

In the dining room: "You stand here unless I tell you to do something. If the family or guests address you, you answer politely."

In the foyer: "I will open the door and greet the guests and then you take their coats and luggage. *Do not forget whose coats and luggage belongs to whom!*"

In the drawing room: "I will pour the drinks and instruct you who to take them to. If you should spill or drop a drink *I will kill you*! Now practise walking with this tray!"

By the time the servants' lunch was being served in the kitchens, Joe's mind was spinning with the sound and demands of Bruton's voice.

He entered the kitchen with Bruton and saw that all the staff were already seated. The only other older person there was a quiet shy-looking woman by the name of Mrs. Farrell who was the housekeeper. Joe reckoned it was Mr. Bruton and Mrs. Crowther who ran the show at Cliffenden.

"Sit here beside me, so I can keep an eye on you," said Bruton, indicating the chair beside him as he took his position at the head of the table.

"How's he working out, Mr. Bruton?" asked Mrs. Crowther as the rich stew and potatoes began to be passed around.

"Shocking, Mrs. Crowther, shocking. I think we would be better with no footman rather than a half-baked one," said Bruton.

"Oh, it wouldn't look right, Mr. Bruton, not having a footman with all those fine guests arriving on New Year's Eve," said Mrs. Crowther.

As Joe began to self-consciously eat the delicious food, he saw he was sitting opposite to the kitchen maid he had heard being called Kathy earlier. She smiled at him and passed him the bread. He dared not smile back or say thank you.

"Fred Astaire was a guest here last summer," said Kathy, who seemed to be addressing him.

"That's right," said Mrs. Crowther. "His sister is married to the Duke of Devonshire and he's a regular visitor to their estate up the road in Lismore."

"He arrived in a Rolls Royce," said Kathy. "We all crept up the stairs to get a glimpse of him. He danced with Miss Cassie. Such a sight!"

Joe managed a quick smile at her and then concentrated on his food.

"Any sign of Miss Cassie back from Dublin yet, Mr. Bruton?" asked Mrs. Crowther.

"Not yet. She's not expected till tomorrow. No doubt enjoying herself at the post-Christmas parties."

"And has Mr. Teddy been seen yet today?"

Bruton's face clouded over. "Not yet, I'm afraid."

CHAPTER 4

After lunch, Bruton left Joe in the kitchen with Kathy to show him how to polish silver for that night's dinner. They stood at the table as the rest of the kitchen maids baked and cooked.

"She hardly ever gets up from her chair," whispered Kathy, nodding over at Mrs. Crowther who was sitting beside the stove with a glass of sherry in her hand. "She just barks orders at the rest of us."

Joe nodded.

"I've seen you around the village a couple of times," smiled Kathy. "When I'm down getting groceries."

"Have you?"

"Where do you live?"

"Just in one of the cottages on the coast road. With my mam."

"Where's your father?" asked Kathy.

"He died when I was just a baby," said Joe. "He was badly wounded in the Great War and died a few years after returning home from complications with the injury. Just me and my mam since then."

"I bet this is a different world from what you're used to?"

"It is," nodded Joe. "Never could have imagined a place like this."

One of the bells started ringing.

"That's the dining room. It's probably Mr. Bruton looking for you, Joe. He's up there preparing for tonight's dinner," said Mrs. Crowther.

Joe nodded and put down the fork he was polishing before he rushed out and up the stairs.

"In here, boy!"

The voice came from the dining room. Joe quickly entered.

Bruton was busy laying the table for the night's dinner and broke off from this duty to go to the drinks table and hand Joe two bottles of wine.

"Place these on the sideboard in the drawing room," said Bruton.

"Yes, sir," said Joe, taking the bottles and leaving the room.

He walked across the hall and through the open double doors that led into the drawing room.

He suddenly stopped as he saw the figure of a woman in front of the tall window. Her back was to him and she was wearing a gold dress. The sun was coming in through the window and seemed to glow around her. She turned around and Joe saw she was a beautiful young woman. She looked surprised to see him and then smiled brightly.

"Hello there! Are you new here?"

"Yes, miss. I'm the new footman."

Joe knew this woman was the daughter of the house, Miss Cassie Fullerton, but he had never seen her up close before. He had only ever seen her drive through the village at frightening speed in her motor car.

She walked towards him from the window, the sunlight continuing to flow around her, making her seem as if she came from another world. He thought her the most beautiful thing he had ever seen. She had soft golden hair, fashionably styled, and blue eyes.

"What's your name?" she asked.

"Joe, miss."

"Well, I hope you're enjoying being here," she said, smiling warmly.

He felt suddenly moved. It was the first time anyone had looked at him as anything other than a curiosity or a nuisance since he arrived.

Someone entered the room behind Joe and, turning his head, he saw it was a young man in a satin dressing gown with tousled sandy hair. He looked like he had just got out of bed.

"Ah, you're back, are you?" said the young man, walking straight past Joe as if he wasn't there and up to the woman. He kissed her cheek.

"Yes, just got back an hour ago. I came straight from the party last night and drove all the way down from Dublin without stopping. I'm still wearing my party dress!"

"Well, it's been a bit dull around here since you've been gone, that I can tell you!"

"I've only been gone two days!"

The young man suddenly looked at Joe as if just seeing him for the first time. "Who is that?"

"That's Joe – he's our new footman."

Joe realised his mouth was wide open at the sight of the two of them and quickly closed it. He had never seen such glamorous people in his life. He didn't even think such people could exist.

Teddy came up to Joe and looked at him. "Well, I hope you last longer than the last chap."

Cassie went to the sofa and, sitting down, lit a cigarette as she crossed her legs.

"He was found sozzled out of his brain on stolen gin," said Teddy.

Cassie gave her brother an accusing look. "I'm still not entirely convinced you didn't play a part in that unfortunate episode, Teddy."

"Nothing to do with me!" Teddy defended himself.

"The poor chap was thrown out into the night without so much as a reference!" said Cassie.

"I hope you don't have a predisposition for gin?" Teddy asked Joe.

"No, sir. I never drink," said Joe.

"Never drink!" Teddy turned to his sister. "He doesn't drink, Cassie!"

"I heard him speak, Teddy." She smiled over at Joe and blew out smoke in his direction. "Very wise of you, Joe. It's the ruination of many a man."

"And woman!" retorted Teddy.

"True," said Cassie.

"So, as the new footman, you're to look after me as part of your chores," said Teddy.

"No, sir – I mean, sir, I'm only here for a few days till a proper footman is found," said Joe.

"Are you not a proper footman?" Cassie looked at him, confused.

"Not really, miss. I'm just filling in."

"Oh, what a pity!" Cassie looked disappointed. "I quite like the look of you."

Joe felt himself go bright red.

"Stop it, Cassie! He's blushing!" Teddy started laughing.

"*Joe!*" Their banter was interrupted by the sound of Bruton calling.

"That's Mr. Bruton calling for me."

"Well, you had better run along then, hadn't you?" said Teddy, amused.

"I hope Bruton is not bullying you. He's a terrible brute," said Cassie.

"Yes, miss, I mean no, miss," Joe said.

He looked down at the wine bottles he was still holding and went to put them on the drinks cabinet. But Teddy reached forward and took them from him.

"I'll mind those for you!" said Teddy. "Very thoughtful of you to bring them!"

Joe nodded before turning and hurrying out of the room. As he made his way to the safety of the dining room he could hear the brother and sister's laughter behind him.

That evening in the dining room Joe stood where Bruton had told him to stand as the family had dinner. Lady Dorothy and Howard were sitting on one side of the table while Cassie and Teddy sat on the other. Bruton served them as Cassie gave them all the news of their friends from Dublin.

"Sounds like you had a marvellous time," said Howard.

"Oh, I did," said Cassie.

"You should have stayed a couple of more days," said Dorothy.

"No, I was anxious to get home," said Cassie.

"Can't imagine why," said Teddy, giving her a knowing look.

"So is everything all sorted for New Year's Eve?" asked Cassie.

"I think so," said Dorothy.

"Who is coming?"

"The usual crew. The Steeles, the Dawsons, Lord and Lady Bilton, Wally Stanton from London –"

"Wally Stanton? Why is he coming?" Cassie suddenly looked displeased.

"Why wouldn't he? He's a close friend of ours," said Howard.

"He's not a close friend of mine," said Cassie.

"But I think he'd like to be!" sniggered Teddy.

Cassie gave him a warning look. "He's such a bore! He's so self-important, and so – *boring*!"

"You may find him boring, Cassie, but the rest of us don't!" Dorothy gave her a withering look.

"Who else?" asked Cassie.

Cassie listened as her mother fired off a list of familiar names.

"What about the Greys?" Cassie asked as Dorothy finished her roll call.

"Ah, yes, the Greys. I decided not to invite them," said Dorothy.

"Not invite them? But you always invite them!" Cassie looked concerned.

"Yes, well, that's the point. I don't want them to feel as if they are a permanent fixture on our guest list," said Dorothy.

"But why not? They always have been before."

"Oh, I just find them hard work. I mean, they have fallen on such hard times at this stage that they can't expect to be invited to Cliffenden and mix with us as if they belong. I mean they were never affluent, but they are the very essence now of the impoverished Anglo-Irish that give the rest of us a bad whiff. Their house is falling apart and they are down to just one member of staff. They are trying to still be gentry, when really they are not anymore. I think we'll steer clear."

"You can't just drop our friends because they are down on their luck!" objected Cassie. "That's terrible behaviour! Tell her, Papa!"

Howard looked at his wife. "It would be very rude not to invite them. We always have before."

Dorothy sighed. "Oh – if I must! But they really do seem to be becoming exceedingly eccentric. Reggie is getting deafer by the day, while Molly is getting dafter. As for their son Bowden, he hardly says a word. But I will put up with deaf, daft and dumb if I must!"

Cassie smiled happily and looked over at Joe. "Joe, fill my wineglass, please, would you?"

Bruton made a quick rush for the wine bottle. "I will do it, miss."

"No, Bruton!" said Cassie. "Let Joe do it. How do you expect him to be able to help serve at New Year's if you don't let him practise before?"

Bruton nodded and stepped out of Joe's way. Joe approached the table, lifted the bottle of wine and filled Cassie's glass. Then, seeing the other glasses were near-empty, he filled the rest of the family's as well.

"Initiative too!" said Teddy. "Who would ever have thought?"

That night Joe left the house by the kitchen door after Bruton had given him permission to go home. As his feet crunched on the snow under the darkening sky, he felt a little dazed. He had never had a day like it before in his life, never been in an environment like it before in his life. He felt like a fish out of water there but somehow he was drawn to the place like a moth to a candle.

As he made his way down the avenue, he stopped and turned to look back at Cliffenden. It looked a picture with all the lights blazing from the windows as it stood in the snow against the darkened navy sky. He could have looked at it for ever but knew his mother would be anxious to see how he was and so continued on his journey home.

"Well?" asked his mother excitedly as he came through the door of their cottage.

"How did it go?"

"I don't know, Mam. It's full of rules and regulations and that Mr. Bruton gave so many orders that I can't remember half of them!"

"All jobs have their rules, Joe – nothing can be done about that. Just try to follow them and not get fired!"

"I know, but if I could at least remember them then I could follow them!"

"Joe! You always have an answer for everything! Having a smart answer to everything is not going to get you a job in this life. Shutting your mouth and following rules will! Do you understand?"

"Yes, Mam."

She helped him take off his coat and looked disappointed to see he was still wearing the same clothes as he was when he'd left the house that morning.

"Oh, I thought I'd see you in your footman's outfit," she said.

"No, Mr. Bruton said I couldn't leave the house with the suit on, as I was only part-time and I might steal it."

"The cheek of him!" said Florrie, affronted. "Nobody ever stole anything in our family."

"I know! That's what's I told him!"

"Joe!" she said, sitting him down and wagging a finger in his face. "Don't answer this Mr. Bruton back ever again. Just nod and agree with him, do you understand me?"

"Yes, Mam," he sighed.

"So," she said, pulling up a chair and sitting beside him. "Tell me all about it – did you actually meet any of the family?"

"Yes, I met them all."

"Oh, Joe! What are they like?" she asked greedily.

"Well, Lady Dorothy looks very prim and proper and she speaks ever so posh. She doesn't smile much, but everyone seems to have great respect for her."

"Go on!"

"Mr. Howard has a kind face, but is very prim and proper as well. Their son, Mr. Teddy – I don't know what to make of him, Mam. He came into the drawing room at lunchtime in his dressing gown."

"No!"

"Yes, and the smell of booze off him would put Guinness brewery to shame!"

"He's supposed to be a wild one, alright. And the daughter, did you meet the daughter?"

"Miss Cassie, yes." Joe's smiled broadly as his eyes twinkled. "She's just beautiful, Mam, and so kind to me. She was the only one who spoke kindly to me at all. She was just after arriving back from a party in Dublin and had driven straight from the party to Cliffenden."

"On her own?"

"Yes, Mam."

"I don't believe it! Go on!"

"She was wearing a fancy gold dress the likes of which I never saw before, the same one she had worn at the party! And she just took out a cigarette and lit it in front of me! She had a silver cigarette-holder, and a silver lighter . . ."

CHAPTER 5

Mrs. Crowther placed the silver tray into Joe's hands.

"Now take this straight up to Mr. Teddy's room."

"But Mr. Bruton said I wasn't to bother with my duties with Mr. Teddy because I wouldn't be here long enough," said Joe.

"Well, somebody has to take Mr. Teddy's breakfast up to him, and I obviously can't send one of my girls. Place it on the table by the window in his room, then open the curtains and say: 'Breakfast is served, sir'."

Joe nodded.

"Then tell him to ring for you when he wants his clothes laid out for the day. You don't even know how to do that but chances are he will spend the day in his dressing gown and not want his clothes laid out at all!" Mrs. Crowther raised her eyes to heaven.

Joe hovered for further instructions.

"Well, off with you!" she snapped.

Joe turned and, steadily holding the tray, left the kitchen and went up the stairs to the main lobby before going up to the first floor and down the corridor to Teddy's room. He listened at the door for any form of activity inside, but all he could hear was snoring. He put the tray down on a sideboard and opened the door. Then he picked up the tray and walked into the room. In the light coming through the curtains he saw the table Mrs. Crowther had mentioned and placed the tray on it. He looked at the bed and saw that Teddy was buried under the blankets somewhere.

Joe went to the windows and drew the curtains before turning to the bed and saying: "Breakfast is served, sir!"

There was no movement from the bed and so he decided to say it again, much more loudly.

"Breakfast is served, sir!"

"I heard you the first time!" growled a voice from under the blankets. Teddy's head emerged from beneath the covers. "What time is it?"

"Nearly noon, sir," said Joe.

Teddy slowly sat up in the bed, shaking his head and rubbing his eyes.

"An unearthly time to wake a man. I had the most dreadful night's sleep. Could hardly get a wink. The howling of the wind all night. Why does the wind always seem to howl when I'm here?"

Joe wasn't sure what to say, so said nothing. There had been no wind howling the previous night to the best of Joe's knowledge.

Teddy climbed out of the bed, reached for his dressing gown and put it on before stumbling over to the table, tossing his hair with his hands.

"What have we got here?" he asked, lifting up the silver cover over the plate on the tray.

"Bacon and sausages and eggs, sir," said Joe.

"*Uggh!*" said Teddy, quickly replacing the cover.

He lifted the teapot and poured tea into the cup.

Then, aghast, he whirled around to Joe. "What's this?"

"Tea, sir."

"*Tea!*" roared Teddy, making Joe jump.

"Y-y-yes, sir."

"Why, man, are you bringing me *tea*?"

Joe felt scared as he saw Teddy's temper. "B-b-because Mrs. Crowther put it on the tray to bring up, sir."

"The old *bitch*!" snapped Teddy, grabbing the teapot and going to the window.

"This is what I think of her *tea*!"

He opened the window and flung the tea from the pot outside.

Cassie walked into the room. "What on earth is the matter, Teddy? I could hear you from down the corridor!"

"This is what is the matter!" Teddy's voice rose further as he shook the silver teapot. "He's woken me up and brought me a pot of tea, and – and – and," he raced to the table and lifted the silver cover, "and a lot of mush!"

"I see," said Cassie calmly before walking over to her brother, and taking the teapot. "Come along, Joe." She picked up the teapot and led him out of the room.

Nervously he followed her out and down the stairs.

"Ignore him – he's always like this in the mornings, particularly before he's had his medicine," said Cassie cheerfully.

She continued down the stairs to the servants' quarters and into the kitchen.

The kitchen staff jumped to attention when they saw Cassie. Mrs. Crowther quickly put down her sherry and stood up.

"Good morning, Miss Cassie, is everything alright?" asked Mrs. Crowther.

"I'm afraid not, Mrs. Crowther. Teddy is in a very foul mood as he wasn't served his usual morning beverage." She went to the sink, rinsed out the teapot, then placed it on the table.

Mrs. Crowther looked embarrassed. "I'm afraid I was acting on instructions to serve Mr. Teddy tea instead of his usual morning, eh, beverage."

"Whose instructions, Mrs. Crowther?"

"Lady Dorothy's, miss."

Cassie threw her eyes to heaven. "The time for Mother to take Teddy in hand was years ago. There's no point in trying to change his ways at this stage. Follow me, Joe."

Joe followed Cassie as she picked up the empty teapot and walked over to a larder. She opened it up, walked in and started to inspect the produce on the shelves inside.

"Ah, here it is," she smiled, taking down a bottle of gin. She then proceeded to pour half the bottle into the teapot which she then handed to Joe.

"Now, take this back up to Teddy. You'll find him in a much better mood this time, once he's had his medicine. He might even eat something!"

Cassie walked out into the kitchen, a bemused Joe following her.

"Just follow the same procedure every morning," she said, "and you'll have no trouble from him. Good day, Mrs. Crowther!"

Cassie walked past the cook, out of the kitchen and up the stairs.

"Where is Teddy?" asked Howard as the Fullertons finished their lunch.

"Still in his room, I imagine," said Cassie.

Howard sighed. "Does that boy never have lunch?"

"Hardly. He only has his breakfast delivered at noon," said Cassie.

"Well, I think now in the New Year we are going to have establish a few ground rules," said Howard. "It's two years since he finished at Cambridge and there's no excuse to continue this life of idleness."

"As I keep saying to Mama, you won't change him now. All you'll do is put him into a foul temper and make life dreadful for the rest of us," said Cassie.

"I don't know why you defend him," said Howard.

"I don't. I merely point out the facts," said Cassie.

Bruton nodded at Joe and Joe attentively began to clear away the dishes.

"Well, he had better bloody well get his arse out of that bed early tomorrow so he's up and ready to greet our guests," insisted Howard.

"Oh, he'll be up for that alright – he'd never miss a party," smiled Cassie.

"And I want you to be there to greet our guests too, Cassie," said Dorothy.

"Of course, where else would I be?"

"And be kind and polite to all of them," insisted Dorothy.

"Am I ever not?"

"Sometimes . . . Some of our guests have made a long journey and I want you to show you appreciate their efforts," said Dorothy.

Cassie looked at her mother accusingly. "If you are making a reference to Wally Stanton, then why not say it?"

"Wally is coming all the way from London to be here, so I think it would be very nice of you to show him you appreciate the effort he made."

"But I don't appreciate the effort at all. He's your guest, not mine. I will be perfectly civil to him, but I will not allow myself to be cornered by him and be forced to listen to his tedious tales of business for longer than five minutes, and that's me being generous . . . Anyway, I'm off!"

Cassie pushed back her chair and stood up.

"Off where?" asked Dorothy alarmed.

"Just for a drive into the village. I need to get supplies," said Cassie.

"You've no need for supplies, Cassie – everything is ordered in."

"I need cigarettes," said Cassie as she continued to the door.

"The snow is beginning to fall heavily, Cassie – you're not driving out in that." Dorothy's tone was insistent.

"Of course I can drive out in it. I drive everywhere in all weathers. I just made the journey down from Dublin yesterday and the roads were terrible."

"My point exactly. You take that automobile far too much for granted. You're an accident waiting to happen. I absolutely forbid you to go!" Dorothy's tone was so severe and agitated that Joe felt himself tremble.

Cassie held her mother's gaze. "I will be absolutely fine as I will take Joe with me."

Joe nearly dropped a plate as he heard his name.

"And what use will he be to you? I'd say he can't ride a bicycle let alone drive," said Dorothy.

"If I should veer off the road, he can push me back on. I'm sure you can spare Joe for a little while, can't you, Bruton?"

"If you can make some use of him, then I'm certain I cannot better that," said Bruton.

"Excellent, come along, Joe," said Cassie as she hurried out the door before her mother engaged her in any more discussion.

Joe looked nervously at Bruton.

"Well, get along, lad!" snapped Bruton.

Joe tightened his overcoat belt as they came out the front entrance and down the steps. Cassie had wrapped a fur coat around herself.

"It's not even snowing anymore," said Cassie as she made her way to the deep-green car. She opened the door and got into the driver's seat.

Joe had never travelled in an automobile and looked at it nervously as he sat in.

She started the engine and tore off down the drive.

"Reach into the glove compartment and hand me a cigarette, Joe," she said.

As Joe reached for the cigarettes he saw it was a full pack and realised she was not in dire need of a supply of cigarettes at all. Joe held the cigarette out to her.

"Be a sweetheart and place it in my mouth," she said, pursing her lips.

He hesitated and then did as she bid.

"Grab my lighter and light me up," she said, nodding to the silver cigarette-lighter in the compartment.

He nervously took the lighter and, reaching over, lit her cigarette up.

"I don't know what I would have done without you, Joe. She was determined to keep me prisoner in the house today under the pretence of bad weather."

"Glad to be of assistance, miss."

Suddenly Cassie took a right at a fork in the road and headed west instead of continuing down the coast road to the village.

"I think you missed the turn, miss," said Joe, worried.

She just turned to him and smiled. "It's your first time in an automobile, isn't it, Joe?"

"Yes, miss."

"Well, in that case, why don't you just sit back and enjoy the ride?"

They eventually arrived at a small manor house which Joe knew to be the Greys'. Cassie pulled in up the road under some trees and turned off the engine. Pulling her fur around her, she sat forward peering at the house. They seemed to sit there for ages as she hungrily drew on her cigarette.

Suddenly in the distance Joe saw a man walking towards some stables situated at the back of the house.

Cassie quickly stubbed out her cigarette. "I just have to run an errand, Joe. You stay here and mind the car. Shouldn't be long." With that, she hopped out of the car and walked quickly towards the stables along a pathway that ran through the trees.

Confused and alarmed, Joe looked on as Cassie disappeared from view.

Hours seemed to have passed by and there was still no sign of Cassie. Joe felt himself becoming increasingly alarmed as the sky was beginning to darken. He was absolutely freezing and blew constantly into his hands to keep them warm. He was terrified that something had happened to Cassie. He remembered Lady Dorothy's dire warning not to venture out that day and he was certain he would get the blame if Cassie had had an accident and slipped and fallen or something else had occurred. He decided he would prefer to leave the car and face Cassie's wrath rather than face Bruton's wrath if he returned home without her. He was just getting out of the car when he saw Cassie come hurrying along the pathway back to the automobile.

She got in and started up the engine. Despite the severe cold, she didn't seem cold at all.

"I was a bit longer than I expected to be," said Cassie as she swung the car around and took off in the direction they had come from. "You poor thing, you must be freezing."

"No, miss, I'm fine."

"What a trooper!" She smiled at him as she tore up the road back to Cliffenden under the darkening sky.

When she pulled up in front of the house, she turned to Joe.

"Oh, and Joe, if anyone asks, we drove around all afternoon together and went for a walk by the sea," she said evenly.

Joe nodded. "Of course, miss."

It was afternoon and the kitchens were empty apart from Joe who was sitting in a small alcove off the main kitchen. All the rest of the staff had retired to their rooms for a rest before they were on duty again in half an hour. As Joe had no bedroom in the house and it was too cold outside to take a wander, he had been hiding in that alcove during the afternoon breaks all week.

He suddenly heard giggles and peeped out to see what was going on. He saw Cassie and Teddy creep into the kitchen. They looked like naughty children as they glanced around.

"Is the coast clear?" checked Teddy.

"Yes," confirmed Cassie.

Joe hid further back into the shadows so he wouldn't be spotted.

"Oh, Teddy, do you think we should?"

"Of course we should!" said Teddy. "Mrs. Crowther is an old bat and she needs to be taught a lesson. How dare she swap my morning gin for tea! She doesn't do anything all day except sit down drinking sweet sherry, bellowing orders at everyone else to do her work for her. If she got up off her lazy arse and did some work herself we wouldn't have to employ half the kitchen staff we do!"

Joe watched as Teddy, who seemed to be holding a bottle, and Cassie made their way over to Mrs. Crowther's chair beside the stove. Teddy reached behind the chair and took out her bottle of sherry. He tiptoed over to the kitchen sink and poured three quarters of the sherry down the sink before taking the bottle he had brought with him and filling the sherry bottle with its contents.

"What are you putting in it?" asked Cassie.

"Paraffin," said Teddy.

"Paraffin! Oh Teddy, you'll kill her!" Cassie was more amused than concerned.

"We'll teach her to interfere with my gin line again," said Teddy as he replaced the bottle behind Mrs. Crowther's chair.

Then the two of them crept out to the hall. Joe continued to hear some muffled whispering and giggling and deduced they were hiding out there to observe.

A few minutes later Mrs. Crowther came into the kitchen from a side door. She was tutting and swearing to herself as she sat down and stoked up the fire in the stove. She reached behind the chair for her sherry bottle and filled her glass to the brim.

Smiling to herself, she leaned forward and took a large mouthful. Then her face contorted. She stood up quickly and spat the mouthful she had taken into the stove. The paraffin she spat ignited into a cloud of fire, causing Mrs. Crowther to scream in fright.

"Mr. Bruton! Mr. Bruton!" she screamed as she raced from the kitchen.

Cassie and Teddy erupted in laughter as they emerged from their hiding place. Joe watched in astonishment as the two of them headed back upstairs, arms around each other's waists, full of mirth.

CHAPTER 6

It was New Year's Eve and the snow which had been on and off all week was now pelting down strongly. Cliffenden had been a hurricane of activity all day as servants rushed around preparing the house for the guests' arrival. Joe didn't seem to stand still for a moment as Bruton barked orders at him. At least he felt useful as he followed Bruton's orders to a tee.

Joe was setting out glasses in the drawing room with Bruton as Cassie sat looking out at the falling snow at a French window, her parents sitting nearby.

"Oh dear, if this snow gets much worse, I'm worried all the guests won't make it here," said Dorothy.

"I'm sure you're worrying unnecessarily," said Howard.

"I'm not so sure. I hope Wally Stanton doesn't get stranded somewhere, after making the journey from London," said Dorothy.

"Hope springs eternal," said Cassie.

Dorothy looked at her daughter sternly. "I really hope you improve your attitude by the time Wally arrives. He's coming all the way from London to see you –"

"*Me?*" said Cassie, alarmed, as she swung around and faced her parents.

"Us, I mean coming to see us," said Dorothy. "The least you can do is spend some time with him."

"I'm afraid Mr. Stanton will give me no other choice. The last time I was in London he followed me around from lunch to the theatre. He had the most annoying habit of showing up wherever I was."

"You should be flattered. Wally is a very influential man," said Howard.

"I was not flattered. He's a pest," said Cassie.

"How dare you speak about Wally like that!" said Dorothy. "Do you know how many people would give anything to be his friend or acquaintance? I, for one, am very pleased he has chosen to be our friend."

"Well, then, you can spend the night entertaining him, Mama," said Cassie.

Dorothy looked at her husband and frowned.

"Just be polite to him, Cassie, that's all we ask," said Howard.

"Am I not polite to everyone? I can't see why I would be any different with him. It's Teddy you need to warn to be polite!"

"I don't think anybody is too bothered about how Teddy behaves anymore – he's past redemption," sighed Howard.

"Did I hear somebody mention my name?" asked Teddy as he strolled into the drawing room, already dressed immaculately in a tuxedo.

"You are all dressed up very early," said Howard.

"Can't let the side down, Papa." Teddy smirked at his sister as he went to the drinks table Bruton and Joe were laying out and, taking a crystal glass, filled it with wine from one of the decanters.

"You look very smart, Teddy." Dorothy smiled at him indulgently.

"And I think I'd better go and have my bath and dress for this evening, as well," said Cassie as she rose up from her seat. She kissed Teddy's cheek and walked out.

Joe was so engrossed in watching them that he almost didn't hear Bruton order him to take the empty trays down to the kitchen. Joe nodded, picked up the trays and walked out into the foyer.

Cassie was beginning to climb the stairs.

"Oh, Joe! Come here a second." She beckoned and he rushed over to her. "Joe, you're in a position to do me a great favour tonight."

"Anything, miss."

"There's a guest coming tonight called Wally Stanton. You really can't miss him – he can be quite loud and has an American accent. Anyway, if you should see me in conversation with him for longer than five minutes, will you just come over to me and tell me there's an urgent telephone call for me?"

"An urgent telephone call," Joe repeated.

"That's right. Keep a watch, will you, and time it. No longer than five minutes left alone with him, alright?"

"Certainly, miss."

"You're a darling, I don't how I managed before you came here!" she said, smiling at him and then continuing up the stairs.

The automobiles started to arrive at six, an array of expensive vehicles delivering stylishly dressed guests. As much as Joe disliked being in Bruton's company, he was overwhelmed by the sight of so many sophisticated people and clung to his side, grateful for the instructions being barked at him by the butler who seemed to know exactly how to address everybody and what to do.

"Good evening, Bruton, good to see you again," said a woman in her fifties.

"Good evening, Lady Bilton, welcome back to Cliffenden," said Bruton, smiling as he took the woman's fur.

"We weren't sure we were even going to make it, Bruton – the weather is shocking," said the man accompanying her as he took off his top hat and handed it to Bruton.

"Indeed, Lord Bilton, the snow is most inconvenient," nodded Bruton who passed their coats to Joe.

"Our chauffeur has our luggage in the car, Bruton," said Lord Bilton.

"We will take care of that, my lord, and have it taken to your room," said Bruton. "The family are in the drawing room if you would care to follow me."

"Very good," said Lady Bilton as she swept past Joe, giving him a brief smile.

Bruton delivered the guests into the drawing room and then came hurrying back to the hall where Joe stood holding the coats.

"Well, don't just stand there like a fool!" snarled Bruton. "Get out and help their driver bring the luggage up to their room!"

"Yes, sir," said Joe and went rushing to the door, then paused, confused as to what to do with the Biltons' coats and hats he was still holding.

"Give them to me, you silly lad!" snapped Bruton.

Joe quickly handed the coats over to Bruton and then rushed out the front door and down the steps to the forecourt where the Biltons' chauffeur was taking out the luggage from the car's boot.

"Ah, reinforcements!" said the chauffeur as he handed two suitcases to Joe and kept the third one for himself.

"You're to follow me," said Joe.

The chauffeur smirked at him. "I thought that might be the general idea!"

Joe turned and walked up the steps through the snow and into the house, followed by the chauffeur.

"Hello again, Mr. Bruton," said the chauffeur.

"Good evening, Mr. Evans."

"I thought I'd be waiting for some help out there till this time next year," said Evans.

"You'll have to forgive us, Mr. Evans – we have a new footman." Bruton made a face and raised his eyes to heaven.

"Oh, I see!" laughed Evans.

"Joe! Take the Biltons' luggage to the Blue Room," ordered Bruton.

"Yes, sir," said Joe as he hurried towards the staircase followed by Evans.

Joe paused and turned to look at Bruton, confused.

"What is it now?" demanded Bruton.

"S-sorry, sir, which is the Blue Room again?"

"For goodness' sake! Second corridor on the left, third door on the right! I went through all this with you today!" Bruton's temper was boiling.

"Yes, sir, sorry sir," said Joe as he hurried up the stairs, followed by an amused Evans.

"And Joe, once you have finished there take Mr. Evans down to the kitchen for Mrs. Crowther to feed him and then get back here as fast as is humanly possible as I see the next guests are already arriving!"

Joe felt tears sting his eyes as he hurried up the stairs.

Nearly all the guests had arrived. Teddy had set up his gramophone and music was spilling out from the drawing room over the laughter and chatter there.

Bruton came back to the front door where Joe had been left in attendance.

"Mr. Teddy is insisting on serving cocktails! At least it gives us a breather. Now, let me see who is not accounted for yet." Bruton checked through the guest book on a side table. "Wally Stanton is yet to arrive, and also the Greys," he mused.

At that moment the front doorbell rang. Bruton checked his appearance in the mirror, walked to the front door and opened it.

Molly and Reggie Grey were standing on the porch with their son Bowden.

Joe knew of the Grey family. As with most of the Protestant gentry in the area, they kept mostly to themselves. They appeared to live in genteel poverty up at their small manor house, the one Cassie had driven to earlier in the week.

He knew Molly to be a jolly woman, a slightly dishevelled, no-nonsense, stout woman in her fifties, who spoke in a deep voice and as if she had several plums lodged in her mouth. Her husband Reggie had been a captain in the Great War, and had been injured badly. He walked now with a severe limp and seemed to have a constant confused look about him. Having now witnessed the sophistication and glamour of the Fullertons, Joe understood Lady Dorothy's reticence about inviting them. They were not like the other people who were guests there that night.

"Here we are!" said Molly as she walked in. "Are we the last to arrive, Bruton?"

"Nearly, but not quite."

"No excuse really, since we live the closest. But a cow was calving and it was a difficult birth, couldn't get away," said Molly as she threw off her coat and handed it to Bruton. "Don't worry –

I gave my hands a good scrub before I came!"

"Nearly damned lost the calf and the cow along with it!" added Reggie.

"Quite!" Bruton managed to smile.

In behind them came their son Bowden. Joe had often seen him drive through the town. Bowden Grey was something of an enigma. It was understood that the gentry did not mix socially with the locals, but they as a rule were always chatty and pleasant, in that condescending way they were known for. But Bowden Grey never even seemed to smile. Joe had seen him drive or walk through the town, never smiling or even nodding to anybody. Whatever business he had to do he seemed to do it with the minimum of interaction. He seemed aloof and in a world of his own. Joe was even amazed that he had come to this social party that night, but figured he might be different when he was amongst his own crowd.

"Mr. Bowden, good to see you again," said Bruton as he took his coat.

"Yes," said Bowden whose dark eyes seemed to be searching the hallway as if looking for somebody.

"So – where's the party, Bruton? I need a hot whiskey immediately!" said Molly.

"Indeed. If you would like to follow me," said Bruton and led them to the drawing room.

Joe stayed at his post in the hallway, waiting for Bruton to bellow his next order at him. Suddenly he looked up at the staircase and saw Cassie elegantly walking down. He nearly gasped as he stared at her. She was dressed in a long deep-red satin dress that left her shoulders and arms bare. Her blonde hair was crimped back and a diamond necklace glistened around her neck. She paused at the bottom of the stairs and seemed nervous as she listened to the music and chatter in the drawing room. Then she walked over to Joe.

"Everything alright, Joe?"

"It seems to be, miss."

"Are the Greys here?" Her face lit up in expectation.

"Yes, they just arrived now."

She smiled. "I thought I saw their car drive up. Has Wally Stanton arrived?"

"Not yet, miss."

The news gave her an even more satisfied smile as she looked out at the pelting snow through the windows. "Well, I can't imagine he'll get here at this stage, not with that weather."

"*Joe, get in here and assist me!*" Bruton appeared at the drawing-room door, looking hassled and angry. "Oh, pardon me, Miss Cassie, I didn't realise you were there." He gave a warning look before disappearing back into the drawing room.

"We had better get to our posts, Joe," said Cassie, making a face at him.

Joe walked across the hall behind Cassie. She stopped a moment before entering the drawing room and appeared to steady herself. Then, smiling, she entered.

Joe saw Molly and Reggie Grey approach Dorothy and Howard.

"Well, well, Dorothy!" said Molly.

"Molly, so glad you could make it." Dorothy smiled falsely and leaned forward to air-kiss her.

"Wouldn't have missed it for the world – it's the only shindig we get invited to anymore that has a bit of glamour," said Molly.

"Only shindig we get invited to full stop," said Reggie. "Although my leg was giving me gip, so I nearly had to stay behind."

"Lord and Lady Bilton seem to have flicked us off their guest list for anything happening at theirs anymore," said Molly. "And I remember her when she was just plain old Sarah Potter . . . we used to call her Potty . . . amazing what a title can do to people's egos. Have they managed to marry their Felicity off yet?"

"Well, we're so glad you managed to come," said Dorothy, ignoring the question. "And Bowden . . . so nice to see you again." She nodded to their son standing behind them.

Bowden nodded back to her.

"Please do help yourself to the refreshments on offer."

"You'll be sorry you said that, Dorothy – Reggie has an appetite like a horse!" said Molly, nudging her husband.

"As long as it's nothing too fancy, otherwise I'll be up all night," warned Reggie.

"Plain fare, Reggie! Stick to plain fair and you'll be alright," said Molly, leading him off to the food.

"He certainly stuck to plain fare when he married her!" Dorothy whispered to Howard.

CHAPTER 7

Cassie was like a beacon of light as she walked through the party, greeting everyone with a smile and a kiss. Joe could see she was a very popular young woman, with the different guests vying for her attention. As Joe circulated amongst the guests with trays of drinks, he found it hard to keep his eyes off her as she effortlessly charmed them. And yet, as she chatted away to people she seemed restless, her eyes never concentrating on the person in front of her. After a while Joe realised the person Cassie's eyes were continually being drawn to was Bowden Grey. The tall, quiet young man who seemed to disappear into the background.

"No, Major, no plans to return to London yet," said Cassie as she spoke to a portly man. "But of course I will be sure to call in to you when I'm there. If you'll excuse me, Major."

Cassie edged away from him and walked across to the room, stopping and chatting briefly with people as she went. Eventually she reached Bowden Grey who was standing beside a French window on his own, smoking a cigarette. And, as Joe watched, Bowden and Cassie became lost in what looked like a very intimate conversation.

"*Joe!*" hissed Bruton, jerking Joe out of his momentary trance. "The doorbell is ringing! Will you go and answer it immediately? I can't leave with the party in full swing!"

"Yes, sir," said Joe, putting the tray he was holding on a side table and hurrying out to the hallway.

The doorbell was ringing incessantly by the time he opened the door.

"For fuck's sake! It's about fucking time!" boomed a loud American voice as a man stepped into the hallway from the falling snow, followed by his chauffeur.

"Sorry, sir," said Joe.

The man was large-framed, with blonde hair, in his early forties.

"I come all the way from London in this confounded weather, on these confounded roads, nearly getting killed on the way, and then am left to stand at the doorway for an eternity!" He shook snow off himself. He took off his coat and scarf and threw them at Joe. "Who the fuck are you? Where's Bruton?"

"I'm Joe the footman, sir. Mr. Bruton is in the drawing room."

"I'm surprised anyone else managed to make it here in this blasted weather."

Joe realised that this must be Wally Stanton. "All here, Mr. Stanton. We were just waiting for you."

On hearing his name Wally stopped for a second and observed Joe.

"Would you like to go to your room to change?" asked Joe.

"No, I bloody well wouldn't. If I'm any later I'll miss the whole bloody party." He turned to the chauffeur. "Take my stuff to my usual room." He turned to Joe. "I *am* staying in my usual room?"

"Yes, sir." Joe hadn't a clue if the room was his usual room, but Wally was so intimidating he didn't want to say anything to anger him. He knew there was only one room left unoccupied – hopefully it would be the room Wally wanted. "Would you care to follow me, Mr. Stanton?" he said, leading Wally across the hallway and into the drawing room.

Wally pushed Joe aside as they entered and took in the party in full flight before him.

"Wally! Thought you'd never get here!" said Teddy, leaving his gramophone and rushing over and embracing him.

"Nearly didn't, Teddy. The car took a skid and we ended up in a ditch," growled Wally.

"I daresay you've ended up in worst places, Wally!" laughed Teddy, taking one of his prepared cocktails and handing it to him. "Here, this will make you feel better."

Wally took the cocktail and downed it in one.

"And another one!" Wally insisted, handing back the empty glass.

Laughing, Teddy took another one and handed it to him.

Wally drank this one more slowly. "It's absolutely foul! What's in it?"

"Gin, rum, whiskey, vodka, vermouth – oh, and orange juice!"

"Is there anything not in it?" asked Wally, grimacing.

"Come, I want to show you all my new records," said Teddy, taking his arm and leading him over to the gramophone.

"Wally! You managed to make it!" said Dorothy, smiling broadly as she came forward and kissed him on the cheek.

"Couldn't let you down, Dorothy," said Wally.

"It wouldn't be the same without you," she said, beaming at him.

"Welcome back to Cliffenden," said Howard, grabbing Wally's hand and shaking it excitedly.

"Now come on! I want to show you my records!" said Teddy, grabbing his arm and leading him over to the gramophone.

Wally's eyes searched the room full of people as Teddy positioned him beside the gramophone. His search stopped as he saw Cassie in the far corner by a French window. He began to smile and then frowned as he saw her in a deep conversation with Bowden Grey.

Teddy was holding up a record. "Young Hilly Keane brought me this one back from New York. Can you believe it? You can't get this record anywhere in Ireland yet!"

Wally glanced at the record. "I brought you over some new records from London," he said.

"Really?" Teddy was delighted. "Well, go fetch them and we can put them on!"

"Send your footman up to my chauffeur and he'll give them to him," said Wally.

"Joe! Get up to Wally's room and get me my present – the records Wally has brought for me," ordered Teddy.

"Yes, sir," said Joe.

He put down the tray of drinks he was holding and quickly left the room. He took the stairs two at a time, though Bruton had told him he must never do that – he must at all times move in a dignified manner. He hurried down the corridor to the room he assumed Wally had been put in. There he found Wally's chauffeur unpacking his luggage. He breathed a sigh of relief: this must be the room Wally wanted.

"Mr. Stanton said I'm to fetch the records he brought over for Mr. Teddy," said Joe.

The chauffeur raised his eyes to heaven, reached into the suitcase and handed the records over. Joe went hurrying back down to the drawing room, terrified Bruton would notice his absence and shout at him. He went over to Teddy and handed him the records.

Teddy looked like a child on Christmas morning as he excitedly looked through his new records.

"Top man! I haven't heard any of these ones yet," said Teddy.

"All newly released," said Wally whose eyes were boring across the room at Cassie who was still deep in conversation with Bowden.

"Bloody marvellous!"

"Say," said Wally, elbowing Teddy, "who is that guy Cassie is speaking to? I haven't seen him before socially."

Teddy guffawed. "Of course you haven't. He's one of our country-bumpkin neighbours."

"What's his name?"

"Bowden Grey." Teddy took off the record that was playing and put one of the new ones on the gramophone.

"What does he do?"

"Nothing by the looks of him. He helps his father run that ramshackle farm, or what's left of it." His foot was tapping away to the new song. "Hey, listen to this! I love it!"

"And what's the relationship between Cassie and him?" persisted Wally.

"Just old chums. We've known him since we were children. We used to play with him, when Mother allowed. She doesn't approve of him."

"I'm not surprised." Wally nodded. "He's lowering the tone of your party."

"Is he?" Teddy looked up momentarily from his gramophone and looked over at Bowden.

"That suit didn't come from Saville Row," said Wally.

"Saville Row?" Teddy guffawed again. "They haven't a pot to piss in, let alone buy from Saville Row, Wally."

"Well, I think you should get rid of them!"

"Easier said than done. Cassie has a peculiar attachment to him and his family. She insists they be invited to events here at Cliffenden."

Wally's face went bright red.

Dorothy looked over at Cassie. She was becoming more and more annoyed.

"She hasn't even said hello to Wally!" she said to Howard.

"I'm sure she will in time," said Howard.

"I'm sure she won't! She'd be content to stay in that corner with Bowden Grey for the rest of the night, if left to her own devices. No – no – I'm going to have to intervene."

She paced over to her daughter and Bowden.

"Ah, Bowden, so lovely you and your family could make tonight," she said, smiling at him.

"Thank you, Lady Dorothy, we were grateful for the invitation," said Bowden.

"I'm sure you were," said Dorothy. She turned to Cassie. "Cassie dear, could you help me look after the guests, please? I've hardly managed to talk to half of them."

"They look perfectly fine," said Cassie dismissively.

"Regardless of that, Cassie, I would like you to assist me." Dorothy's smile remained but her eyes were steel. "I'm sure you won't mind, will you, Bowden?"

"Eh, no, of course not," said Bowden.

"See, Cassie, Bowden is a big boy now and doesn't need you holding his hand for the evening," Dorothy said, reaching out, grabbing Cassie's arm and pulling her away.

Cassie's face became sullen. Her eyes apologised to Bowden as Dorothy marched her away.

"You're hurting me!" Cassie tried to pull away from her mother's grip.

"I warned you before that you need to circulate tonight!"

"You were very rude to Bowden," snapped Cassie.

"No – if he and his motley crew of a family hadn't been invited, then that might have been rude. As it is he can avail of the free food and drink for the night and go home well fed and watered. To ask to be well entertained on top of that is a request too far."

They reached Wally and Teddy by the gramophone where Dorothy practically propelled Cassie at Wally.

"Cassie dear, Wally has managed to battle the elements tonight and make it to Cliffenden!" announced Dorothy with a huge smile.

"Most heroic of you, Wally." Cassie managed to smile at him.

"Cassie!" Wally smiled and stepped towards her. Embracing her, he kissed her cheek. He drew back and looked at her. "So very good to see you again."

"And you, Wally," Cassie said.

"Wally has brought me a gift of all these new records from London," said Teddy, gesturing to the collection on the side table.

"Generous as always, Wally," said Cassie.

"I brought you a present as well, Cassie."

She looked annoyed and embarrassed. "You really shouldn't have."

"Well, I couldn't have neglected you when I got Teddy the records," said Wally. "It's just a little something from Asprey's. Will I fetch it now?"

"No, no, Wally, don't trouble yourself," said Cassie. She glanced over at Bowden who was still at the window, looking out at the snow falling as he smoked a cigarette.

"You are always too generous when you visit us at Cliffenden," said Dorothy. "Isn't he, Cassie?"

"Too generous," said Cassie.

Dorothy looked at Teddy who was busy selecting the next record to put on.

"Oh, Teddy, give that gramophone a break, will you!" said Dorothy.

"Mother!" objected Teddy.

"Come, play a tune on the piano for us and sing a song," insisted Dorothy and she gave him a warning look as he was about to object further.

Realising that Dorothy was manoeuvring for Cassie and Wally to be left alone, Teddy turned off the gramophone and made a face at Cassie as he followed his mother over to the piano.

"Ladies and gentlemen," said Teddy loudly as he theatrically opened the piano lid. "By popular demand, or at least my mother's, I have been asked to sing a song!"

There was laughter and applause from the guests as Teddy sat down to play.

"Joe – a drink!" he shouted.

Joe hastily brought a cocktail over to him.

Teddy placed the cocktail on the piano and then ran his fingers down the keys in a waterfall of sound.

"Ladies and gentlemen – particularly the gentlemen – I'm going to sing you a little cautionary tale about falling in love," said Teddy and the crowd laughed.

He coughed loudly, took a swig of his drink and launched into 'Makin' Whoopee'.

Wally stood close to Cassie.

"You left London without saying goodbye," he said.

"Did I?" She pretended to be engrossed in Teddy's singing.

"One minute you were there, and the next you were gone."

"Yes – I think Teddy was having one of his crises and I just had to get back to Cliffenden to rescue him." She glanced at him and smiled before turning her attention to Teddy again.

"And we were getting on so well – in London," said Wally.

"Yes, you're always such a dear when I'm there," she said, smiling.

"When are you coming back?" he asked.

"Oh gosh, Wally, I hadn't given it any thought. I hadn't planned on making any trip anytime soon."

Wally's face clouded over. "Your mother said you were due over in January."

"Oh, I don't know what she's thinking half the time," said Cassie.

Joe observed Cassie and Wally from across the room. He remembered her command to him earlier. That if she was in conversation with Wally Stanton for more than five minutes he was to interrupt. He had kept one eye on the clock and it was now well over five minutes. But the idea of interrupting Wally Stanton filled him with dread, having now met him with his gruff no-nonsense ways.

He bit his lip and went out to the hallway, waited a minute and then returned and walked confidently up to Cassie.

"Excuse me, Miss Cassie," said Joe.

Wally looked angry at the intrusion. Cassie looked delighted.

"Yes, Joe, what is it?" she asked.

"It's the telephone, miss – somebody is looking to speak to you," said Joe.

"Oh, that's probably my friend Bettina Leslie – she said she'd call me tonight," said Cassie. "If you'll excuse me, Wally."

As Cassie walked past Joe towards the hallway, she winked appreciatively at him.

Out in the hallway Cassie picked up the telephone to take the imaginary call. She glanced back at the drawing-room door to make sure Wally hadn't followed her. Then she looked at her watch and hovered there for a few minutes, pretending to speak on the telephone. Feeling she had spent enough time hiding, she replaced the telephone and crept back into the party. Teddy had finished singing and was back administering the gramophone. She discreetly walked around the edges of the room until she reached the other side where she found Bowden still smoking alone, gazing out the window.

"I'm so sorry about that," she said, smiling apologetically at him.

"You've nothing to be sorry about, Cassie. I completely understand. Your mother doesn't want you wasting your time on me when there are important people for you to be with."

She looked down at the floor. "Don't talk about yourself like that, Bowden. You are as important as anybody else here in this room."

"Just not as rich then," he said, smiling at her.

"Drink, miss?" asked Joe as he passed them by with the tray.

"Yes, thanks, Joe," she said, taking two drinks and passing one to Bowden.

"*Cassie!*" said a voice beside her, and Cassie turned around to see her mother standing there. "If you could assist me with the other guests, please!"

Cassie sighed loudly in frustration and gave Bowden a desperate look. Bowden nodded to her to go.

Cassie reluctantly accompanied her mother away from Bowden and across the room to Wally Stanton.

"I was just saying to Wally earlier what a wonderful dancer you are, Cassie dear," said Dorothy.

"You flatter me, Mama – I'm mediocre at best," frowned Cassie.

"Nonsense," smiled Wally. "You forget we danced in London last time you were there."

"Indeed, how could I forget?" she said, smiling.

"You haven't danced once all night, Cassie – go dance with Wally," said Dorothy.

"You know, I've two left feet at the moment – I think I'll sit it out –"

Dorothy grabbed Cassie's arm and propelled her towards Wally.

"Nonsense! Off you go!"

Cassie glanced over at Bowden as Wally took her in his arms and swept her out to join the other dancing couples.

"Oh Cassie, it feels so good to have you back in my arms," whispered Wally as he gripped her tightly.

"I can't recall ever being in your arms," said Cassie, as she tried to loosen his grip.

"When we danced in Claridges, remember? Was it only just a few short weeks ago? It feels like an eternity."

"Oh, yes – Claridges," she said, nodding.

"You were like Cinderella that night. One minute you were

there, and the next gone," said Wally.

"That's me, Wally, completely unreliable."

Joe looked on as they danced. He didn't know what to do. Cassie had told him to interrupt if she was speaking to Wally for more than five minutes. But she never said anything about dancing with him. As the next song started and Wally seemed to have no intention of releasing her, Joe took one look at Cassie's distressed face and decided to act.

He steadied himself and walked up to them amongst the dancing couples.

Wally looked at him in confusion and snapped, "What is it now?"

"A telephone call for Miss Cassie," said Joe.

"What? Another one?" Wally was irritated.

"I am popular tonight," smiled Cassie, extracting herself from his arms. "Thank you, Joe."

Cassie swept out to the hall again.

"She never seems to be around when I telephone for her," said Wally, looking after her.

As midnight and the New Year approached, Wally was seething with anger. Cassie had purposefully avoided him for almost the entire night. He realised she had gone out of her way to talk to anybody in order not to talk to him. What had enraged him though was that her attention always seemed to be focused on this Bowden Grey.

"*Happy New Year!*" roared Teddy and the crowd began to sing 'Auld Lang Syne'.

Wally found himself squashed between two matronly women who held his hands and shook them energetically as the song was sung. Across the room Cassie was holding hands with Bowden and Teddy as she sang happily.

As the song ended Cassie turned to Bowden and smiled at him. "Happy New Year, Bowden," she whispered as she reached up and kissed his cheek.

Dorothy walked over to Wally and kissed his cheek.

"Happy New Year, Wally!"

"Yes – same to you, I'm sure." His tone was unpleasant.

"Is anything the matter, Wally?" Dorothy looked concerned.

"I feel as if I have made a wasted trip," he said, nodding over to Cassie who was again deep in conversation with Bowden.

Dorothy followed his gaze and became infuriated at the sight of her daughter in yet another intimate tête-à-tête with the Grey boy.

"You know I could have spent New Year's Eve anywhere, Dorothy. The Riviera, Paris, New York," scowled Wally.

"Yes, I'm sure you were not short of invitations."

"But I chose to come and spend it here with you at Cliffenden."

"And we very much appreciate the effort, Wally."

"I don't think all members of your family appreciate the effort to the same extent." Wally put down his glass of champagne. "If you'll excuse me."

Dorothy watched in concern as he strode across the room towards Cassie and Bowden.

"Ah, Cassie there you are!" said Wally loudly as he stepped between her and Bowden, elbowing Bowden out of the way. "Happy New Year, darling!" He reached for Cassie's shoulders and held them tightly as he leaned forward and planted his lips firmly on hers.

She was shocked as his lips bore down heavily on hers. As he continued to forcibly kiss her, she struggled to break free. Finally he released her and she stood there, dazed and embarrassed.

As if Wally only then noticed Bowden for the first time he turned around to him and said, "Fetch us two glasses of champagne, there's a good fellow."

Bowden stared at him, still shocked at the forced kiss.

Wally clicked his fingers in front of Bowden's face. "Didn't you hear me, boy? Two glasses of champagne!"

Bowden glared at him in stunned silence.

Cassie managed to regain her composure. "Bowden isn't a footman, Wally," she snapped.

Wally feigned surprise as he looked Bowden up and down. "Oh, I thought you were one of the new footmen. Sorry, who are you?"

Cassie stepped away from Wally and closer to Bowden. "Wally

Stanton, this is Bowden Grey, a neighbour of ours."

"Oh, I see! I thought you were a servant! " said Wally loudly, causing people nearby to look around. "It's the way you're dressed, you see. I've never seen a chap come to a cocktail party in a suit like that before!"

There were sniggers from the surrounding guests.

"Bowden is a neighbour of ours," repeated Cassie. "A family friend."

"Have we met before?" asked Wally.

"I don't think so. I'm sure I'd remember if we had," said Bowden.

Cassie glanced at Bowden and was relieved to see his face was cool and unemotional, showing no sign of embarrassment.

"You look very familiar to me," said Wally. "Did you go to Cambridge?"

"No?"

"Oxford?"

Bowden shook his head. "Neither."

"Yes, I should have known that. A Cambridge man wouldn't be seen dead dressed like that!"

More sniggers from the guests.

"I might have met you through work? I'm a banker. Are you in that line of business?"

"No, I'm a farmer," said Bowden.

"I see! We've got ourselves a peasant boy!"

"Wally!" begged Cassie.

"We might have met socially?" said Wally. "At Ascot or Wimbledon?"

"No. I've never been to either."

"Did you holiday on the Riviera last summer? I was there for eight weeks."

"As I said, I believe we have never met before," said Bowden evenly.

"Doubtful alright, if you've never even been to Ascot." Wally guffawed and turned to the other guests who were listening.

"I'm too busy on the farm to be able to get to anywhere much," said Bowden.

"Oh, my dear boy, you're wasting away here. You need to get out and see some of the world. Don't hide yourself down here. Get a job abroad – you might even be able to get yourself a decent suit and some style."

"Style doesn't always equal manners," said Bowden as he put down his glass of champagne and turned to Cassie. "I think I had better be going."

Dorothy, who had witnessed the scene, hurried over to them to try and diffuse the situation.

"No, Bowden!" Cassie objected. "There's no need for you to leave."

"I think there is," said Bowden before turning to Wally and nodding. "Mr. Stanton."

Cassie went to follow Bowden but her mother grabbed her arm.

"Let me loose!" snapped Cassie.

"I will not!" whispered Dorothy into her ear, squeezing her arm. "If you think you are following him, you are mistaken."

Cassie watched as Bowden walked across the room and disappeared out into the hallway.

"Seems like a nice guy. Not much to say for himself, mind you!" smiled Wally.

Cassie glared at him. "You were very rude."

"Me – rude? Never! Well, now that there is nothing here to distract you – shall we continue with our dance?"

"I've a headache coming on – I need to have a lie-down –" began Cassie.

"Telephone calls, farmer boys, headaches – I think we've used up all the excuses for one night, don't you? Now, in the words of the song Teddy has just put on – let's face the music and dance!"

Cassie glared at Wally.

Dorothy whispered into her ear. "Cassie, if you think anything of me and your father you will not make this scene any worse and will just dance with Wally! There are people looking on!"

Cassie glared at Wally as he led her out to dance and put his arms tightly around her.

Joe watched as Cassie and Wally danced. Loath as he was to

interrupt Wally Stanton again he remembered Cassie's request. He walked over to the dancing couple.

"You again!" snarled Wally. "What do you want this time?"

"Sorry, Miss Cassie, but there's an urgent telephone call for you."

"At this time of night?" Wally looked incredulous. "Now listen, you – why don't you just piss off!"

Joe blinked several times and went bright red.

"It's alright, Joe," said Cassie. "Can you tell whoever it is to call back tomorrow?"

"Yes, miss." His face burning with embarrassment, Joe retreated.

Finally the guests began to depart or go to their rooms.

"I really need to get some sleep," said Cassie to Wally.

"But the night is still young!" Wally objected.

"No, really, Wally. I've danced with you until I can dance no more," Cassie said wearily. "I'll see you in the morning."

Cassie walked out of the room without saying goodnight to anybody else.

Soon Lady Dorothy and Howard said their goodbyes and went to their room, followed by Wally and the last of the guests. Only Teddy remained up, listening to his gramophone while he drank from the mouth of a champagne bottle.

Bruton and Joe were clearing up around him.

"Leave that till the morning," growled Teddy drunkenly. "Leave me in peace."

"Very good, sir," said Bruton, discreetly raising his eyes to heaven.

Joe followed Bruton out to the hallway.

"Get yourself off home," ordered Bruton. "See you first thing in the morning."

Joe nodded. He went down to the kitchens to get his coat and left. He was exhausted as he got on his bicycle and began to cycle out to the front of the house. There was a blanket of thick snow glistening in the moonlight, but it had stopped falling.

He stopped cycling and looked back at the house. Just then a French window opened at the side. Cassie came out, dressed in a fur coat. He watched as she ran across the patio and down the steps to the gardens. Out from the shadow of a tree stepped a man, and Joe saw that it was Bowden Grey. Cassie went racing across to him and fell into his arms. Joe looked on astonished as the couple kissed passionately, the full moon shining across the sea behind them. He was transfixed by the vision before him. And then, frightened they might spot him, he quickly cycled away down the avenue to his home.

CHAPTER 8

Cassie walked down the stairs and across the hallway into the dining room where she found her parents and Teddy already having breakfast.

"Good morning, Cassie," said Dorothy as she sat down.

"Where is everyone else?" asked Cassie, relieved not to see Wally there.

"Most of the guests asked for breakfast to be brought to their rooms this morning," said Bruton as he began to serve her.

"Plenty of sore heads," said Howard.

"I'm surprised to see you, Teddy, at such an early hour. I thought we wouldn't be seeing you for the rest of the day," said Cassie.

"I never went to bed, been up all night," answered Teddy.

"I see," said Cassie, looking at the nearly empty bottle of champagne beside his breakfast plate.

Joe stepped forward and poured tea into her cup.

"Is Mr. Stanton having breakfast in his room?" asked Dorothy.

"He didn't request it, my lady," answered Bruton.

"Pity," sighed Cassie under her breath.

"I do hope you are courteous to Wally today," said Dorothy.

"Was I not courteous to him last night? He was glued to me like wallpaper," said Cassie unhappily.

"Well, you could try to look a little happier in his company," said Dorothy.

"Lie, in other words," said Cassie. "How long is he staying anyway?"

"He hasn't said," Howard replied. "There is always an open invitation for Wally at Cliffenden."

Cassie didn't try to hide her frustration as she ate her breakfast. As Joe looked on he could see her unhappiness and how the rest of her family were either oblivious to it or simply didn't care.

"Pardon me, my lady," said Bruton. "But, just to inform you, I have made contact with the agency in Dublin and they are sending down some interviewees tomorrow. If you could make time to meet them and approve my choice?"

"Very well, Bruton," said Dorothy.

"Interviewees for what?" asked Cassie.

"For the position of footman, miss," said Bruton.

"But we have Joe," said Cassie.

"Joe was only ever a temporary measure," said Dorothy.

"But he's been perfectly marvellous since he arrived, hasn't he, Bruton?" Cassie said.

"Eh – 'perfectly adequate' would be the preferred term, miss."

Cassie looked over at Joe. "It's stupid to go to the trouble of hiring an agency footman, when we already have Joe."

"Darling, leave the domestic side of things to me," said Dorothy.

"Joe's a treasure! We'd be mad to let him go," objected Cassie.

"He may be a treasure, but he isn't a properly trained footman."

"Oh Mama, you are being ridiculous! He's been wonderful at one of our busiest times of year. He picked everything up so quickly. He has the makings of a wonderful footman – with the right training from Bruton, of course."

"Cassie, Bruton has already set up the interviews," said Dorothy.

"Well, I insist he stays! And if you want me to be civil to Wally for the rest of his stay here, after his dreadful rudeness last night, then I suggest you allow Joe to stay." Cassie looked determined.

"Oh, Cassie, you are a pain!" Dorothy looked over at Joe, weighing up the situation.

"It does seem rather silly to employ another footman when we have one already here," said Howard.

"Oh, very well then," said Dorothy. "Bruton, sort out the arrangements to keep him on permanently, will you?"

"Yes – my lady," said Bruton, looking irritated.

Cassie smiled over at an astonished Joe.

"You're always picking up waifs and strays, Cassie," said Teddy as he emptied the last of his champagne into his glass.

"Good morning, everyone!" said a bright and cheery Wally as he strode into the room.

"Good morning to you, Wally!" Dorothy beamed at him as he took a seat at the table. "Cassie was just saying how much she enjoyed dancing with you last night."

"Really?" Wally smiled at her.

"Yes – really," Cassie managed, remembering her promise to be civil.

Wally reached into his pocket, took out a box and handed it to her.

"What's this?" Cassie asked, looked worried.

"It's the gift from Asprey's I was telling you about."

"You're so kind and generous," Dorothy said, smiling.

"You really shouldn't have bothered," said Cassie. She opened the box and saw a beautiful diamond brooch inside.

"Wow! That set you back a bit," said Teddy, looking over.

"I really can't accept this, Wally – it's far too costly." Cassie handed the box back to him.

"Of course you must accept it! It's just a small token of my fondness for you and all your family."

"Too kind!" beamed Dorothy. "Put it on."

Reluctantly Cassie took out the brooch and pinned it on her dress.

"So what's the plan for today?" asked Wally.

"We're going out riding later," said Teddy.

Wally frowned. "I'm not a good rider."

"Oh, don't worry – we've got an old nag you can ride on. She won't give you any trouble at all." Teddy smirked over at Cassie and their eyes locked in a secret understanding.

"Well, I really don't think –" began Wally.

"Oh do, Wally! Otherwise you'll be stuck in the house while we are off gallivanting," said Cassie enthusiastically.

Surprised and delighted Cassie wanted him to go with them, he smiled at her.

"Well, in that case, how could I refuse?"

That afternoon Teddy and Cassie were standing in the stable yard at the back of Cliffenden, dressed in riding outfits.

"Teddy – do you think we should?" asked Cassie.

"Of course we should! Either that or you get lumbered with him for the rest of the day," said Teddy.

"When you put it like that . . ."

"Hello there!" called Teddy as Wally entered the courtyard, dressed in a riding costume. "You do look smart, Wally. Doesn't he look smart, Cassie?"

"Very!" agreed Cassie.

"Your father lent me the riding clothes. I don't think they fit that well," complained Wally.

"Perfect fit!" said Teddy before turning to the stable lads and shouting, "Bring forth the horses!"

They brought out three horses.

"This is yours," said Teddy, taking the reins of a large black beast and trotting her over to Wally.

"This is the old nag you promised me?" Wally said, eyeing the animal cautiously.

"She's so slow she should have been sent to the knacker's yard years ago and turned into glue!" said Teddy.

"Well – if you're sure," said Wally as one of the stable lads helped him mount.

Wally looked decidedly uncomfortable on the horse.

"One forgets how high a horse is until you are on the damned thing!"

"You look a fine figure on her, doesn't he, Cassie?" said Teddy.

"A most impressive sight," Cassie said, smirking.

"We had better give you a head start, Wally, as she's so slow," said Teddy. "Take her out on a slow trot. Take it steady now – she's not used to the open countryside."

Wally nodded and, taking a firm hold of the reins, turned the horse and began to trot her out of the courtyard. But no sooner had they trotted through the gate when suddenly the horse took flight and started galloping. Wally ferociously tried to pull on the reins but the action only seemed to make the horse run faster.

"*Help!*" screamed Wally. "*Stop the bloody thing!*"

"Oh my word!" roared Teddy as he and Cassie raced across the courtyard and watched as the horse fled across the countryside with Wally holding on for dear life.

Teddy and Cassie collapsed in laughter.

"The horse won't stop till she reaches Dublin!" laughed Teddy.

"Hopefully!" said Cassie.

The stable lads looked on amused, well used to the Fullerton children's pranks.

At last, after Wally disappeared from view, Teddy and Cassie walked back past the horses and stable lads towards the house.

"Sir!" one of the lads called. "Won't ye be needing the horses for your own ride?"

"Of course not!" said Teddy. "It's far too cold to go horse-riding today!"

"Can't imagine why Wally wanted to!" laughed Cassie. "Take the horses back to the stables, boys."

"That's got rid of him for a few hours," said Teddy.

"You are dreadful, Teddy!"

Cassie was still laughing as they put their arms around each other and made their way back into the house.

Joe had been in a state of shock all day since the decision that he was to be made permanent at Cliffenden. It was too much for him to comprehend – that his whole life had been changed in a moment and because of a few words from Cassie. As he did his work around Cliffenden that day he could hardly believe that this was to be his new home, his new life. Bruton had brought him up to the attic bedrooms and showed him a room and informed him that this was his room because he would be expected to move into Cliffenden now he was permanent. It was like a dream. He had been so hypnotised by Cliffenden since arriving that he hadn't allowed himself to think that he would be leaving shortly never to return. And now here he was moving in permanently.

Bruton did not seem that pleased by Joe's appointment. He addressed Joe in the kitchen in front of the other staff as they got on with their work.

"You would not be my first choice as my new footman," Bruton informed him. "In fact you wouldn't be getting a look in if it were left to me."

"Yes, sir, sorry, sir."

"But you are being thrust on me anyhow. The world is changing, standards are falling, and you can't literally get the staff anymore," sighed Bruton. "But do not think I will be lowering my expectations or my standards, lad. I will expect you to be a first-class footman, if I have to kill you on the way!"

Joe remembered his mother's words and just nodded. He could see Kathy smiling happily at him as she kneaded dough on the table.

"You'd better get yourself off home and pack a permanent bag then if you're moving in," said Bruton. "You've got an hour and a half to get back here, and I'll be timing you."

"Yes, sir," said Joe as he rushed out the back door.

"I don't know, Mrs. Crowther," said Bruton. "What is becoming of the place at all?"

"We can only battle on, Mr. Bruton, and try and do our best with the hand we are dealt," said Mrs. Crowther as she sipped her sherry.

"But what a hand, Mrs. Crowther, what a hand!"

CHAPTER 9

Most of the guests had left during New Year's Day and that evening, as dinner was being served, the doorbell rang.

"Go see who it is," Bruton whispered to Joe as he continued to serve gravy.

Joe walked out into the hallway and opened the front door.

There stood Wally Stanton, dishevelled, with his riding coat torn and a dirty face. What's more, he looked very angry as he pushed past Joe.

"Where is everybody?" he demanded.

"At dinner, sir," answered Joe.

"I am going to my room to change. Inform Lady Dorothy and Howard Fullerton that I wish to see them in half an hour for a private talk in the library."

"Yes, sir."

Wally marched across the hallway and up the stairs.

"Who was that, Joe?" asked Lady Dorothy as Joe entered the dining room.

"Mr. Stanton, my lady. He's – he's asked to see you and Mr. Howard in the library in half an hour."

Cassie and Teddy looked at each other guiltily.

"Whatever about?" asked Howard.

"He didn't say, sir."

"Half an hour? We'll hardly have finished our pudding by then," said Dorothy.

"Oh, ignore him, Mama! Let him wait," said Cassie.

"He's been quite rude. Never even informed us he wouldn't make dinner," said Teddy.

"No – no – we shall see what he wants – I hope it's nothing serious," said Dorothy.

The rest of the dinner passed by in idle chatter and after half an hour Dorothy rose.

"If you'll excuse us," she said. "Come, Howard."

She and Howard left the room.

In the library they found Wally dressed in a tuxedo by the roaring fire, drinking a glass of cognac. There was a bad scratch across his face.

"Wally, whatever happened to you?" asked Dorothy as she inspected the injury.

"I was thrown by a horse, Lady Dorothy!"

"How awful for you! One of ours?"

"Of course one of yours!" Wally said crossly. "As soon as I got up on her she took off like a bullet from a gun across country. She didn't stop for miles! And finally threw me into a ditch!"

"How dreadful for you!" Dorothy was shocked.

Howard's eyes widened in amazement.

"I hadn't a clue where I was. And ended up walking for hours, in the snow! Finally I got a lift on a tractor that was pulling a trailer full of horseshit!"

"What an awful experience for you," said Howard.

"I am not a good horseman, as I made plainly clear and your – your children – assured me the horse they were putting me on was an old nag who would give me no trouble!"

"There must have been some mix-up in the stables," said Dorothy, sitting down and pouring herself a glass of cognac.

"There was no mix-up, Lady Dorothy. I suspect I was the victim of a practical joke by Cassie and Teddy. They didn't even come looking for me!"

Howard and Dorothy swapped concerned looks.

"I think you are mistaken, Wally," said Howard.

"Well, I think I'm not! Since I arrived at Cliffenden, Cassie has gone out of her way to ignore or avoid me."

"Another misunderstanding, surely, Wally!" said Dorothy.

"Did your daughter inform you about the last occasion we met in London?" asked Wally.

"Well, no," said Dorothy uncertainly. "She just said you were at a few of the parties she attended in London and you socialised together."

"She didn't tell you about the last night when we were at a dance at Claridges, I take it? She didn't tell you that I proposed to her?"

Dorothy's eyes widened in amazement. "No – no, she didn't."

"And what did she say – when you proposed?" asked Howard, equally stunned.

"She said nothing! She said she was going to the bathroom and would be back in a couple of minutes – and she never reappeared for the rest of the night! The next thing I hear is she's fled London and is back in Ireland!"

"Well, at least she didn't say no!" said Dorothy, whose face had become excited at the thought of a marriage with Wally.

"That might be the case – but most certainly she didn't say yes either!" snapped Wally.

"Perhaps she just needed some time to think about it," suggested Howard. "It's a big decision for a girl to make."

"How much time does she bloody well need?" Wally's impatience was bubbling. "There are plenty of young women who are lining up to marry me, I can assure you!"

"I don't doubt it for a second!" said Dorothy.

"She should be honoured that I have chosen her, I tell you!"

"I'm sure she is!"

"Well, she has a funny way of showing it – giving me the run-around." Wally began to pace up and down. "I arrive at Cliffenden and find Cassie in intimate conversation with this Bowden Grey, whoever the fuck he is."

"A childhood friend of hers, nothing more," Dorothy assured him.

"Well, it didn't look like that from where I was standing. Have I not been a good friend to you?"

"The best!"

"Has my friendship and line of credit not allowed you to continue to live in all this –" he gestured around the room, "grandeur!"

"Your loans have been very much appreciated," Howard said, looked worried and upset.

"Well, I can tell you that Cassie's behaviour is now testing our friendship to the very limit." Wally stopped pacing. "And I hope you understand that."

Dorothy sighed. "You are making that perfectly clear."

"Good! Then I think we understand each other," said Wally and he turned and marched out of the room.

One of the bells on the wall rang as Joe hurriedly brought a tray of empty glasses into the kitchen. He looked up at the bells in confusion, not sure which one had rung.

"That's the library, Joe," said Kathy. "You'd better go see to it as Mr. Bruton is trying to calm down Mr. Stanton's chauffeur who's having a hissy fit over something or nothing."

"Alright."

In the library Joe found Dorothy and Howard sitting, drinking cognac.

"Joe, fetch Miss Cassie for us," said Dorothy.

"Yes, my lady," said Joe.

He made his way across to the drawing room where Cassie and Teddy were leading different teams in a game of charades.

"Miss Cassie, your parents want to see you in the library," said Joe.

"Oh, but I'm in the middle of a game, and I'm winning!" said Cassie.

"Ignore them!" urged Teddy.

"No, I'd better go," sighed Cassie.

She got up and walked out past Joe. At the library door she braced herself and then walked in.

She could see that both of her parents looked stern and unhappy.

"Take a seat, Cassie," said her father.

"No, I won't bother, I'm in the middle of –"

"Sit down!" Dorothy commanded.

Cassie walked slowly into the centre of the room and sat down on the armchair opposite them. This had to be about the trick she and Teddy had played on Wally.

"Well – what's all this about?" she asked.

"It's about Wally," said Dorothy. "He's been to see us and he is understandably most upset."

Cassie tried to look innocent as she took out her cigarette case and lit a cigarette.

"Oh – what about?"

"You know perfectly well what about, Cassie. Why didn't you tell us the horse he was on bolted today?"

"I didn't want to bother you."

"Bother us! How could it not bother us?" Dorothy's voice was raised. "The poor man couldn't control the horse and was carried for miles and finally thrown into a ditch!"

Cassie stifled a giggle.

"It's not funny, Cassie! He could have been killed! What horse did you put him on?"

"Thunder," whispered Cassie.

"*Thunder!*" screeched Dorothy. "But not even an experienced horseman could control Thunder! Let alone a novice like Wally!"

"I'm sorry – I didn't think."

"You're not one bit sorry – it's as Wally said – you did it on purpose," Dorothy accused her.

"And what part did Teddy play in all this?" asked Howard.

"It had nothing to do with Teddy," Cassie said.

"I don't know why you feel the need to defend Teddy all the time," said Howard. "He wouldn't show you or anybody else the same courtesy."

They all sat in silence for a while, then Dorothy spoke again.

"Why didn't you tell us that Wally proposed marriage to you last time you were in London?"

Cassie quickly drew on her cigarette. "I didn't think it important . . . I mean, he wasn't being serious . . . he was playing a joke on me!"

"Well, by his own account, he was being serious, very serious.

And you didn't even give him an answer, but went rushing off into the night – Cinderella-like."

Cassie looked angry. "He had no right to tell you all that rubbish. Of course he wasn't being serious. It would be preposterous for him to even suggest such a thing. It irritates me to even be beside him at dinner, let alone in front of an altar!"

Dorothy sat forward and spoke evenly. "Cassie, I don't think you realise how important a friend Wally has become to this family. He has been very generous in extending credit to us, under very generous terms. If it weren't for Wally I don't know where we and Cliffenden would be by now."

"Well, I don't see what any of that has to do with me."

"It's everything to do with you. If you insult Wally, he will withdraw his friendship and leave us, well, I don't know where."

Cassie stared at the floor.

"You need to be very careful how you handle Wally, Cassie," said Howard. "You cannot continue treating him with the disdain that you do, for all our sakes."

Cassie leaned forward and put out her cigarette in an ashtray. "Very well, I will be charm itself for the rest of his stay."

"Good girl," said Howard.

"Now I really must get back to the game of charades." Cassie stood up.

"And Cassie – I don't like you spending time with Bowden Grey," said Dorothy.

Cassie frowned. "So now it's to be dictated who I may speak to?"

"You should be out and about and mixing with people like Wally. Leave your childhood friendships behind, Cassie – you're an adult now."

Without saying another word, Cassie left the library and headed back to the drawing room where the game of charades was still in full flight.

She had just rejoined her team when an angry-looking Wally entered, dressed in his tuxedo.

"Wally! Where on earth did you get to? We were about to report you as missing in action!" Teddy laughed.

Wally said nothing but stared angrily at Cassie.

"Well, come along, don't dilly-dally, Wally," said Teddy. "You're missing out on the fun. You can be on my team."

Cassie managed to smile at Wally. "No, no – you can be on my team, Wally."

Wally hesitated and then went and sat beside Cassie.

CHAPTER 10

Joe had noticed that the kitchen staff went out the back, to the courtyard there, for their break. He wondered why they chose to go out in the cold. The next day, after lunch was served, he went out for his break there and found Kathy around the corner smoking a cigarette. On hearing someone come up behind her, she jumped and hid the cigarette behind her back.

"Oh, it's only you," she said, relaxing and putting the cigarette back in her mouth and inhaling.

"Just taking my break," he said with a smile.

"Me too!" She indicated her cigarette.

"You smoke!"

"Yes, but don't tell Mrs. Crowther or Mr. Bruton or they will kill me, and probably fire me!"

"Your secret is safe with me!" he assured her.

She offered her cigarettes to him.

"No! I don't smoke," he said.

She giggled. "You will by the time you've worked here a few weeks!"

"Don't think so," he said. "I was wondering why the staff were coming out here for their breaks, instead of staying in the warmth of indoors."

"Now you know!" She smiled at him. "I'm really glad they're keeping you on."

"So am I. It's a great opportunity."

"Well, it's good food, no rent and steady wages – I don't know what opportunity has to do with it."

"Well, getting to work with a family like the Fullertons. I never thought I'd get a chance like that."

"The Fullertons! They're just a bunch of crazy, stuck-up idiots who happened to be born with silver spoons in their gobs!"

"You shouldn't speak about them like that."

"Oh, you'll be speaking about them like that soon enough, I can tell you, when you've had it up to here with their barking orders and expecting you to run yourself into the ground for them, while they drink and dance themselves silly."

"It's the way things are: our betters deserve better," he said.

"Well, they certainly have better – whether they deserve it or not, I'm not too sure." She dropped her cigarette on the ground and stamped it out. "Come on, we'd better get inside."

As he followed Kathy indoors he wasn't sure what to make of her. Inside the house she came across as all deferential and respectful. And yet here she was harbouring a secret dislike of the family who were looking after her. He couldn't understand it. But she had been very kind and helpful to him since he arrived, and that was all that mattered.

The next day Joe knocked on Cassie's door.

"Come in!"

Balancing the tray he was holding in one hand, Joe turned the doorknob and entered.

"Sorry, Miss Cassie. Mrs. Crowther said I was to bring this up to you as you didn't make it down for breakfast."

"Thank you – just put it on that table, will you?" Cassie seemed a little distracted and not in her usual jovial mood. She was at the window gazing out, dressed in outdoor clothes.

"Have all the guests left, Joe?" she asked.

"Yes, miss, they all left after breakfast – except for Mr. Stanton."

She turned and walked towards the table. "Of course. He's probably waiting for me downstairs, is he? Mr. Stanton?"

"He is certainly in the drawing room, miss. I can't say who he is waiting for."

Cassie pulled out the chair at the table and sat down. "I've agreed to go with him to Lismore Castle for the day."

"Very good, miss."

"Is it?"

She lifted the lid on the tray and saw the cooked breakfast there. "Good old Mrs. Crowther. This will set me up for the day."

"Hopefully, miss." Joe hovered nervously before forcing himself to speak up. "Eh, miss, I just wanted to – to thank you for pushing for me to get the permanent job here."

She looked up and smiled at him. "That's perfectly aright, Joe. I'm glad you're staying with us."

She gazed at him, looking as if she was suddenly thinking hard.

"Joe, are you in the house all day – or will you be going out at any stage?"

"Out, miss?"

"Are you due to go down to the village on an errand?"

"No, miss – well, Mr. Bruton didn't say if I was."

"Bugger!" Her face creased in disappointment.

"I get my break in the afternoon, miss – that's if you want me to run an errand on my bicycle for you?"

Her face lit up. "Oh, could you, Joe? You really are a sweetheart."

Leaping to her feet, she hurried to a bureau where she sat and grabbed a sheet of writing paper. Taking a fountain pen, she began to write a letter. Then she folded it into an envelope and handed it to him.

"You know the Grey place? Where we drove to last week?"

"Yes."

"Can you give this note to Bowden Grey – you know, the young man I was talking to at the party?"

"I know him."

"Make sure you don't go up to the house, or are seen by anyone. You'll find Bowden in the hayshed at the stables to the back of the house at four. Can you get there by four?"

"I'll certainly try."

"Excellent!"

Joe folded the envelope, put it into his pocket and turned to go.

"And Joe – not a word to anybody," warned Cassie.

He smiled at her. "Of course not, miss."

Bruton had given Joe a list of chores to do that took forever and he was unable to leave Cliffenden till after four o'clock. Now he pedalled his bicycle as fast as he could towards the Grey farm. As he approached the small manor house he dismounted from his bicycle and, leaving it beside a tree, quickly made his way through the trees to the stables. To the back of the stable yard he saw a large shed which he reckoned must be the hayshed. He opened the big wooden door and slipped inside. He saw Bowden sitting deep in thought on a bale of hay, his eyes staring into the distance as if he didn't belong on this planet. So intense were Bowden's thoughts that he didn't even notice Joe walking towards him and got a start when he stood before him.

Joe felt very uncomfortable. There was something about Bowden Grey that seemed to make everyone uncomfortable. As if he belonged somewhere else and contact with mere mortals was an intrusion into his private world.

"Sorry, sir, Miss Cassie sent me."

Bowden continued to look at Joe without saying anything.

Joe reached into his pocket, took out the letter Cassie had given him and handed it over. "She said to give you this."

Bowden looked at the letter as if it were a bomb and then reached out and took it. Standing up, he went to a corner where he turned his back on Joe and opened the letter.

Joe hovered from foot to foot, not sure what he should do next.

Finally Bowden turned to him. "Tell her it's fine – tell her I'll see her next week, when the coast is clear."

"Very good, sir," smiled Joe and he turned and headed off as quickly as possible.

That evening, Cassie found Wally waiting in the hall for her when she came down to dinner. After a long day with him at Lismore Castle she had really had enough of Wally and wished he would give her room to breathe.

Wally had just offered her his arm to escort her in to dinner when Joe stepped forward.

"Sorry, miss . . ." he began, feeling the need to pass on Bowden's message as soon as possible.

"You *again*!" said Wally. "You're like a ghost hovering around!"

Cassie touched Wally's arm gently and smiled at him. "You go in, Wally. I'll join you in a second."

Wally glared at Joe and went on into the dining room.

"Well, did you give him the letter?" she whispered.

"Yes, miss. I was a bit late but he was still there."

Cassie smiled broadly. "Excellent. What did he say?"

"He said . . ." Joe thought hard so as to get the words right. "He said that it was fine and he would see you next week – when the coast was clear."

Cassie looked delighted. "Thank you, Joe!"

She continued into the dining room, her step light.

"I don't understand something," said Joe as he joined Kathy out in the courtyard.

"What's that?"

"Well, how come Lady Dorothy has a title and the rest of the family don't?"

"That's because Lady Dorothy is the daughter of the Earl of Weybridge, so she was born a lady. But the Fullerton family don't have an actual title."

"I see, I think," said Joe.

"It don't matter a jot to me, title or no title – they're all a bunch of rich bastards in my book who we have to clean up after," said Kathy.

CHAPTER 11

The next few days seemed to pass like an eternity for Cassie. True to her promise to her parents, she was attentive to Wally. She accompanied to him to hunt balls, and made sure to be always sitting beside him at breakfast, lunch and dinner. She smiled as he talked of his boring business affairs, laughed at his ridiculous jokes, and overlooked his rudeness to staff and other people he believed beneath him.

The more she was forced to be nice to him, the more she resented him. How could this man have such control over her family's affairs? Why were they dependent on this oafish brute?

Finally the day came for him to leave, and she felt as if a huge weight was being lifted from her shoulders.

"Is he gone yet?" Cassie asked Joe as she crept down the stairs.

"No, he's in the library and he's left orders for you to be sent to him as soon as you come down."

"Oh God!" she cried in frustration. "Does he never relent?"

Joe looked at her and his heart went out to her.

"I'd better go in. I'll just keep reminding myself he'll be gone in a couple of hours." She sighed as she made her way to the library.

She braced herself, opened the door and walked in.

"Good morning, Wally. I think it's going to be a lovely day – the snow is melting away," she said as she walked past him to the window and smiled out at the sunshine.

"At least we should have an easier trip back to Dublin than the one we had coming here, with the snow going," he said.

"Hopefully. We wouldn't want you to end up in another ditch!" She couldn't help herself. "What time are you leaving?"

"In an hour or so."

"Oh, I must ring for Teddy. He won't be up till this afternoon otherwise, and he would be furious if he missed saying goodbye to you." She turned and walked quickly over to the bell pull.

He grabbed her hand as she walked past him. "No need, I said goodbye to him last night."

She tried to discreetly release her hand from his grip, but he wasn't letting go.

"Cassie – the last few days have made me so happy."

"Yes, we had such fun! I think Teddy –"

"I'm not talking about Teddy, I'm talking about us. Me and you."

She managed to keep smiling, though she was feeling distinctly uncomfortable, and had been dreading he would try to engage her in another one of these conversations.

"You see, I know I could make you happy, if you would just let me."

"Oh, you make me very happy, Wally – you're such a good friend of ours."

"But I'm so much more than just a friend to *you*, Cassie."

"Are you?" She tried again to release her hand but he still held on.

"Have you thought more about my marriage proposal?"

She managed to laugh sweetly. "Oh, Wally, you don't want to get lumbered with the likes of me for a wife! I'd be such a nuisance around the place. And I'd be a liability to you with your business."

"Cassie – I love you."

She gave a loud nervous tinkle of a laugh. "A liability, I tell you!"

As he grabbed her other hand she frantically looked around, wondering how she could remove herself from the situation.

"We could rule the world together," said Wally, moving closer.

"I don't think I want to rule the world, Wally. A few nice frocks, and parties to go to, that's all I need. You need an intelligent, sophisticated woman of the world who can share your tastes –"

Suddenly Wally's mouth was on hers, kissing her roughly. A selfish, greedy kiss, that made her want to scream. The more she struggled and tried to protest, the tighter he gripped her.

Outside the door, Joe had been listening in. He had seen Cassie's discomfort before meeting Wally, and he'd felt the need to make sure she was alright. As he'd heard the words being said on the other side of the door, he'd become more alarmed. Then, when Wally fell silent and Joe heard Cassie's muffled protests, he leapt into action.

He knocked loudly on the door and walked in. Shocked by the intrusion, Wally quickly let go of Cassie who jumped away from him.

"*What the fuck do you want?*" shouted Wally.

Cassie walked quickly to the window, fixing her hair.

"Sorry, sir, I just wanted to ask if you required tea before leaving?"

"No, I don't require bloody tea or anything bloody else from you! *Now will you fuck off!*"

Cassie had quickly gathered herself together. She wiped away a tear that was threatening to spill.

Joe stared at Cassie, his concern for her making him not want to leave.

She turned and smiled at him. "Thank you, Joe. I think tea is what is required right now."

"What's all this commotion?" asked Dorothy as she and Howard walked into the library.

Cassie was relieved to see them. "Nothing, nothing at all," she said. "Joe is just going to bring tea for everyone."

"Lovely, tea sounds just about right," said Dorothy. "Shall we have it in the drawing room?"

Wally's face was red with frustration at all the intrusions.

An hour later Wally's chauffeur had put his luggage into the car and Wally was saying his goodbyes in the hallway.

"Lady Dorothy, Howard, thank you for your hospitality," he said.

"Always a pleasure, Wally," smiled Dorothy.

"Tell Teddy I'll telephone him." He turned to Cassie. "And you're coming to London in a few weeks?"

"Indeed she is!" answered Dorothy for her.

He reached forward, embraced Cassie and whispered into her ear, "We can continue where we let off."

Wally turned, walked out of the house and down to his car.

As Dorothy and Howard walked back to the drawing room Cassie stared after Wally.

"Will I close the door, miss?" asked Joe who was hovering nearby.

"Yes, Joe, close it firmly. Hopefully I won't ever have to see him again."

That afternoon Cassie came rushing down the stairs with her coat and hat on, pulling on her gloves.

"Where do you think you're off to?" asked her mother who was coming out of the drawing room.

"Out!"

"Out where?"

"Out to – none of your business!"

"Cassie!"

"I'm sorry, Mama, but I'm not going to account for my every action to you. Now Wally is gone. And I played the perfect hostess to him for this past week, loath as I was to do it. Now I just want to get back to normal."

Dorothy saw there was anger in her daughter's face.

"Very well – it looks like a nice day for a drive," said Dorothy.

"Indeed it does!" snapped Cassie as she marched past her and out the front door.

The snow had practically melted away under the strong sun and Cassie sped along the country roads, desperate in her haste. She had felt like a trapped bird the past week and she had just been let free again. She had hated every moment she'd spent with Wally. But the incident in the library that morning had disturbed her. His grabbing and manhandling her like that, as if she were some possession of his. Cliffenden might be in debt to him, but that did not mean she was one of the assets he had charge over.

She excitedly drove up to the Greys' house and screeched to a halt outside. She jumped out and walked up to the front door where she sounded the knocker loudly.

A minute later Molly Grey opened the door.

"Hello, Mrs. Grey!" Cassie said cheerily.

"Cassie! What a lovely surprise! We weren't expecting you. Come in, my dear!" Molly beckoned her in.

Cassie walked into the hallway. It had been a grand house in its time, but had a shabby look to it now.

Cassie followed Molly into the drawing room where Molly shooed a cat off the sofa in order to allow Cassie to sit down.

Her husband Reggie was sitting in an armchair reading a newspaper.

"Who is it?" asked Reggie, looking up.

"Can't you see it's Cassie!" said Molly irritably.

"Oh, yes! Hello, Cassie!" Reggie greeted her.

"Hello, Mr. Grey."

"*Sally – tea!*" Molly screamed down the hallway towards the kitchen, to their one remaining servant.

Cassie looked around the room and felt very comfortable. She always loved being at the Greys' house. It was so warm and welcoming, stripped of any protocol, so unlike Cliffenden. She had loved coming here as a child with Teddy and playing all day long with Bowden.

"Well, we had such a lovely night at Cliffenden on New Year's, didn't we, Reggie?"

"Lovely!" confirmed Reggie. "Apart from the indigestion! The food was too rich, Cassie!"

"I warned you to stick to plain fare!" scolded Molly. "It was your own fault by allowing yourself to be tempted by so many tarts! Never seen so many tarts in the one place before . . . it's amazing what young women will wear nowadays!"

Cassie tried not to giggle. "Well, it was lovely to have you."

"Are all the guests gone now?"

"Yes, the last one left this morning," said Cassie. "Where's Bowden?"

"Oh, out and about somewhere, writing poetry probably!" Reggie guffawed at what he saw as his son's peculiarity.

"He's a wonderful poet," Cassie said, smiling.

"Is he?" asked Molly, surprised. "I have to admit I wouldn't know good poetry from bad. Never had much time for poetry, not when there are cows to be calved."

Cassie suddenly stood up. "I think I'll go and find him."

"Oh, eh, yes, dear," Molly said. "He should be around somewhere. But what about your tea?"

"Thank you – I'll have it later."

Cassie left the room and walked down the corridor to the kitchens where she found Sally making tea.

"Hello, Cassie," said Sally with a smile.

"Hello, Sally – do you know where Bowden is?"

"Out the back somewhere."

Cassie walked out through the back door. There was a courtyard out the back which she walked through down to the stables at the other end.

"Bowden!" she called as she got to the stables entrance.

Then she noticed Bowden standing under a tree in a nearby field, gazing out into the distance. She went racing across the field and didn't stop until she threw herself into his arms. She kissed him on the mouth.

He withdrew from her, surprised. "Cassie – someone will see! We're too near the house."

"Let them see! I don't care anymore. We're doing nothing to be ashamed of."

"I don't think your parents would view it like that." He stared at her and then embraced her and kissed her. "Oh, I've missed you this past week. I thought –"

"Come on, let's head towards the beach," she said, taking his hand.

They were soon walking along a secluded stretch of the

shoreline, their coats wrapped tightly around them as the sea lashed against the beach.

"I was so angry with Wally Stanton, Bowden – he was so rude to you at the party."

"I didn't take it personally. I'd say he's rude to everyone."

"There's no excuse for what he did. And then my parents basically ordered me to be his hostess for the following week, for fear he would pull the plug on the finances of Cliffenden."

"Could he?"

"He's certainly in a position to, according to my parents. And I had to put up with his boorishness day in day out – I'd thought he'd never leave! And then I was frightened the day we had arranged to meet that you would think I had stood you up. So that's when I thought I'd get Joe to deliver you the letter, to explain why I couldn't make it."

"You took a chance sending the boy with the letter. How did you know you could trust him?"

"Oh, I knew. I knew from the first moment I met Joe that he's completely trustworthy. He's got a kind face."

"Faces can be deceiving."

"No, they can't. I can always tell what a person is like by their face. I know in an instant. Anyway, we're free of Wally Stanton now, so it can get back to being just us."

He led her over to some rocks and they sat down.

"But for how long, Cassie?"

"What do you mean?"

"How long can we go on like this? Meeting in secret, grabbing opportunities when we can?"

"Well, that's why I drove up to the house today. I'm making a statement: I can see you whenever I want!"

He shook his head sadly. "You know if your family get a whisper of what's going on between us, they will end it. They will force us never to see each other again."

"How can they? I can do what I want."

"In your mind, maybe. They will never accept me. Your mother, the daughter of an earl, wants you to marry to match your station.

I was alright when we were younger, as a plaything for her children – but now, she doesn't want me anywhere near you."

She became angry. "You were never a plaything! You were my best friend in the world. When I'm with you, I feel different. I sometimes look at you, and you're so different from everyone else I've ever met. You're in your own little world, that you only let me into."

He smiled at her and hugged her tightly. "I don't know what I'd do without you," he whispered.

"Well, you'll never have to do without me. Because I belong to you. And, no matter how much Wally Stanton lends to Cliffenden, that will never change."

His face became sad. "You say that now . . . but you'll change. When you see the realities of life, and what someone like you will need from life, that I can never give."

She took his face firmly in both her hands. "You listen to me! I don't care about all that. As long as I have you, I don't care for anything else."

He nodded and smiled at her.

"Come on," she said, standing up and pulling him up from the rock.

Arms around each other, they continued along the beach, oblivious to the cold and wind.

CHAPTER 12

Joe found himself run off his feet in the following weeks as he settled into this strange new exciting world. Soon he couldn't imagine what life was like before he came to Cliffenden. On his days off he would visit his mother in their small cottage, and it seemed so alien to him now, as much as he loved relaxing and spending his day off there.

Bruton was relentless in his supervising of him, as he tried to "whip him into shape". But, as much as the life of the servants downstairs was comfortable and pleasant, he could not wait to go upstairs to do his duties, to escape into the glamorous world of the Fullertons. It was a constant show of excitement and entertainment that he could only watch in awe. There was a constant stream of visitors, often staying overnight, and the Fullertons seemed to relish their role of hosts.

It was of course Teddy and Cassie who most enthralled Joe. They seemed to spend their days in an idyllic life where rules didn't apply. They got up when they wanted to, ate when they wanted to, went to bed when they wanted to, often not appearing back to Cliffenden until three or four in the morning after attending some hunt ball or house party somewhere. Joe would hear the motorcar come roaring up the avenue in the early hours of the morning and he would jump out of his bed in his small room in the attic and rush to the window. It was always Cassie driving back. Teddy would fall out of the car and Cassie would go rushing to pick up her drunken brother from the gravel.

"Teddy! *Shhhh!*" Cassie would urge in a voice nearly as loud as her brother's. "You'll wake up the entire house!"

"*Fuck them!*" Teddy would roar and then screech with laughter.

And the two of them, her in a cocktail dress and fur coat, him in a tuxedo, would stumble up the steps to the front door. Then there would be fumbling with keys and at last he would hear them staggering into the house, and the door closing behind them. By this time Bruton, ever wakeful and security-conscious, would be on his way downstairs, in dressing gown and slippers, to check that the front door was properly locked and to pull the bolts across it.

Joe became used to the telephone ringing and, after Bruton had trained him into answering it, he did so regularly. He became used to Wally Stanton being the caller.

"Good afternoon, Cliffenden," he answered as usual one day.

"It's Wally Stanton. I wish to speak to Cassie."

"One moment, sir, and I'll see if she is available."

He went off to find Cassie. She was in the library with Teddy, immersed in a game of chess.

"Excuse me –" began Joe.

"Shut up! I'm trying to concentrate!" barked Teddy angrily.

"Teddy! Don't be so bloody rude!" Cassie chastised him. "What is it, Joe?"

"It's Mr. Stanton on the telephone for you, miss."

Cassie pulled a face and raised her eyes to heaven. "Tell him I'm busy."

"Yes, miss," said Joe. He was expecting that answer: she told him to say that nearly every day when Wally rang.

As Joe closed the door after him he heard Teddy say, "You can't avoid him forever, you know."

"Can't I?" answered Cassie.

Joe closed the door and went back to the telephone.

"I'm afraid Miss Cassie is busy," said Joe down the receiver.

"*Again?*" roared Wally.

"I'm afraid so, sir."

"Are you that bloody little twerp of a new footman they have?"

"Eh – yes, sir!"

"Are you actually passing on my messages to her?"

"Yes, sir."

"Can you actually tell her to ring me fucking back!"

"Yes, sir."

"If I find out you're not passing on my messages I'll have your arse kicked out of there quicker than you can say shit!"

Joe felt his face go bright red and his hands began to shake with the ferociousness of Wally's temper.

"I'll pass on the message, sir," he said as he gently put down the receiver.

As he turned around, Cassie was coming out of the library. From inside the room, Teddy was whooping with joy at his victory at chess.

Cassie closed the door after her and smiled at Joe. "I had to let him win – he would have been insufferable for the rest of the day otherwise. What did Mr. Stanton have to say for himself?"

"Just the usual, miss, that you are to call him back."

She looked at his reddened face and frowned. "Was he very rude today?"

"He's been worse," said Joe and she gave him a sympathetic look. It was strange but with any other member of the family or household he wouldn't have dared make such a remark. But Cassie seemed to encourage him to be open with her, and she was so easy to be open with.

"I'm sorry, Joe, that you have to put up with his abuse but unfortunately it's better he gives it to you than Bruton. Bruton would report it all back to my mother." She smiled at him and continued on to the stairs.

In the evening, after dinner was served and everything tidied and put away, before all the staff went to bed, there would be an hour of recreation down in the kitchens. The staff would relax as the stove blazed away. If Mr. Bruton was present he would chat to Mrs. Crowther about the day's activities. Some of the staff would be reading a book or a magazine or playing board games.

As Joe played a game of draughts with Kathy at the kitchen table he found his concentration waning.

"Joe!" she snapped. "That's the third time I've won! You're not even trying to win!"

"Sorry! I'm just a bit tired," he said.

"We'll have one more game," she said as she set up the draught board again.

The truth was he wasn't concentrating because he found himself every night during the recreation time wondering what was going on upstairs. Unlike the other staff who all seemed to treasure this time of day, he found it boring. He would much prefer to be party to the Fullertons' lives. As the footman, he was on call during this time if the family required something. And he found himself hoping one of the bells would ring and he would be called upstairs to that other world that he loved so much.

CHAPTER 13

Cassie was having breakfast with her parents while Joe and Bruton served them.

"Have you received many invitations to London?" asked Dorothy.

"Not so many this year," said Cassie.

"You certainly look as if you're getting a lot of invitations with your post," said Howard.

"Not so much."

"Perhaps then it's time you showed your face there, before London society forgets you altogether," suggested Dorothy.

"Hmmm," said Cassie as she pretended to be distracted by something in a copy of *Tatler* she was reading.

"Your Aunt Elizabeth was speaking to me on the telephone last night," said Dorothy. "She said she's redecorated your room at their house in London, waiting for your arrival."

"That's nice."

"You were due to go to London in January, weren't you?" asked Howard.

"I hadn't made any firm arrangements to."

"It's now nearly Easter," said Dorothy.

"Hmmm."

Dorothy became angry. "Cassie! Will you put down that confounded magazine and engage in proper conversation!"

Cassie looked up and closed over the magazine. "Sorry!"

"I really don't know what is wrong with you!" continued

Dorothy. "Why aren't you over in London having a fine old time for yourself like any normal girl?"

"Apart from being to Dublin for a few things, you've been doing nothing!" added Howard.

"Hardly nothing!"

"Burying yourself down here at Cliffenden instead of establishing yourself as a socialite," said Dorothy.

"Bad enough to have one child content to do nothing with his life, but you as well!" said Howard.

"I had a very hectic year last year, and I'm just taking a rest – nothing wrong with that," said Cassie.

"Lady Bilton told me she saw you driving through the village at great speed with Bowden Grey in your passenger seat last week. Is that true?" said Dorothy.

"She's as blind a bat! How can she suddenly see who's in my passenger seat as I drive by – at great speed by her own account?" Cassie said angrily.

"So it wasn't Bowden with you then?" pursued Dorothy.

"Would it really matter if it were?" Cassie was exasperated.

Dorothy raised her hands in the air and brought them firmly down on the table.

Joe flinched at the sight of Lady Dorothy in full anger.

"*Cassie!* I really wish you wouldn't waste your time with that young man!"

"Why not? He's very agreeable."

"He's going nowhere fast!" Dorothy closed her eyes in desperation. "When will you ever stop wasting your time filling your days playing chess and tennis with Teddy and going on jaunts with Bowden?"

Cassie stood up.

"You've not finished your breakfast," Howard pointed out.

Cassie said nothing and walked out of the room.

Howard and Dorothy exchanged exasperated looks.

"Take my plate away, Joe – I've lost my appetite," said Dorothy.

Joe walked around the table, took her plate and put it on a tray on the trolley, and went back to his position.

Bruton came up to him and whispered, "Take a hint, boy! They don't want you here! They want to have a private conversation. Take the tray downstairs."

"Yes, Mr. Bruton," said Joe. He picked up the tray and walked out.

Bruton followed him and closed the dining-room doors behind him.

Joe hurried down to the kitchen and gave the kitchen girls the tray. He watched as a worried Mr. Bruton went off to his office, then he turned and headed upstairs quickly again. He was so worried about Cassie, and the way she had stormed off, that he needed to see her to make sure she was alright.

The post was waiting on the sideboard in the hallway and he quickly sorted it out, putting Cassie's letters to one side. Then he put her letters on a silver salver and went off to find her. She wouldn't be in the drawing room. Maybe she was in the library. He went to the door and, knocking, entered. She was there – pacing up and down at the windows, smoking a cigarette.

"Sorry, miss, I'm just bringing you your post."

She looked over at him and he could see she was still distressed. She walked over to him, picked up her post and riffled through it quickly. She stopped when she came to a certain envelope. Throwing her other letters on the sofa, she stared at the envelope, her face reddening with anger.

"For goodness sake!" she uttered. "Does he never stop? He's so – persistent!"

She marched over to the fireplace and, tearing the envelope in several pieces, flung it into the grate behind the unlit logs. She inhaled from her cigarette in irritation, staring at the torn envelope at the back of the grate.

"Are you alright, miss?" Joe stepped towards her.

She turned around and looked at him. "Yes, I'm sorry, Joe, don't mind me." She smiled at him and looked out the window. "I think it's going to be a beautiful day today, Joe. What do you think?"

"It's certainly shaping up to be, miss."

"I'm not going to spend the day in this house being disapproved of by my parents. Far too nice a day for that. I think we'll go on a picnic – to the beach. Go wake Teddy up and tell him we're going on a picnic."

"He won't take kindly to being disturbed this side of noon, miss."

"Tell him I insist! And then tell Mrs. Crowther to prepare a picnic basket for us – tell her not to forget to put a bottle of gin in for Teddy."

"Very good, miss."

Looking decidedly happier, Cassie walked out into the hallway, Joe following her.

Bruton was coming from behind the stairs.

"Ah, Bruton, there you are," said Cassie. "You can spare Joe for a few hours today, can't you?"

Bruton looked surprised.

"Well, he was scheduled to do a lot of silver polishing for the day, Miss Cassie."

"Far too nice a day to have a young chap polishing silver, Bruton. Myself and Teddy are going on a picnic, and I'm taking Joe with us to serve the food."

"I see!" Bruton said, both his eyebrows rising with incredulity.

Joe stood there, shocked as well.

"I think it will be good training for valet duty, don't you think, Bruton?"

"I'm sure it's irrelevant what I think, Miss Cassie."

"Excellent – in that case, Joe, have Teddy up and ready and the picnic basket stocked and we'll all rendezvous here in an hour." Cassie walked up the stairs. "Don't forget the gin!"

Joe stood hovering, looking at Bruton. He couldn't decide if he looked disgusted or angry. Bruton said nothing but walked off with his lips pursed.

Joe went racing downstairs to organise the picnic basket before going up to wake Teddy.

Joe sat in the back seat of the open-topped motor car beside the full picnic basket, listening to Cassie and Teddy in the front singing

'Oh, I Do Like to Be Beside the Seaside!' at the top of their voices as Cassie drove at alarming speed along the coast road. He mustered the courage to look out the side of the car and nearly felt sick as he looked at the straight drop down the cliffs to the rocks and sea below. It seemed to hold no fear for Cassie as she sped on, further and further away from Cliffenden.

"*And there's lots of girls beside*
 That I'd like to be beside
 Beside the seaside!
 Beside the sea!"

Suddenly Cassie pulled the car over into a grassy layby and came to an abrupt halt.

"Why have you stopped here?" asked Teddy.

"Because there's a beautiful beach down these rocks," said Cassie.

"Oh well, one beach is the same as the next as far as I'm concerned," said Teddy, getting out of the car and stretching.

"Can you manage the basket, Joe?" asked Cassie as she set off down a trail that led down the cliffs to the beach, Teddy behind her.

"Yes, miss!" said Joe, grabbing the basket and the car rug and hurrying after them. He carefully followed them down the path until they reached the bottom where there was a long deserted golden stretch of beach.

"Oh, yes, this is just perfect," said Cassie as she selected a spot near the rocks.

Joe put down the basket and spread the rug out on the sand. Cassie knelt down on the rug while Teddy stretched out on it.

"Open the bloody gin, Joe! I'm dying of thirst here!" said Teddy.

Joe nodded and, opening the basket, quickly got to work on pouring him a full glass and handing it to him.

"Wine for me," said Cassie and Joe opened the bottle and poured her a glass.

Joe lay the tablecloth from the basket out on the sand and started placing the feast Mrs. Crowther had packed for them on it. After he had laid out the food, he stood up and waited there as he did when food was being served at Cliffenden.

"For goodness' sake, what are you doing? Sit down, Joe!" urged Cassie.

He hesitated. It felt so wrong to sit down with them.

"Sit down, Joe!" ordered Teddy. "You're making me nervous and blocking the sunlight!"

Nervously Joe sat down on the sand next to the blanket.

"Now isn't this lovely?" said Cassie as she ate a sandwich and drank her wine. "Joe, have something to eat."

Joe shook his head furiously. "No, I'm alright, miss."

"Don't be silly, Joe! You're missing your own lunch – you have to eat something!"

"No, I'm really fine, miss."

Teddy sat up and, smirking mischievously, said, "You're making him blush again, Cassie."

Cassie reached forward, took a plate and loaded it with food. She held it out to Joe.

"There you go, Joe, that's your lunch."

"I can't, miss."

"Why ever not?" Cassie's eyes widened.

"Well, it's not right, me eating with you – let alone you serving me!"

Teddy roared with laughter. "Well, the good news is the Communists will never take hold of Ireland with the likes of him around!"

"Stop it, Teddy!" said Cassie, seeing Joe's extreme discomfort. She spoke gently as she held out the plate again. "We're not in Cliffenden now, Joe, so it's quite alright. If it makes you feel better, then I *command* you to eat!"

Joe tentatively reached forward and took the plate.

"Well, why stop there!" said Teddy. "Pour him a glass of gin while you're at it!"

"Teddy!" warned Cassie. Then she looked at the bottle of wine. "Though I suppose a small glass of wine wouldn't hurt you, Joe."

Joe shook his head. "I don't drink, miss."

"What – *never*? I thought you were only making that up!" said Teddy. He sat up, poured a glass of wine and handed it to Joe.

"Well, there's a first time for everything!"

"Don't force him, Teddy!" insisted Cassie. "Only if he wants to."

Joe looked at the sparkling white wine fizzing in the glass he was holding, with the sun glistening on it, and he wanted to. He brought the glass up to his lips and drank.

"There you go!" said Teddy, delighted at the successful corruption.

Joe sat there listening to Cassie and Teddy as the afternoon whiled away and he could hardly believe that it was happening. He thought it the best time of his life.

"So, Joe, have you got a girlfriend?" asked Teddy.

"Leave him alone, Teddy! Although I think Kathy the kitchen maid would like to be your girlfriend, Joe."

"No, she wouldn't," Joe said, embarrassed.

"I've seen the way she looks at you," Cassie teased.

"You could do worse," said Teddy. "She's got a fine pair of –"

"Teddy!" warned Cassie.

Suddenly in the distance Joe saw a lone figure walking along the beach. He was almost angry that somebody else was intruding into this little world. Then he noticed that Cassie's expression had changed and her eyes were fixed on the figure.

Joe suddenly realised it was Bowden Grey.

"Look, it's Bowden!" said Teddy.

They watched as he approached.

"Hello, everybody," he said as he reached them.

"Fancy meeting you here!" said Teddy.

"It's such a nice day, I thought I'd come for a walk."

"I bet you did! And so far from your home!" said Teddy knowingly.

"Would you join us for a glass of wine?" said Cassie.

"Eh, no, thank you. There are some seals back behind those rocks. I'm going back to observe them."

Cassie jumped up. "Seals! I'd love to see them. I'll go with you to take a look."

"Don't get lost!" Teddy said, stretching out flat on the rug to have a sleep.

Joe watched as Cassie and Bowden walked so far away they were like little toy figures and then disappeared behind the rocks. He sat there beside the blanket as Teddy slept. He thought Cassie would be gone for only a short while but the hours slid by with no sign of her.

Eventually Teddy woke up and sat up.

"Is Cassie back yet?"

"Not yet, sir. The seals must have swum down the coast and they must have followed them."

Teddy threw back his head and laughed loudly. "Oh, Joe, you're priceless! They haven't gone down to the rocks to look at seals. They've gone down to *f-f-f-fuck*!"

Joe's eyes widened in realisation and he blushed at Teddy's blasé crudeness.

Teddy yawned and stretched back out on the rug. "They'll be gone yonks yet. Might as well get some more shut-eye."

"Where the blazes is she?" demanded Teddy.

The tide was coming in. Joe had packed up the picnic basket and carried it back up the cliff path. He and Teddy were now standing by the car, waiting for Cassie.

"I tell you, if she's not back in five minutes, then we're setting off without her!" said Teddy.

"Oh – do you think that's wise?" said Joe. He wasn't sure if he was more concerned with abandoning Cassie or the thought of Teddy manoeuvring the car along the coast road after the amount of gin he had consumed.

"Wise or not – it's what is going to happen!" said Teddy, clambering into the driver's seat.

Joe was aghast. He really didn't want to get in the car with Teddy. And he didn't want to abandon Cassie.

"Come on, Joe!" said Teddy. "Let's be off, my man!"

Joe looked desperately down towards the beach again and, to his immense relief, saw Cassie clambering up the footpath to the car.

"Sir! Here she is now!"

"Blast! I was looking forward to driving this thing home!"

"I'm so sorry I'm late!" said Cassie when she reached them. "The tide came in and we got caught and had to come back around the rocks."

"A lame excuse, Cassie!" said Teddy as he moved into the passenger seat. "I'm not in a good mood, I can tell you that!"

"Sorry, Teddy," she said as she sat in.

"You get me out to this deserted spot on false pretences and then abandon me, with just *him* for company!" Teddy nodded at Joe who was now in the back seat.

"I'm a dreadful sister, I know!"

"Dreadful is the least of it," said Teddy, sulking.

Cassie quickly started up the engine, turned the car around and started to drive back to Cliffenden.

"I'd have had more fun staring at wallpaper for the day than being left with Joe! Dull, dull, dull!"

Joe tried not to let Teddy's comments affect him. In any case his mind was too preoccupied with what Teddy had said about Cassie earlier. He remembered seeing Bowden and her rush into each other's arms at Cliffenden on New Year's Eve. And how she had driven up to the Greys' house and then disappeared, leaving him in the car for hours that same week. Not to mention the letter he had delivered to Bowden from Cassie. This relationship she was involved in was obviously very strong and very secret with only Teddy being aware, or maybe only suspecting it. The fact that Joe knew it for a fact made him feel very special. He was part of it, a part of Cassie's secret life.

When they got back to Cliffenden it was well into the evening and Joe took the picnic basket down to the kitchen and left it on the table. Mrs. Crowther was by the fire drinking sherry as a couple of the kitchen maids were washing up.

"Joe, you're to go straight into Mr. Bruton's office," said Mrs. Crowther and she pulled a face. "He's not too well pleased – just to warn you."

Joe sighed and made his way out of the kitchen and down the corridor to Bruton's office. He steadied himself and then knocked on the door.

"Come in!"

Joe opened the door and walked in, closing it behind him.

Bruton looked up from his paperwork. "Oh, you're back, are you?"

"Yes, sir, we just arrived back a few minutes ago."

"And what time do you call this to arrive back to your workplace?"

Joe didn't know what to say. "I was with Mr. Teddy and Miss Cassie all day."

"I know where you were! A complete waste of a day, when you should have been here doing your duties."

"Sorry, sir, but it wasn't my idea to go with them," Joe defended himself.

"Oh, I'm sure it wasn't! But go you did anyway!"

"I couldn't disobey Miss Cassie, sir."

Bruton stood up and walked towards him. "I am well aware that you are very inexperienced as a footman, so let me explain something to you. The position of footman does not include you going off gallivanting with the children of the house for the day!"

"I wasn't gallivanting, sir, I was –"

"Shut up!" Bruton shouted, making Joe jump. "It was the family's suggestion that you be kept on here. I would have much preferred to get a footman from an agency with at least some experience. But here you are anyway, in spite of my wishes. So let me make something very plain to you: in the pecking order of this household you, my boy, are at the very bottom. Even the kitchen staff have been here longer and have more experience than you, do you understand that?"

"Yes, sir."

"I've been watching you and I see how your eyes light up when you are upstairs and in the company of the Fullerton family. I am telling you that the Fullerton family are on a different planet from you, do you understand that?"

"Yes, sir."

"Their horses mean more to them than you do. I will not have a footman fraternise with the children of the family."

"I wasn't –"

"Shut up! I will not have you thinking in some way that just

108

because you breathe the same air as them that in some way you are part of their world. Do you understand?"

Joe's face was like stone as he stared ahead and spoke through tight lips. "Yes, sir."

"To put it bluntly, they are everything and you are nothing." Bruton walked back behind his desk. "To try and make up for the lost day's work you are to get up two hours earlier each morning and get to work. Polishing silver! Now, you can go."

"Yes, sir." Joe turned and walked out.

That night Joe sat on the side of his bed in his small room in the attic recalling the day's events. The joy of being on the beach drinking wine with Cassie, feeling like he belonged. And then her being taken away by Bowden for hours. And then Teddy's cruel words about him – *dull, dull, dull*. Followed by Bruton's dressing-down, telling him he was nothing. He didn't want to be nothing. His eyes had been opened since he came to Cliffenden. He had been shown another world, one that he loved.

As per Bruton's demand, Joe was up two hours earlier than everyone else the next morning to begin work. He spent an hour and a half polishing the silver and then went to open all the curtains downstairs. In the library he swished back the curtains and was about to leave the room when he spotted Cassie's torn letter at the back of the grate. No fire had been lit there the previous evening. He thought for a moment and then curiosity got the better of him and he went over and reached into the grate for the bits of envelope. He took out the letter inside and pieced it back together.

He saw the letter was from Wally Stanton.

My Dearest Cassie,

I'm beginning to wonder if you are getting my letters at all? I haven't heard anything back from you. And when I telephone you at Cliffenden, you are never there. And you never return my calls. Where are you, my dearest Cassie? You promised me you would be in London in January, yet you haven't been here.

If you don't come to me soon, then I will have to go to you. You still haven't answered me about my proposal of marriage. I'm waiting for your answer. Why delay things? You are treating me with an indifference that I've never experienced before, and won't tolerate for much longer. You know we are destined to be together. I will not rest until you are mine. And it will happen, Cassie, I can assure you. One day, you will be completely mine. I will have you where I want you, and you will regret treating me this way when I have the control. One day you will be completely in my power, at my mercy –

Joe stopped reading as he heard somebody come down the stairs. He threw the pieces of envelope and letter into the grate. Then he quickly made his way out to the hallway.

CHAPTER 14

Cassie stepped out of the bed naked and went over to the window. She pulled open the curtains and looked out at the view of the sea. She turned around and looked at Bowden who was lying across the bed. They were in a hotel perched on a cliff a few miles away from Cliffenden. It was a small quiet rundown hotel where she was certain they would never run into any of their circle. It had become a regular place for them to meet. She smiled at him and went back to join him on the bed.

He sat up and rested his head on his hand. "What time are you due back to Cliffenden?" he asked.

"Oh, don't talk about that yet, Bowden. We've hours yet."

He looked at his watch. "A couple of hours maybe. They'll expect you back for dinner. Where did you say you were spending the day?"

She sighed. "I said I was visiting friends in Cork. Don't talk about them, Bowden. I don't want to think of my family when I'm with you."

"You don't want reality to intrude into our little world?"

"No, I don't."

He sighed as he leaned towards her and played with her hair. "How much longer do you think we can get away with this?"

"Forever, as far as I'm concerned."

"I imagine you're under intense pressure from your parents to get on with your life."

"It's my life not theirs. And what makes me happy is you.

111

Nothing else." She leaned forward and kissed him.

He closed his eyes. "Imagine if it was just us – just us to worry about in the whole world. And this was our life, every day, for ever more."

"It could be, if we were brave enough."

"What? Announce to your parents that we're getting married. They would never accept it."

"But what could they do?"

"Kick you out, cut off all communication."

"I'd like to believe they think more highly of me than to ever do that."

"But I couldn't do that to you – couldn't cause you anguish in your life."

"The worst anguish you could ever cause me would be not being in my life." She leaned forward again and put her finger on his lips. Her face was pleading. "Let's not talk about that anymore, Bowden. Let's just enjoy what we have now."

He took her in his arms and kissed her passionately as she put her arms around his neck and pulled him closer to her.

They didn't hear the key in the door being rattled from the other side, or hear it drop on a sheet of newspaper that had been slid under the door. They didn't hear the paper being pulled back under the door and the key re-inserted in the lock and turned. They didn't hear the door open or Lady Dorothy and Howard stepping into the room.

As Cassie folded herself around Bowden she glanced up and screamed when she saw her parents looking down at them.

"What the –" said Bowden and, as he turned his head and saw the Fullertons at the side of the bed, he went pale as a ghost.

Cassie reached for the sheet and pulled it over her.

"*What do you think you're doing?*" she screeched as she sat up. Bowden pulled a blanket up around him.

"I know what we're doing! The question is what do *you* think you're doing?" demanded Howard, his face like thunder.

"How dare you come in here! How dare you!" Cassie cried, not knowing whether her tears were from shame, anger or fright.

"Oh, Cassie!" said Dorothy. "I would never have thought you could sink so low!"

"You've no right to just barge into our room like that!" said Cassie.

"We have every right to take whatever measures we have to – to stop you from destroying your life!" said Dorothy.

"I want you to get out of here!" demanded Bowden as he sat up.

"Oh shut up, you stupid bastard!" spat Howard. He reached out and grabbed Bowden's arm, pulling him naked to the floor.

"Don't!" begged Cassie.

"Bowden Grey, I would never have expected this from you!" said Dorothy. "You were always such a nice boy growing up! Having said that, I always knew you came from bad stock."

"Will you please leave!" demanded Bowden as he stood up, grabbing a blanket and wrapping it around his waist.

"Oh, we're not going anywhere," said Dorothy. "You're coming home with us now, Cassie. Put your clothes on."

Cassie wiped away her tears. "You are sadly mistaken if you think I am going anywhere with you!"

"Oh, yes, you are, Cassie!" Howard looked as if he was about to explode. "If you don't leave with us right now, I will tear this hotel down and actually kill both of you – I mean physically kill both of you!"

As Cassie and Bowden stayed rigidly still, Howard exploded and went for Bowden.

"Right! You first!" He grabbed Bowden by the neck and began to shake him.

"*Stop!*" Cassie screamed. "Alright! I'll go with you."

Howard let go of Bowden.

"Darling, are you alright?" Cassie asked Bowden as he tried to recover his breath.

"Get dressed!" commanded Dorothy.

"Will you at least leave me to get dressed?" said Cassie.

"Very well," said Dorothy. "We'll be waiting down in the car. If you are longer than five minutes –"

"I won't be!" promised Cassie.

Dorothy and Howard turned and walked out of the room, closing the door behind them.

Bowden sat down on the bed. They were both shaking, each as pale as the other.

"Oh, Bowden, I'm so sorry!" She broke down in tears. "Did he hurt you?"

"No, no, never mind that." He reached for her and held her in his arms. "Don't go back there, Cassie, don't go with them!"

"I have to! You saw how angry they are. They will kill you if I don't, and me too."

"You can't go with them! Not after this!" pleaded Bowden.

"I have no choice, Bowden. Who knows what they'll do if I don't."

She got out of the bed and started to get dressed, wiping away her tears.

"What will we do now?" he asked.

"I don't know. Let things just calm down, Bowden."

As she finished dressing he stood up and came to her and embraced her.

She kissed him. "I'll see you soon."

She was terrified her parents would re-emerge so she quickly pushed him away. As she opened the door, she looked back at him seated on the bed with the blanket wrapped around him and quickly went before she broke down in tears again. She walked to the end of the corridor and down the winding stairs that led to the empty reception.

The woman on reception looked at Cassie with her mouth open, after hearing all the commotion upstairs. She had no inkling, when she had given the older couple permission to go upstairs, that there was anything amiss. They had simply said they wanted to have a word with their daughter.

"I think, young lady," said the woman, "it might be best that you avoid our establishment in future. We've a strict policy of no hanky-panky here, and I don't want us getting the wrong kind of reputation as a house of ill-repute. Our hotel isn't for your sort! We don't want any floozies here!"

Cassie lowered her head in shame as she quickly walked past her and out the front door. There her parents were sitting stony-faced in the front seat of their automobile. She made her way to the back door and sat in. As her father started the engine, she stared out the window, silently crying.

Joe wasn't sure what had gone on that day. He was busy polishing silver when he saw the Fullertons arrive back. He was looking out the dining-room window and observed Cassie angrily getting out of the back of the car and marching into the house, not waiting for her parents. Through the open dining-room doors he saw her march through the hallway and straight up the stairs. Dorothy and Howard entered the house after her and went into the library, closing the door behind them.

Cassie sat at her dressing table that evening smoking a cigarette. She had fixed her face to look as if she hadn't been crying and now sat angry and waiting for a visit from her mother which she knew was inevitable. It came at seven o'clock with a knock on the door.

Dorothy entered and closed the door after her.

"Oh, you can knock on a door, can you? I thought you were incapable of doing so," said Cassie, not turning around to face her.

"Your father is distraught," said Dorothy. "He's had to take to the bed."

"He's distraught!" Cassie swung around to face her. "How do you think I feel?"

"I'm past caring how you feel, Cassie, after today. It is plain to see you have no regard for this family's thoughts, feelings or reputation, so why should we care about yours?"

"I have never felt such shame or embarrassment in all my life," said Cassie.

"Good! At least there's some moral compass left in you. You need to feel ashamed and embarrassed."

"Not over anything I did! Over what you and Papa did! Barging in on us like that, making a show of me and poor Bowden."

"'Poor Bowden'? I shouldn't worry about him – he's too insignificant. Whatever were you thinking of jumping into bed with the likes of Bowden Grey?"

"I didn't – jump – into bed with him. I'm in love him. I have been for a long while."

Dorothy frowned. "I don't know whether to rejoice that you didn't just jump into bed with anybody, or despair that you think you've fallen in love with Bowden Grey!"

"I don't think it – I know it!"

"I mean, really . . . I know gals these days have far looser morals than in my day. I mean, before the war it was unheard of! I am very happy to say that I went to my marital bed a virgin. It would have been unthinkable for it to be any other way."

"Well, as you said, that was before the war, Mama. And I can assure you things have changed."

"Well, not for the better – that I'm certain of."

"How did you know we were at that hotel? You were obviously having us followed."

"The if ands whys of the whole unfortunate episode are really immaterial –"

"Not to me!"

"The reality is that I have suspected for some time that there is something going on between you and him. And I can assure you that I will do anything and everything in my power to stop this – liaison – from continuing."

"You can't dictate who I see and I don't see."

"Oh, can't I? Don't push me, Cassie. You've seen today what I'm capable of doing, and I will do anything to stop you from ruining your life. I mean – what if you got pregnant?"

"We took precautions."

"Oh, please – spare me the details!"

"You did ask."

"Your father is tonight going to pay a visit to the Grey house and explain to Bowden's parents what exactly has been going on – including finding the two of you in flagrante delicto this afternoon."

"He can't!" Cassie's eyes widened with horror.

"Oh, he can and he will . . . unless you do exactly what I say."

CHAPTER 15

Joe detected a strange atmosphere at Cliffenden over the following days. Cassie stayed mostly in her room, rarely coming down to join the family at mealtimes, and only doing so if there were guests.

One morning Lady Dorothy stopped in the hallway where Joe was sorting the post.

"Joe, in future I want you to bring me Miss Cassie's post in the mornings before giving it to her, do you understand?"

Joe looked at her and nodded. "Yes, my lady."

Joe thought Cassie would be furious when he brought her post to her in the mornings after Lady Dorothy had already riffled through it. But Cassie seemed to accept it unquestioningly. Joe deduced that Bowden never contacted her by post so therefore she didn't care if her mother meddled with her letters. That was why he, Joe, was so important to their relationship.

He usually found her sitting at the window, sadly looking out. Although she was as always polite and pleasant to him, she seemed distracted. If he informed her there was a telephone call for her, she would tell him to say she would ring back, but she never did. He was desperate to ask her was she alright, but knew it wasn't his place. It made him upset to see her not her usual cheerful self but, conscious of Bruton's warning not to fraternise, he forced himself to keep his distance.

One afternoon he was taking out the rubbish to the bins near the stables at the back of the house, when he thought he could hear crying. He went to investigate and followed the soft crying to one of the stables. He opened the door and peeking in saw Cassie there, crying as she stroked a horse. He stood staring at her. He was going to turn and leave her, but the sight of her so unhappy was too much for him to bear and he gently walked into the stable.

"Miss Cassie – is everything alright?"

Cassie got a start and turned to see him. She quickly turned away from him and walked away from the horse, wiping her tears with her hand.

"Oh, Joe, I didn't hear you come in."

"Sorry, miss, I just thought I heard someone in here."

She kept her back to him.

"I'm quite alright, Joe, thank you for asking."

"Is there – is there anything I can get you?"

"No – no, I'm fine."

"Very well, miss, sorry, miss," said Joe and he turned to leave.

But suddenly Cassie began to sob loudly.

"Miss Cassie!" cried Joe, rushing to her.

"I'm sorry, Joe, you shouldn't have to see me like this. I'm really alright – please leave me."

"But I can't leave you like this! I'll fetch Lady Dorothy –"

"*No!*" said Cassie loudly and she swung around to face him.

He got a full look at her face and saw how distressed she was. He suddenly forgot about his position as footman, and Bruton's warnings, and all he could think of was that this young woman who he cared very much about was so upset. He walked a couple of steps towards her.

"What's wrong, Miss Cassie?" His voice was quiet and gentle.

She looked at his caring, kind face. Then she went and sat on a bale of hay.

"What is wrong with me?" she repeated as if she didn't know the answer. "Things that a boy like you could never understand."

"Well, you could try me, miss. I'm a good listener, and my mam always says that a problem shared is a problem halved."

She looked up at him and smiled. "You're a lovely boy, Joe, but my problems aren't for your ears."

Her words irritated him. He found them dismissive, implying that he was unimportant, in the same way Bruton's words did.

He suddenly felt the need to prove himself. "Is it Mr. Grey that has you so wound up, miss? I know that you care about each other an awful lot."

"If you're talking about that letter I had you deliver to him, Joe, it was merely a message about a horse-riding lesson."

"Miss Cassie," he stepped closer to her, "I saw you together, on New Year's Eve, after the party when everyone had gone to bed. I was cycling home and I saw you rush out of the house in the middle of the night to his – well, to his arms."

She looked shocked. "I see!"

"Oh, I never told anyone, Miss Cassie, I promise you that. I'd never tell anybody. I'd never do anything to betray you. You've been nicer to me than anybody ever has been my whole life."

She studied him carefully. She had underestimated their new footman. She had seen him as a naïve lad who was amusing and sweet. When she had driven up to the Grey farm that day with him and got him to deliver the letter to Bowden on that other occasion, she had honestly thought he wouldn't have the cop-on to realise anything was going on. And perhaps he wouldn't have if he hadn't seen her kiss Bowden passionately in the moonlight on New Year's Eve. As she studied him, she saw no malice in him. She still saw him as the same innocent lad, who seemed to be quite devoted to her, more than she ever realised, or had ever given thought to.

"Well," she said, "there's no point in me denying something you saw with your own two eyes."

"I know I'm speaking out of turn here –"

"Well, yes, you are, Joe." She said it kindly but firmly.

"But I just hate to see you so upset. And all I'm saying is, if I can help in any way just ask me!"

She thought for a moment, seeing the earnest look in his eyes. Maybe this lad who she teased so often was her only friend at Cliffenden.

"Have you ever been in love, Joe?"

"No, at least I don't think I have."

She gave a little laugh at his answer. "Well, then you haven't, Joe. Because if you had, you couldn't miss it. It's this all-consuming, devoted feeling. All you want to do is be in the other person's company. Even if they don't speak for hours, or are in terrible form themselves, it doesn't matter – because you're just happy to be with them."

Joe looked pensive. "No – no, I don't think I have been then, if that's the case."

She smiled again at his answer.

"And that's how you feel about Bowden Grey?" he asked.

She nodded sadly. "Absolutely."

"Well, that's good then, if that's how he makes you feel – isn't it?"

She shook her head sadly. "Due to circumstances outside my control, I can't see Bowden again. I've been banned from seeing him by my family. And it's a terrible wrench to me."

"They don't approve?"

"No, they don't. And I think I have been given no choice but to comply with their wishes."

He thought long and hard before speaking. "But if they didn't know you were meeting him, then there would be no problem, would there?"

"But they would know. I mean, they found out about my movements with Bowden, and I thought I was being quite discreet. I never told them I was meeting him."

To Cassie's surprise, Joe pulled up a bale of hay and sat down beside her.

"Yes, Miss Cassie, but you weren't careful enough!"

Her eyes widened as she looked at him.

"You've been driving up to the Grey farm, meeting him in the village. You've been seen with him around the place. Word was bound to get back to your parents sooner or later!"

The whole thing felt quite surreal to Cassie. She had never heard a servant speaking so frankly before, and she would never have suspected that Joe was even capable of voicing an opinion, let alone of pointing out the error of her ways.

"In future, we're going to have to be much more careful!" he said.

"We?" she said, shocked.

"Well, that is if you want me to help? I'll do anything you want, Miss Cassie. Anything at all. I can help you meet Mr. Grey, and nobody would ever know, I swear to you."

Cassie sat thinking hard as she studied his face.

"Alright – I haven't spoken to or seen him since – since a couple of weeks ago. I'm sure he's worried sick about me. Can you just let him know that I'm alright? And find out – find out how he is?"

"Of course I can. It's my afternoon off tomorrow, and I'll make my way up to his place and track him down. Nobody will see me – no fear on that account, Miss Cassie."

She nodded, got up and went to walk out.

Then she stopped and turned to him.

"And tell him – tell him I love him."

CHAPTER 16

Joe stood hidden in trees the next day, looking up at the Grey house for any glimpse of Bowden. But there was none. Finally Molly and Reggie emerged from the front door and, with much fuss and four dogs, got into their clapped-out automobile and headed off down the road.

Seizing his chance, Joe hurried up to the house and started peering through windows. Through the drawing-room window he saw Bowden standing on his own, staring into the fire. Joe made sure there was no sign of their housekeeper and then he knocked on the window.

Startled, Bowden turned around. As he was making no attempt to move, Joe pointed to the front door. Bowden nodded and left the room.

Joe went and waited at the front door until Bowden opened it.

"Hello, Mr. Grey, I'm –"

"I know who you are . . . but what do you want?"

"Miss Cassie sent me."

Bowden nodded and beckoned him in. Joe followed him down the hallway and into a room which seemed to be a study. Bowden shut the door behind them.

Then he stood staring at him and eventually said, "Well?"

"I've got a message from Miss Cassie. She said to say she's alright, and she wanted to know how you are. Oh, and that she loves you."

Bowden seemed confused as he headed over to a whiskey bottle and poured himself a drink. He sat on the edge of a desk and studied Joe.

"And is she? Is she alright?"

"Well, no, she doesn't look alright at all, sir. I found her yesterday in the stables sobbing her heart out."

Bowden's face dropped.

"She's hardly come down from her room. She only joins the family for dinner if there's other guests there. She doesn't even play tennis or chess with Mr. Teddy."

Bowden sighed loudly and whispered to himself, "My poor darling, what trouble I have caused you."

"From what she was saying, Lady Dorothy and Mr. Fullerton have banned her from seeing you ever again."

Bowden nodded and said nothing for a long while. Then he looked at Joe curiously.

"And what has all this got to do with you?"

"Well, you see, Miss Cassie trusts me. I know about you and Miss Cassie and so I'm going to help in any way I can."

"Help in what way?"

"Well, help you to meet each other. She told me how much she is in love with you."

The words seemed to bring happiness to Bowden's face. He got up and began to walk up and down.

"Tell her that I will be at Harrington's Ruin tomorrow night at one in the morning. If she can slip out of Cliffenden, I'll meet her there."

"Harrington's Ruin at one tomorrow night – I'll let her know," said Joe.

Bowden took a pen and paper from the desk and scribbled a note which he handed to Joe.

"Make sure she gets this," he said.

Joe nodded, turned and left quickly.

Cassie had waited impatiently in her room all afternoon for Joe's return. That evening she went down for dinner.

"Ah, you're joining us tonight, are you, Cassie?" said Dorothy.

"Yes," she said, taking her normal seat at the table.

"Have you been sick or something?" said Teddy. "You've spent more time up in your room than I have in mine!"

"I had to catch up on a lot of correspondence," said Cassie.

"Well, I hope you've done all your catching up now and you're not going to be such a bore from now on," said Teddy.

Cassie glanced at her father who looked stern and unforgiving. She felt herself going bright red at the memory of that dreadful day in the hotel and looked away.

"I had a call from Lady Bilton this afternoon – her Felicity is getting engaged," Dorothy announced. "A very suitable match to an earl's son. They are all very happy."

"So they should be!" said Teddy. "Felicity Bilton has a face that always conjures up the image of a cow's behind in my mind. They should be very grateful she's made any match, let alone to an earl's son."

"Teddy!" Dorothy chastised him.

"Felicity Bilton to my mind has always been a very gracious young woman," said Howard sternly. "A very respectable young woman with an impeccable reputation. A credit to her parents."

Cassie felt herself overtaken with embarrassment at the thinly veiled attack on herself.

"She only has an impeccable reputation because nobody ever wanted to do anything with her!" said Teddy, laughing.

"That's enough of all that, Teddy!" Howard's voice was so harsh that even Teddy stopped laughing. "There's been too much silliness at Cliffenden with everyone thinking they can live their lives in whatever fashion pleases them, regardless of morality or common decency. We should all aspire to be like the Biltons, not mock them for doing things right."

"Quite right!" agreed Dorothy. "You can't spend your whole life as if it is either a party, or the hangover from a party, Teddy. You need to change your ways."

Teddy yawned. "To do what exactly? I'm just taking a breather until it all kicks off."

"All what kicks off exactly?" asked Howard.

"The next war! I'm just waiting around for the next war to start – that should give me plenty to do."

"And you shouldn't speak so flippantly, Teddy!" snapped Howard. "You were too young to remember the horrors of the Great War or you wouldn't say such a dreadful thing. There will never be another war, not after the horrors of the last – everyone knows that – at least not in our lifetime."

"So you might start thinking of an alternative future for yourself that does not include going to a fantasy war," said Dorothy.

"Although I can't see what use Teddy would ever be in any war," said Howard.

"Oh, you don't have to have any particular qualities to be cannon fodder," said Teddy. He looked around the table. "Cliffenden seems to have lost its sense of humour all of a sudden. Even Cassie has lost her joie de vivre."

"That might not be a bad thing," said Howard. "You can have too much – joie de vivre."

Cassie anxiously looked around for Joe but he didn't seem to be waiting on them that evening. She sat through the rest of dinner, listening to her parents comparing and contrasting the best qualities of Felicity Bilton. Finally Joe arrived in and assisted with dessert.

As dinner finished and the family retired to the drawing room, Joe began to clear away the dishes.

Cassie held back.

"Did you get to see him?" she whispered.

"Yes, he's fine, Miss Cassie. And I've a message for you. You're to meet him tomorrow night at one in the morning at Harrington's Ruin."

She looked delighted and horrified at the same time.

"Harrington's Ruin? But how am I to get back into the house without anyone noticing? Bruton bolts all the doors on the inside at night unless Teddy and I warn him we'll be returning home late. I know he'd normally be in bed at such a time but he's always snooping round checking on security and he might notice if I left a door unbolted. Worse still, he might bolt it and leave me locked out!"

"I was already thinking about that. I can bring you down the kitchens and let you out the back door, Miss Cassie. And then I can let you in again at a time we fix."

Cassie digested this information. She nodded. "Good, Joe – out the back is safer. Mama is such a light sleeper and their room is at the front of the house. She often sits up during the night just staring out at the sea."

Joe reached into his pocket and handed her the note Bowden had given him.

"He said to give you this," he whispered.

She quickly took the note and slipped it into her pocket.

"We'll discuss it in the morning when you bring me my post," she said quietly.

"Very good, Miss Cassie," Joe said with a smile.

He continued clearing the plates away as Cassie left the room.

Later in her room Cassie excitedly opened the note Bowden had written.

> *My darling Cassie,*
> *I'll be at Harrington's Ruin tomorrow night at one. Try to be there. I'm mad with desperation to see you,*
> *Love, Bowden*

Cassie read and re-read the letter before holding it close to her heart. She walked over to her dressing table. On it was a hexagonal mirrored ornament, about one foot long. It had been a gift to her from her grandmother, the Countess of Weybridge, when she was a child. To the uninformed onlooker it looked just like a pretty ornament. But her grandmother had shown her a secret way to open it. The hexagonal plates were mobile and could be shifted according to a secret sequence that caused it to open up. So it was a safe that precious items could be put in – nobody could ever open it or even guess one could. She had never seen another one like it and nobody else in the family knew it could even open, let alone the code to open it. She opened it up and placed Bowden's letter inside to join some others, before closing it up again. She knew the letter would be safe there, free of any suspicion or fear of discovery.

That night during the recreation hour, Joe was sitting opposite Kathy as she set up a board game. Joe's mind had been on Cassie's rendezvous with Bowden all day. He had met her in the morning and discussed the logistics. It was agreed that the safest option was for Joe to let her out the kitchen door.

"Oh, don't bother setting that up for me," said Joe to Kathy as he went to stand up. "I'm heading to bed early. I'm going up now."

"But we haven't had a game in ages!" said Kathy, just loud enough for him to hear.

"Haven't we? Well, you know how busy I am upstairs," he said.

"And you never come out when I'm having a cigarette break anymore!"

"Don't have the time, Kathy," he said.

"No, no, you don't! You don't have the time for anything anymore, not like when you came here first." She was clearly upset.

"I'm here to work, Kathy. I can't neglect my duties."

"Oh, I know that, Joe." She pulled a nasty face. "You can't neglect your Miss Cassie."

Joe looked at her warily and then headed quickly off to bed.

Joe waited in the darkened kitchen as the whole house slept.

At last he heard somebody come in and whisper, "Joe?"

"Yes, Miss Cassie, I'm here," he said, stepping out of the shadows. He could see she was wrapped up in a fur coat.

He pulled back the heavy bolts and taking the key from its hook, unlocked the door and opened it.

"How long will you be?" he asked.

"I don't know – a couple of hours, I suppose."

"Alright, I'll meet you back here at three so," he said.

"You won't fall asleep and leave me locked out, will you?" she asked, her face creased with concern.

"Of course not – you can rely on me."

She nodded as she stepped outside and pulled the collar of her fur around her. She looked around and nervously smiled at him before setting forth into the night.

Cassie followed the series of footpaths that led along the cliffs to Harrington's Ruin. It was an old medieval fort that now lay, as its name suggested, in ruins. She remembered she used to play there all the time with Teddy and Bowden when they were children. As the ruins came into view she felt her heart pounding with excitement. All that mattered to her was seeing Bowden as she hurried through an arched door and into the ruins.

"Cassie!" said Bowden.

She rushed to him and held him tightly.

"Oh my darling, my darling," he said as he stroked her hair.

She looked into his face. "I'm sorry, Bowden. I don't know what to say to you – my parents barging in on us like that and my father attacking you."

"It wasn't your fault," he said, leading her over to a stone bench and sitting her down beside him.

"I just truly can't believe they stooped so low," she said.

"What have the repercussions been?"

"I'm banned from ever seeing you again. I'm not even allowed to look at you if we should pass on the street."

"Do they not realise that we have feelings for each other?"

"They couldn't care less. It's the fact that we do feel so strongly that makes them adamant that we should never meet again."

He held her hand. "I'm completely unsuitable for you in their eyes."

"I'm afraid you are. Bowden, what are we going to do?"

"We'll figure something out. The boy, the footman, he's to be trusted?"

"Oh, yes, Joe is quite incredible. I'd have never suspected him to be so ingenious and daring," she said.

"He adores you. I can see it when he speaks about you. His eyes light up."

"Do they?" she smiled. "He's a good boy. He's going to let me in the kitchen door at three. We don't have much time together, my love."

Joe waited anxiously at the kitchen door, looking repeatedly at the clock on the wall. It was after half three and no sign of Cassie. He wondered why he ever thought she would be on time. She led her life by her own rules.

There was a quick rap on the door and he unbolted it.

Cassie stepped into the kitchen.

"I was getting worried about you, because you're so late," he said, bolting the door closed and locking it before putting the key back on its hook.

"Am I?" She seemed unconcerned.

"Did you meet him? Was he there?" he asked.

"Oh, yes, he was waiting for me. I'd better get to bed – it's been a long day."

Joe heard footsteps coming down the back stairs.

"Quick!" he said, pushing her into an alcove.

The light turned on in the kitchen and there stood Bruton in his dressing gown.

"What are you doing?" he demanded.

"Sorry, Mr. Bruton, but I thought I heard somebody out back so came down to investigate," said Joe as he pretended to look out one of the windows.

Bruton hurried over to the window and looked out as well.

"Did you see anybody?" he asked.

"No, sir – it was probably just my imagination."

"I don't think it was!"

"No, sir?" Joe croaked and he felt himself perspire.

"I heard somebody outside as well. Some prowler lurking around Cliffenden at night."

Bruton came over and checked the door was bolted. Then he took the key down from its hook on the wall and checked the door was locked before replacing it on the hook.

"We'll have to be vigilant. I'm impressed with your diligence, Joe," said Bruton. "I never thought you'd be alert enough to hear noises out the back during the night. Takes a man of my experience to notice things like that. Now, come on, off to bed with you – you'll be up in a couple of hours."

Joe dutifully followed him out of the kitchen and back up the servants' staircase.

Cassie waited until they were safely gone and then stepped out from the alcove.

CHAPTER 17

"We were very nearly caught by Bruton," said Cassie the next day to Joe.

"Yes, miss, my heart is still not the better for it," he said.

Cassie sighed. "It's so risky. Whatever about me, you would be fired on the spot. I can't let you take that risk, Joe . . . I don't know what we're going to do."

"Felicity, darling! Congratulations on your announcement," said Lady Dorothy as Felicity Bilton was led into the drawing room with her parents.

The Fullertons were throwing a small cocktail party for her engagement.

Dorothy and Howard each gave her a congratulatory kiss on the cheek.

"Yes, we're all thrilled," said Lady Bilton. "She couldn't have met a nicer chap if she tried."

"Cecil would have loved to have been here but he was detained in Dublin," said Felicity.

"Well, I'm sure we'll have plenty of time to meet him now he's going to be one of us!" said Dorothy.

Cassie stood up from the sofa and went to Felicity and embraced her.

"Congrats, Felicity, you deserve it," Cassie said, smiling warmly at her.

"Thank you, Cassie, I still can't believe it. Cecil could have his pick of girls, and he chose me!" Felicity was ecstatic.

"Why wouldn't he?" said Cassie. "You'll make him a wonderful wife."

"Yeah! Well done, Felly!" Teddy called over from the gramophone where he was master of ceremonies.

Joe approached the Biltons with a tray of cocktails and they all took one. Then he circulated the room to the other guests.

Cassie returned to her seat, picked up her cocktail and took a sip. She took out her cigarette case and lit herself a cigarette, smiling at Felicity's obvious happiness . . . and thinking how wonderful it would be to have the man she loved accepted by her family and circle in such a welcoming fashion.

Teddy came and sat down beside Cassie.

"Well, at least you seem a little more cheery than a few weeks ago," said Teddy.

"Do I?" said Cassie, who knew the only reason she was happy was because she had met Bowden and was still assured of his love after the terrible incident in the hotel with her parents.

Teddy's eyes were trained on Felicity as she went around the room accepting everyone's congratulations.

"Say – do you have five pounds going spare?" he asked.

"I guess – do you want it now?"

"No – I'm going to wager you a bet."

"On what?" she asked.

"On whether or not I can seduce Felicity Bilton," he said.

Cassie's head shot around to look at him. "What are you talking about, Teddy?"

"Well, I've been having a bet with myself, so I thought you might like to join the game as well?" His face was full of mischief.

"A bet to do what?"

"I told you – to seduce Felicity!"

"Teddy, I know you live in cloud cuckoo land, but it may have escaped your attention that we are actually here to celebrate Felicity's engagement?"

"I know, that's what makes it all the more exciting to do it tonight."

132

"You cannot be serious!" Cassie was horrified.

"Of course I am. All that piffle Papa was prattling on about Felicity being so virtuous with an impeccable character – well, let's just see how impeccable she is when she is put to the test."

"Teddy!" Cassie warned, her eyes wide with disgust.

"I know! It will be a blast. Let's face it, I don't think it's going to be much of a challenge – poor old Felly has been looking at me with doe-eyes for years – she goes positively ga-ga when she's in my company. It's more of a challenge for me to see if I can go through with it. I'm visualising that cow's behind again just looking at her!" He downed his whiskey in one go and pointed to his empty glass. "I guess another couple of these and it won't matter."

"Teddy, you're being absolutely disgusting – and ridiculous – and I suggest you put any such notions out of your mind before you make a fool of yourself and embarrass poor Felicity into the bargain."

"So you won't wager a bet then?"

"Of course I won't. And I don't wish to discuss your vile suggestion, joke or no joke, again."

Teddy looked at her and his face clouded over. "I don't know what's become of you lately. You used to be so much fun, game for anything – now you're like a damp squib!"

"I'm growing up, Teddy, that's all – perhaps you should try it."

"Growing up? Growing old, more like it! Right, I will go conquer my conquest!" Teddy stood up petulantly. "The Right Honourable Felicity Bilton . . . let's see just how honourable she is."

"Teddy – don't!" Cassie implored but he was gone.

Cassie looked on nervously for the rest of the evening as Teddy completely focused on Felicity. She watched with increasing alarm as he continually refilled her wineglass. And it was true for Teddy – Felicity always did seem to be enamoured of Teddy in the past. Even tonight, at her engagement party, she seemed flattered by his attention.

It was a very warm night and the French windows were open. Eventually Teddy seemed to steer Felicity to the open window and pointed to the stars scattered across the sky.

Cassie could just about overhear Teddy say, "I can't see the North Star – let's go see if we can find it."

And suddenly Felicity was following Teddy out onto the patio as he pointed to the night sky.

Cassie sat in agitated thought as she realised that Teddy meant what he had said. He had no limitations, she knew that. As ten minutes led on to fifteen and there was no sign of them, she decided she needed to take matters into her own hands. She stood up, walked over to the French window and stepped out into the night.

She looked up and down the long patio that ran the length of the house but they weren't there. She walked down to the end of the patio and down the steps that led to the garden. She made her way through the gardens, looking out for them, and then she spotted them leaning against a tree. They were kissing and Teddy was undoing the buttons on Felicity's blouse.

She had a flashback to her parents' intrusion into the hotel room on her and Bowden and how wrong it had been. But this was a totally different matter. She and Bowden were in love. This was just a joke to Teddy and Felicity didn't seem to know what she was doing and risking.

She stepped towards them.

"Felicity – I urge you to think very carefully before you continue with this," she said. "You are risking your future happiness, and you may never get it back."

"What the fuck are you doing here?" said Teddy, turning around surprised.

Felicity looked horrified as the realisation of what she was doing hit her.

"Felicity, don't be stupid. You have a fiancé who is waiting for you," said Cassie.

"Would you ever just piss off and leave us alone!" demanded Teddy.

But Felicity was quickly buttoning up her blouse.

"Teddy, you have absolutely no interest in her, and are only messing with her mind for your own amusement," said Cassie.

Her blouse rebuttoned, Felicity smoothed her hair and then

quickly walked away from the tree and Teddy. She glanced at Cassie, embarrassed, as she walked past her and then hurried back up to the house.

"Well, thank you very much!" snapped Teddy, furious.

"I don't apologise for it, Teddy – you shouldn't play with people like that."

"You can talk! You've joined me in enough pranks over the years – never bothered you then."

"This is different, Teddy. Felicity has finally found happiness and you could have destroyed all that over nothing."

"So what?" Teddy's anger was growing.

"You shouldn't mess with people's hearts – they are not easily fixed."

"You know, you used to be so much fun! Up for anything! Now, ever since you've been hanging about with that boring bloody Bowden Grey, you've turned exactly like him."

"What are you talking about – me and Bowden Grey?"

"Did you really think that I didn't know you were screwing him? I know everything about you! Every sordid little detail! Your seedy little rendezvous in sleazy hotels. And you have the audacity to judge me!"

Realisation crossed Cassie's face. "It was you! You told Mama and Papa about us meeting in the hotel! Why would you do such a thing?"

"Because I don't want you ending up married to a nobody down the road! You know all our futures could rely on your marrying well."

"How could you do that to me?" Cassie's eyes stung with tears. "You and I were so close. We loved each other so much."

"But I do love you, Cassie," his said, his face slightly mocking. "Far too much to see you married to Bowden Grey."

Teddy walked towards her and stopped as he reached her side.

"Cassie, my darling, you might be Bowden's whore, but you'll never be his wife," he whispered into her ear, before continuing back to the house.

CHAPTER 18

Cassie looked out her bedroom window and saw a Rolls Royce parked outside. She hadn't been told they were expecting guests that day and wondered who it was. She left her room and, walking down the corridor, saw a maid making up a bed in the Blue Room.

"Kathy, are we expecting somebody to stay?" she asked the maid.

"Yes, miss."

"Who?"

"Don't know, miss. Mrs. Farrell just told me to make up the room."

Cassie nodded and continued along the corridor and down the staircase. She could hear chatter and laughter coming from the drawing room and made her way over to it. To her horror she saw Wally Stanton there, smoking a cigar, in conversation with her parents. Teddy was busy inspecting a batch of records that presumably Wally had brought him from London.

"Ah, Cassie, come in and say hello! Wally is here," urged Dorothy.

"So I can see," said a startled Cassie as she ventured in.

"Cassie!" declared Wally as he came over to her. Enveloping her in a hug, he kissed her cheek.

As he released her, she quickly moved away from him.

"I didn't realise Wally was visiting us," she said.

"Did we fail to mention?" asked Dorothy.

"Yes, you did!"

"Well, I wrote to you in my letters I was coming," accused Wally.

"Oh, yes . . . so you did," she said quietly, as she thought of the stack of letters he had sent, all of which had ended up in the fire unread.

"You look swell, Cassie, just swell!" said Wally.

"Doesn't she?" said Dorothy.

"How long are you staying?" asked Cassie.

"Well, I'm not so sure," said Wally. "I'm here on business as well as pleasure."

"What kind of business?" asked Cassie.

"The bank sent me over to do an audit on Cliffenden," explained Wally.

"Oh, I see," said Cassie.

"But we hope that it won't get in the way of you having a wonderful time here in Cliffenden. Treat it as your home," said Dorothy.

"I do always so enjoy being here. I see it as a home from home," said Wally as he grinned at Cassie.

"And Wally brought me all these fabulous new records from London, Cassie! Isn't he a gent?" said Teddy. "Come over and take a browse."

"Yes, later," said Cassie.

Bruton entered the room. "Pardon me, Mr. Stanton, but your room is now prepared, for whenever you'd like to freshen up."

Wally threw his cigar into the fireplace. "Might head up for a quick change of clothes now. Been a long journey."

"Do, Wally. And a bottle of your favourite bourbon has been left in your room," said Howard.

"You're just too kind," said Wally and he followed Bruton out of the room.

Cassie waited until he was gone. "I'm heading down to the village. I need cigarettes."

She turned and walked out of the room.

Dorothy quickly got up and followed her into the hallway.

She grabbed her arm. "Where do you think you're going?"

"I told you, to get cigarettes."

"Are you sure that's all you're doing?"

"Oh, don't worry, Mama – I'm not planning on meeting Bowden. I know your spies would report it back to you straight away if I did."

"Good! Make sure you don't disappear for hours and get back here quickly to help us entertain Wally."

"For goodness sake, Mama, he's your guest not mine! I'm not going to play nursemaid to him again."

Dorothy's grip on her arm tightened. "You'll assist us in any way you can. Did you not hear him – he's here to do an audit for the bank! That means all hands on deck for us to pass this audit. And that includes you. It's the least you can do after your shameful shenanigans." Dorothy released her grip and called out loudly, "Joe!"

Joe came out of the dining room where he was polishing silver.

"Yes, my lady?"

"You're to accompany Miss Cassie down to the village to purchase cigarettes. Bruton needs you to assist him, so you are to be away no longer than an hour – is that understood?"

"Yes, my lady."

"I will hold you responsible if you arrive back any later, Joe," warned Dorothy.

"Yes, my lady."

Joe saw the anger on Cassie's face as he followed her through the front door and out to the car. They sat in and she tore off down the drive, narrowly missing Wally's Rolls Royce.

"Is everything alright?" he asked eventually.

"No! That oaf Wally Stanton has arrived. And nobody told me because they knew I'd have gone mad. Not even Teddy. He could have warned me."

"Sorry, Miss Cassie. I knew there was a visitor coming from London, but didn't know who. If I had known how important it was, I'd have told you."

She smiled at him. "I know you would have."

"And – and what's the problem with Mr. Stanton?"

"Apart from being brutish, and boorish and awful – he's also in love with me," said Cassie.

"Oh!"

"Or at least thinks he's in love with me, the fool."

"And you have no feelings for him?"

"Of course I don't!"

"Then maybe it might be clever . . . to let him know?"

"It's not as simple as that, Joe. For reasons that are far too complicated to ever be able to explain to you, I must be exceptionally pleasant to him at all times."

Her dismissive words were slightly wounding to him.

"I see, miss."

"Let's just hope he gets his business done quickly and leaves us in peace soon. I'm not even allowed to escape for the day. We have to be back within the hour."

"Or else I'll be in big trouble," Joe pointed out, worried Cassie might take it into her head to drive off down the coast for hours and he would be left to face the wrath of Lady Dorothy and Bruton.

"Don't worry, we'll be back in time."

That evening, as Cassie walked into the dining room with Wally, she said, "I'm very surprised you came to Cliffenden to do this audit, Wally."

"Are you? Why?"

"Well, I just would have imagined a man as high up and powerful as you wouldn't come personally to do the audit on something as small as Cliffenden, in the greater scheme of things."

"The debt at Cliffenden is not a small thing, Cassie," he said, his face serious. "Not a small thing at all, in the greater scheme of things."

Cassie frowned at his words as she took her seat beside him.

CHAPTER 19

"You're up bright and early, Wally," commented Dorothy as Wally came bounding in for breakfast and took a seat beside Cassie.

"Well, I've a lot to do, Lady Dorothy. An awful lot of bookwork to go through here at Cliffenden to see how the estate is running. Need to make a good start."

"Of course." Dorothy managed to smile.

"Have you left all the books and ledgers in the library as I asked you, Howard?" asked Wally.

"Yes, well, some anyway."

"Some?"

"You've asked for a huge amount of stuff. It will take a while to locate everything."

"I see." Wally frowned. "Well, I'll start with what you've left me. I'm afraid I'm going to have to commandeer your library for the duration of my visit, Lady Dorothy."

"Absolutely, you need to be left in peace . . . however, I do feel so sorry for you, Wally."

"Why?"

"It's such a beautiful day to be cooped up in a library all day."

"Yes, it is," agreed Wally.

"And Cassie was just saying how she had hoped you'd go for a drive with her in the afternoon. She wanted to show you around and spend some time with you."

Cassie glared at her mother.

Wally turned to look at Cassie and beamed. "Really?"

"Eh, yes, of course, Wally," she said.

"Well, I'm sure I will be able to spare some time for you," Wally assured her.

Wally sat at the giant desk in the library, looking at the stack of books and ledgers before him. He looked out through the tall windows and saw Cassie walking quickly through the gardens. He got up from his desk and went to the window. He watched as she made her way over to the stables where the footman Joe was filling the coal bucket from the coal shed. He watched with curiosity as Joe stopped working and they stood quite close together, talking. Cassie seemed quite animated in her speech.

"Can you deliver a letter to Bowden today," Cassie asked Joe, holding out a letter to him.

"I can't! Mr. Bruton has given me a list of things as long as your arm to do, with Mr. Stanton being here. He said I have to be on standby at all times to cater to Mr. Stanton's every wish – that's what Mr. Bruton said."

"Damn Wally!" she spat, looking frantic. "What am I to do? I have to get a message to Bowden."

"It's just not possible for me to get away today, miss. I'm sorry."

Cassie drove through the countryside with Wally beside her in the passenger seat. She felt very uncomfortable as he was sitting sideways facing her and had his arm stretched along the top of the seat behind her.

"Oh, Cassie, I feel exhilarated driving along on a beautiful day through the lovely country air, just you and me."

"Hmmm," said Cassie.

"Why don't you pull over and we can take in the view?"

She put her foot down on the accelerator on hearing this, thinking of the last time she was alone with him and he had lunged at her.

"Oh, there are much nicer views than this one, Wally. I'll stop when we get there!"

He studied her as she drove. "You never came to London. I was expecting you to arrive every week."

"I know. I just had too much on here, Wally."

"Like what?"

"Well – I couldn't leave Teddy for a start. He hasn't been the best these past few months. He can get so down, and he would have got even downer if I just took off."

"Teddy is a grown man, Cassie. It's time you and everyone else stopped treating him with kid gloves as if he were a child. He'll never become responsible with the way you all dance around him."

"I think some people are made to be responsible and others aren't. I'd definitely put Teddy in the second category."

Wally laughed and moved his arm from the back of the seat to around her shoulders. She sat a bit forward to shake off his arm but was unable to.

"And you never wrote to me. And I wrote to you all the time. Why didn't you write back to me?"

"Oh Wally, I'm the most terrible letter writer. I hate writing letters. I never know what to say in them."

"Poor excuse – a simple line would have done."

She thought of the audit. "I know, I'm sorry. I'm dreadful. I'm a complete scatterbrain, can't even write a letter."

He leaned towards her. "You're not dreadful, you're wonderful. Did you get my messages from the times I telephoned?"

"Do you know, I hardly ever see messages that are left for me."

"I knew that little bastard of a footman wasn't passing on my messages!"

"Oh, it's not Joe's fault. He'd write down the messages but I just never check them. Entirely my fault! I've fallen out with several of my best friends over my perceived rudeness!"

He sat back and studied her. "I think you're playing hard to get, Cassie Fullerton."

"Oh no! I'm not playing anything at all!" she said, pushing her foot down further on the accelerator.

CHAPTER 20

Over the next few days Cassie's frustration nearly reached boiling point. Despite Wally's insistence that he had so much to do with the audit, he seemed to manage to find more time to spend in her company than he did poring over the books in the library. Under strict orders from her parents she managed to be polite to him and suffer his company. All the while she was denied contact with Bowden. True to what he'd said, Joe was on standby constantly for Wally and was run off his feet, from the pouring of Wally's bath in the morning to being at his beck and call all day. Joe had been unable to leave Cliffenden and get word to Bowden about what was going on. She could only imagine how worried Bowden would be and that he would be thinking something had happened. The worst thing of all would be if he imagined that she had abandoned him.

Joe was serving drinks in the drawing room after dinner to Wally and the family.

Cassie approached him at the drinks table and asked him to pour her a gin and tonic. Then she whispered, "Do you think you'll manage to get to Bowden tomorrow?"

"I don't know, Miss Cassie. It's my day off the day after though."

Her eyes lit up. "Then at least you'll be able to go then?"

"That is unless Mr. Bruton cancels all leave until Mr. Stanton has left."

"Oh!" Cassie's heart sank.

Across the room Wally was watching Cassie and the footman in their secretive conversation. Over the past few days he had seen the two of them often chatting quietly together or in whispered conversation. It was very unusual to see the daughter of the house being so close to a footman. Their closeness had piqued his interest in Joe. Wally had scarcely given any thought to any footman in his life, including his own one. He wondered why Cassie had such an interest and fondness for this boy, who to his mind was no different or more special than any other servant he had ever encountered. He wondered what was going on.

Especially as Cassie, although at least being charming to him during his stay, was successfully side-tracking any talk of their romance. He would continue to be patient with her, but his patience wouldn't last forever.

He went up to Teddy and sat beside him.

"Cassie seems in very good form," he commented.

"Cassie? Yes, I guess she is."

"I haven't seen that man around."

"What man?"

"What was his name again – Bowden Grey?"

"Bowden!" Teddy gave a laugh. "No, and you won't either. He's been given his marching orders. He was hanging around the place like a bad smell."

Wally smiled broadly. "Good. I didn't like the look of him. Eh, that footman seems very well-in – with the family."

"Joe? One footman is the same as another, I think. He runs a good bath though, I'll give him that."

"What's the plan for today?" Dorothy asked Cassie as she came into her room the next day.

"I was going to call over to Felicity Bilton and see how she's getting on with her wedding plans."

"No, no, Cassie. I'm sure Felicity is getting on just fine and is not in need of any advice from you."

Cassie held her frustration in. "And what would you suggest I do then?"

144

"I thought it might be nice if you took Wally out riding. Not Thunder this time, please!"

"Mama! I've already spent most of the morning with him discussing the minutest detail of Russia's foreign policy. I don't think I can take any more!"

"You can and you will! You will do anything you can to keep Wally out of that library and from going through the details of our finances!"

"Can't Teddy entertain him for a change?"

"Teddy doesn't hold the same attraction for him. Now, come on, get down to the library and entertain him."

Cassie reluctantly stood up.

Cassie knocked on the library door and entered. She found Wally sitting at the desk, reading ledgers and making notes.

"Am I disturbing you?" she asked, hoping the answer would be yes.

"Not at all! Come in! Cassie, you could never disturb me." He stood up, smiling.

"I was just thinking it would be a nice day to go riding?" she said.

Wally's face clouded over at the memory of his last ride at Cliffenden.

"I think I'll pass on that one, thank you all the same," he said.

"Oh, not to worry! I'll see you at dinner then," she said, delighted at the refusal, and turned to leave.

"Cassie, wait!"

She stopped and turned around.

He went and closed the door.

"That doesn't mean I don't want to spend time with you," he said.

She walked into the centre of the room with her arms folded.

"What would you like to do? Another drive?"

"No, I think I've done enough sightseeing as well," he said. "You know, Cassie, we don't always have to be doing something. You're not my tourist guide. It's quite alright for me just staying here and spending time with you."

She gave a laugh. "Well, if you want to be bored to death!"

"You could never bore me, my darling Cassie," he said, reaching behind him and locking the door.

"Why are you locking the door? Joe might want to come in to fix the curtains or something."

"That's why I locked the door. I don't want us to be disturbed. And I don't want you distracted by a drive, or a horse, or a view or a seagull or a passing dog, as has continually happened over the past few days when I try to bring our situation up. I want your complete and utter undivided attention."

"Well, I think you've managed to secure that." She felt herself becoming very nervous as he walked towards her.

"Cassie, I think we've been dodging this bullet for long enough, don't you?"

"What bullet?"

"Us! Me and you – our relationship."

She had managed to successfully avoid this inevitable topic and now there was no escaping it.

Her eyes became pleading. "But Wally, there is no *us*!"

"Of course there is! You know how I feel about you. I made it perfectly clear. I've told you I love you and that I want to marry you."

Before she could say anything he grabbed her and kissed her roughly on the mouth. She struggled to pull herself away from him.

"Cassie, I want you so much," he whispered.

"Wally! Let me go!"

He kissed her again before gasping, "All I think of is you!"

He went to kiss her again but she turned her head. "Wally, you're being ridiculous – now let me go."

"I love you," he said as he kissed her neck again and again.

"Wally! I said let me go!" She struggled against him. "*Wally!*"

She fought against him. Releasing her arm and raising her hand, she slapped him hard across the face.

Shocked, he let her go and held his hand to his cheek.

"For goodness' sake, Wally!" she gasped, walking quickly away from him.

"Why did you hit me?" he asked.

"Why do you think?" She was furious.

"But this is what you want. What we both want!"

"It's not what I want, you stupid man! When have I ever told you or made you think that this is what I wanted?"

Wally's face darkened with anger and he stared at her in fury.

She spoke rapidly and angrily. "You just keep pushing and pushing, not taking the hint, when I'm trying to make it perfectly clear that I have absolutely no interest in you in that way!"

"That's not the impression you gave me when you were in London last year, attending all the parties with me and other nights out!"

"That was before I realised you had a romantic interest in me. As soon as I realised that, I extracted myself from your company very quickly! And besides, we were out in a group a lot of the time, with other people – we never courted or anything like that. I'm sorry if you thought I was leading you on. I really didn't think I was. I thought we were just friends. But I never said or did anything to let you think I was interested in you."

"That's what you say! But you were flirting with me all the time, letting me think you liked me as much as I liked you!"

"You read it all wrong, Wally. That's just my personality at times. I was just being fun and jovial. I'm sorry if you picked it up as flirting."

"But what about when I was here at New Year's and over the past week?"

"I've been polite to you because my parents insisted I should be. I'm sorry, Wally, but now you really do well and truly need to move on!"

He stared at her in silence for a while. "I don't believe you."

"For goodness' sake!"

"What we had last year in London was real. Something has happened since. Somebody has got in the way. Who is he?"

"There is nobody, Wally."

"You're very close to that footman, aren't you?"

"What are you talking about?"

"I've seen you with him. Joe. Secret little chats. What on earth could you have in common with a lad like that?"

"He's a very pleasant boy, who I'm quite fond of," said Cassie and she felt her heart pounding as he was nearing the truth about Bowden.

"Are you sure that's all he is to you?"

Cassie stared at him quizzically. "You can't for a moment be suggesting . . . ? Are you seriously suggesting that I'm having some kind of liaison with a footman?" She started laughing so loudly she nearly cried – she wasn't sure if it was from relief, amusement or horror at the whole situation. "Oh, Wally! Have you lost your mind? That I would be remotely interested in a simple boy like him! A servant!"

Wally felt himself go red with embarrassment. "Well, perhaps not. I apologise."

Cassie shook her head. "I'm going to leave you to get on with your work, Wally. I think I've disturbed you for long enough."

She walked past him to the door, unlocked it and left.

There was a window open in the library, and outside the window Joe had been standing to its side, listening in.

That night he lay on his bed, thinking of the conversation he had overheard between Cassie and Wally. He wasn't so much thinking of the horrible encounter between the two but Cassie's words about him. He remembered her saying she would never be interested in a simple boy like him – a servant. He found her words about him strangely wounding. He knew he shouldn't be upset. He had never ever imagined Cassie thought of him as anything but a servant. But her words were so cruelly dismissive. He knew she didn't mean to be cruel – she was only speaking the truth. And yet he realised she had come to mean so much to him that maybe he had convinced himself that in some small way he meant something to her. The reality of the situation made him feel bad about himself. Tears fell silently down his cheeks.

CHAPTER 21

The next morning Joe was at the kitchen table having breakfast with the rest of the staff and listening to the idle chatter. As soon as the plates were cleared Bruton beckoned to Joe.

"Joe, go run Mr. Stanton's bath. Make sure you run it before Master Teddy's. Let's get our priorities right."

"Sorry, sir, but just to remind you it's my day off today."

Bruton drew himself up to his full height as his face became enraged. "Day off! Do you honestly expect to have a day off when we have such an important visitor at Cliffenden?"

"Yes, sir – I mean, no, sir."

"Your leave is cancelled until Mr. Stanton is safely on his way back to London, my boy."

"Yes, sir," Joe nodded, dreading telling Cassie he couldn't go and see Bowden.

Cassie walked down the corridor from her bedroom and saw Joe approaching her, holding several fluffy white towels.

"Joe?" she asked.

"Mrs. Farrell told me to put these towels in Mr. Stanton's room," he said, then he stepped in close to her and muttered, "Mr. Bruton has said I can't have my day off today, because of Mr. Stanton's visit."

"Bugger!" cried Cassie. She looked around to make sure there was nobody around and then whispered, "But what shall I do? I *must* get a message to him."

149

"I know, miss, but there's nothing I can do. I tried but Mr. Bruton put his foot down."

Cassie's face dissolved in distress. "But what about poor Bowden? He'll be distraught with worry about me. He'll wonder why I'm not making contact!"

Seeing her upset made his heart melt. "There's no chance I'll get out today, miss, but I'll try and get out for an hour over the next couple of days and make my way straight up to the Greys' place to explain everything to Mr. Bowden."

She reached out and placed her hand on his arm, her face pleading. "Oh, will you, Joe? We're depending on you." She quickly removed her hand as she heard somebody come up the stairs and hurried back to her room.

It was the evening of the day after his confrontation with Cassie, and Wally waited in the library for Lady Dorothy and Howard to arrive. He had summoned them.

The door opened and they walked in, all smiles.

"You wanted to see us, Wally?" said Howard.

"Yes. If you could take a seat?"

Dorothy sat down, thinking it strange that she was being asked to sit in her own house.

"Would you like a drink?" asked Wally.

"No, thank you," said Dorothy, thinking it even stranger that she was being offered a drink in her own house.

"I wanted to speak to you as I've completed the audit on Cliffenden," said Wally.

"Well, that is good, Wally – now you can concentrate on enjoying the rest of your time here," said Howard.

"I'm afraid there is nothing good in it and nothing good to report, either to yourselves or back to my bank."

"I see," said Howard, his mind filling with dread. "What seems to be the problem?"

Dorothy was smiling but she was extremely frightened.

"An easier question to answer is what seems *not* to be the problem," said Wally. "Your finances are in dire circumstances. I can't stress to you how dire they are."

"I see," nodded Howard.

"I don't think they have been in great circumstances for a considerable time, Wally, and we must just continue to muddle through," said Dorothy.

"I have to say that your days of muddling through have come to an end. Drastic action is now what is needed."

"What kind of drastic action?" asked Howard.

Wally paced up and down. "Do you have any other assets that I'm not aware of? Any property?"

"No," said Dorothy. "We used to have our house in London, but like most great families we had to get rid of that after the war. Now when we are in London we stay with my sister, Lady Emily. Or Claridges, if it's just a short visit."

"Then you have to take drastic measures," said Wally.

"But what other cuts can we make?" said Howard. "We've already made substantial cuts to the running of Cliffenden over the past years. A house like this should and did have three footmen – now we get by with one."

"And the kitchens are run on a very tight staff. And the estate has the minimum of workers," said Dorothy.

"I don't think you are grasping the seriousness of your situation. The days of getting rid of a footman or a kitchen maid are long gone. Cliffenden will have to go up for sale."

"Oh my God!" cried Dorothy as she reached out and grabbed Howard's hand in shock.

"You cannot be serious?" said Howard, his face paling.

"I'm afraid I am. The bank cannot risk lending you any more money and, to recuperate your losses, the estate and house must be sold."

"But that's unthinkable – Cliffenden has been in my family for generations," said Howard.

"Perhaps, Lady Dorothy, you can call on the assistance of your own esteemed family – your brother, the Earl of Weybridge?" asked Wally.

"The Earl of Weybridge is by no means flush himself," said

Dorothy. "I can't imagine he would be able to come to our aid. And my sisters would not be in the position to help us to such a degree."

"In that case, you have no option: Cliffenden must go," said Wally.

Tears welled up in Howard's eyes.

"But what will we do? Where will we go?" asked Dorothy in desperation.

"I'm sure you'll figure something out," said Wally.

"But we have nowhere to go or means of supporting ourselves," said Howard.

"Everyone must adapt to the changing times," said Wally. "Perhaps Teddy could find a job?"

"Goodness me! As what?" said Dorothy who was in danger of joining her husband and starting to cry too.

"Surely, Wally, there is something you can do for us?" begged Howard. "We are such good friends."

"We are such good friends, but my hands are tied. My loyalty is first to the bank of course."

"I can't believe it, I tell you!" said Dorothy.

"I have tried everything to see if I could help you but I can't see how I can. And now that Cassie and I are truly over – well, it's not like you are relatives of mine, is it?"

"What do you mean, Cassie and you are over?" asked Dorothy.

"Cassie has given me a definitive answer to my marriage proposal which was no, I'm sad to say. I'm afraid, as good a friend as I am of yours, there is a point where I have to put the bank's business first, and that's what I'm doing now."

"*She said no!*" Dorothy's voice was raised.

"In a most unkind way," said Wally. "Now, if she had said yes, and we were to be married, then the circumstances would be entirely different obviously."

"Obviously – eh, how exactly?" Howard asked.

"Well, I certainly could not see my in-laws lose their home. I would have no option but to extend continual credit to Cliffenden and, of course, being a wealthy man, I would want to financially assist my in-laws in getting out of this hole they find themselves in."

Howard and Dorothy stared at Wally, taking it all in.

"But, as it stands, I'm afraid. . . I'm sure you have much to talk about and arrange . . . I'll leave you alone." Turning, he walked over to the door and left the room.

Dorothy went marching into Cassie's room, her face like thunder.

"What have you done to upset Wally?" she demanded.

"Nothing!"

"You turned down his marriage proposal and were very rude to him into the bargain!"

"I had no choice but to set him straight," said Cassie.

"You *silly* girl! Do you know what you've done?"

"Yes, perfectly. I've finished this stupid charade that you have been forcing me to play with Wally. I can't take it anymore."

"Wally has just told myself and your father the result of his audit. He has told us that we have reached the end of the line."

"What do you mean?"

"He has told us that Cliffenden must be sold."

"Oh!" Cassie's hand covered her mouth in shock.

"He's not offering us any lifeline."

"The bastard!"

"He said he's just doing his job and has helped us as far as he can . . . due to the fact that you turned down his marriage proposal."

"What do you mean?"

"That if you were marrying him it would be a different situation entirely, as we would then be his relatives and he could not let us descend into such a crisis."

Cassie was incredulous. "So he's taking his hurt pride out on my family?"

"Your father has taken to the bed – he's beside himself, he just can't cope with this. Why, oh, why did you turn him down?"

"Oh, Mama! I had no option!"

"And would life married to Wally be so very bad? A life of comfort and luxury and your every wish taken care of? You would never need to worry about a thing again!"

"No, it's a ridiculous situation. I don't love him, don't even like him. Even less after this appalling behaviour."

Dorothy sneered at her. "Love! What does a girl like you know about love?"

"More than you think, Mama."

Dorothy raised her eyes in desperation. "Please tell me you're not referring to Bowden Grey?"

"I am in love with him, Mama."

"Oh Cassie! You're not in love with him – it's just a passing infatuation. What kind of a life could Bowden ever hope to offer you?"

"A life of love and happiness."

"You know nothing of such things. Love is very overrated, Cassie. Bowden can offer you nothing. When money worries come in the door, love flies out the window."

"Why are you laying all this on me? Teddy is your heir – *he* should be the one you are speaking to about this situation."

"What use could Teddy ever possibly be to any situation? You're our lifeline – you're the person who can save us from all this."

Cassie was angry and incredulous. "By prostituting myself?"

"Don't be so stupid, Cassie!" Dorothy suddenly sat on the bed and burst into tears.

Cassie stared at her in disbelief. She had never seen her mother cry before in all her life and here she was in floods of anguished tears.

Cassie went over and sat beside her. She put her arm around her.

"I'm sorry it's come to this, Mama."

"I don't know . . . what we're . . . going to do!" Dorothy said between sobs. "We'll have nothing . . . nowhere to go even . . . what will become of us?"

"I'll talk to Wally, try to appeal to his better nature," said Cassie.

"Don't, Cassie. All you'll do is anger him and make it worse."

CHAPTER 22

Dorothy and Howard came down the stairs and saw Wally standing beside a man they had never seen before. They were inspecting the paintings hanging on the wall and the man had a notebook and pen and was writing down figures.

"Wally?" asked Howard as they reached them.

"Ah, Dorothy and Howard, this is Ewan Hiddles. He's been sent by the bank to do an evaluation of everything."

"So pleased to meet you," said Ewan as he reached out his hand to them, smiling.

"That's a portrait of my grandmother," said Howard. "Why are you looking at it?"

Seeing his outstretched hand was being ignored, Ewan awkwardly dropped it to his side. "I'm valuing it. It's a fine piece, Victorian. It's a pity the artist isn't more well-known though."

"Wally?" Dorothy asked, ignoring Ewan.

"I'm sorry. I should have explained everything better yesterday. Naturally all the contents of Cliffenden will be part of the sale as well. We must try to get the best price for everything for the bank to regain its money."

Dorothy and Howard looked on in frightened horror.

"But these are my things, my belongings, passed down to me from generations of my family," said Howard, his voice weak.

Wally pulled a sympathetic face. "*Were* your things, Howard, I'm afraid. The bank really has the say of what happens to them now. I was hoping that myself and Ewan could enter your bedroom sometime today? At a time that's convenient of course."

"Whatever for?" asked Dorothy, shocked.

"To value your jewellery collection of course, Dorothy," said Wally, smiling.

He then walked past them and into the drawing room.

Ewan looked at them awkwardly, smiled at them and then quickly followed Wally.

Cassie walked into the drawing room and found Wally there, looking out the French window.

"Oh, you're still here, are you?" she said coolly.

He turned to her and smiled. "Yes, where else would I be?" He walked over to a decanter and poured himself a drink.

"I know my parents always told you to make yourself at home, but I think you're really taking advantage of our hospitality at this stage."

He looked surprised. "Actually, considering Cliffenden is practically owned by my bank, it's us that are being very generous to you, allowing you to stay until the sale goes through."

She took out her cigarette box and nervously lit herself a cigarette.

"When are you returning to London?" she asked.

"Well, I can't say for sure. I'll be staying here until the sale has successfully gone through, naturally. We hope for our business to be concluded here as quickly as possible. Perhaps, though, you should start looking for other living arrangements now in preparation for your move."

He walked past her, smiling again at her.

"You're breaking their hearts, you know," she said.

"I know . . . and breaking hearts is such a very sad thing to do, isn't it?" he said and continued out of the room.

"I thought the expression was 'Hell hath no fury like a *woman* scorned', not a man!" she spat.

He paused momentarily, and then walked out.

There was a terrible atmosphere in the house. Joe could sense it as he went about his work. Lady Dorothy and Howard seemed to look depressed and upset all the time. Cassie was keeping out of the way. All the staff seemed on edge and Bruton was in foul temper. If Bruton knew what was going on he wasn't saying anything. Wally Stanton was greeting a series of strange men who spent their time examining the furniture, the house or the grounds. Only Teddy seemed to be oblivious to what was going on while he went about his daily life as if everything was normal.

Joe was bringing the rubbish down to the stables in the afternoon.

"*Joe*!" came an urgent whisper from somewhere behind the stables.

Joe looked around the corner of the stables and to his shock saw Bowden crouched there by the gable wall.

"Mr. Bowden!" said Joe as he went rushing to him. "You shouldn't be here! Somebody might see you!"

"What the fuck is going on? Where's Cassie? I've heard nothing from her!"

"All our time off has been cancelled due to Mr. Stanton's visit. We have to be on call to cater to his every whim. I couldn't get out of the house to deliver any messages to you."

Bowden looked up at the house, worried. "Wally Stanton is here?"

"Yes."

"Cassie never said he was coming."

"She didn't know – he just arrived one day. I don't know what's going on in the house, Mr. Bowden, but there's a very strange atmosphere."

"I bet there is. Well, I've had enough of this – I'm going in to see her," said Bowden and he started taking long strides towards the house.

"No!" pleaded Joe as he ran alongside him. "You can't!"

Bowden ignored him as he kept walking.

"Mr. Bowden! Mr. Bowden! You don't understand what's going on in there!"

"No, but I'm going to find out."

"You'll get Miss Cassie into further trouble!"

"I don't care!"

Joe suddenly reached out, grabbed Bowden's arms and pushed him up against the wall to halt his stride. As he held Bowden forcefully against the wall, Joe wasn't sure which one was more shocked by his actions.

"I'm sorry, Mr. Bowden, but I can't let you go in there. The whole house is like a furnace ready to explode and, if you just walk in there now, you'll be the one to cause the explosion!"

Bowden thought for a while and then said, "Alright, let me go."

Joe released him, looking ashamed. "I'm sorry, Mr. Bowden. I'd no right to do that."

"No, you didn't, but you were just trying to protect Cassie. But I have to see her soon, otherwise I shall go mad. Arrange it, Joe."

Joe thought for a moment. "Be there at that spot by the gable wall of the stables at nine this evening. They should still be at dinner and Miss Cassie will be able to slip out for a few minutes without anyone noticing, I hope."

Bowden looked visibly relieved and placed his hand on Joe's shoulder. "Thank you, Joe – you're a good man."

"Now go, quickly, before anybody sees you!" begged Joe.

Bowden nodded and turned quickly to go.

Back inside, Joe hurried through the house, going from room to room searching for Cassie. He finally found her in the conservatory at the back of the house nestled in a corner behind some plants, staring out across the gardens to the sea.

"Miss Cassie," he said, rushing over to her, "I've seen Mr. Bowden!"

"Where?"

"He was out the back behind the stables and called me over."

She looked relieved but frightened. "Is he still there?"

"No, he's gone now."

"Did anyone see him?"

"No."

"Did you explain everything to him?"

Joe nodded vigorously. "Told him all about Mr. Stanton and

how Bruton had cancelled all time off and I couldn't make contact with him for you."

"How is he?"

"Not great, Miss Cassie – beside himself with worry about you. He was going to come marching into the house looking for you!"

"Oh my gosh!" Cassie was horrified at the thought of the repercussions.

"It's alright – I calmed him down and he's gone home. But I've arranged for you to see him tonight at nine around the side of the stables."

Cassie was delighted and terrified at the thought. "Bless you, Joe!"

"I'll tell you there's a telephone call when dessert is served and you can sneak out to meet him. And don't forget to bring your front-door keys down to dinner to let yourself back into the house. But you can't be long, Miss Cassie, or they'll know something is up."

Cassie nodded. "I'll be quick and I'll be careful."

Teddy walked into the conservatory and called "Cassie!"

She looked out from behind the plants where she was seated, holding a book.

"What are you doing hiding here? Been looking for you everywhere," said Teddy as he walked over to her.

"I'm seeking some peace from the endless stream of strange men Wally is parading through the house," said Cassie.

"Some of them are a bit of entertainment actually. Did you meet the antiques dealer who was here today? He told me he spent two years in a prison in the Arab world somewhere when he was arrested while looking for artefacts. Imagine? Two years held captive in the desert! I think I should go mad if that had happened to me. They accused him of stealing them."

"He probably did!"

"He gave me a really fine box of cigars."

Cassie snapped her book shut in frustration. "Fraternising with the enemy! Teddy! Have Mama and Papa not told you yet, or have you not figured it out for yourself, what all these men are doing here with Wally?"

"Yes, evaluating everything for the bank," he yawned.

"They are selling Cliffenden from under us! Are you not worried sick?"

"What good would me worrying myself sick do any of us? It wouldn't make any difference to the future of Cliffenden if I worried myself sick, now would it?"

"Teddy, you are so irresponsible!"

"I'm just being realistic. Besides I'm not the one being irresponsible – you are!"

"What are you talking about?"

"As I understand it, the whole mess could be solved in a jiffy if you just agreed to marry Wally."

Cassie's mouth dropped open.

Teddy bent down to her and whispered, "You won't be able to fight it forever, sweetheart. Why not just say yes now, and save us all the bother of going through this any longer. The Persian rug in the library will be finished for good if another travelling salesman traipses across it with muddy shoes doing his evaluations!"

He smiled at her, gave her a kiss on the cheek and walked out.

That evening Joe stood in attendance while the family and Wally had dinner. Wally dominated the conversation and seemed in joyous mood as he swapped jokes and anecdotes with an equally happy Teddy. Lady Dorothy and Howard were much quieter, but were trying to be polite. Cassie didn't even try to be polite as she threw Wally filthy looks.

"I mean the reality is Hitler is an amazing politician in my opinion," said Wally loudly. "Anyone who can pull Germany back from the brink as he has done deserves a lot of credit, I think."

"He looks a bit mad to me," said Teddy. "All that ranting and raving. I wonder does anybody ever listen to what he actually says?"

"Plenty of enthusiasm, it's what we lack in our politicians. Nobody seems to get excited about anything anymore – nobody's ready to drive change," said Wally.

"Some of us are happy with the way things are, Wally – we don't want change," said Dorothy.

"I don't think what the likes of us want is of any interest to Wally anymore, Mama," said Cassie. "It's all about profit and getting what he wants."

Wally raised his glass and smirked over at her.

"What's for dessert, Bruton?" asked Teddy, pushing his empty plate away.

"Mr. Crowther has made apple frangipane, sir."

"*Yuk!* You can tell her I don't want any of that muck. Frangipane reminds me of boarding school."

"Did you go to boarding school, Wally?" asked Dorothy, forcing herself to be civil. With everything going on, she couldn't remember or care less where Wally had gone to school, but was sticking to neutral topics.

"No," said Wally.

"You were lucky!" said Teddy. "I was packed off at twelve. I didn't know what I was letting myself in for."

"I think it was more of a case the school didn't know what it was letting itself in for with you, Teddy," said his mother. "We had a terrible time with him. I spent more time there listening to the irate headmaster than I did at Cliffenden."

Joe looked at the time and it was approaching nine. He collected the empty plates and rushed off to the kitchen with them. He gathered the tray of desserts and headed back to the dining room where Bruton was serving dessert wine.

"Excuse me, Miss Cassie, but there's a telephone call for you," he said as he re-entered the room.

"Oh, thank you, Joe," said Cassie and she stood up.

"Cassie, where are your manners? Tell them to telephone back after dessert, Joe," said Dorothy.

"I think manners is the least of our concerns around here, don't you, Mama?" said Cassie as she gave Wally a withering look and walked out of the room.

While Bruton poured the wine, Joe rapidly served the desserts, then went out to the hall.

Cassie was waiting for him there, pretending to be talking on the telephone.

They hurried to the front door and Joe unbolted it.

"Have you got your keys?" Joe whispered.

For answer Cassie waved her silver evening bag at him.

"Okay," Joe whispered. "I'll leave the door unbolted so just let yourself in when you're finished. I'll keep an eye on the door and make sure Bruton doesn't bolt it again but I mightn't be right here in the hall when you get back. And please, Miss Cassie, don't be long!"

Cassie nodded and slipped out. She found herself racing around the side of the house and towards the stables, praying that Bowden would be there.

She rounded the gable of the stables and saw him waiting.

"Bowden!" she cried and ran into his arms.

They kissed each other frantically.

"I can't stay long," she warned.

"Oh, I missed you so much," he said as he led her around the back of the stables into a field.

"I couldn't get any messages to you."

He silenced her with a kiss. "I know, my love – Joe explained everything to me. What's been going on? Wally Stanton is at Cliffenden?"

"Bowden, it's been dreadful!" Tears started to fall down her face. "He forced the issue with me about marrying him, and I set him straight and said I had no interest in him whatsoever. Now he's – the bastard – he's pulling the plug on Cliffenden and forcing us to sell everything!"

He grabbed her tightly. "He can't do that!"

"He can! He can do anything he wants. Cliffenden is in such a mess financially that he can do anything he wants. Mama and Papa are distraught, and they are blaming me for not marrying him and securing all our futures."

"That's so unfair!"

"They're desperate and they're looking for somebody to blame, and they are blaming me. I don't know what to do. Oh, Bowden,

162

tell me what to do!"

He held her shoulders tightly as he stared into her face.

"Cassie, I'm going away."

"What? Going where?"

"America."

"You're leaving me?" she said incredulously.

"No, my darling, no! Don't you see? I want you to come with me. We can never have any future here. We have to get away from our families and this place. Start anew, just the two of us, how we always wanted it to be."

"But how will we live? What would we do with ourselves?"

His dark eyes looked sad. "Would it matter? As long as we have each other. I don't expect you to say yes immediately. I know I'm asking you to leave your family and everything you know. And Stanton is offering you a life of luxury."

"He can keep it! All I want is you!" She kissed him.

"What are you saying?" he asked, almost too nervous to ask.

"I'm saying yes! Yes, I will go with you. Anywhere you want!"

"My darling!" He held her tightly. "But I want you to think about it carefully over the next few days. Really think about it. It's not a decision you can make easily. And in the cold light of day you might see it very differently."

"I don't need to think about it. I want to go with you."

He gazed into her eyes and said seriously, "We can't tell anybody, Cassie. If your parents or Wally Stanton realise what we're up to they'll stop us from going. And, of course, when we do go, they may pursue us. For that reason I think we should take the ferry to England and arrange our passage to America from there. That way we'll be less traceable."

"Yes, we'll drive to Dublin and leave the car there," Cassie said excitedly. "We'll be on that ferry before they know we're gone!"

"Okay, but I need to plan everything, and you need to think everything through carefully."

"I might not be able to get out of Cliffenden again with Stanton staying, so I'll get Joe to stay in contact with you. Now, I'd better go back before they miss me."

They kissed once more and she dragged herself away from him and went running back to the house. As she reached the corner of the house, she turned and saw him standing in the distance under the darkening sky. She waved at him. He raised an arm in the air and waved back.

CHAPTER 23

"Joe!" whispered Cassie.

Joe looked around and saw Cassie peeping out of her bedroom door, beckoning to him.

He quickly went over to her and she held the door open for him to enter.

She locked the door behind him.

"Is everything alright, Miss Cassie?"

He was surprised to see her face was lit up with excitement. It was the first time he had seen her look so happy for a while.

"Everything is perfect, Joe!"

"It went well with your meeting Mr. Bowden last night?"

She nodded happily. "Joe, I need your help."

"Anything, Miss Cassie."

"I'm leaving."

"Leaving what?"

"Cliffenden – for good!"

"Where are you going to?" Joe's heart was sinking.

"Bowden is leaving and I'm leaving with him. We're going to elope!"

Joe's eyes widened in amazement and horror. "I don't understand – elope where?"

"Probably America. Somewhere we can live our lives together and in peace without all this interference. We just want to be together, that's all. And we shall never be allowed to if we stay here. So we're taking matters, and our destinies, into our own hands."

"Miss Cassie – have you thought this through? Does Mr.

Bowden have any means to support you?"

"Not a bean, but who cares about things like that! We'll have enough for our passage to get far away from here. That's all we need."

"But you don't know what kind of a life you're letting yourself in for. You don't know what it's like not to have anything. All you know is your luxurious life here at Cliffenden and in your circle. You're making a terrible mistake!"

Cassie looked at him, surprised by his outburst. "I know what I'm doing, Joe. I don't need you to tell me otherwise."

"Sorry, miss."

Cassie took out a cigarette and lit it as she walked past him to look out the window.

"Besides, our luxurious life here at Cliffenden isn't going to be here for much longer, if Wally Stanton has his way."

"What do you mean?"

"Stanton is forcing us to sell Cliffenden, and everything else, to recoup the losses for his bank. Nobody knows and you're not to tell anybody."

Joe was speechless. Since he had come to Cliffenden, he had been so bowled over by this other world that it seemed untouchable in its refined glamour and wealth. For it to be pulled away by anybody was unthinkable.

"But – but I thought Mr. Stanton was a close friend of the family – how could he do that to you?"

"He was a close friend – until I turned down his marriage proposal." She dragged on her cigarette and turned to face him. "He's been trying to trap me into a marriage with him, and when I told him it would never happen he turned nasty – very nasty indeed."

"But poor Mr. Howard and Lady Dorothy! They must be beside themselves!"

Cassie looked sad. "They are, poor darlings. They shouldn't be treated like this, but I can't marry that man just to save Cliffenden, Joe!"

"Of course not, miss," Joe said, his heart going out to her.

"So we're leaving. Myself and Bowden are running away, as it were. And I need you to help plot our escape. You might call it deserting a sinking ship but I'm not finished with Stanton yet. I'm going to teach that bastard a very valuable lesson."

Cassie sauntered into the library where Wally was sitting at the desk.

"Oh, I'm sorry, I didn't realise you were here," she said, turning to leave.

"You don't have to leave on my account – it's still your house, for now," said Wally.

She walked over to the shelves of books and began to browse, finally taking out a travel book.

"Planning on going anywhere nice?" he asked.

"I haven't decided yet," she said as she flicked through the book. "I always wanted to go to Kenya – Papa has distant cousins there. I believe they have a fantastic social life."

"Kenya? I thought you would have more things on your mind than travelling to Kenya, with your family on the verge of losing Cliffenden?"

"True, but I have to think about my life after Cliffenden is gone. As you said yourself, I need to make arrangements – we all do."

He sat back and smirked at her. "And your arrangements are to be – Kenya?"

"Perhaps – or perhaps not! The world is my oyster."

"I think you'll find the world is not an oyster when you have no money, which will be the case soon for the Fullertons!"

"The world is always an oyster for a girl like me, Wally – you should know that."

As she continued to flick through the book he studied her, becoming intrigued.

"And what do you think you'll live on when you reach Kenya? Distant cousins' hospitality can run out quite quickly, you know."

"Well, my distant cousins aren't the only people I know in Kenya."

"Who else do you know?"

"Do you know Philip Carter, the polo player?"

"I don't know him but I've heard of him. I believe he's a shit polo player."

"Perhaps, but he's very handsome and owns half of the Happy Valley. We knocked around together quite a lot when I was in London last year."

Wally found himself becoming enflamed with jealousy.

She closed the book and put it under her arm, then walked to the door smiling at him before saying, "Wally, did you honestly think yours was the only marriage proposal I got in London last year?"

Cassie was laughing as she spoke on the telephone in the hallway.

"Oh, you are terrible! Dreadful, I tell you! Shocking!" She erupted in laughter.

Wally stood at the library door, trying to listen. He came out of the library as Cassie was concluding her telephone call.

"Alright, darling Philip. Yes, speak to you next week," said Cassie and she hung up the telephone.

"You're in a good mood," he commented.

"Yes."

"That telephone call seemed to cheer you up?"

"Yes, it did." She went to walk past him.

"Philip? Was that your friend Philip Carter?"

"It was, as a matter of fact, not that it's any of your business."

"Expensive business, telephone calls to Kenya. I don't think you should load Cliffenden with any more expenses."

"Rest assured, Philip telephoned me. He always telephones me, not the other way round."

Wally found himself becoming enraged with jealousy. "So you take his calls, but you wouldn't take mine?"

"If that is how it looks, then I won't argue with you."

"And what's he got that I don't? He might own half of the Happy-fucking-Valley, but I can assure you I'm much richer than him!"

Cassie looked at him coolly. "He's kind, Wally . . . he's kind. He doesn't just demand everything in life and expect to have it. He knows how to treat a girl with respect. He knows how to treat me."

She walked quickly away from him.

Cassie walked into the drawing room that night, dressed in a long silver slinky gown that stretched to the floor. She took Wally's breath away. He thought she looked like a Hollywood movie star.

"Gosh, sis! Going anywhere special tonight?" asked Teddy.

"No, just for dinner with you all," said Cassie.

Dorothy raised her eyes upwards and sipped on her sherry. She whispered to Howard. "I believe we have raised two fluff brains! We're about to lose Cliffenden and all our son is interested in is playing that gramophone all day and our daughter dresses as if she is about to be presented at court!"

"Dinner is served!" announced Bruton.

As everyone got up and left the room Wally called Cassie back.

"Yes, Wally?"

"I just thought you should know. I put in an urgent request with my bank to put a stay on the sale of Cliffenden."

Cassie's eyes widened. "But how – why should you do such a thing?"

"I'm trying to do my best for you all, for you – I guess it's just because I'm . . . kind."

Cassie grabbed both his hands. "Oh Wally! Do you think you can pull it off?"

"I'm not sure. I can try my best for you. It all depends how negotiations go over the next couple of weeks."

She smiled at him and hugged him. "Oh, I don't know how I'd ever repay you, Wally, if you could manage to do this for us. I never dreamed you could be so . . . kind." She slipped her arm through his and led him to the dining room.

CHAPTER 24

Dorothy looked out the drawing-room window at Wally and Cassie playing tennis in the gardens.

"I don't know what's got into her," she said to Howard. "Before, she couldn't get away from him enough, and now she's out playing tennis with him."

"And they went on a long drive yesterday," said Howard.

"Could she finally be seeing sense? And realising that her future and all our futures rely on her being with Wally?"

"Oh, I sincerely hope so," said Howard, sinking his head into his hands with stress.

"But if we were to be married, Wally, where should we live?" asked Cassie as they strolled arm in arm along the beach.

"Well, my house in London is always there, but it all depends where my work takes me of course. I'm stationed in many places around the world."

"It all sounds very exciting, I suppose," said Cassie.

"Oh, it would be. You couldn't have a more exciting life than with me, I can guarantee you that."

"I really don't know . . . it's such a big decision! I was never very good at making decisions."

Wally held his patience and didn't snap. "Why don't I just make the decision for you, and we get married!"

"But I don't know if I could truly make you happy!"

"You will, don't worry about it . . . We had better get back to the house. I'm expecting an important telephone call."

"Alright . . . oh, and Wally, any word yet from the bank about extending the credit for Cliffenden?"

He looked at her and his eyes narrowed. "Not yet . . . they haven't made their decision yet. I'm waiting for your decision first."

Joe knocked on Wally's door.

"Come in!"

Joe walked in.

"Sorry, sir, just here to run your bath."

"Oh yes, go ahead," said Wally who was wearing a silk dressing gown.

Joe nodded and walked quickly into the bathroom off the bedroom. He tried not to stay any longer than he had to in Wally's company. The man was rude and obnoxious and spoke to him and all the other servants as if they were slaves.

Joe turned on the taps in the bath and began to test the water as he poured bath oils in.

Wally sauntered in and sat down on the ornate chair there, studying Joe. He lit up a cigar.

"Joe, isn't it?"

"That's right, sir."

"Have you been at Cliffenden long?"

"A good while at this stage, sir."

"Do you like it here?"

"Oh, very much, sir. The Fullertons are a wonderful family to work for."

"Yes, they are smashing, aren't they? You seem to be quite close to Cassie?"

Joe felt himself go red. "Miss Cassie is a wonderful lady."

"She is swell, isn't she? I think she's quite fond of you."

"I'm only a footman, sir, so I'm sure she gives me no thought at all."

"True, but I do think she likes you. What's your ambition in life, Joe?"

"Ambition? I never give that any thought, sir. I just do my job

171

here and know I'm lucky to be here."

"I think you have a lot of potential, Joe."

Joe looked over at him, confused.

"I think you might make a very good butler one day," said Wally.

"I never thought about it, sir. You need years of experience before you can even think of becoming a butler."

"It all depends on how quick or slow you are, and I think you're very quick."

Joe turned off the taps as the bath was filled and stood up straight.

Wally stood up and walked over to him. "I'm not sure if you are aware of the situation between me and Cassie?"

Joe tried to look innocent. "No, sir."

"Oh come, come, Joe. Your loyalty to Cassie is touching, it really is. But I don't think for one moment that you're not aware of the fact that I am romantically involved with her . . . She's such an indecisive girl. She can't seem to make her mind up one way or the other about things. I suppose it's an endearing quality. If Cassie does agree to becoming my wife, then I should like to take you with us."

"With you, sir?"

"Well, I know she'll miss you when she comes to live with me. So I would like you to come and work for me, for us, in my house."

Joe shook his head in bewilderment. "As what?"

"As our butler," said Wally.

Joe's eyes widened and his mouth dropped open.

"Opportunities like this don't come along often for a young lad like you. You should grab it with both hands."

"But – but – I don't know what to say! You'd make me your butler?"

"When Cassie marries me you will come and live with us as our butler. You'd like that, wouldn't you, Joe?"

"Y-y-y-yes."

"Then you've got to help me out here, Joe. You've got to help me convince Cassie to marry me."

Wally reached forward and tested the water in the bath with his hand.

"Perfect!" he said. "You can go. But, Joe, don't tell anyone what I've said. It's our secret."

Joe nodded and quickly left.

Joe was stunned by Wally's proposal. It was true for him – opportunities like that did not come around very often. He had never even dreamed of such an opportunity, especially without years of experience. And yet here he was being offered the position. More importantly, it meant that he would still be with Cassie. Working for her forever. He had never liked Wally Stanton. But then he didn't like Bruton either and had to put up with him all day. And if he was butler he would be in charge of a household, of the servants. He could scarcely believe it. He shook his head and brought himself firmly down to earth. This was all a dream that could or would never happen. Cassie was never going to marry Wally Stanton. She hated him. It was the last thing in the world she was going to do. She was going to run away with Bowden Grey and Cliffenden forever. And leave Joe forever. And once she was gone, Cliffenden would be gone soon after. Instead of day-dreaming about being a butler in Wally and Cassie's house, he had to face the reality that his and everybody else's days at Cliffenden were drawing to a fast close. And, instead of having a bright future, he was facing a bleak one.

CHAPTER 25

"You seem to be getting on very well with Mr. Stanton," Joe said as he polished the ornaments in the library where Cassie had been talking about Bowden with him for the previous half hour.

"It's all an act, Joe. I'm pretending to be nice to him and he's pretending to be nice to me."

"But I think he might think it's more than you just being nice to him."

"Good! That's what I want him to think. I'm trying to secure a couple of years of extra credit for Cliffenden before I leave with Bowden. And the only way I can do that is pretend that I'm contemplating marrying him. A couple of years' credit should be enough time for Mama and Papa to try to turn this place around. It's as much as I can do for them, and then I can leave with Bowden with a clear conscience."

"Do you think you'll secure the credit from Mr. Stanton?"

"I don't know how far I have to go with this game with him but I won't stop until I get it."

"He'll be very angry when he finds out you were playing him along," warned Joe.

"I won't care by then. I'll be far away with Bowden and the papers will be signed to save Cliffenden for another couple of years."

"It's a very dangerous game you're playing, Miss Cassie."

"It's the only way I know how to play it."

"Don't you think – don't you think Mr. Stanton might not be all that bad?"

"He's repulsive! A ruthless vicious man who will stop at nothing to get what he wants. His behaviour to us has been appalling. I'm looking forward to never seeing him again."

"But – but he seems to be much politer and nicer this past while."

"I told you it's only pretence, Joe. He thinks that's how he'll woo me."

"I'd say he has a beautiful home, Miss Cassie. And you'd never want for anything married to him."

"Except for Bowden, who I love."

"It's just –"

"Joe!" snapped Cassie. "I don't want to speak about Stanton anymore. He irritates me beyond expression."

"Yes, miss – sorry, miss."

Cassie had always considered herself a very good chess player and an even better poker player. And she realised she had to rely on all those skills when dealing with Wally. He was a very clever man who was hard to outwit. And, as Joe had said, she was playing a dangerous game. She continued courting him, and he continued to be evasive about the bank paperwork to extend the credit to Cliffenden. Her frustration was bubbling as they continued to dance around the two issues of the credit and the engagement, neither she nor Wally agreeing to either outright. As she thought of the deep love she had for Bowden, she wondered how Wally would want a marriage with her with the knowledge that her previous behaviour clearly showed she didn't care for him. But she realised Wally didn't look at life like that. For Wally, people were like everything else – possessions to be had. Wally didn't care what Cassie's feelings were.

They were walking through the gardens.

"Your workload at your bank must be mounting up with you being away from it for so long," commented Cassie.

"It can wait. Besides, I'm managing to do a lot of work from here."

Cassie had seen the deliveries of large packages of paperwork that came in the post to Wally each day from the bank. She burned with curiosity to know if amongst the packages was the credit extension for Cliffenden. She decided to come right out and ask.

"Any word on the paperwork for Cliffenden?"

"Oh, yes, it arrived a few days ago," he said nonchalantly.

"Did it? You never said!" she said excitedly.

"Did I not?"

"But that's wonderful! You can just sign it and have it returned."

Wally stopped walking and sat down on a nearby bench, crossing his legs and laying his arms out across the back of the bench.

"Hmmm . . . I'm really putting myself out on a limb with this one."

"I know and we appreciate it so much." She went and sat beside him, smiling happily.

"Cassie?" His face was smug as he pulled his arms back from behind the bench and took her hands.

"Yes, Wally?"

"Will you marry me?" His face was self-satisfied and conceited.

She managed to continue to smile through tight lips as she realised he had successfully cornered her. She thought of the bank paperwork sitting somewhere in his room ready to be signed by him.

"Yes, of course I will, Wally," she said.

"Oh, my darling! You've made me the happiest man alive," he said, pulling her to him and kissing her firmly.

"Well, I could not be happier!" said Dorothy that evening after Wally announced the engagement to the family, standing beside Cassie, his arm around her waist.

Cassie saw her father's face visibly relieved and looking ten years younger instantly.

"Oh, congratulations!" said Howard, shaking Wally's hand and kissing Cassie's cheek.

"I apologise. I really should have asked your permission first," said Wally.

"No need for that!" said Teddy. "Papa would have tied her up in a ribbon with a bow for you at this stage."

"Teddy, do try to behave," said Dorothy, looking irritated. She went over and kissed Wally's cheek. "Welcome to the family, Wally. And Cassie . . . you have made me so proud!"

"Proud as punch!" said Teddy who came and offered his own congratulations.

"This calls for champagne," said Howard, quickly tugging the bell pull.

"What a good idea!" said Teddy.

"It's all so sudden, I need to get my head around it," said Dorothy who looked light-headed with relief.

"It's not *so* sudden," commented Teddy. "He's been sniffing around her for ages."

Dorothy's patience finally snapped from the pressure of the last few weeks. "Teddy, if you don't stop with your crass remarks you'll be sorry, I swear!"

"No, Teddy is right," said Wally as he smiled down at Cassie. "My – fiancée – certainly did keep me waiting. I like to think she was making me fight for her love."

"One way of looking at it," said Teddy under his breath.

Joe entered the room.

"Joe, fetch a bottle of champagne at once!" said Howard.

"Yes, sir," said Joe, looking in surprise at the scene of Wally standing with his arm around Cassie.

He turned quickly and rushed down to the cellars, wondering what on earth was going on. He selected a bottle and returned to the drawing room.

"Will I open the bottle now, sir?" asked Joe.

"Yes, do," said Howard.

Joe opened the bottle of champagne and filled the glasses on a tray. Then he offered a glass to everyone in the room.

"We're celebrating my engagement to Miss Cassie, Joe," said Wally as he took his glass.

"Oh!" Joe was shocked. "Congratulations, sir – and to you, Miss Cassie."

177

"Thank you, Joe," said Cassie, taking her glass.

"Why don't you join us and have a celebratory drink, Joe," suggested Wally. "That would be okay, wouldn't it, Dorothy?"

"Ah, yes – I suppose so." Dorothy was uncomfortable and surprised by the suggestion.

"It would be a waste of good champagne on him. He doesn't even drink," said Teddy.

"Regardless, I think it would be nice for him to toast our engagement. I know what a loyal servant Joe is," said Wally.

"Thank you, sir." Joe nodded. He went back to the drinks table and poured himself half a glass of champagne.

"And I propose the toast," said Howard. "To Cassie and Wally!"

Everyone raised their glasses. "To Cassie and Wally!"

"I hope you don't mind, Dorothy, but I took the liberty of contacting *The Times* in London myself today to place the engagement announcement in tomorrow's newspaper."

"*The Times*!" Cassie cried, choking on her champagne.

"Yes, I know the announcement is usually placed by the bride's parents, but I thought I'd save you the job," said Wally.

"Oh, yes, I see." Dorothy was taken aback. "But it's customary to tell relatives and friends first."

"Well, I thought there's no point in waiting around about these things."

"Apparently so!" said Dorothy. "I shall be quite busy tonight phoning everybody to let them know before they read about it in the newspaper in the morning."

"I think you might have mentioned it to me before doing that," said Cassie, astonished.

"Did I not? I'm sorry, my darling." Wally leaned forward and kissed her lips.

"Actually, Dorothy, before you telephone everybody, I was thinking we could have our engagement party here at Cliffenden next week. I was hoping Saturday?"

"That doesn't give us much time," said Dorothy nervously.

"For seasoned hosts like you, plenty of time. Besides you'll have

Bruton and Joe on top of the whole thing quick sharp," said Wally.

"But –" began Dorothy.

"That's absolutely fine," Howard cut in over his wife and smiled. "We very much look forward to hosting our Cassie's engagement party here next week."

"Thank you, Howard," said Wally.

"Well, I don't think I really want to have an engagement party quite so soon," said Cassie, very alarmed at the tide of events that was now threatening to overtake her.

"Just leave the whole thing to me, my sweet," said Wally. "You won't have to do a thing. All you'll have to do is show up and look pretty."

Cassie forced herself to hold back on the tirade of abuse she wanted to fire at him. She smiled sweetly and sipped her champagne.

"We must get those papers signed for Cliffenden tomorrow if we get a chance," she said. "So we can relax and put the servants' minds at rest that their jobs are safe."

"Oh, yes, that," said Wally. "There's a paper missing, I'm afraid, amongst the paperwork."

"Missing?"

"Yes, don't worry about it. Mr. Dickens from the bank is bringing it over."

"Mr. Dickens from the bank? When?"

"Well, he's invited to our engagement party, so he'll be bringing it then," said Wally.

Joe was sleeping when his door opened.

"Joe!" whispered a woman's voice.

He sat up.

"Who's that?" he called.

"*Shhh!*" said Cassie, coming in and closing the door behind her. She tiptoed quickly over to his bed and sat down on the edge of it.

"Miss Cassie! What are you doing here? You shouldn't be here! Mr. Bruton is only three rooms down! And Mrs. Farrell next door!"

"Never mind that. Listen to me – I'm in a dreadful situation!"

The moonlight coming through the window illuminated her face.

"What's going on, Miss Cassie? You've agreed to marry Mr. Stanton?"

"The bastard forced my hand! I had no choice but to say I would marry him or else he would have left for London and Cliffenden would have been lost forever!"

"So you are marrying him?"

"I've no intention of marrying him. I just said it to keep my plan alive. But now he's gone and announced it in tomorrow's papers. Bowden's parents will see it. They pore over the births, engagements and obituary section of the papers every day. It's the highlight of their day to see if they spot anybody they know!"

"What are you going to do?"

"I asked Wally again tonight about signing the papers for Cliffenden. And he's come up with another excuse saying that a paper is missing and a director from his bank, a Mr. Dickens, who is coming to the engagement party next week, will bring it with him and he'll sign it then. He's taking no chances with it at all! He's making sure our whole engagement is announced to family, friends, everybody in society, before he signs the papers – to make sure I don't back out. He doesn't trust me at all!"

"Maybe for good reason," ventured Joe.

"This is what I want you to do – go to Bowden tomorrow and explain that the engagement is not real and I'm being forced into it to save Cliffenden. Then tell him we must escape from here as soon as Wally signs the bloody papers."

"But, Miss Cassie, are you planning on running away the night of your engagement party?"

"As soon as is humanly possible."

"But – but – what if the papers don't get signed that day?"

"They will, Joe. Wally knows he can't put it off any longer. He won't risk a scene or me cancelling the party or just not showing up. We've entered into an unspoken bargain, and he knows what's being bartered."

"But you'll be ruined in society!"

"That's my ace card, Joe. Wally doesn't think I will risk being ruined by pulling out of the marriage arrangements once we've announced it to the world. But I don't care about being ruined! I don't care about all that. I only care about Bowden and being with him for the rest of my life. So you must go to him tomorrow and explain all this."

"And what if, as soon as you're gone, he tears up the papers that are signed, Miss Cassie?"

"He can't do that. They are legally binding documents and my father will have his copy. There's nothing he can do."

"But I don't know if I'll be able to get out of the house tomorrow. Mr. Bruton –"

"Joe!" Cassie reached out and grabbed his hand. "You just *have* to! If you think anything of me at all, you'll see Bowden tomorrow."

Joe nodded. "Alright, Miss, I'll try my best!"

"Thank you," she said, getting up and quietly tiptoeing out of the room again.

CHAPTER 26

The whole mood of the house seemed to have lifted with the announcement of the engagement. Lady Dorothy and Howard were elated. Even Bruton seemed to be in better form. Joe waited until his afternoon duties were completed before knocking on Burton's office door.

"Yes?"

"Mr. Bruton, would it be alright if I go down to the village for a couple of hours? I've got some stuff to do."

"No, you can't. There's plenty of items that need attending to here with the engagement party scheduled for next week. That must take precedence over your – stuff!"

Joe nodded and was about to turn when he thought of Cassie's desperate plea to him.

"Sorry, Mr. Bruton, but – but I haven't had my day off since Mr. Stanton arrived and I really need to see my mother. I really have to go!"

Bruton looked at him, surprised by the outburst.

"Very well, but make sure you are back within two hours."

"Thank you, sir!"

As Joe rushed out of the house and on to his bicycle he wasn't sure if he was more surprised that he had stood up to Bruton or that Bruton had conceded to him. He reached the gateway of Cliffenden and furiously cycled towards the Greys' place.

He didn't have time to be lurking around, waiting for Bowden to appear, and cycled round the back and knocked on the back door. The Greys' cook opened it, a dishevelled woman wiping her hands on her apron.

"I need to see Mr. Bowden Grey."

"Who are you?"

"Can you just tell him there's somebody here to see him!" Joe said in exasperation.

"He's not here. He's gone for a walk down by the river. Goodness knows what time he'll be back, what with the way he's been lately. His head was always in the clouds, but lately –"

Joe turned and rushed away towards the river.

"You're very welcome!" cried the cook after him.

Joe was running along the river bank, scanning the landscape for any sight of Bowden. Finally he saw a lonesome figure sitting watching the water flow by.

"Mr. Bowden!" said Joe, out of breath as he reached him.

"Joe!" Bowden jumped up.

As Joe tried to catch his breath, he noticed that Bowden looked as if he had tears in his eyes.

"What's going on? I saw in the papers today that Cassie has got engaged to Stanton?" The tears in his eyes were threatening to spill over.

"Stanton forced her hand and said he wouldn't sign the papers to save Cliffenden if she didn't agree to marry him."

"So they are getting married?" Bowden's heart felt as if it was being ripped in two.

"No, she's only saying she is until the papers are signed – which should be next week when the man from the bank arrives with them the day of the engagement party."

"Engagement party!"

"Yes."

"But how is she going to get out of this?" Bowden demanded. "We were meant to elope together."

"And that's what she's going to do, once the papers are signed."

Bowden sank down on the bank again. "I can't take much more of this. All I want is to be with her. Not seeing her is killing me. But – but are you sure she doesn't mean to marry Stanton?"

"She says she loves you and to just wait until next week and you can go and start your new life together."

"If I didn't know her so well, I'd . . . I'd think she was making a fool out of me . . . leading me on, instead of being honest with me, too cowardly to tell me the truth that we have no future together."

"She said to say she loves you, Mr. Bowden."

Bowden nodded. "Tell her I love her too."

"I will," nodded Joe. "I'd better get back or I'll be in trouble with Mr. Bruton."

"Of course when we were married it was cited as the wedding of the year," said Dorothy as she discussed the engagement party that night with the family.

"It was very hard on Dorothy – we were no sooner married than I had to go off to the war," said Howard.

"It was much harder for you, my dear, going to war. But we managed," smiled Dorothy. "Wonderful for you two that you can start your married life without it being marred by anything like that."

As Cassie sat beside Wally, she imagined if she had ever been stuck in a marriage with Wally, she would have been very happy to wave him off to war.

"All the invitations have gone out now for the engagement party. Have you invited everybody you need to, Wally?" asked Dorothy.

"Of course – everyone I need to."

"You didn't forget to invite Mr. Dickens from your bank?" Cassie asked.

"Of course not."

As Cassie imagined everyone's faces when it was realised that she had bolted, she almost felt sorry for Wally. Certainly for her parents, who would consider the whole thing as bringing a great shame on the family. But she was doing all this for them, to save their home, she reminded herself. And as for Wally, he had behaved so ruthlessly, continually bullying her into this situation, that any sympathy she had for him quickly evaporated. He was a man who needed to learn how to be humble. But the most important thing for her was that she would soon be with her Bowden, and none of them could interfere in her life ever again. She anxiously waited for a moment alone with Joe and got her opportunity when they rose to go for dinner.

"Well?" she asked nervously.

"I explained everything to him. And told him that you would be leaving with him next week as soon as the papers were signed."

"He realises the engagement is a charade?"

"I explained it all to him," said Joe.

Cassie relaxed and gave a sigh of relief.

Cliffenden was a hive of activity for the following week. Joe was run off his feet as the house prepared for the engagement party. As he watched everyone's excitement he could hardly imagine what the aftermath of Cassie's departure would be like. What would be the consequences following her elopement with Bowden? Lady Dorothy and Howard would be devastated. Wally enraged. Society scandalised. Only Teddy, Joe imagined, would trundle on oblivious to the disaster. At least Cliffenden would be saved, but it would never be the same again. Especially for Joe, as he realised how important Cassie had become to him. He couldn't believe he would never see her again. And it would all be so different if she just went ahead and married Wally. Not only would all their lives be happy, but Joe's own future would include Cassie and a wonderful position as head of Wally's household. It was like a bright future being snatched away from him.

It was the day before the engagement party and Joe was out emptying the bins when he heard his name called. Going around the corner of the stables he saw Bowden there.

Joe hurried over to him.

"There are guests already arriving for the party tomorrow, Mr. Bowden – you might be spotted," warned Joe.

"I'm not staying. I just wanted to give you this to hand to Cassie." Bowden handed Joe an envelope. "Make sure she gets it."

Joe nodded and tucked the envelope into his inside pocket.

Cassie had spent the week, when she wasn't pretending to be the devoted fiancée, deciding what she needed to take away with her. She packed a suitcase with the clothes she felt she needed and added some valuables – her jewellery and some money – things that she felt would see them into the short-term future and pay for their passage to America.

She was so happy and excited at the prospect of her new life with Bowden that she scarcely gave any thought to the fact that she would not be seeing her home or family again. It had become so stressful for her that she realised she would be just glad to be away. She anxiously awaited Mr. Dicken's arrival and for the paperwork to be finally signed.

"What are you wearing tomorrow for the party?" asked Wally.

"Oh, I was thinking my green gown," said Cassie, wondering why he should enquire what she would wear, apart from the fact he was just seeing her as a possession to be shown off.

"I prefer your blue gown, far more sophisticated," he said.

She bit back a snide reply. "In that case – blue it shall be!"

As she thought of her beloved Bowden she knew he would never care what she was wearing, as long as she was with him.

That evening Joe sat in his room, looking at the envelope Bowden had given him. It was a blank envelope with not even Cassie's name written on it. His curiosity was burning as to what was in the envelope. As he toyed with it he suddenly decided to open it. He could get another envelope and just put the letter inside it and hand it to Cassie; she would be none the wiser. He took out the letter and with slightly shaking hands opened it and read it.

My darling Cassie,

I have missed you so much this past while, I can't put it into words. All I can think of is no matter how hard it has been for me not seeing you, it has been so much worse for you. Trapped in Cliffenden under your family's constant supervision and pretending to be nice to Wally Stanton. My heart was broken when I read you were engaged to him in the paper. I couldn't believe it, and yet I knew the intense pressure you were under to save Cliffenden, and thought you must have had to cave in. Joe then explained you are not really engaged to him, at least in your heart.

I dream of being alone together, away from here, far away from the prying eyes and the rules we are forced to live with.

I know you are waiting on paperwork to be signed to save Cliffenden but, I wonder, darling, will that be the end of it? Will you ever be free? Will they ever let you go? And when we do elope this weekend, if we do, what life will you have with me? You are leaving everything behind, my darling. Is it fair to ask this of you? And once you bolt from your engagement, the ensuing scandal will mean you can never return.

I want you to think about this carefully, darling. Because, if you come with me, I want to never see a moment of regret in your eyes.

Joe said the paperwork is to be signed tomorrow for Cliffenden, which should allow you to leave with your family's future secure. But I want you to know I will never blame you or be angry with you if you feel at this late stage that you can't go with me. Regardless of what you decide, I am leaving here tomorrow. I can't take this secrecy and double life anymore. I'm leaving on the eight o'clock evening train for Dublin.

I will never be coming back. I wish with all my heart that you will be on that platform at the same time as me to go and start our new life together. When I arrive in Dublin I will be staying at a guest house for the next two weeks before I take the ferry to England. As we agreed, it's better we leave for America from England as our journey will be less traceable should Wally Stanton or your parents try to pursue us. The address in Dublin is 7 Sandford Road, Ranelagh. If you are held up and can't be on the platform for the train tomorrow, you know where I'll be for you to join me and we can set sail to America together in two weeks' time.

And I'll love you forever,
Bowden

Joe stared at the letter. Bowden was definitely going and had given Cassie an ultimatum. To leave with him forever, or never see him again. Joe wondered if perhaps Bowden feared Cassie wasn't being truthful with him. Maybe he thought Cassie didn't have the courage to go and he loved her so much he was giving her an easy way out. Joe pondered those words: giving her an easy way out.

CHAPTER 27

The next morning Cassie got up and felt her heart pounding from the excitement. She just had to get through the day and she would be gone that evening, she hoped. In a way the whole thing suited her; she always hated goodbyes. She had managed to sneak her suitcase out the previous day and it was now hidden in the boot of the car, ready for her departure. As she walked down the stairs she wondered where she would be that time tomorrow.

"Good morning, Wally," she said as she came down the stairs, smiling.

"Good morning, Cassie. And what a beautiful day it is. Let me lead you in to breakfast."

"How gallant!" she said as she took his arm.

Joe saw them walking in arm and arm as he served breakfast and found it impossible to believe they were not a couple in love. He'd had a sleepless night, tossing and turning, with the contents of Bowden's letter going through his mind. He didn't know why he hadn't delivered it to Cassie straight away. Or certainly before she had retired to bed. But something was stopping him from doing it. He felt Cassie really didn't know what she was doing with this insane plan to run away. He couldn't even think of Cliffenden without her. Of his life without her. All their happiness depended on her staying. And even Bowden was nearly saying it in his letter. That she would be better off staying and not leaving with him.

"Coffee, please, Joe," said Cassie, jolting him out of his trance.

189

He jumped to attention. "Certainly, Miss Cassie."

As the guests arrived during the day, Cassie played the perfect hostess, warmly introducing Wally to everyone he didn't know, and being charming to his friends and family on being introduced to them. She was keeping a beady eye out for this elusive Mr. Dickens from Wally's bank and was thrilled when the bespectacled man finally arrived at four in the afternoon.

"Mr. Dickens! I've heard so much about you! I'm delighted you managed to come," said Cassie.

"Well, Wally is an old friend of mine. Wouldn't dream of missing this important event in his life. Well done, Wally old chap!"

"Yes, I know!" said Wally, looking proud.

"Well, now that you're here, Mr. Dickens, let's get this ghastly bit of work out of the way before we can enjoy ourselves," urged Cassie.

"Ghastly work?" Dickens looked confused.

"Yes, the missing paper for Cliffenden," said Cassie.

"Sorry?" Dickens looked even more confused.

Wally coughed and frowned at Dickens, nodding at him. "You know, the paper I told you to bring, which wasn't in my file."

"Oh, yes, that paper!" said Dickens.

"Well, I'll fetch my parents and we'll get the thing signed in the library and get it out of the way," said Cassie, realising that Wally hadn't been missing any paper at all and had just used it as an excuse to put her off.

Wally made a face. "Cassie, this is our engagement party. We can do that tomorrow."

"No, Wally, it's hanging over my head like a bad smell. I want it done now," said Cassie.

"Oh, it's Saturday, it's my engagement day. The last thing I want is to be looking at papers today."

Cassie felt her temper flare but kept her voice low and stern. "I want it to done *now*, Wally. Look, you've got what you wanted. We're engaged, we're having the party. Now I'm tired of having the financial insecurity of Cliffenden hanging over my head and I want it done now!"

Wally looked at Cassie's angry face and smiled briefly at her. "Very well, my sweet. I'll get the paperwork and meet your parents in the library in ten minutes."

"Thank you!"

Cassie looked on as Wally signed the paperwork, followed by Howard and Lady Dorothy, at the desk in the library.

"And there is your copy," said Wally, handing Howard some papers.

"Thank you, Wally. We're so grateful for what you've done," said Dorothy.

"Why wouldn't I? You're family now," said Wally, smiling over at Cassie. "Satisfied, my love?"

"Yes, very," said Cassie, feeling elated.

Joe had hardly spoken to Cassie all day and his nerves were nearly shattered as the realisation of what he was doing dawned on him. He was sabotaging their future. Bowden would be gone by eight that evening and she was letting him go without the knowledge of what was happening because he had kept the letter. Also he couldn't imagine what would happen to him if she discovered what he had done. But he was saving her future, as well as his own.

As Cassie mingled with friends and family she took it all in. She watched her parents, looking so happy and relieved now Cliffenden's future was secure. They could continue living here as they always had and Teddy could continue doing whatever Teddy did. Of course they would be horrified and scandalised when they realised she had run off with Bowden. But in time they would realise she couldn't have done anything but be with the man she loved. She hoped that one day they would see past their disappointment and anger to recognise this thing she had done in securing Cliffenden for them. She would miss them all terribly, but she couldn't go on without Bowden anymore.

She looked at Joe busy serving people. He had been such a great help to her. She was so incredibly fond of him that she would miss him dearly. She wasn't going to say goodbye to him because she just wanted to slip away. But once she was settled with Bowden she would write a long letter to him, telling him how much he had meant to her and how she and Bowden would always be grateful for the part he played in bringing them together.

Guests had been coming and going all day, settling into their rooms, and by seven people were retiring to change and get ready for the party. Cassie thought it was the ideal time to slip away. She left the drawing room and went up the stairs to her room. She had left her coat and hat in the car so she wouldn't be seen walking out of the house in outdoor clothes and draw attention to herself. She took out the letter she had written, explaining everything to her parents, and left it on her desk for them to find.

She waited half an hour until she was sure everybody would be in their rooms, having a nap, taking baths, laying out clothes for the night ahead. She then left her room and headed quickly down the stairs and across the hallway to the front door. She slipped out and around the gable of the house to where she had parked the car. She hurriedly pulled her coat on, got in and set off down the drive past the array of expensive cars parked there. As she turned out of the gateway she didn't look back. She headed to the Grey home.

As she swerved into the Greys' forecourt she thought she had to let Bowden know that they couldn't waste time in case they discovered she was gone from Cliffenden and sent out a search party. She smiled to herself as she knew Bowden wouldn't need to be told such a thing. He would be as anxious to leave as she was. He would throw a few things into a suitcase, if he hadn't packed already, and they would be on the road. She would leave the car somewhere in Dublin and let her parents know where to collect it.

She sprang out of the car and skipped over to the front door.

She rapped the knocker a few times. The door was opened by Reggie.

"Oh, hello, Mr. Grey, could you tell Bowden I'm here please," she said, a broad smile on her face.

He looked at her, perplexed. "But Bowden is gone, my dear."

"Gone? Gone where?"

"Who is it, Reggie?" asked Molly, coming out of the drawing room with four overexcited dogs. "Oh Cassie – what are you doing here?"

"I just want to see Bowden, please, Mrs. Grey."

"*Get down!*" Molly screamed at the dogs. She ushered them back into the drawing room and slammed the door shut on them. "Those brutes! You know, I discovered this morning they have been making a lavatory out of my knitting basket. And I had been just in the middle of knitting a polo-neck sweater for Reggie . . . all ruined now, of course."

Cassie tried to keep her patience.

"Now, how can we help you, Cassie?" asked Molly.

By now Cassie couldn't keep the frustration out of her voice. "Bowden! I want to see Bowden, please!"

"But did you not tell her he's left, Reggie?" Molly asked.

"I did, I tell you!" Reggie defended himself.

Cassie's face creased in confusion. "Left for where?"

"America," informed Molly.

"*America!*"

"Yes, New York," said Molly.

"Chicago!" corrected Reggie.

"*New York!*" insisted Molly.

"Well, yes, but he wouldn't have gone yet," Cassie said.

"He has, Cassie. He left a couple of hours ago. Took the last Dublin train this evening," said Molly.

"I know, but – did he leave a message?"

"No. For whom?" asked Molly, bewildered.

"A letter or something for me?" Cassie was desperate.

"No!" said Molly and Reggie in unison.

"We're heartbroken he's gone, place won't be the same without him," said Reggie.

"But we didn't want to hold him back," said Molly stoically. "There's nothing for him here, and we had to let him go. I don't know why he's stayed as long as he did. There was nothing keeping him here, but he seemed to be holding on, for whatever reason."

"And he's been so morose recently. I'm glad he's now free to make his own way in the world, without two old giddy-goats like us holding him back," Reggie said.

Cassie stood in silence.

"Are you alright, Cassie dear – you've gone quite pale?" said Molly.

"He can't have gone! He wouldn't have gone without me!" said Cassie quietly.

"What? What?" Reggie strained to hear her.

"Do you need to sit down? Maybe a stiff drink?" asked Molly, wondering what on earth was the matter with the girl.

"No, I . . ." Cassie trailed off.

"Did I not hear a rumour that it's your engagement tonight? That you're marrying that Mr. Stanton?" said Molly.

"The American chap," added Reggie.

"For goodness sake, she knows who he is, Reggie! She's marrying him!" snapped Molly.

"Yes, I . . . I'm sorry. It's all a misunderstanding. I'm sorry for disturbing you," said Cassie and she turned and ran to her car.

Bowden stood on the platform of the train station looking at his watch. It was almost eight o'clock and no sign of Cassie. He walked up and down the platform, his heart pounding. Any second now she would arrive on the platform, smiling and laughing and running into his arms. He heard a whistle and saw the train coming down the track.

"Cassie – where are you?" he whispered to himself.

The train pulled up at the platform and a few passengers got off.

"All aboard for Dublin!" shouted the station master.

Bowden stood still, staring at the entrance of the platform in a trance.

"Sorry, sir, but are you getting on this train?"

Bowden turned to see it was the station master talking to him.

"Sir? If you are, you need to get on now. The train is about to depart," warned the station master.

Bowden nodded and, picking up his suitcase, made his way to a carriage and opened the door. He hesitated, then stepped into the carriage. He put his case on the rack and turning, opened the window and put his head out, desperately searching the length of the platform for Cassie.

The station master blew his whistle and waved a flag and the train began to pull away from the station. Bowden continued to stare at the platform as the train picked up speed quickly, leaving it behind, his two hands gripping the window, his eyes filled with tears.

CHAPTER 28

Cassie drove slowly back to Cliffenden in a trance.

"He can't have left. He wouldn't have left without me," she kept repeating to herself.

But he had. He hadn't waited for her. He had slipped way without even saying goodbye. Run away without even telling her he was going. She reached the gateway to Cliffenden and stalled the car. She looked up at all the cars parked in the distance at the house. All the people there waiting for her. She slowly turned the car into the driveway. She continued up to the house, parked the car around the gable of the house and got out. She took off her coat and left it in the car, then made her way to the back.

She reached the kitchen door and walked in. The kitchen staff were all busy at work preparing the food for the night's events. Mrs. Crowther sat by the stove, sherry glass in hand. All the talk and work came to an abrupt halt when they saw Cassie.

"Miss Cassie!" exclaimed Mrs. Crowther, quickly putting down her sherry. "Can we help you?"

Cassie ignored them all and walked through the kitchen and down the corridor that led to the servants' stairs. She walked up the stairs and made her way down to her bedroom. Once there, she closed the door and stumbled over to her dressing table. She sat down, staring at herself in the mirror in a trance, not even seeing the tears falling down her face.

The bedroom door opened and Dorothy swept in.

She took one look at her daughter sitting slumped with her back to her and wondered what was going on.

"Cassie?"

Cassie quickly reached for the envelope containing the letter she had left for her parents and put it in a drawer.

Dorothy made her way to Cassie. "Cassie! Why haven't you changed? Why aren't you ready? Don't you realise what time it is?"

Dorothy saw Cassie had been crying and began to panic that her daughter was having second thoughts.

"What time is it?" asked Cassie absentmindedly.

"Cassie, it's nine thirty! All the guests are already downstairs waiting for you! What on earth do you think you're playing at?"

Cassie continued looking at her reflection in the mirror.

Dorothy decided that whatever was wrong with her daughter, she didn't want to find out, not with a house full of guests waiting downstairs.

She quickly grabbed Cassie's wrist and pulled her to her feet.

"Come on, Cassie, let's get you ready as quickly as possible!"

As Joe helped to lay out the sumptuous buffet in the dining room, his nerves were shattered. He kept thinking that Cassie and Bowden would somehow discover about the undelivered letter. He was thinking up excuses in his head to explain why he hadn't delivered it. He was getting anxious as the clock struck ten and there was still no sign of Cassie, even though all the guests were assembled and the party was in full swing.

Suddenly he heard applause from the hallway and rushed out to see Cassie walking down the stairs with Dorothy.

"Thank you . . . thank you," Cassie said to the guests as she made her way through the well-wishers and into the drawing room.

"And here she is now!" said Wally and he cut through the crowd to greet her. He took her hand and declared, "Ladies and gentlemen – my fiancée!"

The crowd clapped their approval as Wally moved in and kissed her. As he pulled away from her he whispered harshly, "You didn't wear the blue dress!"

She ignored him and continued to smile meekly as Wally led her around to everybody to accept congratulations.

As the night wore on, Joe desperately sought a moment to talk to Cassie, but she was surrounded by people.

There was a tinkle of a fork against a glass which brought quiet to the room. To Joe's surprise it was Bruton, and to his even bigger surprise Bruton was smiling from ear to ear. He'd never seen Bruton smile before. Assembled behind Bruton were all the household staff.

"Lady Dorothy, Mr. Howard, I just wanted to say on behalf of all the servants and staff here at Cliffenden that we wish Miss Cassie and Mr. Stanton all the happiness in the world. We've known Miss Cassie since she was a child, and she means a great deal to all of us."

"I hope I do too!" roared Teddy across the room to laughter.

"In equal measure, Mr. Teddy." Bruton even allowed himself a laugh.

As Joe looked at Cassie being held firmly by Wally, he realised she was the only person in the room not smiling.

"And as a token of our affection for Miss Cassie, and of course having secured Lady Dorothy's permission, Kathy here is going to sing a song," said Bruton.

Dorothy nodded her approval.

Kathy stood nervously beside Bruton.

"Well! Get on with it, girl!" ordered Bruton, pushing her forward.

Kathy stepped bashfully forward and cleared her voice. Then she started to sing. Joe thought her voice the sweetest, saddest voice he had ever heard. It resonated as she sang through the verses of 'She Moved through the Fair'.

"The people were saying
No two e'er were wed
But one had a sorrow
That was never said
And I smiled as she passed
With her goods and her gear

And that was the last time
That I saw my dear.

Last night she came to me
My dead love came in
So softly she came
That her feet made no din
As she laid her hand on me
And this she did say
It will not be long, love,
Till our wedding day."

"Beautiful! Well done, Kathy!" Dorothy led the approval.

Wally looked at Cassie and saw a tear trickling down her cheek.

"What's this, my dear?" he said, reaching for the tear and wiping it away. "Could this mean you are actually truly happy?"

He bent down and kissed her.

As Teddy led the increasingly drunken antics of the party, Cassie escaped through the French window and stood at the end of the patio looking out at the sea.

Joe had spotted her leaving and, seizing an opportunity, followed her out. He saw the lonely figure at the end of the patio and made his way over to her.

"Are you alright, Miss Cassie?"

"He's gone, Joe. Bowden has left me."

Joe felt his heart pound. "I don't understand?"

"I was leaving this evening, the papers had been signed for Cliffenden. So I drove up to collect him from his home – but he had already gone."

"Did he – did he leave any message?"

"Nothing, nothing at all."

Joe felt his body relax. "Perhaps it's for the best, Miss Cassie. He probably thought you'd be better off married to Mr. Stanton."

"How could he ever think such a thing? He knew he was my whole world. We were so close. We didn't even have to talk – we understood what the other was thinking. And for him to just desert me, without even telling me . . . to abandon me . . . he's broken my heart . . . I'll never trust another person as long I live . . . I'll only ever put myself first from now on."

During the night, Cassie lay in her bed in the semi-darkness, only the moonlight illuminating the room. The party was over, most people gone to bed. She was drifting in and out of sleep. As she looked to the window she saw it was open and there was a figure standing there. She didn't move as the figure walked towards her and then sat down on the side of her bed.

"Bowden!" she cried as she sat up quickly in shock. She reached out to touch him but then he was gone and the window was closed.

She lay back against her pillows and closed her eyes, silently crying.

Joe lay in his bed, everything that had happened swirling through his head. Cassie might think she was heartbroken now. But soon she would realise that what had happened was for the best. He knew that. He had done the right thing in keeping the letter. He knew he had. Suddenly his bedroom door opened and a woman came in and quickly closed the door behind her.

"Cassie?" he said, his mouth open.

"What are you talking about – Cassie? Have you gone mad?" asked the woman and he realised it was Kathy.

"What are you doing here?" he asked, sitting up in the bed.

She crept over to the bed. "I've come to see you!"

"Kathy, Bruton might wake up! The slightest thing wakes him! And Mrs. Farrell is just next door!"

"They won't wake tonight, I can promise you. Not with the amount of sherry they and Mrs. Crowther put away down in the kitchens after the party ended. Never saw Bruton have a drink before, let alone that amount of drink!" She took an open bottle of wine from behind her back and took a drink from it, before plonking it on the side table beside the bed.

"Is that one of Mr. Bruton's bottles from the cellar? He will kill you!"

"He'll have too much of a hangover in the morning to notice. Now, shove over!" Lifting the blankets, she got into the bed beside him.

She reached forward and kissed him before pulling back, smiling at him and saying, "We can talk about our wedding plans in the morning!"

CHAPTER 29

Six Months Later

Cliffenden was wrapped in a blanket of snow. Joe remembered the snow that was there the year before when he had arrived in Cliffenden. It didn't seem like a year, it seemed like an eternity. The weeks and months after the engagement party had been taken up with plans for Cassie's wedding. Cassie and her mother travelled to London a lot to make the wedding plans, for it had been decided that it would take place there. Joe was slightly disappointed as he would have loved to have been waiting at the wedding breakfast and seen Cassie get married at Cliffenden.

Cassie never mentioned Bowden again to him. It was as if Bowden had never existed. Joe liked to think that was because she was now happily engaged to Wally and delighted and looking forward to her new life. But when he looked into her eyes, he knew that wasn't the truth.

Joe couldn't wait to start his new life as butler for Wally and Cassie. He had attentively studied Bruton in all things, learning what was to be expected of him and what he should be doing. Bruton seemed very impressed with Joe's new-found interest in the profession. But Bruton or nobody else knew that he would soon be butler for the Stanton household.

It was Christmas and the week before the wedding in London. Wally had come to Cliffenden to spend Christmas with his fiancée and her family. Joe was extra polite and attentive to Wally, making sure to impress him and for him to know he was more than capable for the position about to be entrusted to him. He kept waiting for

Wally to bring the matter up, but he hadn't yet. Joe decided he must have a lot on his mind with the wedding in a few days.

It was two days after Christmas and Wally was setting off back to London.

"I'll see you all in London in a couple of days," he said to the Fullertons and he reached over and kissed Cassie. "Goodbye, my dear."

"Safe journey, Wally. Joe is taking your cases out to your car," said Dorothy.

Joe crunched through the snow out to Wally's Rolls Royce and placed the suitcases in the boot. Wally's chauffeur was about to get out of the car to have the back door open for Wally.

"It's alright, stay where you are!" Joe called. "I'll open the door for Mr. Stanton!"

The chauffeur nodded and sat back into the driver's seat. Joe held the door open and decided this was his opportunity to broach the subject of his new position. Wally came out of the front door and walked down the steps and over to the car.

"Thank you, Joe," said Wally as he went to sit in.

"Sorry, Mr. Stanton, if I could just have a word?" asked Joe.

Wally paused and looked at him. "Yes?"

"It's just with you getting married to Miss Cassie in a few days, I wanted to ask when you wanted me to start work in your house, just so I can give enough notice here at Cliffenden?"

"Start work?" Wally looked confused.

"As butler," said Joe.

"Ah, yes, as butler," Wally said, frowning. Then he smiled. "Actually, Joe, my bank is posting me to Singapore as soon as Cassie and I are married. That's the thing with a job like mine – you can be sent anywhere around the world at any time. We're due to be in Singapore for quite some time, so we won't have any need for a butler in London."

Joe's mouth dropped open.

"You know, it's probably just as well. As you said yourself, Joe, you really need years of experience before becoming a butler, experience you don't have yet. But I do thank you for looking after Miss Cassie so well here at Cliffenden. I know she's quite fond of you, old chap. But she'll have me to look after her from now on." Wally clapped his hand on Joe's shoulder and smiled before sitting into the car.

Joe stood there, stunned.

"Joe – the door!" snapped Wally.

Joe slammed the door shut. The chauffeur started the engine and drove down the driveway, leaving Joe standing staring after it in the falling snow.

PART TWO

England 1988

CHAPTER 30

Joe sat in his office in London preparing himself for the afternoon ahead. In front of him on his desk was the file he had got from the DPP on Cassandra Fullerton. He had forensically gone through it, inhaling every detail.

His secretary knocked on his door and popped her head around it.

"Mr. Grady, your taxi is waiting for you," she said.

"Okay, I'll be down in a minute."

He tidied the file away and placed it in his briefcase. As he was about to leave the office, he stopped at the mirror and looked at himself. It was almost fifty years since he had seen Cassie. As he studied himself he tried to remember what he looked like back then at Cliffenden. He had no photographs of himself from the time but he had been only a boy then so he must have changed considerably after so long a time. In fact, as he looked at his neatly cut silver hair, his pin-striped suit, the wrinkles around his eyes, he knew he had metamorphosed from his days as a footman at Cliffenden. But, apart from the physical changing, it was the expression in his eyes that was now so different. His eyes now looked cunning, informed, experienced. Not those of the wide-eyed innocent he was at Cliffenden.

He left the office and walked through his reception and out to the corridor. He got the lift down to the building's foyer and walked out to the street where his taxi was waiting.

"Holloway prison," said Joe, sitting into the back.

"Yes, sir," said the driver as he turned on the meter.

As the taxi drove through the streets of the city centre, Joe found himself becoming nervous. He had met hundreds and thousands of clients over the years and never felt a jot of emotion on meeting them but he was feeling intimidated at the thought of meeting Cassie again. She knew him when he was a lowly footman and not what he had become in the intermittent years.

The taxi pulled up outside the prison and he got out and paid the driver. He looked up at the dark forbidding building and it was impossible for him to imagine the Cassie Fullerton he knew in such an institution.

He went up to the entrance and signed himself in.

"I'm here to see my client, Cassandra Fullerton – there has been an appointment made," he said.

The clerk checked through the record and nodded. "She's waiting for you, if you could follow me."

"Very good," said Joe and he followed the man through a maze of corridors.

He had visited prisons many times and he never ceased to wonder at what dreadful places they were. He couldn't imagine how Cassie had survived since she had been arrested. Having said that, he realised it had been nearly fifty years since she had been last seen by anyone who knew her or the public. Goodness knows what kind of a life she'd had in the meantime.

"She's a bit of a cause célèbre for you, this one, Mr. Grady," said the clerk.

"Cause célèbre?"

"Yes, all the publicity she has received."

Joe decided it was an opportunity to pick the clerk's brains.

"Has she read much of the publicity she has generated?" he asked.

"The newspapers are readily available for her to read, but I'm not sure if she's read them. She has remained mostly in her room. She doesn't mix with the other prisoners much, if at all. I suppose she has little in common with the usual types we have in the remand centre."

"What have her spirits been like?"

"She's been polite, but has kept herself distant – as I said, keeps mostly to her room."

The clerk reached a door and stopped.

"Here we are," he said and opened the door for him.

Joe steadied himself and walked through.

"If you need anything, just ring the bell," said the clerk and he closed the door.

There was a simple table in the room and two chairs. She wasn't sitting at the table. She was standing with her back to him as she looked out the window. All the photos that appeared in the press of her had been taken in the thirties and forties – they hadn't managed to get any photos of her now.

He was almost frightened to address her. He actually hoped that she would turn around and it wouldn't be her. That they hadn't caught Cassie Fullerton, and that this was all a mistake. That she was living somewhere exotic abroad, and life hadn't caught up with this former beauty.

"Mrs. Stanton?" Joe said gently.

The woman turned around. It was Cassie alright. But not the one he remembered. Cassie had aged considerably. Her hair was now silver blonde, cut in a bob, not the glamorous tresses he remembered. Her face was etched with many tiny fine lines, but she still had a refined beauty that was disguised by years of . . . years of what, Joe wondered. The most remarkable thing he noticed was that she was dressed in a plain grey skirt and V-neck wool jumper. He had never seen her in anything not expensive and glamorous before.

"Yes?" she said, looking at him, confused.

He had wondered if she would recognise him, remember him. He had wondered if seeing him again might give her a big shock, and bring back memories of her youth at Cliffenden. But from what he could see, she didn't recall him at all. Even if Cassie could remember the footman who had served her at Cliffenden, he realised he probably looked even more different from those days than she did.

"Mrs. Stanton, I'm Joe Grady." He wondered if saying his name would make her instantly remember him. But again this was not the case. He wondered then if she had ever even heard his surname – she knew him just as 'Joe the footman'.

"Who are you?" she asked.

"I'm your lawyer, your barrister," he explained.

"But you're not the barrister I was dealing with before," she said. She still spoke in the clipped posh tones of her youth, but her voice seemed weaker.

"No, I'm taking over your case, if you're happy for me to do so?"

"I don't understand – I thought the last fellow had been appointed by the courts?"

"He was. But, as I said, I'm taking over your case."

"I see – why?"

"He was unable to continue. I am happy to represent you – that is if you are happy for me to represent you?"

"Well, the last fellow looked as if he should still be in short pants, so anyone over the age of twenty-five is a bonus, I suppose," she said.

He smiled and moved closer to the table.

"I have no money to pay you," she said. "So I think you might be wasting your time with me." She moved towards the table herself.

"That is all taken care of – please don't worry about that," he said.

"How very strange," she said.

He smiled to himself. It was just the way she would address something back at Cliffenden. Something that she might not have understood and wasn't going to spend too long trying to understand it.

"I presume by the poor British tax payer?" she checked.

"That's right," he lied.

"Shall we sit down?" he suggested.

She nodded and they each took a seat either side of the table.

"You've been treated well here? Have you any complaints?" he asked.

"No, perfectly fine. It's not The Ritz, mind you . . ."

He smiled at her and nodded. "Did your previous lawyer explain to you that it's an extradition hearing you are facing in London as the crime was committed in France?"

"Yes, he explained all that. So not only will I cost the British tax payer money to defend me, but then I'll go on to do the same to the French tax payer as well."

"I think the initial thing is to get you out of here and released on bail," he said.

"I'd say that won't happen. They spent almost fifty years trying to find me – they're not going to release me back into the wilderness now."

"We can but try, Mrs. Stanton," said Joe and he saw her wince. "You'd prefer me not to address you as such?"

"Yes, I'd prefer if you didn't. I was never comfortable being Mrs. Stanton and the press have chosen to call me by my proper name, Cassandra Fullerton, so . . ."

"Then shall I call you – Cassandra?"

"Cassie," she said.

Hearing her call herself that as she looked so alone and isolated, he had to fight the need to reach out and hug her.

"Well, Cassie, we must apply for bail. It will probably be set quite high. You've said you have no money. Do you have any relatives who could assist?"

"Not a soul, I'm afraid. My cousin is the Earl of Weybridge, but I doubt he will be my knight in shining armour. I saw he already gave an interview to the *Daily Mail* saying he wanted nothing to do with me and that I'd brought shame on the family for decades. He's opened the family stately home to the public, you see, since the sixties I understand, turned it into a kind of posh Disneyland and thinks I might be bad for business. My mother would be horrified to see her ancestral home belittled. Having said that, if he marketed me properly I might attract some ghoulish new tourists."

"I see. Have you any closer relatives? You had a brother, I believe?"

"Teddy? Teddy was killed in the war."

"Oh, I am sorry," said Joe who felt his heart sink as he remembered the dashing hilarious young man who had filled Cliffenden with joy and mischief.

"Why don't you go and try and find the person who killed him?" said Cassie. "He was shot in battle. Somebody killed him. There were so many people killed back then that I just don't know what all the fuss is about the person that I'm supposed to have killed. It's a strange irony, isn't it? Give a person a war and you can excuse a million deaths. As Stalin said, one death is a tragedy, a million is a statistic."

Joe decided to try and stick to the point of raising her bail. "And your own parents' home in Ireland?" He shuffled through papers he had taken out of his briefcase. "I believe it was called Cliffenden."

"My parents died years ago and I don't know what became of Cliffenden, Mr. Grady. You must remember I've been on the run and had no contact with my family or friends since the forties. "

"I do understand that, forgive me."

"Cliffenden was always run on a shoestring anyway, so I imagine there was nothing left in the estate after my parents passed away. It was probably all taken by the Irish government in taxes. I've had too many other things on my mind since my arrest to investigate what happened to it."

"You were friends with some very wealthy people when you were a young woman. Could any of them assist you now?"

"All my set are either dead, broke or senile. And any that aren't, like my dear cousin the earl, don't want to have any association with me. Perhaps you need to get it into your head, Mr. Grady, that I do not have anything, least of all anyone who cares about me to that extent."

She spoke matter of factly, but hearing her words made him sink into a dreadful sadness. For a young woman who was so loved and sought after to have ended up like this!

"Thank you for informing me of your situation," he said. "I shall apply for bail at the quickest opportunity."

"But why? It seems quite pointless, does it not?"

"We may get a sympathetic judge on the day." He smiled at her, realising he was probably giving her false hope. "He may set the bail terms very low."

"I can't see much sympathy out there for me at the moment, not judging by people's reactions to me."

"Try not to dwell on it, Cassie. Please trust me," he said, standing up, picking up his briefcase and shaking her hand. "I'll be in contact with you shortly."

He smiled at her and left the room.

Outside in the corridor an officer had been waiting for him.

"Finished?" he asked.

Joe nodded and was escorted out of the building where the clerk had arranged a taxi for him. Joe got the taxi to take him straight home.

CHAPTER 31

Joe was speaking to Cassie in a room at the court buildings before they were due in court for the bail hearing.

"For all intents and purposes, the hearing will be the same as a trial. The Crown Prosecution Services have appointed a barrister in order to prosecute you and all the evidence will be presented in court. The only difference is that your case will be tried before a judge as opposed to a jury."

"And, if I am then extradited to France, I have to go through the whole thing again?" asked Cassie.

"Well, if the judge orders your extradition then the evidence presented to the court in London will pretty much have already sealed your fate. The judge will not extradite you unless he really believes you are guilty. That's why these proceedings to stop your extradition are so important. We have appealed your extradition, pleading that you are not guilty, and today we are requesting bail pending the hearing."

"Will I be required to take the stand?" she asked.

"You need not say anything," he said. "Just leave everything to me and I'll do the talking."

"That will disappoint the assembled press. They can't wait to hear me speak."

"Well, they will get plenty of opportunity later. For now we need to concentrate on getting you out of the prison."

She looked bewildered and for the first time, worried. "To go where?"

The court clerk knocked and came in. "You're up now, Mr. Grady."

"Very well," said Joe.

Cassie stood up and he allowed her to walk out ahead of him. They walked down the long corridor and into the packed courtroom.

He saw Cassie flinch with nerves as she entered, at the sight of all the press in the public area who became visibly excited on seeing her.

"This will not take long," Joe whispered to her and beckoned her to take a seat beside him.

"All rise," said the court clerk and the whole room rose until the judge sat down.

"He doesn't look in a very good mood," whispered Cassie.

"Good, then he won't keep us long here deciding," said Joe.

The proceedings started and the barrister for the prosecution stood.

"My lord, we could not oppose the defendant being released more strongly. This is a woman who has been on the run, in hiding for nearly fifty years. She poses a significant flight risk, regardless of what you set the bail terms as. In fact, I can only think of the elusive Lord Lucan as being more of a flight risk should he ever be brought to custody."

The public-gallery crowd laughed as he sat down.

Joe rose to his feet. "My lord, my client poses no flight risk at all. She has, to put it in her own words, nowhere to go."

The prosecution barrister rose to his feet. "For a woman with nowhere to go, she has managed to remain quite invisible for almost five decades, my lord. I'm sure a woman of her guise and cunning would find an escape route just as quickly now as she did then."

Joe raised his voice. "My lord, my client is no longer a young woman. She is being kept in basic surroundings that cannot be good for her health. She is not a risk or a danger to the public. I suggest it would be churlish to keep her in those conditions."

"Churlish or not," said the judge, "the defendant is accused of a most heinous crime – an accusation she has not chosen to address despite having many years to do so to clear her name, if her name could be cleared."

"My client has every intention of now clearing her name, my lord. And I ask for you to release her to enable her to prepare for clearing her name."

"Very well. I set the bail at one hundred thousand pounds and a place to stay that is to the absolute approval of the court. Where is it suggested she will be staying?"

"My client will lodge the hundred-thousand-pounds bail money. And she will be staying at my address."

The public gallery erupted in talk.

"Silence!" shouted the judge.

"Given my reputation in the legal system, I trust I will be approved as a guardian?" said Joe.

Cassie stared at Joe in confusion and surprise.

"Say it isn't so, Joe!" said Ann down the phone to him.

"Say what isn't so, my dear?"

"This! What I read in the evening paper – that you are offering that woman, Cassandra Fullerton, a roof over her head!"

"Well, as you must know yourself, Ann, if you read it in the paper then it must be correct."

"Give me a straight answer, Joe. *Is* it correct?

"Yes, it is."

"But why? Why would you do such a thing?"

"I have my reasons."

"Well, I'd like to know what they are!"

"I'm a bit busy at the moment to go into all that," said Joe.

"You're always a bit busy to go into anything! Seriously, Joe, why are you even representing her?"

"Because I don't believe she's guilty."

"You're the only person in the country who doesn't. And where exactly do you mean to put her? Are you bringing her down here to Cambridge? Am I expected to look at her face while I have my scrambled eggs in the morning?"

"Of course not! She'll be staying at the apartment in the city. You won't ever have to see her or have anything to do with her. Unless you come to the apartment which, let's face it, you never do."

"It's out of the question! Have you lost your marbles? You simply can't harbour this criminal."

"It's too late. I've already lodged the paperwork. She'll be released into my care this evening."

"Well, I don't know how you'll sleep in your bed at night, I really don't. Knowing there's a murderess sleeping down the corridor from you. I hope you keep your door locked!"

"I will, don't worry, dear."

"Worry! I'm beside myself with worry. We'll be the talk of the bridge club. And I'm due there this evening!"

"Why don't you take Timothy with you? I'm sure he'll offer you support." Joe said the words nonchalantly, even though the thought of Ann's affair with Timothy Mason was cutting him like a knife.

As Ann ignored Joe's mention of Timothy and began to rant down the phone at him, Joe raised his eyes to heaven and placed the receiver on his desk to allow her to vent without him having to listen to her.

Finally he picked the receiver up again.

"Joe? Joe? Are you there?"

"Yes, listening to your every word, dear."

"Anyway, I realise I'm wasting my time talking to you. You'll just do what you want to, like you always do. But don't come crying to me when you're found murdered in your bed! I'll only tell you I told you so!"

"I'll bear that in mind. Now I'd better go."

"Goodbye!" Ann slammed down the phone.

Joe waited inside the prison entrance with two prison officers for Cassie to be brought to him. He finally saw her being escorted towards him carrying a small suitcase and dressed in a simple black dress and coat.

"Hello, again," he said and smiled at her.

"Hello," she said, looking at him nervously.

"I think I should warn you that there's a posse of press outside waiting for you," said Joe.

"I see," said Cassie as she looked down at the ground.

"Unfortunately we can nothing about that – they are entitled to be there. But I do have a car waiting for us to make the process as quick as possible," said Joe, nodding at the prison officers to acknowledge their assistance with the upcoming exit.

She nodded and braced herself as one of the prison officers opened the door. Joe put his arm around Cassie and hurried her through with a prison officer on the other side of her.

The photographers immediately began to snap her photo as she rushed along, looking down at the ground, with Joe shielding her face with his briefcase.

"Did you do it?" cried one of the journalists.

"Cassie! Give us a quick smile!" roared a photographer.

"We're making no comment today," said Joe as he rushed Cassie to the car where the driver was waiting with the back door open. Joe manoeuvred her into the back seat and sat in himself beside her. The driver rushed to the front and drove off quickly from the scrum.

"Are you alright?" Joe asked her.

She just nodded while staring out the window as they made their way to the city centre. She never said a word as they drove through the city but continued to look out the window, almost looking at modern-day London as if it were a different world. Joe realised it was a different world from the London she frequented as a young socialite.

The car pulled up outside a high apartment block on the Embankment overlooking the Thames.

"We're here," said Joe as he got out of the car and went around to the other side to open her door. Old habits die hard, he mused to himself.

As she stood gazing up at the apartment block, he had a few words with the driver who then took off.

"If you'd like to follow me?" Joe said as the doorman opened the glass doors for them.

"Good afternoon, Mr. Grady."

"Sam," acknowledged Joe as they walked past him and through a giant cream-tiled foyer to one of the lifts at the end wall.

He pressed for the lift and the door opened. She looked at him hesitantly before stepping into the lift. He realised how frightened and confused she must be – from being in an alien environment like prison to now being in a luxury apartment block with a man who, in her mind, she had never met before and knew nothing about.

He smiled reassuringly. "It's alright, Cassie. You're quite safe." He pressed the top button. "Top floor," he said.

"Are you going to throw me from the roof?" she asked with a wry smile.

"No! I'd then lose my hundred-thousand bail money. It's in my interest to keep you safe." The lift door opened. "This way!"

She followed him down the corridor and into his apartment. They walked through a narrow, exquisitely furnished hallway with doors leading off it. He opened the end door and beckoned her in.

Inside was a huge living room with wooden floors and modern cream furniture. She could see it was the penthouse and that there was a wall of windows and a balcony that wrapped around the apartment.

She walked through the room and took in the view that looked out across London, St Paul's Cathedral's dome dominating the skyline across the Thames.

"It certainly beats the view from my cell," she said.

He smiled at her. "Pippa!" he called and a few seconds later a woman in her fifties, blonde and neat, came out from a corridor off the room.

"Ah, you're back, Mr. Grady," said Pippa, looking curiously at Cassie.

"Yes, Pippa, this is Cassie who I told you would be staying here for a bit. Cassie, this is my housekeeper, Pippa."

"Nice to meet you!" said Pippa, smiling broadly in an attempt to disguise what she felt about all the articles she had read about this woman.

"Pippa, Miss Cassie has had a bit of a tiring day, so she might like to freshen up," said Joe. "Can you show her to her room, please?"

"Certainly. If you want to follow me?"

Cassie crossed over to the housekeeper, staring at Joe, and followed her down the corridor.

"I fixed the guestroom up for you. It's a lovely room, and if you need anything just yell," said Pippa. "I'm here till about seven most evenings. Just long enough to make sure Mr. Grady has his dinner, then I'm off home. He likes the peace and quiet at night so he can concentrate on his work."

"I wonder why he wants me here then?" said Cassie as she followed Pippa into a bright spacious bedroom with a view over the Thames.

Pippa just smiled at her. She knew Joe liked to take his work home with him, but he never actually took the defendant home with him as well. Pippa knew Joe lived for his work, but in her mind this was taking it too far. She had made sure to hide all the sharp carving knives in the kitchen.

Cassie walked cautiously around the room, taking it all in.

"Is everything alright?" asked Pippa.

"Yes – thank you."

Pippa walked over to the wardrobe and opened it. Inside was an array of women's clothes.

"Mr. Grady asked me to do some shopping for you. Buy you some new clothes. He gave me your sizes. I wasn't quite sure what your taste was. All I saw was photos of you in the papers from the thirties and forties . . ." Pippa trailed off as she looked at Cassie's simple clothes and found it hard to equate this woman with the vision in a series of slinky gowns the papers kept publishing. Pippa had bought some glamorous clothes thinking Cassie would still have the same taste as in her youth, but clearly she didn't. It was no wonder she had managed to stay undetected for so long, she thought.

The camera never lies, she thought, but old photos certainly do!

"Anyway, I'll let you freshen up – the ensuite is through there." She indicated the bathroom before hastily exiting.

CHAPTER 32

"Did she say anything?" asked Joe as Pippa served up dinner on the glass table at the end of the living room.

"Hardly a thing," said Pippa. "She just looked around. Will I tell her that dinner is served?"

"No, I'll do it – you can go home now. I'll see you tomorrow."

"Very well, Mr. Grady."

Joe went to the corridor.

"Cassie! Dinner is served!" he called down the corridor. More memories of Cliffenden, he thought to himself.

Pippa was standing there in her hat and coat, looking a little worried.

"Well! Off with you home, Pippa. Your husband will wonder where you've got to," said Joe, shooing her away.

"Yes – are you sure you'll be alright, Mr. Grady?"

"Quite sure, Pippa, I'm a big boy now," said Joe.

"Well, call me if you need . . . just call me if there's any trouble!"

"I will, but Pippa there's a twenty-four hour doorman in this building, so I will call him first as he can come to my rescue quicker. Now go home!"

Pippa nodded and quickly left.

Joe walked over to the table, sat down and poured two glasses of wine.

A few seconds later Cassie walked in, wearing a cream satin dress Pippa had bought her.

"Ah, you look refreshed," he said, thinking she looked

221

startlingly different in the dress.

She ventured over to the table and sat down opposite him.

"I had a long bath," she said. "Trying to get the smell of that place off me."

He nodded sympathetically. "It can stay with you a while, that smell. Hard to get rid of the memory of it."

"I think I shall never forget it," said Cassie.

Joe hoped that smell would not become part of her everyday life in the future.

"The clothes fitted alright, it seems?" he asked.

"Yes, thank you."

"I got your sizes from the prison and then set Pippa free in Harrods with my credit card for a couple of hours." He leaned forward and smiled. "I wasn't sure if she knew what she was doing!"

"I suppose she had a strange combination to cater to – mixing prison and Harrods chic," she said.

He laughed and continued to eat, glad to see the dry wit he remembered her having was still there.

As he ate, Cassie was curiously studying him.

She glanced at the walls and saw photos of him with a woman she presumed was his wife. Other photos were of a young man and woman who she assumed were his children.

"Is that your wife?" she asked, looking at the photo.

"Yes – Ann."

"She's beautiful."

"Well – she's likes to think so!"

"She doesn't live here?"

"No."

"You're divorced?"

"Eh, no, she lives in our house in the country. This is my city pad for when I'm in London for my work," he explained.

"I see . . . and do you let all the people you defend stay here then?"

"No – no, I don't."

"Then why am I here?"

"As you said, you had nowhere else to go," he said.

She put down her fork and knife and walked over to a cabinet where she picked up an old black-and-white photo of Joe and Ann on their wedding day.

"Miss Cassie," she said.

"Sorry?"

"You told the housekeeper to show 'Miss Cassie' to her room," she said.

Joe said nothing as she studied the wedding photo and then turned around to him.

"Joe – Joe our footman?" she whispered.

He put down his fork and nodded. "Yes."

She stared at him in disbelief.

"It can't be!" she said, nearing him and staring at him.

"It is – Miss Cassie." His voice was a whisper.

"But – but – when were you thinking of telling me?"

"I was going to tell you tonight. I just didn't want to startle you before I had you out of that prison and settled in here," he explained. "You look like you've seen a ghost."

"In a way – I have," she said.

She turned away, walked quickly over to the balcony and gazed at the sun setting across the London skyline.

"What must you think of me?" she said. "Seeing me like this."

"I don't think anything, Cassie, nothing at all," he reassured her.

"I don't have much left, but I do have my pride! Joe – my young footman – seeing me like this."

"But I'm not your young footman anymore," he said.

She turned around, gestured to the luxurious room and said, "Clearly!"

She turned and looked at her reflection in the pane of the glass.

"I look so old, so drab. Not even Pippa's glamorous dress can disguise that! I don't want anybody from those days seeing me now. You should have told me who you were before I agreed to meet you!"

"Would you have then refused to meet me?"

"Yes! Of course!"

He got up and walked over to her. He saw her eyes were filled with the first emotion he had seen her display since meeting her.

"Cassie –"

"I don't want you representing me! Anybody but you!"

"Even the barrister who should be in short pants?" he said, trying to make light of it.

"Yes! Don't you know how humiliating this is for me? Far more than the prison, or the stuff they write about me in the press – or anything else!"

"Cassie!" he said softly. "You're being silly."

"I'm not being silly! I'm being truthful!" She quickly walked away from him and sat on the couch, her face in her hands. "And this is why you wanted to represent me? And why you put up the bail money and brought me to stay in your home? Because – because why exactly? To see what had become of me? To lord it over me?"

"No!" He went and sat beside her. "I would never want to lord it over you, Cassie! Why would I? You were never anything but kind and considerate and lovely to me at Cliffenden. I just want to help you, that's all. Nothing more. You need a friend, and I just want to help you, like you once helped me."

"You owe me nothing," she said.

"I owe you a lot, Cassie. If it weren't for you, your family and Cliffenden, then I wouldn't be where I am today. You set me off on the right path for life."

"If Cliffenden sent you on the right path for life, then it sent me on the wrong one. Could our destinies be any more different or cruel?"

"You've had a shock. I know seeing me again after all these years has probably hit you sideways. I just want you to rest for the next couple of days, and get over the ordeal that you've been through since your arrest. There's no pressure on you. Nobody will bother you here. It's an oasis for you, in the same way your home at Cliffenden was an oasis for me."

He reached out, took her hand and squeezed it.

"Your wife is on the phone, Mr. Grady," said his secretary.

"Okay, put her through," sighed Joe. He was sitting at his desk in his office.

"Well – how's your girlfriend?" said Ann straight away.

"If you mean my client, she's resting," answered Joe.

"At the penthouse?"

"Where else?"

"Well, at least she hasn't killed you yet. I suppose we should be grateful for small mercies."

"I never realised how much you cared." His voice dripped sarcasm.

"Well, has she admitted she did it yet or not?"

"You know I can't discuss a client's case with anybody."

"That's what I've always liked about you, Joe – your professionalism."

"Well, I'm glad you like something about me," said Joe.

"Anyway, I don't have time to discuss that woman any longer – I'm due at the tennis club. Now, about this weekend."

"What about it?"

"There's a barbeque at the Majors' – Saturday, three o'clock."

"Ann, you know I can't make it."

"And why?"

"Because I can't leave Cassie."

"*Cassie*! Since when has she become *Cassie*?"

"Cassandra. I can't leave her on her own. I'm standing over her for the bail and I can't just head off because I have to attend a barbeque in the shires."

"I don't believe it! Are you trying to tell me that you have to stay at the penthouse until they lock her up and throw away the key for good?"

"Or until she is proven innocent and they release her, which would be the outcome I would prefer."

"And how long is all this going to go on for *exactly*?" Ann's voice was brimming with frustration.

"I can't say, but certainly longer than this weekend, so if you could pass on my apologies to the Majors, and I hope they don't overdo the steaks like they did last time."

"*Ahhh!*" shouted Ann in frustration and slammed down the phone.

Joe shook his head, almost in amusement, as he replaced the receiver.

Joe finished his work at the office early and headed back to the penthouse. Cassie had indeed been resting since she had come to stay. She seemed to be sleeping a lot and he realised she must be exhausted after everything that had happened to her. He got the lift up to the penthouse and let himself in.

He dropped into the kitchen first where Pippa was busy preparing dinner.

"Everything alright?"

"Yes, Mr. Grady fine. She's just been pottering around all day, watching television, reading magazines."

"I see, that's good. Pippa, you can head off home early now, if you want. I'll finish the dinner."

"Are you sure?"

"Certain."

Pippa nodded. She tidied up and then went to get her coat. She knew when Joe Grady said to do something, it was best not to question it.

Joe walked into the living room and saw the balcony windows open with Cassie sitting out on the balcony staring at the view. He walked out to her.

"Hi," he said with a friendly smile.

She looked startled. "Oh, hello, sorry, I was a million miles away," she said as he sat down at the garden table with her.

"Penny for them?" he asked.

"I was just thinking back to Cliffenden. Meeting you again has stirred up all the memories."

Joe smirked at her. "Mrs. Crowther and her sherry!"

Cassie giggled. "She never did a day's work in all her time at Cliffenden!"

"Mr. Bruton and his strict ways!"

"Gosh – did that man ever smile?"

"He absolutely terrified me!" admitted Joe. "I remember starting at Cliffenden and being petrified of him! He used to berate me all day long!"

"I think he'd be very proud of you now. They were such happy times, really. We were so happy, and I don't think we even knew it. Except for Teddy. I think he realised it. I mean, people thought he was irresponsible and silly. I think he knew how to grab happiness when he could."

"You mentioned he was killed in the war?"

"Yes. I read his obituary at the time in the paper which said he was killed in battle in North Africa. Maybe he had a sense of what was going to come. I remember he said once that he would end up as cannon fodder in the next war, poor Teddy."

Joe sat back and realised this was an opportunity to bring up the case.

"You say you read about Teddy's death in the paper? I take it that was because you weren't in contact with your family at that point? You had gone into hiding after the murder?"

Cassie bristled and looked straight ahead at the skyline.

"Cassie – I know this is very painful for you to talk about. But we are going to have to talk about it at some stage. We have a case to defend."

She flicked her hair back from her face. "I really do not want to talk about it."

He leaned forward and smiled encouragingly. "Not even to me? Your favourite footman Joe?"

She continued to stare ahead.

"Come on, Cassie. You know you used to confide in me about everything."

"That was a very long time ago."

"But still – if there's anyone you can trust, you can trust me, Miss Cassie. You know I'd never betray you." He felt consumed with guilt as he said it, remembering his ultimate betrayal of her and Bowden. "We don't have to talk about the – incident – yet but maybe we could talk about your life after you left Cliffenden? When you married Wally Stanton? Maybe we could start there?"

She sat staring ahead for a long time and he sat looking at her. Realising she was not going to speak, he went to stand up.

"It all happened so fast," she suddenly said.

Surprised, he sat down again. "What did?"

"The wedding to Wally. One minute I was at Cliffenden and the next I was married to Wally. I didn't want to marry him. I was trapped into it. You know that – you must remember that?"

"Of course I do. And was the marriage happy?"

"No, but I just got on with it. After we left Singapore we went to live in London, so I continued with my friends and relatives in the way I had before I was married – Cassie Fullerton, the socialite. Then we moved to Paris. Wally was transferred there as part of his job, heading a big bank. And I loved Paris. I'd always wanted to live there. Though I hadn't imagined living there married to Wally. And I certainly hadn't imagined living there with the war. But I was young. Our youth is always special, isn't it? Even if Paris was being invaded . . ."

PART THREE

France 1940's

CHAPTER 33

Cassie frantically raced into her bedroom and began opening her wardrobes, followed by their maid Michelle, a petite dark girl with a very pretty face and deep-green eyes.

Cassie began rummaging through her clothes and quickly selecting items and throwing them on the bed.

"Where is Pierre? Where are the suitcases?" she demanded.

"Will I check on him, Madame Stanton?"

"Yes, do! And tell him to hurry! I'll try Wally at the bank again."

As a terrified-looking Michelle rushed out of the room, Cassie picked up the telephone and got a connection to Wally's bank.

"Brigitte? It's Cassie Stanton here. Where is my husband? What? He hasn't been in the office all day? As soon as he arrives back, will you tell him to ring me *urgently*." Cassie replaced the receiver and raced to the wardrobes again and began to throw clothes onto the floor.

"What is going on here? Looks like a bomb has hit the place," said Wally, sauntering into the room.

"Wally! Where have you been? I've been leaving messages for you everywhere I could think of!"

"You knew I was away on business," said Wally, unconcerned.

Pierre walked in with two suitcases.

"Thank goodness!" said Cassie, grabbing the cases. Putting them on the bed she began to fling clothes in.

"What are you doing?" Wally asked.

"Packing obviously. We must leave immediately!"

231

"Pierre, you can take those cases back to the attic – they are not needed," said Wally.

"What do you mean – not needed? We have to get out of here – we don't have much time!" insisted Cassie.

Wally went over to the bed, took up the cases and emptied the contents on the ground before handing them back to Pierre.

"You can leave us," he commanded.

"What do you think you're doing? Bring those cases back, Pierre!" demanded Cassie.

Wally gestured to Pierre to leave quickly, which he did.

Wally turned to look at his near-hysterical wife.

"Cassie, will you calm down!" he half-shouted.

"Calm down! The Germans are a few miles down the road and you're telling me to calm down! We have to get out of Paris immediately! Out of France!"

"We're not going anywhere, Cassie."

"Are you insane! I should never have listened to you when war was declared last year. I should have insisted we left France then. Now we're in danger of being trapped here! What was I thinking of to listen to you? You said the Germans would never get across the French border and here they are on our doorstep!" Cassie was pacing up and down in anger.

Wally marched over to her and grabbed her two shoulders aggressively.

"Cassie, let them come! It won't affect us," he said.

"Have you lost your mind? The city is about to be invaded, there was bombing a couple of nights ago – we'll be bombed and killed and –"

"I have it on very good authority that Paris is about to be declared an open city."

"What does that mean?"

"The French are not going to put up any resistance, in order to save the city and its citizens from being blitzed. The Germans will be merely marching into the city unobstructed."

"I don't believe it! They would never give in like that," said Cassie.

"That is what is happening. Better than the city being razed to the ground, isn't it?"

"Regardless, Wally, we need to get moving. We can't stay here."

"Why not? We are both neutral citizens: you hold an Irish passport and I an American one. This war has nothing to do with us."

"Nothing to do with us! How can you say that, with Teddy, poor Teddy, and all my relatives fighting for the other side!"

"There is and never has been anything 'poor' about Teddy. He is a spoilt petulant man-child who thinks everything in life is one big game. I have no doubt he has wrangled himself a cushy position that will ensure he will never be in danger or see any military action."

"You weren't being so dismissive of him when you were showering records and other gifts on him, trying to ingratiate yourself with my family. I'm very proud of Teddy. For once in his life, he's done the right thing."

"The fact remains we are neutrals, and we can't just up sticks and leave," said Wally.

"Why not?"

"Because my bank would not allow it. I have been entrusted with the French division of our bank and I can't just run away from it because my wife's got the jitters. More than ever I have to stay to ensure the smooth running of the bank during this emergency – isn't that what the Irish call this war?"

"Emergency! You're putting our lives in jeopardy because of your job!"

"Our lives are not in jeopardy, we are quite safe. Now could you please calm down? You're unnerving the already unnerved staff."

"I can't believe you!"

Wally went over, opened his cigar box and lit himself a cigar.

"Besides, where do you think you are running to?" asked Wally.

"Back to London, of course."

"And how do you propose to get there? How do you propose to get across the channel?"

"To the south then!"

"The roads, trains, are jammed with people fleeing and refugees. You haven't a hope of getting there – and, even if you do, we're far safer here in Paris, now it's to be declared an open city, than being in London and suffering the blitz every night."

Cassie took out her cigarettes and lit one, her hand shaking as she raised it to her mouth. "But what are we to do?"

"Sit tight and lead our lives as normally as possible. Now France has fallen, the British can't hold out for much longer and will look for peace very soon. Then the whole war will be over and we can get back to our normal lives."

"That won't happen, Wally!" insisted Cassie.

"It will. You're just going to have to trust me – what other option have you got?" he said, smirking smugly at her.

Cassie marched past him, opened the door and yelled, "*Michelle!*"

A few moments later Michelle walked in. "*Oui, Madame?*"

"Michelle, can you put all my clothes back into the wardrobe," she said with a nervous energy. "My husband has decided that we are all quite safe in Paris. Nothing will happen to us! We may sleep sound in our beds!"

"Cassie!" Wally chastised her.

"And when you're finished with the clothes, Michelle, do we have a fiddle in the house?"

"A what, Madame?"

"A fiddle! You know – a violin. If we do, can you bring it to my husband so he can play as Nero did while Paris burns!" She stormed out of the room.

Wally followed her quickly along the landing outside and down the staircase.

"You shouldn't speak in front of the servants like that!" he said.

"You have no need to tell me how to speak in front of servants. I grew up with a household of them at Cliffenden."

"Yes, well, you're not in Cliffenden now."

"More's the pity! At least I would be safe there and not in any fear of being bombed!" She walked into the drawing room and, lifting a decanter, poured herself a glass of wine which she downed

234

in one before turning and facing him. "Where have you *been* these past couple of days?"

"I told you – on business," he said, closing over the door.

"With the city about to be invaded?" She was incredulous.

"It's precisely because the city is being invaded that I needed to see to business. We had to empty the safe deposit boxes, hide everything away safely for clients."

"And what about my safety? Didn't you think of me here alone when the bombs fell?" Cassie demanded.

"No bombs fell near here, did they? You see, you were perfectly safe."

"How did it ever come to this?" Cassie was shocked.

The Germans had swept through France with frightening speed.

Cassie stood amongst the crowd of people on the footpath of the Champs-Élysées. They were all looking on silently as the German army marched past them toward the Arc de Triomphe. They seemed to go on forever. Lines and lines of marching soldiers, followed by rows and rows of tanks, followed again by marching soldiers. She saw the man standing next to her, a man in his late fifties, was silently crying. She suddenly slipped her hand into his and held it tight. He seemed so in shock by what was happening he didn't even notice the gesture of kindness.

Wally had been right. The government, or what was left of the government, had declared Paris an open city. This action had enabled the German army to just march in unopposed.

She finally pulled herself away from the parade and made her way through the throngs of people. To avoid the crowds she kept to the back streets. The same solemn atmosphere existed there as she passed small shops, boulangeries, and cafés that were closed, the shutters locked. As she walked along she wished she was in Cliffenden. She used to love the Parisian streets – she would lose herself for hours there. But now everything seemed frightening and surreal and she longed for the security and comfort of home. She hadn't been back to Cliffenden much since she married Wally, just an occasional short visit.

She now realised that after Bowden ran off on her she had gone into a kind of shock. She just couldn't believe he could do that to her. Bowden, who she loved so much and who she had thought loved her equally, just to disappear. Without an explanation. Without anything. She had never believed he would be capable of such cruelty. Or that he could ever have doubted how much she loved him, which he obviously did from his actions. She had sleepwalked into the marriage with Wally afterwards. She had allowed herself to be marched up the aisle without resistance, in the same way Paris had allowed itself to be marched into by the German army. Her confidence had been shattered and she didn't see any other life for herself without Bowden by her side.

After the marriage, when Wally said they were moving to Singapore, it seemed like a welcome opportunity. She needed to get far away from Cliffenden and all memories of Bowden. What better place to go than to the other side of the world to try and forget him? Life in Singapore had been a genteel existence of colonial living as they merged into the expatriate community. They spent as much time in the famous Raffles Hotel as they did in their own home. After Singapore, they had been sent back to London for a long time where she had restarted her life with her friends and relatives, much like on her visits before her marriage. Then Wally had been posted to Paris where they had been for the past eighteen months.

Life with Wally was what she had expected it to be. He was obsessed with money and power, and showed little affection for her. He was demanding and prone to fly into jealous rages. He always had to be in control. There was no romance in their lovemaking. She felt he treated her just like another one of his possessions.

He had lusted after her for so long she thought she might have been a disappointment in the end.

She had learned to fight back. People looked on and thought they were the ideal couple, that they had everything. Wally enjoyed that image, he cultivated it, and expected her to do the same. She tried not to think about Bowden anymore. Her deep love for him had transformed into something else; it was tinged with bitterness and sadness, hurt and betrayal.

And yet he still played on her mind. She wondered where he was, what he was doing, who he was with.

She and Wally had rented a lovely bright spacious house in the affluent Neuilly-sur-Seine neighbourhood of Paris and she tried not to think of Bowden anymore.

Cassie made her way to the building which was the headquarters of Wally's bank. She walked through the ornate building's front door. The foyer was hushed that day without the usual busy bustle going on. She walked past the receptionists and security guard who didn't even acknowledge her. Usually they would be overly courteous to her as Wally's wife. But today they all seemed in a trance, their eyes misty and faces disbelieving like everyone in Paris.

She got into the lift and went to the top floor. As she walked down the wide plush corridor to Wally's office she bumped into Luc Labelle, a lawyer who worked at Wally's bank.

"Ah, Cassie," he said, kissing both her cheeks.

"Hello, Luc, how are you?"

He gave a Gallic shrug. "Like everyone else today in Paris, Cassie, devastated."

Cassie nodded. "It's hard to believe. I just came from the Champs-Élysées and watched them parade by. It's happened so *fast*. Where are Simone and the children today?"

"At home. I told them not to go out today."

Cassie had become very fond of Luc and his wife Simone. Luc had been a lawyer working in the bank for some time before Wally took over. As was Wally's gift in life, he had spotted Luc's potential and brilliance and promoted him quickly to head of legal affairs. Cassie didn't know whether she admired or despised Wally's manipulation of people. Ever since she had got to know him he knew how to identify people who could help him and then use them to his advantage. Even with her, Wally had played Teddy like a toy in order to become acquainted with her, and then dropped him as soon as he got what he wanted. She had seen Wally operate like this many times since she had married him. He would pretend to be the best friend of somebody who could be useful to him and shower them with gifts, invitations or promotions until they had served their purpose – and then they were unceremoniously dumped. And Wally didn't look back. Luc Labelle was the latest in this long line. Since Wally arrived at the Parisian bank, Luc had been his eyes and ears. Wally had been reliant on him to know all aspects of the bank and to execute his polices. Luc did the work and Wally took the praise and credit, Cassie thought. In the meantime, Cassie herself had become friendly with both Luc and his wife, who she found kind and down to earth. She fought the niggling desire to warn Luc of Wally's true character, but knew she never could.

"You are here to see Wally?" Luc asked.

"Yes, is he in his office?"

"I believe so."

Cassie smiled at him and walked on. Wally's secretary Vera wasn't at her normal desk and Cassie knocked on Wally's door and entered. Wally was sitting behind his desk, his back to her, swinging from left to right on his swivel-chair as he laughed and joked on the telephone to somebody.

Hearing the door open, he looked around and waved for her to come in. She walked in as he continued his conversation on the telephone.

"Well, I think rather than the occupation affecting business, it's going to expand it. Let's face it all those German troops are bringing a lot of money into the economy . . . certainly I'll keep you informed . . . alright, talk to you later."

Wally hung up the telephone and looked at her.

"You must be the only person in Paris who is laughing today," said Cassie.

"I can't be seen to unsettle investors," said Wally.

She looked at him and shook her head in dismay.

"Where's Vera?" she asked.

"I sent her home. She was of no use to me today, sitting out there weeping. I can't be looking at her sitting there maudlin all day."

"I see," she said. "It might have been an idea to close the bank altogether today for your employees' sake. Everything else seems closed."

"Why would I do that? Everything will be back to normal in a few days and all those other places will be opened again and will find themselves busier than ever with their new influx of German customers."

He stood up, got his coat and put it on.

She looked at him, alarmed. "I hope you won't be having any German customers!"

"Come along, Cassie, and let's get home – we'll be late for dinner," he said as he put his arm around her and led her out.

CHAPTER 34

Paris wasn't back to normal as Wally had predicted, not in the way Cassie saw it, but it was certainly open for business again. German soldiers seemed to be everywhere. Sitting drinking coffee amongst the Parisians outside the cafés, going to the cinema, shopping in the boutiques. Cassie wondered if the clothes they were buying were for their wives at home or for the new girlfriends they were quickly finding in Paris. The Nazi flags were being hoisted up on the buildings everywhere. It certainly wasn't normal, but life was going on.

Cassie began to wonder if Wally was right and the war would be over soon, and this was just the reality of their new future.

Wally sat at his desk in his office, going through paperwork with Luc Labelle.

He finished putting his signatures to the papers and handed them back to Luc.

"Make sure these go out today," he instructed.

"Yes, I will," said Luc, standing up and turning to leave.

"Oh, myself and my wife are entertaining some clients at Maxim's tonight – I'd like you and that charming wife of yours to be there too," said Wally.

Luc looked uncomfortable. "I would love to – it's just my wife is a little unsettled since the occupation. She doesn't like going out at night."

"Well, then, it will be good for her to get out of the apartment.

Come by our house for eight and we can go together in our car."

Luc went to say something but realised Wally was issuing an order and there was no point in arguing.

Cassie sat at her dressing table in their room, putting on her diamond earrings.

"Who are these clients tonight?" she asked.

Wally came out of the bathroom, tying his cufflinks. He was dressed in a tuxedo.

"Just the Verduns and the Gardins, quite tedious people, but important. They seem to like Luc and so I thought it would be good to bring him along."

"Well, Luc is very charming," agreed Cassie.

Wally came over to her and kissed her neck. "Of course he is – why else do you think I gave him the job?"

She stood up and walked in front of him out of the room and down the stairs. They went into the drawing room to find Luc and his wife Simone had already arrived.

"Hello there," said Cassie. She kissed them both. "Good to see you again."

Cassie thought Simone Labelle was a very beautiful woman, sophisticated and elegant. She was very slim, with brown hair and green eyes. With her husband's blonde good looks, Cassie thought them a handsome couple.

Simone was on the sofa, sipping a glass of wine Michelle had poured for her.

Cassie sat down beside her and took a glass of wine from Michelle.

"You look lovely tonight, Simone," said Cassie.

"Do I? Thank you," said Simone, who always seemed to have an unsure nervousness about her.

"Well, you look lovely always," smiled Cassie, trying to make her feel at ease. She wondered if Simone was always nervous or if it was just when she was in Wally's company. Wally had that effect on people, Cassie knew.

"Hello, Simone!" said Wally.

"Good evening, Wally," she said, accepting a kiss from him on the cheek.

As Wally and Luc began to discuss business, Cassie reached over and took the other woman's hand.

"And how are you keeping?" she asked.

"Trying to keep things as normal as possible for the children with all this going on," said Simone.

Cassie nodded sympathetically. "As hard as it is for us adults, it must be very confusing and frightening for children."

Luc overheard the conversation and said, "At least the bombs aren't falling here like in London."

"That's very true," said Cassie.

"And besides," said Wally, "it's all been sorted now. The French government has relocated to Vichy and will run the south of the country while the north here will remain under German supervision."

"That is not the French government in Vichy," spat Simone. "It is a puppet government of the Nazis!"

Wally looked at her, surprised. "Well, it's the only French government there is!"

"Hasn't de Gaulle relocated to London to continue the fight from there?" Cassie pointed out.

"What fight? The fight is over!" said Wally.

Simone went to say something but Luc gave her a warning look and she closed her mouth.

"Anyway, enough of this war talk and politics!" said Cassie. "Let us just have a nice evening out and forget all about it for just one night."

Wally looked at his watch and quickly put down his glass of wine. "And we had better be going."

Simone stood up. "If I may just use your bathroom first?"

Wally looked at her, annoyed. "You'll have to wait until we get to the restaurant – we're already running late!"

Simone looked down at the floor.

"For goodness sake, Wally! If Simone wants to use the bathroom then let her!" snapped Cassie.

Wally glared at her.

"No!" Simone gave a little laugh. "It's not an emergency, I can assure you. I was only going to fix my lipstick. I can wait till Maxim's."

"Excellent! Then let's get going," said Wally.

Cassie stood up and, as she walked past Wally, she gave him a filthy look.

CHAPTER 35

The chauffeur pulled up outside of Maxim's restaurant and got out to let the party out. As Cassie stepped out of the car she saw there were groups of soldiers congregating outside the restaurant, laughing and smoking cigarettes. Cassie walked confidently to the door with Wally, followed by Luc with his arm around Simone's waist.

"Good evening, Madame," said a soldier who blocked the entrance.

Cassie glared at him and said nothing.

"Good evening," said Wally with a smile.

"Allow me," said the soldier and, smiling, he opened the door for them.

Cassie walked through, ignoring him.

"Thank you," smiled Wally, then as they moved into the restaurant he whispered in Cassie's ear, "Try to be polite!"

"Piss off!" Cassie whispered back.

"Good to see you again, Monsieur Stanton, and Madame Stanton," greeted the maître d'. "Your guests are already here."

"I told you we were late," Wally snapped at Cassie.

Cassie ignored him and, as she walked through the restaurant following the maitre d', she got a shock. Apart from a scattering of well-heeled Parisians who were the regular clientele, the restaurant was filled with German officers enjoying the city's best cuisine.

"I wish I hadn't come," whispered Simone to her husband who tightened his grip on her waist.

"We're so sorry we're late!" said Wally to his clients.

"I'd like to say it was our fault, but the Germans have put road blocks up everywhere which delayed us," said Cassie.

"Will you keep your voice down!" Wally hissed in Cassie's ear. "You remember my wife Cassie?" he then said loudly to his clients.

Cassie went around and greeted the clients warmly before taking a seat at the top of the table with Wally. She saw Simone looking quite pale and called over to her. "Simone, do sit beside me!"

Simone smiled appreciatively and occupied the seat to Cassie's other side and Luc sat down beside her.

"Well, I imagine Maxim's has never had a night like this before," said Cassie as she looked around the restaurant at the soldiers who were all laughing loudly and enjoying themselves.

They were handed menus and ordered. Cassie knew what was expected of her and chatted away to Wally's clients, trying to ignore the increasingly loud noise from the other diners.

As they finished their main course Cassie noticed that Simone was unusually quiet and she said to her, "Are you alright?"

"Yes, I'm fine. I just wonder what's going to happen next? With the occupation?"

"Well, Wally says nothing. This is it."

Simone's eyes narrowed. "How can you say that? Look what they're doing to Warsaw. We're not safe . . . well, maybe you are with your neutral passport. But what of the rest of us?"

"Try not to think about it, Simone. You have to go on as best you can, for the sake of your children if nothing else. My brother Teddy has the most amazing ability to never worry about anything. He believes that worrying about something will not change the outcome one way or the other."

"Where is he now?"

Cassie's smile faltered. "He's fighting for the British."

Simone nodded, took a sip of her wine and smiled weakly. "You're right, of course."

"Hello, Wally!" a loud voice suddenly boomed.

Cassie looked up to see the speaker was a high-ranking German officer.

"Stefan, good to see you!" said Wally, standing up and shaking his hand warmly.

"You're having a good night?" the German asked.

"Yes, very much so. Let me introduce you to everybody. This is Monsieur and Madame Verdun, Monsieur Gardin – Luc you know already –"

Luc stood up and shook his hand. "Hello, Stefan."

Wally continued, "This is Luc's wife Simone."

Stefan reached over, took Simone's hand and kissed it. Cassie saw Simone shiver at his touch.

"And this is my wife Cassie. Cassie, this is Oberst Stefan Bayer."

Stefan took Cassie's hand and kissed it. "Ah, the famous Cassie Fullerton."

"I didn't realise I was that famous," said Cassie, pulling back her hand.

"But who hasn't heard of Cassie Fullerton, the aristocrat known for her outlandish behaviour?" He smiled mockingly at her.

"Any outlandish behaviour was before I was married – marriage to Wally has calmed me down considerably. Oberst Stefan Bayer? What exactly is an oberst?"

"My rank is equivalent to that of a colonel in the British army," he said.

"Very senior," smiled Wally.

"I used to see your picture a lot in *Tatler* magazine," said Stefan.

"I didn't realise *Tatler* had such wide readership."

"We Germans always have a thing for the aristocracy. Hitler himself is good friends with one of Mitford girls. Do you know the Mitford girls?"

"Only very vaguely," said Cassie.

"Of course she knows them," said Wally.

"And I have heard that you give the best dinner parties in Paris. I look forward to my invitation to your house," said Stefan.

Cassie looked at him coolly. "Why wait for an invitation? I think it's more of your habit to just walk in uninvited."

There was a hush around the table as Stefan's face soured for a moment and then he smiled again.

"Your wife is enchanting, Wally. I look forward to getting to know her so much better. Now, if you'll excuse me." Stefan turned and walked back to his table.

As Wally sat down he glared at Cassie in anger.

Cassie ignored him and said to the table, "Has anybody been to the theatre recently – or has that been taken over by the Nazis as well?"

They exited from Maxim's and got into the awaiting car.

Away from his clients, Wally sat stony-faced.

"Maybe Simone and I should get a taxi," said Luc, sitting uncomfortably in the car with Wally's cold silence dominating the atmosphere.

"Not at all!" said Cassie. "Are there any taxis left in Paris? You could be waiting for hours for one. They are probably all taken by the –"

"*Will you stop*!" Wally shouted suddenly, making everyone jump. He then looked out the window again, stony-faced.

Cassie reached into her purse and took out a cigarette. "Does anyone mind if I smoke?"

Luc was the only one who spoke. "No, of course not."

"Thank you!" she said, putting it in her mouth and lighting it.

Then she looked out the other window silently.

After they dropped Luc and Simone off they drove back in silence to their house. When the car pulled up Cassie got out quickly and walked indoors, followed in quick pursuit by Wally.

Cassie walked into the drawing room and poured herself a cognac.

Michelle came in.

"Good evening, Madame, Monsieur," she said. "Can I get you anything?"

"No! Leave us!" snapped Wally.

Seeing the atmosphere, Michelle quickly retreated.

Wally went to the doors and slammed them shut.

"*What do you think you were doing tonight*?" he shouted at Cassie.

"Entertaining your clients, as per usual," she snapped back.

"All those insults and remarks you were making about the

Germans! You can't speak like that anymore. You're not in Cliffenden now, able to say or do whatever you want whenever you want, like a silly child. You cannot speak like that in Paris anymore!"

Cassie's voice was raised too. "What can they do? They may be able to bully and coerce everyone else, but I for one will speak my mind!"

He marched over to her and stood before her, shaking with anger. "You will keep your remarks and comments to yourself. This is not a city where people speak their minds anymore. You're putting us in danger, you stupid woman!"

"What danger? You said yourself we are neutrals."

"Nobody, not even neutrals, can get away with speaking like that to a top officer in the army."

"*Then if it's so dangerous why are we still bloody here?*" Cassie shouted back at him. "I told you we needed to leave Paris, and you insisted we stay, because of your bloody job!"

"My bloody job, as you call it, that keeps you in diamonds and furs and kept your precious Cliffenden from going down the Swanee, along with your family of fools with their airs and graces!"

Outside in the foyer Michelle and the chauffeur made faces of concern at each other as Wally and Cassie's voices grew louder and louder.

That night Cassie lay awake in the darkened bedroom. Wally slept beside her. She got up and walked over the windowsill and sat on it. She could see the houses and buildings of Paris stretch on forever beyond their gardens. She could hear the rattle of gunfire somewhere in the distance and laughter and shouting from German voices nearer by. She thought about Simone and Luc and their obvious love for each other. It reminded her of the way she used to be with Bowden. As she thought of the aggressive row she'd had with Wally that night tears began to slip down her face. She quickly wiped away the tears and refused to allow herself to think along those lines. Bowden was gone, long gone, he had deserted her. He wasn't worth wasting her tears on. Wally was her life, however difficult it was.

CHAPTER 36

Cassie picked up the telephone and waited for the connection to the Labelles.

She had been thinking about Simone. The woman was so agitated with the occupation. Cassie knew everyone was agitated and distraught, but she was worried about Simone. Luc had mentioned to her that Simone rarely left the apartment.

"*Bonjour.*"

"Hello, Simone, it's Cassie here."

"Oh, hello, Cassie – is everything alright?"

"Yes, yes, I just wanted to invite you out today. I'm doing some shopping and I thought you might like to join me?"

"Ah – thank you but no, Cassie. I have too much on with the children."

"But the children are in school till this afternoon. I'll have you safely back home by then, I promise."

"I don't think so – I'm not feeling the best today."

"I'm not putting pressure on you, but I think it might do you the world of good to get out for a bit?"

There was silence from Simone's end. Then she said, "Thank you, Cassie. Perhaps if you give me an hour to get ready?"

"Wonderful! I'll collect you."

The chauffeur drove them through the centre of Paris.

"I was thinking we might like to go to Dior first?" suggested Cassie.

Simone smiled at her. "I don't think I'm in need of any new

clothes particularly, so wherever suits you." She looked out at the city streets which were dominated by German military personnel. "With all this going on, clothes are really the least of my worries."

"Perhaps you think I'm very shallow, suggesting to go shopping in a war?" Cassie realised her actions might be disrespectful.

"No, what are you doing differently from everybody else? I would never have believed the city could just continue to operate the way it has during the Nazi occupation. But people still need to feed themselves, earn a living, clothe themselves. Luc still has to go to the bank every day and do his work."

"But you're not, are you, Simone? You're not even leaving your apartment?"

"Yes, I do. I do my shopping and me and the children go to the park."

Cassie could tell she was lying. Cassie hoped getting her out that day would encourage her to be more confident.

Cassie and Simone sat on an ornate sofa in one of the luxurious rooms at Dior while a series of models came out, modelling different fashions for them.

"Oh, that is glamorous, isn't it?" said Cassie as the model twirled in a dark-green gown.

"Yes, very," agreed Simone.

Cassie always thought Simone a very elegant and fashionable woman and she was glad to see that the display of fashion did seem to be managing to distract her that day.

Cassie could hear a loud German accent that seemed familiar boom down the corridor and as she looked she saw Stefan Bayer passing by the doorway, on his arm a young woman who Cassie knew to be a well-known Parisian model.

Seeing Cassie and Simone, Stefan halted.

"You are so generous, Stefan! You've already brought me to Chanel this morning," said the model who looked delighted with herself.

"Well, we can't have you not looking well at the Ritz this evening," said Stefan as he led her into the room.

"Ah, ladies, how very nice to see you again," he said, smiling.

"Oberst Bayer." Cassie nodded coolly, but mindful of Wally's dire warning she didn't scowl at him as she wanted to.

"Out doing some shopping?" he asked.

"That's what it looks like, doesn't it?" said Cassie. "I wouldn't have thought you were the type of man who would have been interested in ladies' fashion."

"Then you misjudge me, Cassie. Everything concerning women interests me. I think women should be allowed to look as beautiful as possible, and therefore fashion should be encouraged."

"He has great taste!" gushed the model on his arm.

"Really?" said Cassie, raising an eyebrow.

"I don't know what I would have done if Stefan had not been with me today. He knows exactly what suits me best," the model said, smiling at him.

"Even the Führer has an interest in fashion," commented Stefan.

"I really would never have guessed," said Cassie.

"We are planning on moving all the fashion houses from Paris to Berlin," said Stefan.

"But how could you do that?" Cassie was aghast.

"Quite easy with a little organisation. We will change the capital of culture and fashion from Paris to Berlin. We think Berlin deserves the title," he said happily.

The sales assistant came in. "Pardon, Oberst Bayer, your room is waiting."

"Ladies, I bid you farewell and no doubt I will see you soon," he said and led the model out of the room.

"Well, whatever next?" said Cassie, turning to look at Simone.

Simone had turned very pale and was trembling.

"Simone, are you alright?"

"Yes, just a little cold."

Cassie reached out and felt her hand to find it was freezing despite the room being warm. As laughter echoed from the next room, Cassie asked, "Would you like to leave?"

Simone nodded and they quickly got up and left.

"Where would you like to go next?" asked Cassie as they sat into the back of the car.

Simone turned to her. "Would you think me very rude if I went home?"

"No, of course not. Are you ill? Do you need to see a doctor?"

"I'm fine. I just need a little lie-down," said Simone.

Cassie told the chauffeur to drive to the Labelles' apartment.

"I will come in with you, to make sure you get in alright," said Cassie as the car pulled up outside the apartment building.

"No, I'm fine," Simone objected.

"You're still as pale as a ghost – I insist," said Cassie.

They entered the building and got into a small lift that brought them to the third floor. Simone opened the door and they entered. The apartment was stylish and elegant.

"Where's your maid? I'll tell her to get you a glass of water," said Cassie as they entered the drawing room.

"No, I'm fine. Our maid left and I haven't been able to find another," said Simone as she went to a decanter of cognac sitting on the table and poured herself a glass. She downed it in one go and then poured herself another.

"No maid? Well, I'll ask our housekeeper if she knows anybody looking for a job –"

"No!" Simone interrupted abruptly, taking Cassie by surprise. Then she smiled and sat down on the sofa. "No, it's fine, Cassie. I'm enjoying not having one around all the time at the moment, to be honest."

"I see," said Cassie, sitting down on the armchair opposite her and lighting a cigarette. "It must be hard for you doing everything yourself, with no help with the children?"

"We manage just fine."

"Do you feel better now?" asked Cassie, seeing the colour begin to return to Simone's cheeks.

Simone nodded. "Yes – I don't know what came over me."

Cassie sat back, crossed her legs and smiled, trying to lighten the mood. "Making Berlin the capital of fashion – can you imagine such a thing? To just wave a wand and think you can transport the whole French fashion industry to another country? Ridiculous!"

"It's not as ridiculous as you think, Cassie," Simone began animatedly. "They can do anything they want now. They have all the power. If they would only stop at fashion and clothes! They are already looting all the art and everything else of value from France and transporting it back to Germany. How long now till they start transporting people?"

"That will not happen, Simone – it would never be allowed."

"There are no rules anymore – anything is allowed! They have already put a freeze on all Jewish bank accounts in France."

"Whatever do you mean?"

"Jewish accounts are frozen. The Jews can't get access to their own money. They are only allowed small withdrawals. The Germans have put a gigantic fine on the Jewish community in France that must be paid for by their accounts."

"Absurd! They can't just steal people's money."

"Ask Wally if you don't believe me!" snapped Simone.

"Wally? You mean to tell me they have done this in Wally's bank as well?" Cassie was horrified.

Simone suddenly looked terrified. "Please don't say I told you! I shouldn't be discussing the bank – it's not my business. Luc would get into terrible trouble if it got out I'd said anything."

Cassie came over and sat beside her and took her hand. "Please, don't worry. I won't say you told me anything."

"Promise me?"

"Of course."

"You're very kind . . . and I'm very stupid. Luc always says I get nervous and then say too much. I get carried away."

"Well, I've always spoken my mind, so it's not a trait I dislike in other people."

"It's not wise to speak your mind in France anymore," said Simone.

"So I've been told. But I hope we still can, amongst friends."

Simone smiled and squeezed Cassie's hand "You've had a very charmed life, haven't you? Nothing has ever gone wrong for you. You're so confident and sure of yourself. I wish I could be like you."

"Looks can be deceptive, Simone. Be happy with what you've got."

CHAPTER 37

Cassie picked up the telephone and got a connection to Helen Neumann, the wife of a Jewish industrialist who was one of Wally's clients. They had socialised many times together in the past.

"Hello, Helen, it's Cassie Stanton here," Cassie said in a friendly fashion.

"Yes?" came the cold reply.

"I haven't seen you or Laurent for so long I thought I'd give you a call to see how you are?"

"How we are?" screeched the woman down the line. "How do you think we are? With your husband's bank taking our money!" The line went dead.

Wally came into the house and walked into the drawing room where Cassie sat waiting for him.

"Why aren't you dressed? We have to leave in thirty minutes for the theatre," he said.

"I was speaking to Helen Neumann today," said Cassie.

He looked at her, startled. "What were you speaking to her for?"

"I telephoned her. I wanted to see how she was – we haven't seen them for so long."

"And how was she?" asked Wally, unconcerned.

"She hung up on me," said Cassie.

"Well, you shouldn't have telephoned her."

"Why not? I didn't know you had frozen their bank accounts," Cassie spat.

Wally sighed heavily. "I didn't freeze them, the Nazis did."

"But you did the actual freezing!"

"And what was I supposed to do? Disobey their order?"

"Yes, of course! You can't just stop people from accessing their money!"

"They can draw down a monthly allowance," said Wally.

"How dare they! How dare you! The Neumanns are very nice people – they were very hospitable to us when we moved to Paris first."

"That was a different era. I've told you before – everything has changed."

"And do you agree with this act?"

"Well, no –"

"But you are complicit in it. What does your headquarters in New York say about this?"

"They have said we must follow the orders of the new regime," said Wally.

"But how can we look the Neumanns and our other Jewish friends in the eye ever again?"

"We won't have to look them in the eye. It's not our business. It wouldn't be safe for us to be seen being friendly with them anymore," said Wally.

"How can you just abandon people like that? You used to ass-kiss them and now you've frozen their money and left them to their fate."

"They are not my responsibility! Everyone has been abandoned to their fate! There's no oil, no coal, no food for the general populace. It's a matter of survival, and I intend to survive," said Wally, losing his temper and speaking angrily.

"I think you intend to do much more than survive, Wally. I think you intend to prosper with this new regime. That's all you've ever cared about – getting what you want for yourself!"

"Well, if you are so opposed to our lifestyle then you may go and join the other housewives queuing at the shops for food, instead of having a pantry full of food delivered to the door, my dear wife. Money talks, Cassie, more so now than ever. Now, can you please quickly get ready or we'll be late for the theatre!"

"I won't be going to the theatre tonight, Wally – you'll have to go on your own."

He glared at her before turning and storming off. "Very well – please your bloody self!" He turned before leaving and spat, "When did you ever care about politics or business? You said yourself many times you had no interest in politics! All you ever cared about at Cliffenden was parties and drinking and making a fool of yourself with Teddy!"

He stormed out.

"That's what you think, Wally," she whispered to herself, wishing with all her heart she could be back there during those days at Cliffenden with Teddy, and her parents, and Bowden.

"Simone! How could you!" shouted Luc, distressed, as he paced up and down the apartment's drawing room.

"I just blurted it out!" said Simone, shaking slightly. "I was so agitated with seeing that German officer in the store, and – and she seemed so naïve about everything that was going on –"

"*Anything* that I tell you from work or elsewhere must remain absolutely private, Simone! If Wally should find out that you told Cassie that!"

"Oh, Luc, you don't think he will, do you?" Simone was terrified of the consequences.

"I hope not – I don't think so. If Cassie said she wouldn't say anything then I believe she will be true to her word. But you must not ever put us in such danger again, Simone!"

"I know! I'm so sorry, Luc."

"You don't know how ruthless Wally can be. If I ever displeased him he would just throw me out without a second thought. I'm only as good as I am useful to him, do you understand?"

"Yes, I know that, Luc. That's why I went with Cassie shopping in the first place, so as to keep in with them."

Luc came over to his wife, sat down beside her and held her in his arms. "It was good you went – we have to come across as being as normal as possible. But you can't act like that in front of her again. She may become suspicious, and we have so much to lose. Force yourself to be strong in their company."

"I don't want to be in their company. I just want to stay here in the apartment safe until this war is over."

"But the war is already over, Simone, at least for France. And we have to pretend everything is normal when we are out," he said, pulling back from her and taking her face in his hands. "Do you understand me?"

"Yes." She managed to smile at him.

CHAPTER 38

It was afternoon and the chauffeur pulled up outside the department store Galleries Lafayette.

"I shouldn't be long," said Cassie as she got out and the chauffeur nodded.

Stefan Bayer was across the street and watched as Cassie's graceful figure walked across the pavement and into the store. Stefan turned to the two policemen who were with him and began to talk to them.

A couple of minutes later one of the policemen went up to the chauffeur.

"You can't park here, move along!" said the policeman.

"But I'll only be a couple of minutes more – my employer said she wouldn't be long," said the chauffeur.

"Now!" demanded the policeman.

Reluctantly the chauffeur pulled out into the traffic and went to drive around the block in order to collect Cassie on his way back around.

Cassie picked up a couple of scarves at one of the counters under the huge glass-and-steel dome that dominated the building. After paying she made her way back to the front door. The store seemed so much emptier now as the rations and war reparations being demanded began to affect the general public. She passed a gang of officers, with their new French girlfriends in tow, coming into the store as she walked out onto the pavement. She was surprised to see the car was not there and began to look up and down the street but could not spot it. She began to walk down the street, looking out for the vehicle.

"Pardon, Madame, may I see your papers, please," said one of two policemen who sidled up beside her.

Cassie looked at him, surprised.

"Papers? What papers are you looking for?"

"Your residency papers, passport, Aryan Certificate," said the man.

"Why do you want to see papers?" Cassie asked, annoyed.

"Please just show us your papers, Madame."

"Well, I don't have any on me, as it happens. I'm just out doing a bit of shopping – why on earth would I need an Aryan certificate?"

"I see. Could you come with us, please," said one of the policemen, taking her arm.

"Go with you where?" she demanded, trying to shake off his arm.

"To the station."

"No, I will not! How dare you! I don't know where my chauffeur has gone to." She was desperately looking up and down the street for him. "I left him here ten minutes ago!"

"Madame, we will not ask you again – please accompany us now!" demanded the policeman.

"This is the most ridiculous thing I have ever encountered!" she said as the men marched her to an awaiting car, as onlookers stopped to stare at the commotion. She dropped her shopping bag on the pavement and it was left there as she was driven away.

Stefan Bayer stepped out of a side street from where he had observed the whole episode.

"I've already told you! My name is Cassie Fullerton Stanton and I was out shopping!"

Cassie was sitting in a room at the police station, facing two policemen who were sitting on the other side of a desk from her.

"But where are your papers to prove who you are?" asked the policeman.

"At home! If you take me home I'll show you them! Although I really think you have a cheek to drag me in here as if I was some – common criminal!" Cassie took out her cigarettes and went to light one.

"No smoking, please!"

"For goodness' sake!" Cassie raised her eyes to heaven and threw her cigarettes back into her handbag. "Is there anything one is actually allowed to do in this country anymore?"

"Are you Jewish?" asked the policeman.

"I don't see that that's any of your business!" snapped Cassie. "What concern is it of yours?"

"So you are Jewish?"

"How long are you going to keep me here?" she demanded.

"Will you answer the question – are you Jewish?" The policeman's voice had risen.

Cassie kept her voice very calm. "I have told you my name is Cassie Fullerton Stanton. I am an Irish National and my husband is an American citizen. I have given you his work number. Now will you please telephone him to confirm who I actually am, in order that I can leave this shithole!"

"You're not being very cooperative. Perhaps you have something to hide?"

"What could I possibly have to hide? Except my embarrassment at being marched off the street into a police car!"

"If you are a neutral citizen as you claim, then what is your business being in Paris?"

Cassie sighed in fury. "Because my husband's job is here! Believe me, if it was up to me I'd be somewhere – anywhere – else!"

"Perhaps it suits your purposes to remain in Paris?"

"What are you talking about?"

"Being the wife of a banker is a good disguise for you to go about your business as a spy for the British."

"A spy!" She started to laugh. "That's absurd! The British would want to be very desperate to employ me as a spy!"

"Ah, but you've just said it yourself – the British are desperate. You are aware that all Jews have been required by law to register with the authorities?"

"I am aware of that abnormality, yes."

"Then I ask you again: are you Jewish?"

"You have no right to question me in this way! I am a neutral citizen of a neutral country."

The policeman closed over the papers in front of him. "Yes, so you say, but you have no papers to prove what you say. Which means you could be anybody. We are allowed to detain you and send you to an internment centre until then."

"*What?*" Cassie shouted.

The telephone rang on Wally's desk and he picked it up.

"Wally Stanton?"

"Yes," said Wally as he continued writing notes on the paper in front of him.

"This is the police."

Wally looked up from his paperwork. "Yes, how can I help you?"

"We have a woman here who is claiming to be your wife."

"My wife! What on earth is she doing with you?"

"She was picked up this afternoon without any papers on her."

Wally raised his eyes to heaven. "I see. In that case it most probably is my wife."

"We need you to come down to the station to identify her and bring her papers with you."

"I see – give me the address." Wally scribbled down the address on paper and then hung up the telephone. "Cassie!" he muttered to himself under his breath, annoyed at the inconvenience of it all.

He stood up and went to put on his coat, then stopped and thought for a while. He then took off his coat and sat back at his desk.

"Fuck her," he said, laughing to himself.

It was getting dark outside and Cassie's initial anger was now turning to concern and stress. She had known the Gestapo and the French authorities under their orders were arresting people and sending them to detention centres. She had heard of the dreadful things and conditions in those centres. She had thought that, being a neutral and having no involvement in anything political, such a thing would never enter her world. And yet here she was being threatened to be sent off to a detention centre without anybody even knowing where she had gone. She suddenly for the first time in her life felt very vulnerable and alone. She had grown up with such security and connections that she had never felt fear before. And yet here she was isolated, with nobody to call on except Wally who seemed to have vanished.

"Are you sure you spoke to my husband?" demanded Cassie.

"Yes, several hours ago."

"Then where is he?"

"You tell me! It is getting late, Madame, and we must make arrangements for tonight for you. You will be transferred to –"

At that moment there was a knock on the door and a policeman showed Wally in.

"Wally! Where have you been till now?" Cassie said, not sure if the tears that were threatening were from anger or relief.

Wally ignored her and handed Cassie's passport and papers to the policeman behind the desk. "I believe this is what you're looking for."

The policeman took the passport and studied it.

"Your wife has been very un-cooperative, Monsieur Stanton," said the policeman. "She has refused to answer basic questions."

"Like what?" Wally gave Cassie a filthy look.

"Like – is she Jewish?"

"Gentlemen, I can assure you that my wife is not Jewish," Wally said. "As you can see from her papers."

"After today, she has drawn much suspicion on herself as to what her activities are here in Paris," said the policeman.

"My activities! Are you thick or something?" Cassie erupted.

"Madame!" shouted the policeman.

"What appears to be the problem here?" said a male voice and Cassie turned around to see Stefan Bayer walk through the door.

"Stefan!" said Wally.

"I saw you come into the building, Wally. Is anything wrong?"

"It's all a bit of a misunderstanding, Stefan. Cassie was out shopping today and forgot to take her papers with her."

"I've been given the most terrible time!" Cassie said.

Stefan addressed the policemen. "It's quite alright. These are good friends of mine. I can vouch for them. There is no need to detain them any longer."

"Now – can I go?" demanded Cassie as she stood up.

The policeman nodded. "Of course."

Cassie went marching out, followed by Wally and Stefan.

"I'm so sorry – if I had known you were here I'd have been able to intervene so much earlier," said Stefan.

"We are very grateful to you for speaking up for us, aren't we, Cassie?" said Wally.

Cassie was feeling a wave of relief sweep over her to be free of that room and the questioning. She gave Stefan a firm smile. "Yes – thank you, Stefan."

"What are friends for?" smiled Stefan as he put his arms around them and led them to the front door. "And now, I would like to invite you out for dinner this week."

Cassie desperately wanted to say no, but realised she couldn't.

"No, Stefan – *we* would like to invite you to our house for dinner with a few of our close friends," said Wally.

"Wonderful! At last I get an invitation to Cassie Fullerton's dinner table!"

"Don't start!" begged Cassie as she sat into the back of the car with Wally.

"What were you thinking of, going out without your papers?" demanded Wally angrily.

"I forgot! I didn't think!"

"No – too wound up in yourself to think about anything else! No regard for me, dragging me into a police station to rescue you like that!"

"And what took you so long? They notified you hours ago I had been arrested!"

"I was in meetings – I didn't get the message till late," he lied.

"They were threatening to send me off to one those detention centres." Cassie felt like bursting out crying but was forcing herself not to. All she wanted was a comforting hug and a good cry on a shoulder, and all she was getting was Wally's furious and jeering face.

"And they would have been perfectly in their rights to do so. And what were you thinking not co-operating with them once they arrested you? Are you a complete imbecile?"

Tears were now coming down Cassie's cheeks, but Wally seemed oblivious to them.

"I felt they had no right to ask me what they were asking," she defended herself.

"They can do what they want," said Wally. "If it wasn't for Stefan stepping in, they probably would have detained you, you were so hostile."

"And now you've invited that Nazi into our home!"

"Yes, and you are going to be the perfect hostess to him – is that understood?"

"Why did I listen to you? Why didn't I insist we leave Paris?"

"Because I wouldn't have gone – and I wouldn't have let you go. Here we are and here we'll stay."

CHAPTER 39

Luc sat in Wally's office going through papers.

"And all the accounts have now been successfully frozen from the Jewish clients?" asked Wally.

"Yes," said Luc.

"I'm sure it will only be a short-term measure," said Wally as he browsed through papers.

"No, it won't," Luc said pointedly. "The exact same thing will happen here as in German and Poland. It's only the beginning. The round-up of Jews has already started."

"Only dissidents, lawyers, journalists, people a threat to the new order. Besides, that's really none of our concern. We are obliged to obey the law."

Luc nodded, gathered his files and stood up to go.

"Oh and Luc, you and Simone are invited to our house on Saturday night."

"What's the occasion?"

"We're throwing a dinner party for Stefan Bayer. Well, as he's now one of the most important men in Paris it's important to be friends with him."

"I see."

"Also, he did us an immense favour. Cassie got herself arrested and –"

"Arrested? For what?" Luc face dropped.

"She went out shopping without her passport, silly bitch. She was randomly stopped and arrested."

"Is she alright?" Luc's face was etched with concern.

"Oh, quite alright. She only has herself to blame for her rudeness to the police officers. She still thinks she's the Queen of England or something. Anyway Stefan stepped in to loosen the bureaucracy."

"I see. Poor Cassie!"

"So dinner at our house Saturday, seven sharp," said Wally.

"I'm afraid Simone hasn't been feeling too well this week. I doubt she will be up to going out. I'll have to check with her and get back to you."

"I'm not asking you, Luc, I'm telling you," Wally said with a frown.

Luc swallowed the torrent of abuse he wanted to hurl at Wally and smiled. "In that case, we'll look forward to it – thank you for the invitation." He turned to leave.

"Oh, and Luc?"

"Yes?"

"The Jewish employees at the bank – why are they still here?"

"Oh – there's been too much going on with everything else."

"Well, can you dismiss them as quickly as possible? We don't want to be seen to be working against the new regime, do we?"

"But it's not so easy, Wally. Many have been with us for years. I need to go through their contracts and –"

"Ignore all that, Luc! The statute says they cannot be employed in commercial work. We can't risk continuing employing them. It could risk the new business I'm organising with the German authorities."

Luc nodded and walked slowly away.

Cassie walked through the markets with Michelle. She used to love selecting the beautiful produce on display. Now, as she passed yet another anti-Jewish poster, it had lost its appeal. Especially since she had been arrested for doing nothing more than shopping. It had brought home to her how dangerous everything now was. But the whole world had changed and become a dangerous place. As she thought about Cliffenden, she couldn't imagine that anything had changed there. She couldn't imagine anything ever changing at Cliffenden.

And now here she was being forced to entertain Stefan Bayer.

"Monsieur Stanton says that this dinner party is the most important one that you have held since you came to Paris," commented Michelle as she followed Cassie through the stalls.

"Certainly the most unexpected," said Cassie as she paused to look at some tomatoes.

"Monsieur Stanton says that this Saturday evening must be a fabulous display for the guests."

"We can only try our best," said Cassie.

"Monsieur Stanton says –"

"Michelle! You don't have to keep quoting Monsieur Stanton to me! I'm fully aware of his thoughts on everything – he never shuts up expressing them!"

"Yes, Madame. Pardon, Madame."

CHAPTER 40

"I can't go! I won't go!" cried Simone.

It was the evening of the party at the Stantons'. Simone stood in the drawing room of their apartment dressed in a cocktail dress. Luc was in his tuxedo.

"Simone! We have to go, we have no choice," said Luc.

He looked at his wife who was trembling. Last-minute nerves had taken her over.

She sat down quickly. "Tell them I got a migraine. That I had to go to bed."

"I can't, Simone. Wally will go mad."

"Let him go mad! I don't care!"

Luc went over to her and sank to his knees in front of her. "And what if he should fire me? What would we do then? Where could we go?"

"I just can't sit at the same table as Bayer for the night and pretend everything is alright."

He reached forward and held her shoulders. "Yes, you can. It's just a few hours of acting, that's all."

"I can't!"

"For the children, Simone – you have to for the children."

At the house, Cassie had been busy all day making sure everything was in place for the evening. Their cook was preparing a sumptuous feast of duckling.

Cassie was sitting at her dressing table, fixing her make-up for the night, when Wally walked in.

"What are you wearing?" he asked.

She looked down at the deep-green gown she was wearing and replied sarcastically, "A dress!"

"No, no, that's not suitable at all," he said.

Cassie paused as she applied her lipstick and raised her eyes to heaven. "What is not suitable about it – exactly?"

"Stefan Bayer is a man who likes glamour – that's not alluring enough."

"Well, I'm not changing now," stated Cassie as she continued to apply her lipstick. "And I am certainly not going to change because my dress is not – *alluring* – enough for Stefan Bayer."

"Oh, yes, you are," said Wally as he went to her wardrobes and began riffling through the gowns there.

She sighed loudly. "What are you doing, Wally?"

He pulled out a long slinky gold off-the-shoulder gown and held it up.

"This is more like it," he said.

"Wally! I'm not going to a film premiere!"

He flung the gown onto the bed. "Change into that, will you?"

She swung around and glared at him. "You really are the most impossible man, Wally!"

He looked at his watch. "You don't have much time."

"I'm not changing my bloody dress!" insisted Cassie.

Michelle walked in at that moment. "Would Madame like me to assist her to change her dress?"

"No!" snapped Cassie.

"Yes!" snapped Wally.

Cassie got up and marched over to him. "I know that dictators have become all the fashion in Europe at the moment, but that doesn't entitle you to become one too!"

"For fuck's sake, Cassie, can't you just do what you're told for once! This is an important night for the bank."

"Fuck your bank!"

Wally turned around to Michelle. "Can you leave us please, Michelle?"

"Certainly, Monsieur," said Michelle who hastily retreated and closed the door. She stood listening outside as Cassie and Wally's argument developed into a shouting match.

"*Merde!*" whispered Michelle to herself as their voices screeched at each other.

Twenty minutes later Michelle was downstairs and she turned to see Wally and Cassie walk down the staircase together. Cassie, frowning and agitated, was wearing the gold gown Wally had picked for her.

Cassie and Wally stood in the hallway. Most of the guests had already arrived and were chatting and being served drinks in the drawing room.

Pierre opened the door. Stefan walked confidently in and over to them, accompanied by two officers.

"Am I the last to arrive?" he asked, smiling.

"Not quite," said Wally, shaking his hand.

"Ah, Cassie!" said Stefan, taking her hand and kissing it.

"Good evening, Stefan," she said.

"You look far more relaxed and better than the last time I saw you," said Stefan.

"Well, a police station for several hours plays havoc with the complexion," she said.

Stefan laughed and offered her his arm. "All a misunderstanding, I'm sure. Whenever you are in trouble, I hope you telephone me quickly to help you. That's what friends are for."

She took his arm and said as she led him into the drawing room, "I do not plan to be in any more trouble, I can assure you."

"Let me introduce you to everybody, Stefan," smiled Wally.

"Excellent," said Stefan, looking at the display of Parisian high society before him. "I think I might know some of them already."

Luc led Simone up the drive to the Stantons' house. Amongst the array of cars parked outside, Stefan's car took pride of place outside the front door. His chauffeur was busy polishing it. Simone shuddered as she saw the Nazi flag on the bonnet of the car.

"We'll be fine," Luc whispered to her as he smiled at the chauffeur and said, "Good evening."

"I thought you might have liked to bring your lady friend with you?" Cassie said to Stefan as she drank a glass of champagne with him in the drawing room.

"My lady friend?"

"The model I met you with that day."

"Ah, her! She was merely an acquaintance, hardly a friend."

"I see," said Cassie, fighting herself not to deliver a dozen remarks that were passing through her mind.

"I have to say you look marvellous tonight, Cassie," smiled Stefan. "You're a very lucky guy, Wally."

"Aren't I?" said Wally smugly. "I had to fight hard to win her hand."

"He's not lying." She smiled as she thought of the antics that led to their engagement.

"Tell me, is it true you once did a screen test to be a film star?" Stefan asked.

"No, that's not true at all. I couldn't act to save my life," said Cassie, whose smile hid her growing concern that Stefan seemed to have such an interest in her past and her. She didn't like it when men became too impressed by her. She knew from Wally it usually ended in her being unhappy.

"Having said that, Cassie knows a lot of film stars. She used to party with them in London before she married," said Wally.

Cassie spotted Luc and Simone entering the room.

"If you'll excuse me for one moment," said Cassie and she headed over to them.

"Thank you for coming," she said, kissing each of them on the cheek.

"*Luc!*" Wally shouted from the other side of the room.

"Pardon me, ladies, but I'm being beckoned," said Luc. He gave a reassuring smile to Simone and walked across to Wally and Stefan.

"I heard you had been picked up by the police – are you

alright?" Simone asked Cassie.

"Oh, yes, I'm fine now. I've got over the shock of it," said Cassie. "Very unpleasant experience. I won't be going anywhere now without my passport."

"That would be wise," said Simone.

"How are the children?"

Simone smiled. "They are fine."

"It must be hard protecting them from everything going on."

"We do our best."

There was much laughter around the dinner table as the guests enjoyed their meal.

"I wonder, Stefan – there seem to be so many soldiers in Paris – are there any fighting the war?" asked Cassie.

"A lot of them are here to enjoy the city before they go back to the front," said Stefan.

"That's right," said Wally. "It's a good break for them."

"You mean Paris has become a kind of tourist destination for German soldiers?" asked Cassie.

"We use the expression '*Everyone once in Paris*'. All German soldiers deserve to have a break at least once in Paris. Where better for them to recharge their batteries before going to fight again?" He smiled at her. "Could I ask a favour, Cassie?"

"I'm sure you can ask," answered Cassie.

"Could I have my photo taken with you? I always like to have my photo taken with my friends."

"Well, I don't –" began Cassie.

"Of course you can, Stefan," interrupted Wally.

"Excellent," Stefan said. He turned to one of his officers and whispered to him. The officer nodded and hurriedly left.

"I don't want to have my photo taken with him!" Cassie whispered to Wally.

"Just do it!" snapped Wally.

A minute later the officer arrived back with a camera.

"Ah, here we are!" said Stefan. "Perhaps one of us three together first?"

Wally stepped in beside Cassie and Stefan while the officer took photos.

"And now if I could have one of me and Cassie?" said Stefan.

Wally stepped out of the way and Cassie felt Stefan put his arm around her waist.

"Smile, please!" said the officer as he held the camera up.

"Yes, smile, Cassie," said Stefan as he tightened his grip on her waist.

It was nearly two in the morning and the party was still showing no signs of ending. Cassie stood at the back of the drawing room with Simone, looking on at the merriment in the room.

"We really must be going," said Simone. "We have to get back to the children."

"I wish they would all go, Simone!"

Simone looked at Luc who was deep in conversation with Stefan and another couple of officers.

"I wonder what they're talking about?" mused Cassie.

Simone held her tongue, remembering Luc's warning to her never to divulge bank business to Cassie. But Simone knew the bank was being used to transfer funds from France to Germany. Funds expropriated from families and businesses in France. Stolen funds.

Simone turned and looked out the French windows. "Your gardens are so beautiful, Cassie."

Cassie turned and looked out the glass panes as well.

"Yes, an oasis of calm in a city of chaos," said Cassie.

As Cassie looked out at the gardens her gaze was drawn to the corridor that led to the kitchens that ran out from the back of the house. She saw Wally there in the corridor talking to Michelle. Something in the way they were positioned made her continue to look on curiously. Wally was whispering into Michelle's ear. Suddenly his hand went around her and gripped her behind. Michelle leaned forward and whispered something in his ear.

Simone, who had been the watching the scenario also, looked at Cassie in dismay.

Cassie quickly turned around and faced into the room.

"Cassie . . ." said Simone, not knowing what to say.

Cassie blinked a few times as the image of her husband groping the more than willing maid flashed through her head.

Simone reached forward and put a sympathetic hand on her arm. "Cassie – I'm so sorry."

Cassie looked at Simone, shook her hand off and spoke sharply to her. "What are you sorry about? What have you done to be sorry about?"

Realising Cassie was being defensive, Simone said, "It's none of my business."

"No, it's not! And why are you still here? I thought you had children you needed to get back to?" Cassie blinked away tears of embarrassment and walked quickly away.

Cassie sat at the dressing table in their room, removing her make-up. Wally came out of the bathroom, wearing a silk dressing gown.

"Well, I think tonight was an unqualified success," he said.

"Do you?"

"Stefan was very pleased with it."

"I don't think entertaining Nazi officers for a night is going to be a moment in my life I will look back on with pride."

"Well, I'm very happy."

"As long as you're happy, Wally, that's all that matters."

Wally took off his dressing gown and got into bed.

"I was thinking I might get rid of Michelle," said Cassie, reaching forward and lifting her glass of water to take a sip.

"What?" snapped Wally.

"Michelle. I don't think she's a very good maid. I think I'll give her notice tomorrow. She isn't patch on the staff we had at Cliffenden."

"You'll do no such thing! Michelle is a very good maid, especially as she puts up with your rubbish all day long. She's a treasure. We'll keep her!"

Cassie turned around to face her husband. "Why did you marry me, Wally?"

"Because I love you, my darling."

"Wally, you don't even know what love is. Now you've been married to me for a long while, you must realise that marriage to me wasn't worth the chase."

"I don't know what you're talking about."

"I can't truly make you happy, Wally. You know the circumstances of our marriage. You blackmailed me into marrying you in order to save Cliffenden."

"I did no such thing. Our courting before we got married was the happiest time of our lives."

"You're either delusional, or – or is your pride and vanity so much that you can't accept the real circumstances of our marriage?"

Wally's face turned very sour. "I no longer wish to discuss this, Cassie. Our life is what it is and it is not going to change."

"But why?" Her voice was desperate. "I don't understand what happiness this marriage is bringing either of us. Am I just a possession you won't let go of?"

"You're my wife, Cassie. I've always tolerated you and your silly daydreams. I know what life was like for you in Cliffenden. You and Teddy thinking everything was one big joke. Such irresponsible people. But it's time you grew up and started acting like a woman and a wife, and not some silly child who thinks she can do what she wants. And speaking of children, it's high time we had some."

"Oh – Wally!" She raised her eyes to heaven.

"Time we had a family of our own. That should make you up grow pretty quickly. A girl who looks like you, and a boy who looks like me. A perfect family."

"Heaven help us. Another of you! It's just all about image with you . . . I think we should get divorced."

"*Divorced!*" he roared across the room.

"I don't think there's any point in going on with this sham of a marriage anymore. Why don't you release me, Wally? We might be able to find some kind of happiness yet."

Wally jumped out of the bed and walked menacingly towards her.

"Now listen, you! I don't want to ever hear those words from you again. Release you! You should be very glad you're married to me. I provide you with a wonderful life. Anything you want. And all I expect from you is to show some loyalty, to present yourself well to the world for my benefit!" He began to flick her hair nastily back. "Where would you be, if it wasn't for me? Your family would have lost everything only I stepped in to save you."

"Wally!" She tried to push his offending hand back.

"When I married you I gave Cliffenden a financial settlement to secure its future. I kept my side of the bargain, and you're going to keep yours!"

Smiling at her, he bent down and kissed her neck before turning and going back to bed.

Outside the door Michelle had been listening to every word.

PART FOUR

England 1988

CHAPTER 41

Joe had made a lot of progress with Cassie, getting her to open up about her life when she left Cliffenden and her married life with Wally. As he had anticipated, it was an unhappy marriage. There didn't seem to be any love between them. He had hoped that once she had settled into married life with Wally a love might have developed between them, especially when Bowden was no longer around to distract her. But that didn't seem to be the case. It made his heart sink as he was the cause of the break-up with Bowden. He had got her to open up somewhat and that was an achievement in itself, but she still had not discussed the crime she was accused of or the circumstances surrounding it. He hoped to push her a little further that day. If he could just get the facts from her point of view, then at least he would know what he was dealing with.

He made a pot of coffee and carried it out of the kitchen and into the living room. Through the glass windows he saw Cassie sitting out on the balcony, lost in thought, a soft wind blowing through her hair.

He placed the coffee pot and two cups down on the coffee table.

"Coffee?" he called.

She looked around, stood up and entered the living room. She smiled at him and sat down on the couch.

"Smells wonderful," she said as he poured her a cup.

She raised the cup, smelled it and took a drink. "You know, I never take coffee for granted. Not since being in Paris during the war. It was hard to get. When we couldn't get the real thing we drank this substitute drink that was made out of roasted barley and chicory."

"From what you were saying, your life in Paris didn't involve much suffering though?"

"Wally's money made sure we could get most things we wanted. Isn't that one of the things that I'm accused of and hated for in the press? That I was living it up collaborating with the Nazis while everyone else suffered?"

"You're not being tried for collaboration, Cassie – it doesn't matter what people say about you in that regard."

"Of course it does! It's building me up to be the scarlet woman – the woman of sin. From reading through the newspapers I think they care more about my lifestyle in Paris than the murder I am supposed to have committed."

"Let's talk a little more about your lifestyle in Paris. You've given me an understanding about what your marriage with Wally was like. From what you say the newspapers were correct in that you were friends and had connections with the Nazis in Paris."

"Well, it wasn't just us, it wasn't just me! You had to! Many people were co-operating with the occupying forces."

Joe hid his delight. It was the first time Cassie had managed to in any way defend herself. If he could only provoke this so she would defend herself from the crime.

"I completely understand. We do what we have to do," said Joe. "Tell me a little more about your dealings with the Nazis. And your friendship with Oberst Stefan Bayer."

Cassie said nothing but stared into space. Joe got up and fetched a newspaper and put it on the coffee table in front of her. In the newspaper there was a photo of Cassie in a Parisian nightclub from the forties standing next to a handsome Nazi officer who had his arm around her, while he held a glass of wine in his other hand. They were both smiling and enjoying themselves.

"That's him, isn't it? Stefan Bayer?" said Joe.

"How many times has that photo been printed in newspapers and books over the years? Damning me forever."

"Were you Bayer's lover as has been reported?" asked Joe.

Cassie frowned and he saw an invisible wall go up between them.

"Cassie?" he pushed gently.

She suddenly smiled at him. "What's intriguing me is you, Joe. How did our little footman in Cliffenden become a top barrister and achieve all this?"

"My history isn't going to help you win your case, Cassie."

"I know, but indulge me. I've already told you about my life after I left Cliffenden. Please tell me about yours."

He sat back and sipped his coffee.

CHAPTER 42

For Joe, a light seemed to go off at Cliffenden once Cassie left. It just wasn't the same without her. He heard all about her glorious wedding in London to Wally Stanton. Saw the photos in the newspapers and magazines. Read about her life after she was married in the same newspapers and magazines, or heard the Fullerton family discuss her latest travels. But all he felt was that he had been robbed of his bright future by being backstabbed by Wally Stanton. He now realised Wally had never had any intention of making him butler at his house once he married Cassie. It was just a ploy to get him on board in assisting him in getting Cassie to agree to marry him. And how his ploy had worked! To a degree that Wally would never know. A ploy that encouraged him not to deliver that letter from Bowden on the eve of his departure. Which led Cassie to believe she had been deserted by Bowden and allowed her to sleepwalk into marriage with Wally.

Yes, Joe had thought he was also acting in Cassie's best interest, thinking she would be better off with a life with Wally. But he had expected to be part of that life too. He had been outwitted, outsmarted by Wally Stanton. And why would he not be outsmarted? He was only a footman.

So life went on at Cliffenden in the couple of years after Cassie's marriage. It actually went on quite joyously for everyone else. Lady Dorothy and Howard were thrilled Cassie was married to Wally, and the marriage had secured Cliffenden's future, with Wally's financial contribution. The parties continued, the entertaining continued. Teddy continued much the same as he always did. Drunk half the time, hung-over the rest. He continued with his fickle ways, oblivious to everyone else. Mrs. Crowther continued to supervise breakfasts, lunches and dinners, while never getting up off her chair. Mr. Bruton continued to bark orders at him, and nothing was ever good enough. Mrs. Farrell continued to go about her business, quiet as a mouse, intimidated by Bruton and Mrs. Crowther. And all the time Joe thought back to when Cassie was the most important part of his life and how he, through being the messenger between her and Bowden, had been the central part of her life. He missed it dreadfully, the excitement of his role in that illicit relationship.

Joe had always been good at school, but with his background it was never a possibility to go any further with his education. As a way to pass his free time he asked Howard permission to borrow books from the library, to which Howard agreed. Joe found he had a thirst for knowledge and read the books whenever he got a chance, improving his literacy skills and knowledge.

And then suddenly the war exploded. Germany had invaded Poland and then it seemed everyone was declaring war on each other to Joe's mind. Except for Ireland of course which declared neutrality. So even the war didn't change things in Ireland or at Cliffenden. Except that everyone was worried about Cassie, stationed in Paris with Wally who seemed to have no intention of leaving to everyone's dismay. And then of course Teddy enlisted in the British army. It was expected of him, with his class and his Anglo-Irish background. Ireland might be neutral but the Fullertons weren't, not in their hearts and backgrounds anyway.

"Didn't think he'd have it in him," said Mrs. Crowther over lunch one day in the kitchens as Teddy was being prepared to be sent off to war. "I thought he might just sit the emergency out here in a sea of gin."

"No, Mrs. Crowther, he'd never be able to hold his head up in society again if he did," said Bruton. "No – all his cousins and friends are gone to war, and his father fought in the last war. It's the natural progression of things. Mr. Teddy might be a little haphazard but he knows what he has to do when the chips are down."

"Lady Dorothy is putting on a brave face, but I heard her crying in her room last night," said Mrs. Crowther.

"Poor Lady Dorothy, and not even Miss Cassie around to comfort her," sighed Bruton.

"It might be quite exciting for him to go to the war," said Joe, looking up from his lunch. "I think he's nearly been waiting for it all his life."

"Don't be so daft, lad!" snapped Bruton. "There's nothing exciting about having your head blown off! You should just be grateful that Ireland is staying out of the whole damned thing and you don't have to go off like they do in Britain."

But Joe didn't feel grateful, not in the least. As he and the rest of the staff assembled in front of the house to wave Teddy off to war, half-sloshed as he got into the car, he felt envious.

"*Give my regards to Broadway!*" sang Teddy as he waved a white handkerchief out of the window of the car as it drove down the avenue from Cliffenden.

"Goodness me!" said Lady Dorothy to Howard as she watched in despair as Teddy was driven off. "Will he even be able to see straight to shoot?"

"Don't worry – he'll be given all the proper training," Howard assured her.

"Well, nobody has managed to ever put manners on him before, so I doubt the British army will either!" said Dorothy.

From then on, lunch consisted of Mr. Bruton reading out the latest war reports from the newspaper, and dinner consisted of listening to the latest reports on the wireless, the new radio that had been installed in the kitchen and had kind of taken over from the conversation that used to be constant there. It all was mounting to a growing restlessness in Joe. With Cassie and now Teddy gone there was no excitement there anymore.

And then there was Kathy, the chambermaid, who he'd had a couple of flings with and now seemed to think they were together for life. Despite his avoidance of the subject she constantly discussed their marriage plans.

"I wonder which room in the attic they'll give us when we marry?" she would say. And then one day the bombshell: "I think we'll announce our engagement to Lady Dorothy and Mr. Howard tomorrow. We've put it off for long enough."

Joe panicked as he saw the rest of his life as being bossed around by Bruton and living in an attic room with Kathy. He would be trapped there forever. He had loved Cliffenden, but looking at the Fullertons he knew there was so much more to life. And he wanted it. He wanted more.

He was pouring tea for Lady Dorothy and Howard in the drawing room that day.

"Oh, Howard make yourself available at three tomorrow, will you? Kathy has asked to see both of us," said Dorothy.

"What about? Does she want a pay rise?"

"Haven't a clue, but she says it's important."

Joe nearly spilled the tea as he heard this and then suddenly he was blurting out, "Sorry, Lady Dorothy, sorry, Mr. Howard, but I want to go!"

Dorothy looked at him in bewilderment. "What's wrong with you, Joe? Go where?"

"To the war!" Joe nearly shouted.

Dorothy looked at him patiently. "But, Joe, Ireland isn't in the war. There's no need for you to go anywhere."

"I know! But I want to join up the British army, like Mr. Teddy did!"

Dorothy remained patient. "Mr. Teddy is an aristocrat, Joe. It was expected of him, with our British connections to the Royal family."

"I know that, my lady, but there's lots of normal Irish lads joining up with the British as well! Lots from the village have joined up. I want to too!"

Howard looked at him seriously. "Have you thought about this, Joe? It's a very serious thing, joining up."

"I'm not a child, Mr. Howard. I know what I want. And I want to go and fight the Nazis!"

Dorothy and Howard looked at each other.

"Well, if that's what you feel you must do, then that is what you must do," said Dorothy.

"Very heroic of you, Joe – we're all very proud of you," said Howard as he came over to him and patted him on the shoulder.

"Will you make the arrangements, sir? I wouldn't know what to do."

"Of course. I'll contact a chum of mine in the army at once and we'll get it sorted out," Howard assured him.

Joe found the hardest part of leaving for the war was saying goodbye to his mother. She had been so proud of him being a footman at Cliffenden and he knew she would never understand that he now wanted more in life. When he told her he was going to war she was astounded.

"But why would you go to war when you don't have to?" she said, devastated.

"My father did," he said. "He fought in the Great War."

"Yes, and got badly wounded for his efforts! And died a few short years after from his injuries, leaving us alone! Why leave that wonderful place Cliffenden when you should be down on your knees giving thanks to be there!"

"It's just something I must do," he said.

He was overcome with guilt as he looked at her sitting beside the fire in the small cottage he had grown up in. He knew, as her only child, the loss of him leaving would be overwhelming for her. But as he reached out and took her hands in his, Joe could see an understanding in her eyes along with the sadness.

"Just be careful . . . and be happy," she whispered, almost as if she knew he would never return to her.

And so, by the next week, instead of Joe announcing his engagement to Kathy, he was being waved off to the war instead.

The staff again assembled at the front of Cliffenden.

Kathy was in floods of tears. "You'll write to me?"

"Every day!"

286

"My mother says you're a disgrace! She says no Irishman should go off and fight for the British!" said Kathy.

"But I'm fighting for world freedom from tyranny, Kathy, just like it says on the wireless!" said Joe.

Mrs. Crowther stepped forward, pushed Kathy aside and gave him a hug with tears in her eyes. "I've got that used to you around the place, I don't know what to say! But I'll give you a bit of advice – if you ever get stressed, just pour yourself a glass of sherry! Cures everything!"

"Thank you, Mrs. Crowther, I'll bear that in mind."

"Look after yourself," said Bruton who to Joe's shock was only just managing to keep a stiff upper lip. "Wherever they send you, always remember the etiquette and manners you have been taught here. I'm very pleased to report that we did turn that sow's ear into a silken purse."

Joe nodded and then he quickly raced away to the car that Howard had arranged to collect him. As the car drove away, he waved back to them, knowing that whatever happened he would never see them or Cliffenden again.

Three years later and Joe was sitting in an office in an old chateau in northern France as the Allied troops were advancing into Europe. As he sat there going through paperwork, he remembered Bruton's words on his departure: *"We did turn that sow's ear into a silken purse."*

A couple of days after leaving Cliffenden, he had found himself in London after Howard had made all the arrangements for him to join the British army. There he was in uniform walking down the majestic streets of London. It was a different world from Cliffenden. And he was excited. Joe knew the war was dreadful, he knew London was being bombed constantly, but he was young and free with a massive adventure before him. The streets of London were packed with soldiers and nurses and everyone seemed united to defeat the common enemy. London was a like a great train station with people stopping off before they were sent or arrived back from the war. It was a world away from emptying coal, shining silver and running baths. And he knew he had made the right decision. There was training, there were parties, there were girls and everyone was living for the day, not sure there would be a tomorrow. Most of the privates in the army were easy to make friends with and he found himself fitting in quickly. And yet something set him apart from them, and it took him a long time to realise what it was. Most were from the same background and education as him but they did treat him a little differently.

And then one day one of the privates said to him, "Well, you're not like the rest of us, Joe – you're posh!"

Joe had been taken aback. He had never been thought of or called posh even once in his life. He was a footman, no more or no less. Then he realised it was his years at Cliffenden. He might have been at the bottom of the ladder at Cliffenden, but it had been his life over the past few years. And living in that stately mansion had obviously filtered through to him. He had somehow picked up their ways. His years at Cliffenden had made him somebody different. Joe supposed if these privates met Mr. Bruton they would consider him to be very 'posh'.

The war years went on and Joe was stationed in North Africa for a long time and saw action there. And then, as the war turned, he was part of the troops advancing through Northern France. He had obviously stood out to the officers as well because he was requested to do errands for them. He was used to doing errands at Cliffenden and so made sure they were done right. One of the officers was a man called Hugh Gordonville. Hugh was very impressed with the way Joe carried out his orders.

"Where did you learn to do things so efficiently?" Hugh asked him one day.

"I was a footman, sir, in a stately home. There was no question of doing anything inefficiently there."

"I see. What stately house?"

"Cliffenden in Ireland."

Hugh nodded with his eyes opening wide. "Cliffenden . . . the Fullerton family."

"That's right, sir."

"Did you know Cassie Fullerton?"

Cassie had become a character of intrigue in the newspapers, the socialite that had gone missing after the terrible murder.

"I did indeed, sir. I had great time for her."

"That's very loyal of you, Joe, considering what everyone says about her."

"I don't believe a word of it, sir."

Hugh had looked at him speculatively. "You know, I think you're exactly what I'm looking for, Joe. I need a secretary to assist me in administrating the court martials. Would you be interested in it?"

"Yes, sir!"

"Good – it will keep you away from the front line, anyway."

And so Joe found himself working for Hugh on court martials. And how busy he was! The army had commandeered a château in northern France and it was there that the cases were brought in front of a board of officers to be tried. Joe found the system of court-martialling intriguing. The soldiers who were fighting the war weren't subject to the law of the country they were fighting in, nor their home country. They were subject to an international military law that was prevalent wherever the army was. The crimes that came before the board ranged from everything from being drunk and disorderly to desertion.

"It's absolutely imperative that strict discipline is kept in the ranks," Hugh said to Joe. "We might be winning the war but a few bad apples here and there could rot the entire barrel and jeopardise our victory."

Joe took it all on board as he meticulously prepared the cases being tried and put together the details, statements and evidence. He knew how important his work was because on a serious charge like desertion the result would be death by a firing squad. He felt a responsibility and sometimes, as he would sit in on the court martials, he would cringe as vital evidence that he had prepared for a prosecuting or a defence officer would be overlooked. He would sit there frustrated, fighting the desire to stand up and point out the mistakes being made. As he continued with his work he learned to put the vital evidence in big bold print on the front of the files, as he realised the officers didn't bother reading through the files and often skimmed over them.

One day he was sitting in what used to be a grand dining room and was now being used as a military court, listening to a young corporal being tried for desertion.

Hugh Gordonville was leading the panel of officers judging the corporal and was delivering his verdict.

"Harry Doughty, you were found escaping through the Ardennes Woods without leave of absence. It is a clear case of desertion. You will be taken to the courtyard here at the Chateau de Filleville, at eight o'clock in the morning, where you will be shot by members of your own regiment."

"No!" shouted Joe, suddenly standing up.

"What is the meaning of this?" demanded Hugh.

"I'm sorry, sir, but the defence officer has missed a vital piece of evidence. There is a statement from a local publican on the file that has not been presented to the court and has been overlooked by the Defence. The local publican has testified that Harry Doughty, the accused, was exceedingly drunk the night before in his bar with a group of other soldiers who were granted leave socialising. The publican has testified that Private Doughty was incoherent when he left the bar and, even though the private asked the publican which direction the base was, he couldn't tell his left from his right due to being inebriated and staggered off in the wrong direction – to the Ardennes Woods where he obviously collapsed and slept the night, only to be found the next morning by a passing platoon who assumed he was a deserter. The fact he asked which way the base was means he had every intention of making it back to base."

Hugh looked at Joe, astonished, and then snapped, "Show me the file and this letter from the publican."

Joe ran over to him and, riffling through the file, produced the letter which Hugh read quickly. Hugh gave the defence officer a withering look before turning and conferring with the rest of the panel.

"Harry Doughty," Hugh began again, "you have been found

guilty of being drunk and disorderly and not returning to base by the curfew time. Your penalty will be . . ."

Joe sat down, relieved.

Afterwards Harry Doughty came up to him, nearly crying. "I can't thank you enough. You saved my life! I was so pissed I didn't know what I was doing or who I'd been speaking to. I owe you a drink, many drinks."

"Perhaps you might stay away from drink for a while?" said Joe, smiling.

"Best I do."

"I'd better rush. I've been summoned to Major Gordonville's office."

Joe rushed up the stairs and down the corridor to Hugh's office where he found a furious Hugh Gordonville.

"How dare you interrupt proceedings in that manner! Who do you think you are?"

"I had to, sir, or else he would have been killed!"

"If you ever interfere in a court martial in that way again I will have you court-martialled yourself, is that understood?"

"Yes, sir!"

Hugh sighed, sat down behind his desk and studied Joe.

"Where did this brain of yours come from, Joe, this attention to detail?"

"Don't know, sir. Polishing silver at Cliffenden, perhaps?"

Hugh smirked and handed him a bunch of files. "Get them back to me by tomorrow."

"Yes, sir!" Joe took the files and rushed out the door.

Joe sat in his office in the chateau, looking out at the courtyard, thinking how Harry Doughty could have been killed there the next day. He felt empowered. He had saved a life. He liked that feeling.

And then the war was over. And all the solders, the ones who had survived, headed home to their jobs in factories, farms and offices. But Joe had no intention of heading home to Ireland when he arrived back on the train to London. He knew when he left Ireland he wouldn't be returning except briefly to see his mother. But, sadly, his mother had died of a heart attack a year before.

The war had given him a new confidence and clear vision of what he wanted in life. He contemplated what job he could get. He didn't want to work in a stately home like he did before the war. Besides, the stately homes seemed to be closing down with the new Labour government and their stringent tax laws. He worked for a while in Claridges Hotel as a porter. It was similar to his work at Cliffenden, showing wealthy people to their rooms and making sure they were alright.

But what he loved was working on those cases for the court martial during the war at the Chateau Filleville. He missed it. He went to night school to get an education. He thought of those officers defending and prosecuting the soldiers at the court martials and he knew that's what he wanted to do. But it seemed an impossible dream. Even with the new opportunities opening for working-class people after the war, the law seemed to be strictly reserved for the upper and upper-middle classes who already had connections with the profession. How could he ever dream of getting there? By sheer hard work, he decided.

He continued with his night studies and managed to get a job as a clerk in a solicitor's office. This is what he enjoyed, what he loved. And as had happened with Hugh Gordonville, his bosses realised his aptitude and continued to hand him more of their footwork to do. They realised he could cut through the paperwork quickly and get to the crux of a matter. He then transferred to being a clerk at a barrister's chambers. He worked harder and longer than everybody else, doing the donkey work on the cases. He gained respect from the barristers in the chambers who realised he could be trusted to give an opinion on a case or a solution to a problem. He looked at these barristers in the same way he looked at the Fullerton family at Cliffenden. They were a different world to him that he served and catered to.

One barrister in the practice was an older man called Conrad Drake who had been keeping an eye on Joe and the work he was doing. One day he called him into his office.

"Have you ever considered taking the law exams yourself?"

asked Conrad.

"No, I haven't," he answered truthfully.

"I know you have been attending night school. Perhaps you might consider doing a law degree?"

Joe looked at him, stunned.

"You are certainly intelligent enough, and I think you have the right aptitude to be a very good barrister," said Conrad.

"But I didn't go to university – people from my background don't go to university," said Joe.

"Well, you shouldn't let that get in your way if that's what you want to do. You can do a part-time degree and work here at the same time. You've made a lot of contacts here – they could start your profession for you once you are qualified."

The commitment to becoming a barrister took many years and sometimes he wondered if life was passing him by as he saw all his friends out enjoying themselves while he was stuck in studying. But he loved it and he was doing something he never thought possible for somebody like him.

All his dreams came true when he passed his law exams and was called to the bar. Joseph Grady, Barrister at Law. It was a title he continually repeated to himself but never really believed it. In his heart he was still a footman. But it was when he started winning case after case and getting a name for himself that he realised the others in his profession were never going to accept he was one of them either. The old boy network never really accepted him.

"They see you as a threat," advised Conrad Drake to him one day. "You'll always be just a clerk here in their eyes. If I was you I'd change to another chambers where you can start anew."

And that's what Joe did. He started in a new chambers and continued building a name for himself. But he knew deep down he was still not one of them as they discussed which schools they went to and what families they were from.

It was 1955 when he met Ann. It was after he had won a big case and he was out celebrating with his clients and the other barristers in a restaurant in Chelsea. She walked in, wearing a red halter-neck dress, and came right up to the table.

"Joe, this is my cousin, Ann," said one of the barristers he worked with.

"I'm so pleased to meet you!" said Ann in her clipped accent as she sat down beside him. "I hear you're one of the best young barristers in London."

"Am I?" he said.

"So I hear." She leaned forward with her cigarette in her mouth and he fumbled for his lighter and lit it up.

She gazed at him, intrigued, and he became self-conscious.

"So," she said. "Tell me all about yourself."

He didn't want to talk about himself at all. What he wanted to do was find out all about her. Luckily, she was quite self-absorbed, and he quickly discovered could talk about herself indefinitely. But he didn't mind that at all. He liked listening to her. Her father owned a factory outside London and she seemed to come from a very comfortable and privileged background. She was very sure of herself and he imagined never had a day of self-doubt in her life. In her mid-twenties, she was at least ten years younger than him. Ann seemed drawn to him for the night and barely paid any attention to the others at the table. Even when the others all left, they remained sharing a bottle of wine. By the end of the night, he was trying to build up his confidence to see her again. He was sure she would decline, and was thrilled when she said yes.

Joe and Ann were married a year later. Their courtship had been fairly whirlwind. She was the first woman he met that he knew he wanted to spend the rest of his life with. He never really talked about his own origins or background and she was very self-consumed and more interested in herself. She had a clear vision of what she wanted in life. She wanted a successful life with a man who was steady and dedicated and admired by her set. She found that in Joe. They had their daughter Pamela first and then their son George followed quite soon after. Joe's career went from strength to strength and they lived a very affluent life in a beautiful house outside London.

To the world they had everything but Joe realised a few years into the marriage that they were very different people. Ann's life was all about the upper-middle-class social scene she came from and she expected him to be part of it and enjoy it as much as she did.

The truth was it bored him. Sometimes he couldn't understand himself, because he felt he should feel lucky to be part of this world. But he didn't feel part of it. He might have married into it and been financially successful but he knew they didn't really accept him as one of theirs. He was an outsider, and he felt like an outsider. But Ann was so attached to it that she wouldn't hear about them moving or doing anything else. And so the years went by and they grew apart. He spent more time at work and bought the penthouse in London for more convenience. So they even physically spent less time together.

But their marriage worked, he convinced himself. They were still happy with each other; they just did their own thing. That was until their daughter Pamela's engagement night when he came upon Ann in their bedroom with their old friend Timothy and realised they were having an affair. It made him realise just how far he and Ann had grown apart when he heard Ann basically describe their marriage as a marriage of convenience to Timothy. Here he was, now in his sixties, and that young footman at Cliffenden would never have believed what he had achieved if he could see him now. And yet happiness had eluded him.

He had not put in the time with his family that he should have over the decades, becoming more detached from them as time went by. His relationship with his daughter Pamela was polite but distant, and his relationship with his son George, who was somewhere in California at that moment, could be openly hostile.

He couldn't help thinking that his own happiness had been jinxed because of what he did to Cassie and Bowden back at Cliffenden. He had destroyed their happiness. Purposefully set out to stop them eloping. He had put his own ambitions and wants ahead of theirs and betrayed them in the most terrible way. He wished he could change what he had done then. He had followed the story of Cassie Fullerton over the years. She was regularly in the papers, the cousin of the Earl of Weybridge, the glamorous socialite who had committed murder and then gone on the run. She had become a figure of mystery like Lord Lucan. The facts of the murder had always been blurred and the way she had just disappeared afterwards made it all more mysterious. Many theories had been bandied about over the years – that she was living in the outback in Australia, that she was living the high life in Rio de Janeiro. That she had been smuggled out of Nazi France by her well-connected relatives and now lived in deepest darkest Africa. That she had committed suicide and thrown herself into the Seine after the murder. That she had been the lover of a Nazi officer and they had fled together to start a new life. So many theories. And then she had suddenly been discovered running a small hotel in the north-east of England in a remote and very un-exotic seaside town under an alias. All those outlandish and colourful theories had been proven to be incorrect. But the history of what had happened still remained. And only Cassie knew the truth.

CHAPTER 43

As Joe retold the story of his life he knew he wasn't being honest with Cassie. Not telling the whole truth. He stuck to the facts. He left Cliffenden to serve in the war. Assisted with the court martials in France. Returned to London and started as a clerk in a law practice and slowly worked his way up. Met Ann and had two children and lived in the country. That was the version he told her. He didn't tell her about the long lonely struggle to the top. He didn't tell her that he and Ann had little in common and their marriage was in severe difficulty. He didn't tell her his relationship with his children was strained. He most certainly didn't tell her the guilt he carried over ruining her relationship with Bowden. She remained ignorant to all these things. It was unfair of him, he knew, to demand that she trusted him now to represent her when he had betrayed her in the past so badly. But then he realised he had been dishonest all his life.

Cassie had sat intrigued, listening to him.

"Amazing. You have had a wonderful life, Joe. You should be very proud. But – you deserve it."

"I'm not sure if I do deserve it," he said. "Anyway, that's enough about me, Cassie. Let's go back to talking about your life in Paris with Wally. You were talking about your friendship with the Nazi officer Oberst Stefan Bayer –"

Suddenly he was interrupted by the front door opening and slamming. He sighed loudly – he had told Pippa not to come in that day as he felt Cassie would open up more if it was just him in the apartment.

They heard fast heavy footsteps come down the corridor and then a young man in his early twenties come bounding in. Cassie got a start. The young man was the image of Joe when he had been a footman at Cliffenden. She looked at the young man in awe. He was tall and well built, with brown hair and dark eyes – just as she remembered Joe.

"George! What are you doing here?" asked Joe, stunned to see his son there.

"Oh, hi, Dad. I didn't realise you were home so I got the doorman to let me in," said George.

"Aren't you supposed to be in Los Angeles?" asked Joe.

"Yeah, I'm finished there now. Been there, seen it, done it!" George said, flinging his bag on the floor and throwing himself in an armchair.

"You could have let us know you were coming home!" snapped Joe.

"Didn't I? It was a spur of the moment kind of thing. I'm exhausted! The flight took forever! What's there to eat?" George looked at Cassie curiously and said, "Hi there!"

"Hello," said Cassie.

"Are you Dad's new housekeeper?" asked George.

Joe went red in the face with embarrassment. For Miss Cassie to be mistaken for his housekeeper by his son! She really didn't need the humiliation.

Joe stood up, grabbed George's arm and yanked him to his feet.

"*Owww!*" yelped George.

"If you could excuse us a moment, Cassie, I just need a word with my son," said Joe, directing him out of the room.

"Lovely to see you too, Dad!" George said sarcastically as they reached the kitchen.

"Why didn't you let us know you were coming home?" demanded Joe.

"I told you – I forgot!"

"You really are too much! You swan off to California for months, hardly a postcard or a telephone call for weeks and then you just barge in unannounced!"

"I didn't realise I needed an invitation to come into my home!"

"This isn't your home, this is my work place! Your home is in Cambridge where your mother has been worried sick about you because you never bothered to let us know how you are! Does she even know you're home?"

"No! I thought I'd surprise her!"

"George! You'll give one of us a heart attack one of these days!"

"Don't be so dramatic, Dad!" said George as he opened the fridge and began to rummage through it.

"You need to get straight home and see your mother, and put her out of her worry!" insisted Joe, slamming the fridge door shut.

"Dad! I'm starving! And exhausted! I've got jet lag!"

"Pity about you! Months in the sun in California doing nothing! When I was your age –"

"I know, I know, I know! You had to walk millions of miles in the snow to get somewhere! Dad, please, will you stop? I'm not in the mood to listen to it!"

"Well, you can't stay here!"

"*What*?"

"You heard me, you can't stay here. I'm in the middle of a big case and I can't have interruptions from you. I'll call you a taxi and it will take you to the station to get a train home to your mother." Joe opened his wallet and took out some cash which he put in George's shirt pocket.

"Buying me off? No! I'm not going home just yet. I've some things to do in London first."

"Like what?"

"I'm meeting some friends tonight."

"More socialising! George! Does it ever stop?"

George's face had become angry. "You should try it sometime, Dad. You know, you might just enjoy yourself for once in your life."

"Your mother does enough socialising for the two of us."

"I will try and stay out of your way as much as possible, as you clearly don't want me here. But here I am staying!"

Joe became flustered. "Out of the question!"

"And who exactly is that woman in there?" demanded George. "If she's not the new housekeeper?"

"A client," said Joe.

"Are you sure that's all she is? Does Mum know she's staying here?"

"Of course she does! What are you implying?"

"Nothing – I'm sure!" George's voice dripped sarcasm. "Just thought you'd have had better taste, that's all! What age is she?"

"*George!*" roared Joe in anger.

There was a cough at the door and they both turned around to see Cassie standing there with the coffee pot.

"Sorry, I'm just bringing in the coffee pot – don't mind me," she said, coming in and placing the coffee pot on the island.

Joe and George looked at her in embarrassment, realising she had overheard everything.

"I'm Cassie," she said, stretching out her hand to George. "You must be Joe's son. He neglected to introduce us. I'm a client of your father's."

George looked at her hand and then shook it.

"It's quite refreshing to meet somebody who doesn't know who I am," she said. "It's clear you've been out of the country for some time, otherwise you would have seen me in the newspapers."

"Sorry?" George looked confused.

"I'm up for murder."

"Oh!" George didn't know what to say.

"So, other than your father's inhospitality, it might be another reason why you don't want to stay here, just for your own safety?"

"I don't scare easy," said George.

"Good!" She looked at Joe and said, "Then perhaps it might be nice if he did stay for a while. You haven't seen him in a long time. I certainly wouldn't mind . . . he reminds me very much of somebody I knew a very long time ago."

"That's settled then," said George happily. "Right, I'm off! I'll unpack later. I don't know what time I'll be back, so don't wait up!"

And then he bounded out of the kitchen and few seconds later they heard the front door slam.

"I can only apologise! I wasn't expecting him at all . . . if I had known . . ." said Joe as he followed her out and back into the living room.

"No need to explain, Joe. I heard everything," she said with a smile, sitting back down on the couch.

"Well, then I really do need to apologise," he said, mortified that George had accused her of being some kind of mistress, not to mention the comment he made on her appearance and age.

"Don't be silly. I found him entertaining. Do you remember what it was like to be that carefree and young?" she said, crossing her legs and looking out the windows. "I envy him."

"I'm afraid he's a little too carefree and acts too young for his age. It's time he grew up a little."

"He's the spit of you," she commented. "At that age."

"He might be physically like me, but in every other aspect he is like his mother."

Cassie studied him. "And is that a bad thing?"

She had caught him off guard.

"No – no, of course not."

"We all have family problems, Joe, nothing to be ashamed of. When you were at Cliffenden you were privy to all of ours. It's strange that it's come full circle and I'm now privy to yours."

CHAPTER 44

Joe was despairing about Cassie. No matter how he tried he could not get her to speak about the case. He had tried gentle coaxing and she refused to open up. It didn't help with George interrupting with his coming and goings. They were running out of time and he had no defence prepared for her.

She sat opposite him in the penthouse living room.

The file was open in front of him on the coffee table.

"According to the police reports you have been living in Morecambe Bay since the fifties under the alias of Sarah King?" He had already been over this ground with her with little result, but he had no choice but to keep tapping away at her story in the hope something new might emerge.

"If the police report says it, then it must be true," she said.

He hid his frustration. "The newspapers have interviewed people in Morecambe Bay and said that you lived there very quietly, kept yourself to yourself, running a small hotel."

She smiled wryly. "Well, I was a woman on the run. I would have been stupid to draw too much attention to myself, wouldn't I?"

"How did you come to be in Morecambe Bay? Why did you settle there?"

"It seemed as good a place to be as any. Besides, it was beside the sea. I've always like being beside the sea. I grew up beside the sea at Cliffenden."

"And how did you become Sarah King? How did you get that name?"

"It seemed as good a name as any," she said.

"Yes, but you didn't just pick it out of a hat, I take it? I mean, you had a national insurance number with the name Sarah King? How did you get all that?"

She sighed loudly. "It's all so long ago – does it really matter?"

Joe bit his lower lip in frustration. "Okay . . . let's talk about how you were discovered. You're living your life quietly and anonymously, running a small hotel in Morecambe Bay – how was it uncovered that you were Cassie Fullerton?"

She shook her head. "Don't play games with me, Joe. You know how I was uncovered – that part is all in the police report."

"I need you to verify it!" he snapped.

"I was sitting on reception in my small hotel, looking out at the sea, and next thing a woman was booking into the hotel and she was French! And she recognised me from Paris! After all those bloody years, she recognised me!"

Joe riffled through the papers in the file. "That would be Francine Delors?"

"Yes. She had been the young daughter of the family that lived next door to me and Wally in Paris. She and her family had been on a tour of the English coast and were stopping a night in my hotel. Just one night! And all this came out."

"It must have been a shock for you to be uncovered?"

"Well, I didn't recognise her! But she called the police and suddenly there they were asking me was I Cassandra Fullerton."

"And you didn't think to deny it?"

"No . . . what was the point? I was sick of running. You don't know what it's like to live your life on the run. Always looking over your shoulder. I genuinely believed nobody would ever be in Morecambe Bay who could ever recognise me. But then that wouldn't be the first mistake I've made in my life."

"Alright, now we are clear on the circumstance of your arrest. Now let's go back to your life in Paris in 1941."

Cassie suddenly stood up and paced over to the windows.

"What's wrong?" he asked.

"What's wrong? All this is what is wrong! Questions, questions,

questions! Will you stop asking all these questions?"

"I can't! It's my job!"

She turned around and glared at him angrily. "I never asked you to take this job! You took it on yourself!"

"But now I have it I want to do it right!"

Her eyes became angry. "You can't do it right! There's nothing to say! It's a very long time ago and what is the point of going through it all now?"

He got up and marched angrily over to her. "Because you are facing trial. The questions that I ask you here will be nothing compared to the way they will cross-examine you in the witness box."

"I don't have to take the witness box!" she spat.

"Of course you do! You've pleaded not guilty and appealed your extradition to France –"

"No! You pleaded not guilty on my behalf and appealed my extradition!"

"So what are you telling me – that you want to plead guilty?"

"No! I don't want to plead at all! Let them do what they want to me. I haven't spoken about it for decades and I'm not going to start now just because they have found me."

"Then you are looking at a substantial prison sentence!" he warned.

"You just don't get it, do you? I don't care anymore! I'm past caring. They can do what they want to me, say what they want about me. It's all the same to me!" With that she stormed off out of the room.

It was after midnight when George opened the door and walked into the penthouse. He walked down the corridor to the living room and found Cassie sitting there on her own, staring out the windows at the skyline under the night sky. The lights were dimmed in the room.

She turned around and looked at him. "Hello."

"Hi there!" he said, walking awkwardly into the room. "Has Dad gone to bed?"

"No, he's not at home."

"Where is he?"

"I don't know. He said he was going out for a walk. That was some time ago."

"I see," he said, hovering at the end of the couch. Since he had arrived back from Los Angeles he had discovered exactly who his father's houseguest was and all about her. It was all his friends kept talking about, trying to find out what he knew. True to his promise to his father, he tried to keep out of her way as much as possible.

"Please take a seat," she said, gesturing to the couch opposite her.

He paused and then sat down. "What's he doing out walking at this time of night?"

"I don't know. I think he's frustrated," she said.

He laughed. "He's always frustrated about one thing or another. Usually he doesn't go walking out at midnight though."

"How do you know? From what I can understand he spends a lot of time here in London on his own. Maybe he's out for midnight walks all the time."

"No, he's always in bed by ten, no matter where he is. He's a creature of habit, never strays away from his strict rules. Anyway – what has him frustrated tonight?"

"I have."

"Oh?"

"He's trying to defend me in a case, and I'm not cooperating with him."

"Why not?"

"As far as I'm concerned it's a fait accompli. They're going to throw the book at me, and there's no point in putting on a circus for the press on the way."

"Does that mean a long prison sentence?"

"Probably."

"Won't you mind that?"

"I've been in my own prison for a very long time . . . maybe it will be good to give that prison structure, actual prison walls."

He watched her carefully. "You've suffered a lot, haven't you?"

"The worst thing I've suffered is loneliness. But perhaps we all suffer from that to some degree. I think your father does."

"Dad! Dad doesn't suffer from loneliness! He's never happier than when he's on his own!"

"Maybe you don't know him very well."

"I'm sorry – Cassie – but I know everything there is to know about him. I've been listening to him going on all my life! You can't just waltz in here and start talking about him as if you know him. You know *nothing* about him!"

"Actually, that is where you are wrong. I do know him. Or at least I did know him. I knew him a very long time ago, long before you were born."

George's eyes widened in amazement. "From where?"

She realised she was saying too much. Joe was a very private man and he would not want her talking about his time at Cliffenden. Did his son even know he was once a footman?

"It doesn't matter. I only knew him fleetingly."

"Did you know Mum as well?"

"No."

George looked at her cautiously. "I don't know what you know about Mum and Dad's marriage, but your being here isn't helping much."

"I'm sorry – I really don't mean to cause any trouble," she said, becoming alarmed.

"I'm sure you don't mean to, but trouble is what you're causing –" He stopped as he saw she was becoming upset.

"The trial is starting tomorrow, George. I expect it will be over very quickly and your father won't have to see me again and I won't intrude in your lives anymore. I am truly sorry for the inconvenience I have caused."

She got up, holding back the tears, and went quickly to her bedroom.

"Oh shit!" said George to himself, feeling guilty at upsetting her.

Later that night George was sitting out on the balcony drinking a can of beer. Joe had still not arrived back at the penthouse. Typical

of him, George thought, leaving him alone with a psycho-
murderess. He thought he heard a noise and turned around to see
if his father had arrived home but there was nobody there. After a
while he stood up and looked over the balcony to see if there was
any sign of his father in the street below. He saw a woman crossing
the street from the apartment building and walking down the other
side of the street along the river embankment. She was carrying a
suitcase.

"Oh *shit*!"

He turned and raced out of the apartment.

He slammed the button several times to call the lift. "Come on!
Come on!"

The doors opened, he jumped in and hit the button for the
ground floor. He went racing through the foyer, past the doorman
and out into the street. He peered down the street and saw the
woman in the distance. He went running as fast as he could after
her.

"*Cassie! Cassie!*" he yelled as he drew nearer to her.

She stopped walking and turned to face him.

"Where the *fuck* do you think you're going?" he gasped as he
reached her.

"Just let me go, George – just pretend you didn't see me."

"I can't! My dad will kill me! Literally kill me!"

"He won't. It has nothing to do with you!"

"He'll know I said something! And he'll kill me! He really will –
throw me off the balcony! I didn't mean to make you feel
uncomfortable with what I said earlier."

"It's nothing to do with what you said, George. I just need to go.
I've caused enough problems for your father, I don't want to cause
any more. This is the best way. I don't want to cause any trouble
between your parents."

"You're not causing any trouble! Well, no more trouble than
there was anyway. They've been on the rocks for years!"

"I'll only bring more trouble to your father's door. He doesn't
deserve that. It's best if I just go now."

"But go where? Everyone will be looking for you!"

"I can disappear very quickly. I've years of experience of it," said Cassie.

"But what about Dad? He'll be devastated! Not to mention his reputation will be damaged because he was supposed to be minding you. Not to mention he'll lose the hundred-thousand pounds bail money, and then Mum will really kill him for being so stupid. And they'll definitely break up! You just can't do it!"

She stood there staring at him and eventually said, "Of course. I didn't think about all that . . . I'm not thinking straight."

"You don't have to think straight. That's what you have Dad for! Let him do the thinking for you, he's very good at it. If you just bloody trusted him!"

"Does he know how much you care about him?" she asked.

George sighed loudly. "Just come on back to the apartment. Please. Whatever you have to go through in the trial tomorrow, you'll get through it, with him by your side."

She nodded and to George's utter relief she began to walk back with him. He took her suitcase and walked alongside her.

CHAPTER 45

George had decided to leave his father's penthouse as the trial began. He really didn't want to add to his father's stress which seemed to be at boiling point over the Cassie Fullerton trial. Then there had been the whole episode when he had just managed to stop Cassie from doing a moonlight flit. Cassie and he had agreed not to mention it to Joe. The stress of her nearly absconding and the thought of how he might have had to explain it to his father had shattered his nerves. George realised the whole situation was too hot to handle and he had better get out of it. So he packed his bag and went home to Cambridge where his mother was only too delighted to have him and was fussing over his every move.

"You know, it's just as well you left Los Angeles when you did, George. I was reading an article the other day and you would not believe the consequences for your skin should it be exposed to too much Californian sun. Especially with your father's Irish complexion. You could have ended up being burned to a crisp!"

"There's such a thing as sun lotion," he pointed out.

"Well, I hope you used plenty of it," said Ann.

George laughed to himself. They were out in the back garden and it was a very sunny day. Ann was stretched out on a sun lounger beside the swimming pool, trying to get a tan with no sun lotion at all.

"Any word from Dad?" asked George.

"No, and there won't be until he's finished with this Cassie Fullerton trial. I can't wait until it's over and things get back to normal."

"What is normal? He'll only be on to his next case and wrapped up in that," he said.

Ann sighed. "True. I give up on him, I really do."

George studied his mother as she lay there with her large sunglasses on.

"Did you not think of going up to visit him in London?" asked George.

"Goodness me, I've too much on here, George! I can't be rushing off to London just because he can't make the time to come and see us. Besides, the crowds in London have become so bothersome. I don't like the pace of life there anymore."

"Dad does."

"Hmmm."

"I think he would have liked us to move to London."

"Ha! The chances of that have always been slim to none!"

"I don't think he likes all the county set here."

"Tough! That's not my problem. It's where I was born and bred. My golly gosh, they've all tried hard enough with him over the years!"

"I wish he didn't work so hard," said George. "He looked tired."

"Did he?"

"I wish – I wish –" George felt himself become upset and then quickly took control of himself.

Ann sat up and looked at him. "What do you wish. George?"

"I wish he could enjoy his life more."

Ann lay back down on the sun lounger. "Oh, he enjoys his life plenty, George – don't you worry about that!"

"Do you think he's lonely?"

"Lonely!" Ann started to laugh loudly. "Of course he's not lonely. He likes his own company too much, so how on earth could he be lonely? If he wanted company he could be down here and out at the tennis club, or bridge club, or a cocktail party every night, instead of being alone with his files in his penthouse!"

"But that's just it, isn't it? Maybe he feels uncomfortable at all your social dos. You can be your most lonely in a crowd."

"Have you picked up all this psycho-babble in Los Angeles, George? You'll be doing yoga next!"

"No – it was just something Cassie said."

Ann sat up abruptly and raised her sunglasses. "*Cassie?*"

"Yes, you know, Cassie Fullerton."

"I know who Cassie Fullerton is, George! What is she doing commenting on your father's life? I would have thought she had more things to worry about considering she's facing the next one hundred years in prison!"

"Well, I think they are quite close."

"What do you mean – *close*?" demanded Ann.

"Oh, I'm not suggesting anything inappropriate. But I believe they knew each other years ago. Before he married you."

"Who said?"

"She said."

"*She said?*"

"That's what I said!"

"How would your father possibly have known Cassandra Fullerton? In what guise?"

"I don't know, she didn't expand. And Dad didn't say anything," said George.

"No – he wouldn't!" She began chewing on the frame of her sunglasses. "It would all make sense though, wouldn't it? Putting up the bail money, and having her stay at the apartment."

George started laughing. "You'd better watch out, Mum! You might have competition!"

"Oh, don't be so ridiculous ! Your father wouldn't dream of . . . he wouldn't have it in him!"

George stood up. "Anyway, I'm going in. Too much sun being bad for you and everything. What are you off to tonight?"

Ann seemed lost in thought as she chewed her sunglasses.

"Mum?" he said more loudly.

"What?" she said irritably.

"What are you up to tonight?"

"Bridge."

"Who are you partnering? Timothy Mason?" he asked, giving

her a quizzical look before turning and walking indoors.

As the hearing day started, Joe felt he had never gone into court before so ill prepared or unready to put up a defence. No matter how he tried, Cassie had remained resolute in not discussing the details. Now, as they prepared to enter court, she didn't look nervous or upset. She just stood there with a slightly serene look, as if she was not involved in these proceedings she was central to. They were called and they made their way into the courtroom.

The courtroom was packed, mainly with members of the press, anxious to finally get to the bottom of the Cassie Fullerton mystery.

As the judge spoke about the proceedings, Joe glanced over at Cassie who still remained aloof. Maybe if she could look a little contrite, the judge might go easier on her, he thought, and not extradite her.

The prosecution barrister was Sidney Sanderson. Joe knew Sidney well, and also knew he was a highly experienced and astute barrister.

Sidney got up and opened the case. Then he called the first witness for the prosecution.

"My lord, I call Michelle Badut," said Sidney.

A woman in her sixties, with jet-black hair and a glamorous appearance made her way to the stand and took the oath.

"Madame Badut, could you explain your relationship with the accused?" said Sidney as he approached the stand.

Michelle's French accent was strong as she spoke but her English was excellent. "Yes, I was engaged as her maid when she lived in Paris."

"And when was that exactly?"

"I began work for her and her husband when they first came to live in Paris which was in 1939. I remained in their employment until the autumn of 1941."

"Which was a very difficult period?"

"Of course. It was the time of the invasion and the occupation by the Germans."

"How did the war affect the Stanton household?"

"Not to any hard degree, from what I could see. They didn't suffer like the rest of Paris. They were neutrals, so I think they thought they were apart from it."

"They weren't in any danger from the Nazis?"

"No! They wouldn't have stayed if they were. In fact, I would say it was the opposite."

"What do you mean?"

"If they had been French they would have been collaborators," said Michelle. "They often entertained Nazi high-ranking officers at the house, where the champagne and caviar flowed into the night."

The crowd in the public gallery began to talk loudly at the rumours finally being confirmed.

Joe rose to his feet. "Objection, my lord. I really can't see where this line of questioning is going. Ms Fullerton is not being tried as a Nazi collaborator and all these details are doing is titillating the public in order to sully my client's name and risking colouring the court's perception of my client's character with gossip that has no relevance to the case at hand."

"On the contrary, my lord," said Sidney. "My line of questioning is very relevant to the case in hand. Firstly we need to know the history of the Stanton house in the lead-up to the murder. And secondly I am establishing Ms. Fullerton's connection with one particular Nazi officer, Stefan Bayer, which as we know is very central to the case."

"I will allow the questioning to continue but, Mr. Sanders, please do not dwell on the champagne and caviar lifestyle the accused is supposed to have led in Paris at the time. There has been enough talk of that over the years in the press and there is no need to add any more details."

"Yes, my lord, thank you, my lord," said Sidney as Joe sat down again.

"Shall we continue then?" said Sidney to Michelle. "Can you tell me about the relationships that existed in the house?"

PART FIVE

France 1940s

CHAPTER 46

Michelle Badut did not like Cassandra Fullerton Stanton from the first moment she met her. And that was when she began to work for Cassie and Wally in their beautiful home. Michelle was only twenty years of age at the time. It wasn't anything that Cassie had done or said to her. In fact, she was always very pleasant and polite to her, unlike the last woman she had worked for who had bossed and ordered her about all the day. No, Cassie was at all times civil to her. But then she knew Cassie had been brought up in a household of servants and knew how to treat them properly. Not like her previous bourgeois boss. It was just Cassie herself she disliked. Here was this woman who had been handed everything in life and never had to do a day's work. She had gone from her privileged life with her aristocratic family to marrying the very successful Wally and she swanned around as if it were her birth-right. She spent her days attending fashion shows and shopping and being driven around by Pierre, their chauffeur.

She spent her nights dressed up, going to the theatre or restaurants. And then when the Nazis invaded and the occupation began, even this didn't seem to alter her lifestyle as the Stantons ingratiated themselves with the new powers that ran Paris. While the rest of Paris suffered and were being persecuted and could barely feed themselves, Cassie was watching her diet and avoiding rich food. Perhaps the main reason Michelle disliked her was because she was married to Wally. Michelle had taken an instant liking to Wally. She felt an instant attraction to him. He was

317

everything she loved in a man. Tall, commanding, handsome and rich. How could a little farm girl from the provinces not be impressed by such a man? But Michelle could tell Cassie was not impressed by her husband to the same degree she was. She could tell quite quickly that Cassie was not in love with her husband. She had obviously married him for his money and because he could provide her with what she was looking for in life. It sickened Michelle that such a woman existed. And that she had to clean up all day after the likes of her.

She didn't know why Wally had bothered to marry her at all, when it was obvious she didn't love him. It was obviously just because she was Cassie Fullerton, and she was the big catch to land.

Michelle might only be a peasant girl from the provinces, but she knew her own attractiveness. She knew how pretty and sexy she was. She had been told enough times. She could tell that Wally found her pretty and sexy. She had caught him glancing at her a few times, when he thought he was safe. Whenever she had caught him looking at her, she would smile back at him. She began to flirt in an innocent way with him at first to see if he was responsive. He was very responsive. And then she started flirting more provocatively with him. She would accidentally touch his hand when she was clearing his plate away or rub up against him if she was passing by him.

Then one day she went into his office when Cassie was out visiting friends.

"Have you finished with your tea, monsieur?" she asked.

"Yes, you can take it away," he said.

She knew the teapot was half full and only lukewarm at this stage and, as she lifted it, she let it fall on him, spilling tea all down his shirt and trousers.

"*You stupid bitch!*" he roared.

"Oh, Monsieur Stanton! I'm so sorry! How can I ever forgive myself?" she squealed.

"I'm ruined!" he shouted, standing up.

"I'm so sorry!" she said as she grabbed a napkin and began to quickly rub the tea-drenched shirt. "Are you burned?" she asked as put her hands up against the shirt on his chest.

"I'm wet through!" he said.

"But I hope it hasn't burned you!" she said and she unbuttoned his shirt and quickly felt his skin underneath. "I don't think it's too bad. The burn."

She looked up at him as her hand still rested on his skin. He stared down at her. She didn't remove her hand but continued to stare at him and then suddenly he grabbed her and pushed her on the desk, kissing her passionately.

And that was how their affair started. Conducted right under his wife's nose. He would even leave their bed during the night and come down to her room. And Michelle was quite sure that Cassie was too stupid and self-absorbed to ever even guess there was something going on.

As their affair continued, Michelle realised she was falling in love with Wally. And she began to resent Cassie all the more. Not only for being married to Wally, but not appreciating being married to Wally. Michele had an aunt who was sick and she used to go and stay with her once a week. She took to saying she needed to stay with her twice a week sometimes. On the second night, Wally and she would book into a hotel.

They would sit having dinner in the lavish hotel room and she soon realised that this was the life she had been born to have.

"She doesn't deserve you," she said as he filled her champagne glass.

"Probably not," agreed Wally.

"You give her everything, and she's still not happy!" cried Michelle.

"Cassie has been used to everything all her life, you must remember."

"If I was married to a man like you, I'd know how to appreciate you."

Michelle used to listen in to their arguments at the doors all the time. And then she heard a magical row between them one night when Cassie was begging him for a divorce. She told him they weren't happy and they should just part.

But he got very angry and told her he would never let her go.

Wally and Cassie often entertained the Nazi elite in the city. There was one particular commander who was very senior called Stefan Bayer. He was doing a lot of banking through Wally's bank. But Michelle had spotted that Stefan was very taken with Cassie.

Soon Stefan started paying Cassie visits when Wally was away on business and showering her with gifts. And the two would head out together on their own for nights out. Michelle was disgusted. If a Frenchwoman was doing the same she would be labelled a whore and a collaborator. But Wally didn't seem to notice or even care.

Then one evening Michelle walked into the drawing room in the house and found Stefan with his arms around Cassie and they were kissing. Cassie was startled at Michelle's interruption and they jumped apart from each other and pretended to act normally. Michelle knew she now had the ammunition to break Wally and Cassie up for good.

Michelle waited for her moment when Wally was in the house on his own and Cassie was out. He was working in his office when she came in.

"Hello there," he said, getting up and putting his hands around her and drawing her close.

"I've something to tell you," she said.

"Huh?"

"It's about your wife."

"Go on?" he said curiously.

"She's having an affair . . . with Stefan Bayer."

He stared at her in disbelief and then he started laughing loudly, released her from his grip, and went back to sit at his desk where he continued his work.

She moved quickly towards him. "Did you not hear me? She's screwing Bayer – right under your nose!"

"Don't be so stupid, Michelle, and go and get me a coffee."

She felt enraged at his reaction and grabbed the papers he was working on and screwed them up. "Are you so blind?" she demanded. "She's cheating on you behind your back. She doesn't love you. She never has. Get it into your thick head that she is having an affair. You need to throw her out! Your marriage is a sham!"

A dark look came over his eyes as he stared at her in silent fury. She became frightened as he stood up and glared at her.

"What do you know about anything?" he said menacingly and she began to back away from him. "What do you know about my wife? Or my marriage?"

"I'm telling you for your own good!" she defended herself as she continued to back away from him.

He grabbed her by the hair and pulled her head back. "Coming to me with these lies! I know my wife, and she is many things, but she is not an adulteress!"

"She is! I saw her with my own eyes!"

He had backed her up against the wall and suddenly he put his hand around her neck.

"Wally! You're hurting me!"

"I am not Wally to you! I'm Monsieur Stanton – do you understand me? If you go around spreading lies about my wife again, I will tell Stefan Bayer what you are accusing him of. Do you know what the Gestapo do with people who cross them? Do you know what he would do with you if I told him what you said?"

"Please – no – "

"Did you expect me to leave her for you? That I would leave Cassandra for the likes of you? Now you get this into *your* thick head. You were nothing more to me than a plaything. A hobby, and one that has become quite boring recently. You're not the first plaything I've had, and you won't be the last. And if you thought for a moment that I would leave Cassie Fullerton, who it took me years to convince to marry me, for the likes of you, a peasant girl, then you are sadly and madly deluded – *do you understand me?*"

"Y-y-yes!"

He released her and she grabbed her neck.

He went and sat back behind his desk and said, "Now, get me that coffee."

Michelle was bitter after her confrontation with Wally. Bitter and frightened. She had been used by him. She'd thought she'd meant something to him, but he had made it clear she had not meant a thing. Her resentment of Cassie grew even more. What had she got that she hadn't?

One day Michelle went to enter Cassie's room to enquire whether she would be going out or would require lunch. At that moment Cassie was inside the door and was about to lock it. Cassie looked flustered and quickly got rid of her. As Michelle heard Cassie lock the bedroom door, curiosity got the better of her and she peeped through the keyhole.

She saw Cassie walk into her dressing room and emerge with one of the many bags she kept there. As Michelle looked on she saw Cassie open the bag, take out a large amount of money and count it on the bed.

Later, when Cassie was out, Michelle took the opportunity to go into her room. She went into the dressing room and searched through the many bags Cassie kept there until she found the one containing the money.

As she counted through it she realised there were tens of thousands of francs there.

Her mind raced as to why the money was there. The Stantons kept very little money in the house and any money they did have there Wally kept in a safe in his office. Why was this money being kept in one of Cassie's bags? And also she knew Wally was far too careful to keep that much money lying around. This money was being hidden from Wally, she knew.

She put the money back and thought about what she should do.

A couple of days later Wally was in his office when she brought in the coffee and left it on the table. Cassie was safely out of the house again.

"Pack a bag for me, Michelle. I'll be away on business for the next couple of nights."

"Certainly, Monsieur. Pardon, Monsieur Stanton, but I just want to ask what you want me to do with the money? Is it for your business trip and will I pack it for you? Shouldn't you put it in your briefcase?"

"What money?"

"The money in your wife's dressing room."

"What money are you talking about?" he asked impatiently.

"The tens of thousands of francs in the wardrobe, Monsieur."

Wally nearly dropped his cup as he looked at her. "What the fuck are you talking about?"

"The money, Monsieur – it's in Madame's bag in her wardrobe."

"If you are bullshitting me again!" he threatened.

"I'm not, Monsieur! I promise!"

He stood up abruptly and pointed to the door. "Show me!"

She walked out and up the stairs, down to their bedroom and into Cassie's dressing room.

"Well?" he demanded.

She reached into the wardrobe and started rummaging through the bags there till she found the right one. She took it and handed it to him.

He opened the bag and looked in. There was nothing inside but old magazines.

He threw the bag at her in disgust. "This has to stop!" he shouted.

She panicked as she looked through the bag. "Monsieur! I swear this bag was stacked full of money! I swear to you!"

"You're lying! Cassie wouldn't have that kind of money. Our money is all in our bank accounts."

"I swear to you, it was here! I don't know what she's done with it!"

He grabbed her and shook her. "I've a good mind to hand you over to the Gestapo! You're just a nasty little bitch!"

Michelle started crying. "I swear, Wally, I swear it was there! I'm telling you the truth. I thought it might have something to do with you! But obviously not! She's planning on something, I'm warning you!"

He flung her down on the bed. He watched her crying for a few moments, then turned and walked away.

For the rest of the afternoon, Wally was in his office. Michelle listened at the door and she could hear him ringing around his banks, checking his accounts. He suddenly emerged out of the office and went tearing back up to their bedroom and she could hear much noise from there.

At that moment Cassie came in through the front door. Michelle realised there was going to be war between them and decided it might be safer if she was out of the house.

"Did Monsieur Stanton leave for Cherbourg on time?" Cassie asked Michelle, handing Michelle her coat.

"No, he's upstairs . . . Monsieur Stanton is in a very bad mood, Madame."

"Is he?" Cassie frowned.

"Madame, my aunt is not very well this evening . . . will you be needing me for the rest of the evening?"

Cassie looked at her witheringly. "No. You can go to her."

Michelle watched as she went upstairs to the bedroom, then hurried to hang up Cassie's coat. A few moments later she heard Cassie and Wally embroiled in a screaming match.

She prepared to leave the house and, before she left, she went and listened at the bottom of the stairs.

"You're leaving me and you've stolen my money to get away and set up a new life for yourself!" Wally was shouting at her. *"You're leaving me, aren't you?"*

Michelle smiled to herself and left the house for the night.

Early the next morning Michelle arrived at the house and passed Pierre who was washing the car in the driveway.

"Bonjour, Pierre!" she said happily.

"Bonjour, Michelle."

She let herself into the house. She wondered if Wally had left for his business trip the evening before or cancelled it due to the break-up of his marriage.

She went down to the kitchens where the cook was preparing for the day.

"Has Madame had her breakfast yet?" asked Michelle.

"No, she hasn't come down yet or rung for me," said the cook.

She's gone, thought Michelle in delight. She wondered what happened in the end. Did Cassie walk out or did Wally eventually kick her out?

"Has Monsieur Stanton left?" she asked

"I've haven't seen him all morning, so he must be gone since last night on his business trip."

Michelle smiled to herself and said, "I'll go and see."

As she walked up the stairs she was mapping her future in her head. Poor Wally had been deserted by his philandering wife. He would need her now to help him through all this. She was sure he didn't go away on his trip after breaking up with Cassie and was probably in bed feeling sorry for himself.

She knocked on the door. There was no answer.

She knocked again.

Silence.

She cautiously opened the door a crack.

"Hello?" she called.

No answer.

She stepped into the room. The bed was empty – not only that but it looked as if it hadn't been slept in.

She walked across the room and suddenly saw what looked like blood on the thick cream carpet. There was a trail of blood leading to the bathroom.

She walked over to the bathroom and knocked on the door.

"Madame, are you in there?" she asked. "Monsieur?"

She tried to open the door but found it locked and the key missing.

She went downstairs and back to the kitchen where she found Pierre having coffee with the cook.

"Something has happened upstairs. There's blood on the carpet and the door to the bathroom is locked – no key."

Pierre shrugged. He went and got some tools and followed her upstairs to the bedroom. He began to work on the bathroom lock until he had unpicked it.

He and Michelle stepped into the room.

Wally's body was lying on the floor in a pool of blood.

Michelle's scream echoed through the house.

PART SIX

England 1988

CHAPTER 47

Joe listened intently to Michelle Badut giving her evidence to the prosecution. He realised she made a valid and good witness, with a very practised delivery. She also looked very well and affluent, he had to admit. As Sidney Sanderson sat down after interviewing her, Joe stood up to cross-examine her.

"Madame Badut, it must have been very hard for you when your relationship with Wally Stanton ended and you remained working for him and his wife," said Joe.

"It wasn't easy, but I got on with it," said Michelle.

"But you must have been very bitter – to realise that you had effectively been used by Wally Stanton and he had no intention of ever leaving his wife for you."

"That was his decision, a decision that ultimately cost him his life."

"That is your assertion, Madame Badut, and it is up to the court to decide, not you," Joe said and he began to pace up and down in front of her. "Your evidence has always been central to this case. There were three people in the house the night that Wally Stanton was killed. Wally is obviously dead and so cannot tell us what happened. But you have said and have given us a clear delivery of what happened in the house that night. But, Madame Badut, your evidence is really only circumstantial, is it not? I mean you didn't see Cassie Fullerton kill her husband. According to you, you left the house when they were still arguing. Who knows what happened after that?"

"I think the fact she fled says it all. Why not stay and defend herself?" said Michelle.

"Maybe for a variety of reasons we can never understand. But, since you were in the house that night Wally was killed, and you had been his spurned lover, who is to say that you didn't murder Wally Stanton yourself?"

"Objection, my lord!" shouted Sidney, jumping to his feet.

"Mr. Grady, may I remind you that the witness is not on trial here, nor has there been any accusation against her. You really should know better!" warned the judge.

"Of course, my lord. I'm just trying to point out how dangerous circumstantial evidence can be," said Joe.

"Well, if you could just stick to the facts as known!" cautioned the judge.

"Of course, my lord."

Michelle glared angrily at Joe. "Her fingerprints were all over the murder weapon – that's enough evidence for you!" she snapped.

"The murder weapon was an everyday household item – her fingerprints would have been all over it anyway. I daresay as the maid your own fingerprints were all over the murder weapon as well!"

"Mr. Grady!" warned the judge harshly.

"I'm sorry, my lord, but I'm just trying to point out that for Ms Fullerton to be convicted of murder, then it has to be proven beyond reasonable doubt."

"And what about the hundred thousand francs?" said Michelle.

"I will ask the questions, Madame Badut, not you," said Joe, realising this witness did not understand or was ignoring court proceedings.

Michelle continued with a rant. "She had taken out one hundred thousand francs from their account without telling him, as she planned to leave him and divorce him. And when he didn't allow her to do that – she killed him!"

"Madame Badut!" interjected the judge strongly. "It is not your place to give your opinion in my court but to simply answer the questions put to you! Refrain! I am not interested in your conjecture. Please stick to the facts."

Michelle sat back sulking as Joe continued.

"Yes, we've heard your evidence already, Madame Badut – your very precise and detailed evidence."

"My memory is perfect," said Michelle.

"Indeed – and why wouldn't it be? You have recounted the story many, many times over the years, haven't you? In fact your involvement in the Stanton murder has provided you with a very good income over the years, hasn't it? Three bestselling books about the matter to date, as well as many interviews to the press."

"People wanted to know what happened – I was providing a service," said Michelle.

"A very good service. And now with Cassie Fullerton's arrest and the trial, there is massive new interest in the case, is there not? Plenty of new lucrative book deals ahead?"

Aware Joe was trying to discredit Michelle, Sidney rose to his feet. "My Lord, I can't quite fathom what any of this has to do with the case."

"I'm just saying that Madame Badut has a vested interest in the case – she is not an impartial bystander."

"Continue," said the judge.

Joe tried his best to discredit Michelle Badut for the rest of her cross-examination. But he wasn't sure really what impact it would have. The fact of the matter was that most things Michelle was saying were backed up by evidence presented to the court. The police investigation did find Cassie's fingerprints on the murder weapon. The bank official at the time did confirm that Cassie had taken out one hundred thousand francs from their bank account without Wally's consent in the week before his murder. And there were statements from the Stantons' other staff, the cook and the chauffeur Pierre, now long dead, that the two did have a volatile and hostile marriage. Also several socialites in Paris, after the war, had confirmed that Cassie was often seen in the company of the Nazi Stefan Bayer and there was even photographic evidence of them together, showing them looking like lovers. Bayer had been sent to the Russian front in the closing years of the war where he had been killed.

The rest of the day in court was taken up with presenting this evidence: statements taken at the time, a bank employee from the bank confirming the hundred thousand francs taken out by Cassie, and representatives from the Paris police force confirming all the evidence and details taken at the time. Throughout it all, Cassie remained impassive with no flicker of emotion. Not even when she saw her former servant and husband's lover, Michelle, bray for her blood.

As they were driven back to the penthouse after the day's events, Cassie and Joe sat in silence.

CHAPTER 48

That evening after eating, Cassie stood at the windows looking out at the city. It was raining hard and water was lashing against the panes.

Joe was sitting on the couch, looking at her.

"It must be very strange seeing your maid again after all these years?" he said.

"No more strange than it is seeing you again. It's funny, isn't it – one of my old servants trying to save me and the other trying to hang me."

"She's obviously very jealous of you, which is what I was trying to show in court."

Cassie laughed harshly. "What on earth is there to be jealous of?"

"At the time she obviously was – a lot of people were jealous of you back then."

"Well, I'm sure they would all be very pleased to see me now in that case."

"I'm going to try and bargain with the prosecution so they don't call you as a witness," he said.

"Let them call me – I just won't say anything. The same as I will do if *you* try to call me as a witness."

His frustration brimmed over. "Cassie! Do you not realise the seriousness of the situation you are in? It looks like a straight case of premeditated murder! It looks like you planned the whole bloody thing! You hated your husband, you were having an affair with a Nazi. You took out a huge amount of money unbeknownst to him the week before, and had your escape route already planned. How else did you get out of Paris and even France during the Nazi occupation when everyone was looking for you?"

Suddenly the front door was heard opening and closing.

Joe swung around to see Ann walking in.

"Ann!"

"Hello, Joe."

Joe got to his feet, very thrown by her unexpected appearance.

"Aren't you going to introduce me to your guest?" said Ann.

Cassie had turned and was staring at Ann.

"Cassie, this is my wife Ann," said Joe.

Ann walked over to Cassie, smiling. "I'm so pleased to meet you! I've heard so much about you."

Cassie took her hand and shook it. "I'm very pleased to meet you, as well. You're a very lucky woman."

Ann laughed lightly. "I always get nervous when another woman tells me I'm lucky. I always worry she might try to grab something I have!"

Cassie smiled and just nodded. "I'm going to leave the two of you to talk. I'm very tired so I'm going to go for a lie-down."

Ann watched as Cassie left the room.

"Well, I can't see what all the fuss is about myself," said Ann, taking off her coat and throwing it over a chair.

Joe took his seat on the couch again and Ann sat beside him.

"Ann – what are you doing here?"

"I thought I'd better pay you a visit and find out exactly what is going on."

"Ann, I'm in the middle of a murder case! I can't have you here right now."

"Well, I know you find me a distraction when you're working and, since you're always working, that's all the time. But I thought I'd better check on you . . . George said you were looking tired . . . and you are, very tired!"

"I'm absolutely fine."

"Well, you don't look it. I think this whole Cassie Fullerton case is a bridge too far for you, Joe. You haven't been able to separate yourself from the case – clearly since she's living in your home! You need to keep yourself emotionally detached from the cases you work on, and you've crossed the line with her!"

"I have kept myself emotionally detached – you're being stupid."

"Really? Really? George tells me that you seemingly knew Cassie Fullerton before you were married to me."

Joe looked stunned. "How did he know that?"

"George got it out of her. Don't look so amazed, Joe. George is like me – cleverer than he looks!"

Joe looked away from her.

"So – so – how did you know her? Is she an ex-girlfriend? Were you in a relationship? Is that what all this is about?"

"Don't be so ridiculous, Ann! Of course not!"

"Well, I'd like to know exactly what the nature of your relationship was, considering she is now living under your roof."

"Nothing – nothing at all – I worked for her, that's all."

"Worked for her – that's all? In what guise?"

"At her family's stately home, Cliffenden. I was the footman there, before the war."

"I see!" Ann raised both eyebrows.

"Oh, come on, Ann, don't look so surprised. You knew I worked in service before the war," he said, annoyed. "Regardless of how much we have tried to hide it from our friends and contemporaries."

"Indeed, though I was never quite sure how well we actually did hide it, if I'm honest. People can smell these things a mile off."

"Well, it didn't stop you from marrying me, did it?"

She sighed. "Of course it didn't, why would it?"

They sat in silence for a while.

"Even if you did work for her family – so what? Why are you going so out of your way to defend and protect her now?"

"I feel I owe her."

"You owe her nothing!"

"That's what she said."

"Well, then!"

"I can't explain it. If you had known Cassie back then . . . She used to just walk into a room and light it up. I can't bear to think of what she has become, how she has ended up."

There was another silence.

"Strange, isn't it?" she said eventually.

"What is?"

"That you introduced her to me, and not the other way round."

"What are you talking about?"

"When I came in, you said – 'Cassie, this is my wife Ann,' instead of saying it the other way round – you should have said 'Ann, this is my friend/client, whatever she is, Cassie'."

"What does it matter?"

"Oh, it matters a lot, Joe. It's who you attach the most importance to that you address first."

"You are being utterly ridiculous."

"I'm not, Joe . . . you attached more importance to her than you did to me."

"Nonsense!"

"Oh, I'm right, I know. The way you described her – how she was when she was young – you had a look in your eyes. I've certainly never seen that look in your eyes when you talk about me, or to me."

"Cassie is now just a client to me – the esteem I held her in years ago is gone."

"I don't believe you. Why else have we not seen sight of you at home since she has come to stay here?"

"Because I can't leave her during the case!"

"A poor defence, Joe, for such an experienced barrister. I think I was right."

"What do you mean?"

"Well, I might have been wrong that she was an ex-girlfriend, but you don't have to be in a relationship to be in love with someone . . . you were obviously in love with this Cassie Fullerton, and perhaps you still are?"

"I never heard of such a silly thing! She and I were in two

different worlds! I was just the footman, and she was –"

"And she was Cassie Fullerton. Why would you not be in love with her? Sounds like everyone else was. I wonder will we survive this, Joe?"

"Survive what?"

"Survive her arrival into our lives? Let's face it, we've been tugging in different directions for long enough. Maybe we just need a little catalyst like her to bring us finality."

"Finality? You mean our marriage?" he said, looking at her incredulously.

"No, I mean the price of butter, you twit!" she snapped.

He looked down at the ground.

Her face softened as she reached out and took his hand. "I don't mean her, not really. I mean *you* . . . you've just always put everything else before me and the children. And she's just the latest thing."

He was still staring at the ground. "I always put you first. Everything I do is for you and the children, has always been for you."

"There's no point in that, if you're not there to share it with us, Joe," she said softly.

"I just come from such a different place than you do. I felt if I didn't keep running to the top . . ."

"Oh, Joe, I know you so well, but maybe you don't know me at all? I guess I'm not as easy to read as one of those files that arrive on your desk."

"You probably would have been better off with somebody else – somebody like Timothy Mason," he said, looking into her eyes.

Her face went red and she quickly looked away as she dropped his hand.

She stood up abruptly. "Anyway, I'll be off."

"Off where?" he asked, surprised.

"Oh, I've booked into Claridges for the night."

"You're not staying here?" He was amazed.

"No, I never planned to. I was just dropping in to see if you were alright. I knew I couldn't stay here with you, not the night before

337

you're due on a big trial. You'd get no sleep and no rest with me twittering on." She quickly put on her coat and buttoned it up. "I'm of course not putting all the blame on you for – for how we are. I know my faults too, don't know how you've put up with me even. It's as I said – we've just been tugging in different directions for an awfully long time." She looked out at the rain splashing against the windows and said, "The weather's changed, hasn't it? And it was such a lovely summer."

She bent down and kissed his cheek.

"I'll talk to you later. Good luck with the case tomorrow."

She smiled kindly at him and walked out.

CHAPTER 49

The next morning Joe stood in a corridor in the courts talking to Sidney Sanders.

"There is absolutely no point in calling Cassie as a witness, as she will just refuse to speak," Joe said.

"Is she adamant on that?"

"Quite adamant."

"So she's not going to defend herself at all?"

"No."

"Is she changing her plea to guilty then?"

"No, she's not."

"I've never heard anything more frustrating. A defendant not prepared to defend herself!"

"Well, that is what we have here," confirmed Joe.

"And you're not going to call her?"

"No."

"You'd better not be bullshitting me, Joe. This better not be one of your tricks."

"It's not!"

"If you pull one of your rabbit-out-of-the-hat jobs on me, I will cross-examine her and tear her to pieces!"

"You already have, Sidney. The French maid did that for you. She's writing her next sequel as we speak, I have no doubt. How she put Cassie Fullerton behind bars, a sure bestseller."

"Alright . . . alright. If that's the deal, then that's the deal." Sidney gave him a warning look and took off, his barrister's gown flying behind him.

Sighing to himself, Joe headed back to the room Cassie was in.

A court clerk came up to him.

"Sorry, Mr. Grady, but there's a woman who wants to speak to you," said the clerk.

"I really don't have time." Joe went to walk on.

"She says it's in connection with the case. She says it's urgent," pursued the clerk.

"Where is she?" he asked.

"If you follow me," said the clerk.

"Let's make it quick," said Joe.

They hurried down the sweeping stairs to the lobby below where an elegant brunette in her forties was waiting for him.

He viewed her carefully.

"Mr. Grady, thank you for meeting me," she said.

He shook her hand cautiously. She looked like a journalist. He hated journalists. What's more, she was French. A French journalist trying to get some details on the case, he imagined.

Joe stood in court and looked at the packed courtroom. He looked at Cassie who was sitting in her normal position, immune to the procedures around her.

"I call to the stand Cassie Fullerton Stanton," he said loudly and clearly.

The public gallery erupted in noise.

"Silence!" ordered the judge, bringing hush to the proceedings.

Cassie stared at him in shock.

"If you could take the stand, please," he said to her.

She sat stock still, staring at him. He was ignoring what she had ordered, what they had agreed.

"Mrs. Stanton, please take the stand," said the judge.

Cassie slowly stood up, walked across the courtroom and took the stand.

"Please take the oath," said Joe, hardly able to look at her. He had betrayed her.

Not for the first time, he thought, as he remembered Bowden

Grey's letter.

As Cassie was sworn in he looked at Sidney Sanders who was glaring furiously at him. Joe realised this had better not backfire, or Sidney would tear her apart when cross-examining her.

Cassie sat composed in the stand as Joe approached her.

"Are you alright?" he asked.

"As alright as I could be, under these circumstances," said Cassie.

"This has been a very difficult few days for you, I'm sure, listening to what everyone has said about you in court."

"It's their choice to say what they said."

"I wonder, Cassie, if you recognise anybody in the court?"

"What do you mean?"

"Other than me, and the other lawyers, and your former maid who testified against you. Could you cast your eyes around the court and see if you recognise anybody?"

Cassie took her time looking around the court and then said, "No."

"Sure?"

"Quite sure."

"It has been a long time since you've seen her, but do you recognise this woman?" Joe walked over to the French brunette he had met earlier and pointed her out.

Cassie stared at the woman and then shrugged. "No, I don't recognise her at all."

Joe nodded and then slowly walked towards Cassie.

"Perhaps this might help your memory," he said and he produced a photograph and handed it to her.

Cassie stared at the photo in silence.

"Does this photo remind you of anybody?" asked Joe.

Cassie looked up at him but remained silent.

"Now, in your own time," said Joe, "I want to hear what your life was like back in Paris, when you were married to Wally Stanton."

PART SEVEN

France 1940s

CHAPTER 50

Cassie didn't know why she was so despondent after she discovered that Wally was conducting an affair with their maid Michelle under their roof. She had always been fully aware of the mechanics of her marriage to Wally. It had never been based on love. Perhaps it was just that the affair so bluntly advertised to her that he had so little respect for her. But she had always known that Wally had very little regard for her. She was just somebody he wanted to own. And he would never consent to a divorce. And even if she did leave him where would she go? Back to Cliffenden? To her parents who would be utterly horrified and disgraced that she had walked out on her marriage? How would she even get to Cliffenden? Travel across the English Channel was non-existent because of the war. Perhaps that was one of the reasons Wally had insisted they stay in Paris. It left her more isolated, more under his control. When she thought of the war and the suffering of millions across the continent she felt guilty. Were her concerns for her happiness minor compared to their suffering? She realised they were. She was safe and, as Wally said, living a comfortable life. Was that the best one could hope for in these dreadful times?

Wally walked into their bedroom after arriving back from work, looking at his watch.

"Oh, is that the time? We had better hurry or we'll be late," he said.

"Late for what?"

"We're going to a club with Stefan Bayer," he said.

"You never said."

"Did I not? Do change into something quickly, Cassie. We don't want to be late for Stefan."

"Wally, I really do not want to spend the evening with that man."

"Well, that's too bad, because that is what we are doing."

"Have you thought how this will make us look? Cavorting with the Nazis?"

"Everyone's doing it."

"How it will look to our friends in London when it gets out?"

"Cassie, our friends in London will all be tripping over each other to cavort with the Nazis is a few months' time when the war is over and the Germans have won. I'm just getting in ahead of the pack, as I always do," said Wally as he quickly changed into his tuxedo.

Pierre dropped them outside the club and Wally and Cassie walked inside. There was a woman singing on the stage with the most striking voice Cassie had ever heard. Cassie was mesmerised by her as they were shown to a table where Stefan was waiting for them.

"Wally, so good to see you again," said Stefan, shaking his hand.

"And you – you are so good to invite us," said Wally, sitting down.

"The least I could do after your hospitality last week," said Stefan before turning his attention to Cassie. "And Cassie, so good to see you again."

He kissed both her cheeks.

She just smiled at him and sat down.

"What an extraordinary singer," said Cassie, looking at the stage.

"Yes, her name is Edith Piaf. I think she's going to be a big star," said Stefan.

"I'm sure she is," said Cassie looking at the clientele who were mostly German soldiers. Perhaps Wally was right, she thought, maybe this was the future.

"I took the liberty of ordering the wine," said Stefan, reaching for the bottle on the table and filling both their glasses. "To your good health," he toasted.

"And yours!" said Wally.

The evening progressed with Wally and Stefan discussing work. As Cassie remained transfixed by Edith Piaf's singing, she became aware that Stefan seemed to be observing her a lot of the time. She felt very uncomfortable in his company.

A couple of hours later the manager came to Wally and began to whisper in his ear. Wally seemed to become agitated as he conversed.

"Is there a problem?" asked Stefan.

"I'm afraid there is. An urgent message for me from my bank. There's been a break-in. I have to go there at once."

"How dreadful!" said Stefan.

"Yes, I'd better go – the police are already there."

Stefan clicked his fingers and one of his officers came straight over.

"Give Mr. Stanton's car an escort to his work place. There has been a break-in – assist him in any way you can."

"Thank you, Stefan," said Wally.

Cassie stood up and picked up her bag.

"Where are you going?" asked Wally.

"Home," answered Cassie.

"Cassie, Pierre is taking me to the bank – he won't be able to take you home."

"Well, I'll go to the bank with you," said Cassie.

"I can't have you there in the middle of a crisis," said Wally irritably.

"Please!" said Stefan, standing up. "I will take Cassie home."

"Excellent, thank you, Stefan," said Wally.

"No!" said Cassie, alarmed.

"Stefan, thank you so much for the offer," said Wally, ignoring her. "We really appreciate it. In fact, why don't you two stay a while longer? Your evening shouldn't be ruined just because I've been called away."

"Absolutely. Cassie is in very safe hands with me," said Stefan, leaning over and filling her glass with wine.

As Wally rushed off, Cassie reluctantly sat down again.

"Now – where were we?" said Stefan, leaning across the table to her.

Two hours had gone by, and Cassie wondered if Stefan would ever suggest they go home. She had heard every story from his past and all the time he was gazing at her in a fashion that made her very uncomfortable. He was flirting outrageously with her, and she was trying to ignore it.

"Have you been to Biarritz?" asked Stefan.

"No."

"Oh, it's the most beautiful place. I was there last weekend. I flew down. It's a good resort for the soldiers to relax in," said Stefan.

"I'm sure," said Cassie.

"One day I'll take you to Biarritz," promised Stefan.

She looked at him coolly. "Wouldn't that be lovely?"

He smiled at her, reached forward and put his hand on hers. "I can't think of anybody nicer to take there. Shall we go?"

He sat smiling at her as she viewed his hand resting on hers.

She smiled at him and leaned forward. "Stefan?"

"Yes."

"I know since the Germans have arrived in Paris they have taken everything they desire as their right. The spoils of war. But may I just tell you, in no uncertain terms, that I am not included in that – booty!" Cassie pulled back her hand abruptly.

The smile fell off Stefan's face.

"Do you know how many women would be only too delighted to be here with me tonight?" he said.

"Good – go find them, wine and dine them and whisk them off to Biarritz!"

"I will not be dismissed like this. You are insulting me."

"No, you are insulting me!" she said.

"I don't think you realise how important I am. I have power over your lives in Paris."

"We are neutral. Your power does not stretch over us," said Cassie.

"That's what you think! I could have you thrown out of France like that!" He clicked his fingers. "I can cancel your residency permits and you would have to leave France straight away."

"Oh, Stefan, please do! I've been trying to get Wally to leave since you invaded! If you could cancel our permits then he'd have no choice but to leave!" She sat back, smiling smugly at him.

"Don't think you're so clever, Cassie Fullerton. Don't ever underestimate me. You don't know what I'm capable of."

"Are you threatening me?"

"I'm just pointing out the facts to you."

She stood up abruptly.

"I'm going home," she said.

He stood up. "I'll have the car brought to the front."

"No! I'm not going with you, thank you all the same. I'll find my own transport," she said and walked quickly away.

The next day Cassie thought about the audacity of Stefan Bayer. That he would assume that a married woman, albeit an unhappily married woman, would consider him in that way. His threats to have her and Wally deported did not frighten her. In fact she really did wish that their permits in France were cancelled and she and Wally would have no choice then but to leave. She imagined Wally would be furious if such a thing occurred, but she would be delighted.

She didn't even think of telling Wally that Stefan had propositioned her. She wouldn't put him in the position of risking his contracts with the Nazis with the need to defend his wife's honour. Besides, she really didn't want to know for sure whether Wally would put his business dealings with the Nazis ahead of his wife's honour. In fact, if she told Wally what had happened, she imagined he would blame her or accuse her of trying to jeopardise their future in Paris by exaggerating what had happened or making it up. She knew where she stood in their marriage, and didn't need further proof. His affair with their maid gave her all the evidence she needed. She thought of Simone Labelle and how she too had witnessed Wally's interaction with Michelle. Cassie realised she had been very rude and dismissive of Simone that night at the party in the house. It wasn't Simone's fault that they had witnessed Wally and Michelle together. Cassie had just felt defensive and humiliated that Simone had witnessed what a sham her marriage was. But it wasn't her fault, and Cassie felt she had to make amends to her.

Cassie knocked on the apartment door of the Labelles. There was no answer. She knocked again. A woman came out of the neighbouring apartment.

"*Bonjour*," said Cassie. "I think I've missed Madame Labelle."

"No," shrugged the neighbour. "I saw her earlier – she's in there, I believe."

The neighbour continued to the lift and went downstairs.

Cassie tried once more. She knocked loudly and called, "Simone! It's Cassie! Are you home?"

A minute later Cassie heard the bolt unlock and Simone was standing there.

"I'm sorry, I was having a nap, Cassie. I didn't hear you. Please come in."

"You must be a deep sleeper!" smiled Cassie, walking into the hallway.

Simone closed the front door and led Cassie into the sitting room.

"Hello there!" smiled Cassie as she saw the two Labelle children, Daphne and Jean, playing there.

"Hello, Cassie!" they said and came running to her to give her a hug.

"I've kept them out of school. They're not feeling too well," said Simone.

"Oh, I'm sorry to hear that," said Cassie as she stroked the girl's hair. She had to admit the children didn't look unwell. As much as she liked Simone, she did wonder if she was a bit neurotic.

"Cassie, can we have our photo taken with you?" asked Jean.

Simone smiled. "Luc got a new camera and Jean is obsessed with it. He wants to take photos of everything."

"Of course. I'd be honoured to have my photo taken with such a handsome boy," said Cassie.

Simone smiled as she went to fetch the camera.

The two children sat either side of Cassie and they all smiled while Simone took their photo.

"Now, go down to your rooms to play," said Simone to the children.

"I'll see you a little later," said Cassie and they skipped away.

Cassie went and sat on the sofa.

"How are you?" asked Simone, sitting beside her.

"Oh, fine," said Cassie and then her face went serious. "I really just wanted to apologise for my behaviour last Saturday. I was very rude to you."

Simone waved a dismissive hand in the air. "Nothing to apologise for, Cassie. I didn't even notice you being rude."

"Liar!" Cassie smiled at her softly.

"Well, you were under a lot of pressure hosting the party. I understood how much pressure you were under."

"I think we both know that's not the reason I flew off the handle."

Simone smiled sympathetically at her. "I'm trying to be diplomatic."

"And I appreciate that. But there's no reason for you to pretend that you didn't see what we both saw."

"I haven't told a soul!" Simone suddenly blurted out. "Not a soul! Not even Luc. It's none of my business and I'm not one to gossip."

"Thank you, Simone. I do appreciate that. My pride is wounded enough."

Simone paused and then ventured, "Did you know?"

"That he was screwing Michelle? No. And I think I would have been better off not finding out."

"Did you confront him?"

Cassie sighed and sat back into the sofa. "No . . . I didn't see what the point of doing so would be. Wally and I are not like you and Luc. Our marriage is . . ." Cassie paused while she thought of the right words. "Our marriage is what it is."

Simone nodded. "I can't imagine he's the easiest man to live with."

"I'm used to his ways at this stage. At least that's what I tell myself."

"And what of the maid? Are you going to get rid of her?"

"He wouldn't allow me to if I tried. I did suggest it – casually – saying she was incompetent. But he was having none of it and told me so in no uncertain terms. To be honest, the maid isn't the real problem. I can assure you she means nothing to him. He will tire of her very quickly, if he hasn't already done so, and get rid of her in a moment, saving me the bother of doing so."

"I used to be very envious of you," said Simone.

"I warned you not to be," said Cassie. "But don't feel sorry for me either. I have the life I chose for myself and in many ways I'm very lucky, when I think of the suffering of other people. I heard there was another raid this morning. They swooped on an area and went to all the homes and arrested Jews and other so-called undesirables."

Simone's bottom lip began to quiver and she suddenly stood up.

"I'll get us some tea and something to eat," she said brightly.

"That would be nice," smiled Cassie.

"I won't be long."

"You didn't manage to get a replacement for your own maid yet?" asked Cassie.

"No," said Simone.

"Maybe you're just as well considering my circumstances! Though I doubt you'd ever have anything to worry about along those lines with Luc."

Cassie sat back in thought after Simone left the room. It actually felt good to discuss her marriage with somebody. To put it in words to an understanding ear that didn't judge you or the situation. She looked around the sitting room and, as always, got a warm feeling. The Labelles' home seemed to be filled with love.

As she admired the tastefully decorated room, something

glinting in the sun on a sideboard caught her eye. It was the corner of a glass object and it looked somehow familiar. She got up and walked over to the sideboard. She pulled away a few books and saw that the object was a mirrored hexagonal ornament. Her face lit up – it was just the same as the one she'd had at Cliffenden. She carefully pulled it out and examined it. To the eye it was just a pretty ornament, the same as the one she had owned. The memories came flooding back to her of her one at Cliffenden and how she had used it to hide things over the years that nobody would know or guess it contained. She remembered storing Bowden's letters in it. Curiosity got the better of her and she wanted to see if it opened the same as hers. It was the same size as her one at Cliffenden, about a foot in length. She began to move the hexagonal shapes in the sequence that used to open her own hexagon. To her delight the top half of the hexagon lifted in her hands. Then she gazed in amazement at the contents of the bottom half. Inside was a small menorah – a gold candelabrum – with six candles lying beside it that looked as if they had been recently lit. And on the front of the menorah was the Star of David. She stared at it as her mind raced.

"I'm afraid I have no sugar," said Simone, entering the room.

Cassie spun around. Simone was carrying a tray. She stopped abruptly as she saw Cassie standing over the opened hexagon and dropped the tray in fright.

"You are Jewish," said Cassie, hardly believing the words she was saying herself.

Simone stood there, as pale as a ghost.

On hearing the crash, the children came rushing in.

"Mama, are you alright?" they asked.

Simone looked at her distressed children and the broken teapot and cups on the floor.

"Yes, I'm fine, my darlings," she said, managing to smile at them. "Just being clumsy. You go back and play. There's nothing to worry about."

They ran off out of the room again and Simone closed the door.

The two women were left staring at each other

"What are you doing? Spying on us!" Simone accused Cassie.

"No – no! I had one of these myself once and I was just checking if it – if it was the same as mine."

Simone rushed over, pushed Cassie out of the way and quickly put the hexagon back together.

Cassie couldn't tell whether Simone was angry or just terrified.

"Does anybody know?" asked Cassie.

"Know what?" snapped Simone.

"That you're Jewish?"

"What are you talking about? You're insane! We're not Jewish."

"It all makes sense now. Why the children are never at school. Why you hardly ever leave the apartment. How terrified you are when you are out."

Simone sank down on the sofa, buried her face into her hands and started to cry.

"I knew this moment would come," she managed between sobs.

Cassie rushed to her and put her arm around her. "Simone!"

Simone turned and grabbed both Cassie's hands. "You mustn't tell anybody! Please, I'll do anything you want – please don't tell anybody!"

Cassie looked at her panicked face in horror. "Of course I won't tell anybody. I promise."

"Not even Wally?"

"Especially not Wally."

"But nobody can find out, ever!"

"Well, they won't from me, Simone. Be assured of that."

Simone wiped away her tears. "Can I really trust you?"

"I won't tell anybody, you can trust me. But who else knows?"

"Nobody, not a soul. They can't!"

"But how have you managed to conceal the truth?"

"We moved to Paris several years ago from Alsace-Lorraine. We were near the German border and so we saw what was happening in Germany to Jews and felt we needed to get away and start again. So we came to Paris where we knew nobody. Luc said, with what was happening in Europe, it was too dangerous to be Jewish, or to be known as Jewish. So we kept away from the Jewish community here. We didn't participate in any Jewish activities and passed ourselves off as Catholics. Nobody assumed any different. We sent the children to Catholic schools and started our new life here, hiding who we actually were."

"Except for the menorah." Cassie glanced at the closed hexagon.

"It's a family treasure, passed from generation to generation of my family. I couldn't bear to get rid of it. Luc and I celebrate our own faith here at home, just the two of us, every Sabbath. It's the only symbol of Jewishness we have in the house. We thought nobody would ever find it in the hexagon."

"I'm sorry for intruding like I did – I didn't think."

"Luc says if Wally found out the truth he would be fired straight away."

Cassie nodded. "Luc is right, Simone. Wally wouldn't think twice about it. He has no loyalty to anyone but himself."

"And now the situation has got so dangerous for us, Cassie. We destroyed all papers showing we were Jewish, but this has left us with no papers at all. If the police should stop us, we have nothing to show them and they will investigate and discover our origins."

"But it might only be a matter of time then until they find out who you are!"

"Yes, the truth will eventually come out." Simone started to cry again.

Cassie put her arms around Simone and held her close, trying to comfort her as she thought about the two little children playing down the corridor.

CHAPTER 51

Cassie sat in the back of the car as Pierre drove her home after leaving the Labelles'. Although she tried to put on a front of being strong in front of Simone, she was reeling from the revelation. It had never occurred to her that they were Jewish. She could only imagine the daily cloud of terror they lived their lives under. The fear of being discovered and apprehended every moment of their lives. Luc losing his position in the bank was now only a minor worry, since they risked fear of being arrested. Her heart went out to them and the children.

As they drove along a boulevard there was a commotion on the other side of the street.

Cassie leaned forward. "Pierre, pull over for a moment."

Pierre parked the car over by the pavement. Cassie wound down her window and watched. Across the street there were German soldiers holding guns and machine-guns. They were ushering people out of an apartment building. The solders were shouting orders at them that Cassie couldn't quite make out. Other soldiers were randomly stopping people in the streets, again shouting at them. The people were scrabbling in their bags and producing papers. The people from the apartment building were being herded into the lorry, along with a couple from the street.

As the soldiers closed up the back of the lorry, Cassie wound up her window.

"Pierre, take me home quickly," she said.

Pierre started the car and drove off.

It was only a matter of time until the Labelles were discovered, she thought. She couldn't allow anything to happen to them. They weren't on their own anymore. They had Cassie Fullerton behind them.

When Cassie arrived back at the house she sat and thought about the Labelles' situation.

There was a knock on the front door and she could hear Michelle going to answer it. A minute later Michelle opened the drawing-room door.

"Pardon, Madame, but Oberst Stefan Bayer is here to see you."

Cassie frowned. "Very well – show him in."

A few seconds later Stefan walked in, holding a huge bouquet of flowers.

"Is there anything else you need, Madame?" asked Michelle.

"No, thank you," Cassie said.

Michelle closed the door, leaving the two of them alone.

"Cassie," he said as he approached her, looking sheepish, holding out the bouquet, "a token of my apology."

Cassie looked at the flowers coolly. Her mind was racing. She couldn't risk now having Wally's and her permits cancelled and being forced to leave Paris. Not now she knew about the Labelles' situation. They needed her help.

She stood up and took the flowers. "They are quite beautiful."

She walked over to a side table, put them on it and turned to face him.

"I feel last night we ended up insulting each other unintentionally," said Stefan.

Cassie chose to play her cards very carefully, mindful of the power Stefan wielded.

"Did we?" she asked.

"I might have overstepped the line with you, and I do apologise for that."

"Being the conquerors in a war can sometimes inflate people's egos, Stefan. I think that's what has happened to you."

"I got a little carried away – the wine, the music, alone with a very beautiful woman," said Stefan.

"Tell me, the break-in at my husband's bank, was that a little trick pulled by you in order for us to be left alone?"

"Some women would be flattered that I went to such lengths to be left alone with them."

"I am not most women," she said.

"That I realise now. I've just been such an admirer of yours for so long. Can I help it if I am a little in love with you?"

"Love?" She started to laugh. "Let's not get ahead of ourselves, Stefan. You trying your luck for a quick romp with me is one thing, love is quite another!"

"I just want you to see that I am a genuine person. That I wasn't insulting you, or assuming you were easy and cheap."

"One thing I've never been is cheap, Stefan."

As she looked at him, she realised he didn't look embarrassed or repentant.

"And all the girls do like a man in uniform," he said.

"I'm afraid that depends on the uniform," she said. "By the way, how do you know I haven't told Wally what happened?"

"Perhaps you have. But I don't think you have. I'm very good at reading people, and I'm seeing a huge coldness between you and Wally."

As she stared at him she wondered that her unhappiness was so apparent – so apparent that Stefan had seen it written across her face and hence had tried his luck with her. But, as she looked at him there in her drawing room, he might seem charming and nice, but she had seen in the club last night how nasty he could be.

He could have her kicked out of France that very day if she didn't pretend to play along with him. And now she knew the Labelles' plight, she couldn't just abandon them.

"Shall I order tea?" she said with a smile.

"That would be lovely, Cassie," he said, smiling and sitting down.

"How could you be so stupid?" Luc shouted as he paced frantically up and down the Labelles' sitting room.

"I'd never have thought she would have even spotted the hexagon, and you know yourself how impossible it is to open. But she managed – she had one the exact same in Ireland."

"Why did you leave her on her own?" he demanded.

"I – I – I can't forgive myself."

Luc ran his hands through his hair in despair. He stopped pacing suddenly. "Do you think she suspected all along? Do you think she was sent here to find out the truth?"

"No, I believe her."

"Maybe Wally has known all along and sent her to investigate. He's so in now with Nazi party we're banking for them!"

Simone's left hand played nervously with her necklace. "I trust her. She promised she would say nothing, not even to Wally. She even said it herself – 'especially not Wally'."

"How can you trust anybody in this new world? A world that hates us. Now that one person in Paris knows the truth, we're no longer safe here."

"But what can we do, Luc? We have no passports, no papers, our birth certificates are destroyed. We can't leave, can't go anywhere. We're trapped. It's all my fault." She started to cry.

He went to her and held her in his arms. "Stop, darling, the children will hear you. As you said we can't go or escape anywhere . . . but it will be alright, I'm sure of it."

CHAPTER 52

Cassie lifted the telephone and got a connection to the Labelles'.

"Hello, Simone, it's Cassie."

"Hello." There were nerves in Simone's voice and Cassie realised she was hoping she wasn't stupid enough to say anything over the telephone.

"It's a nice day, isn't it?"

"Yes."

"I got the children a little present and I wanted to drop it over. I was hoping you and Luc would be there this evening?"

"I – I'm not so sure."

"Oh, I *must* give it to them, Simone," stressed Cassie.

There was a pause.

"Very well – Luc should be home at eight – you can see the children then."

"I won't be late," said Cassie.

Cassie knocked on the Labelles' door and a moment later Luc opened it.

"Good evening, Luc."

"Cassie." He was looking at her warily as he gestured for her to come in.

She stepped in and kissed him on both cheeks. He looked up and down the corridor then closed and bolted the door. She walked ahead of him into the sitting room where she found Simone waiting for her on the sofa.

Cassie just smiled at her and placed a bag on the table. "The presents for the children."

Simone nodded. "You're very good to them . . . they're in bed now . . . we'll let them have them in the morning."

Realising the gifts were a cover for Cassie to come and discuss her discovery, they had not kept the children up to meet her.

As Cassie sat down on an armchair, Luc went and sat beside his wife, putting his arm around her.

"I wanted to come by, Luc, just to reassure you that you have nothing to worry about from me. I will never tell a soul," said Cassie.

Luc nodded. "I would have preferred you not to find out."

"Of course, but, you know, maybe it's for the best," said Cassie.

"How – how could it possibly be for the best? Our secret has been locked here within these walls, and now an outsider knows. I feel very exposed."

"All I can ask is that you trust me, Luc. I'd never do anything to harm you."

"Even if it means keeping a secret from your husband?"

"Oh, I've kept bigger secrets than this from Wally, you can be assured of that. I say it might be for the best that I found out, because I may be able to help you."

Luc shrugged. "How could you possibly help us?"

"Well, that's what I'm here to talk to you about. To discuss what we are going to do."

Luc looked at her incredulously. "What we are going to do? We're going to do nothing. We're going to go on as we are, and hope for the best."

"It's too dangerous a situation to just leave to hope, Luc. There must be something we can do."

"Why are you saying *we*? This has nothing to do with you!" snapped Luc.

"But that's what I'm trying to tell you. You don't have to handle this anymore on your own, Luc – the strain must have been killing you – I'm here to help, if I can think of some way to help."

"The best way you can help us is to turn around and leave now," said Luc. "Never mention this again to us or anyone else. Leave us in peace!"

"But there is no peace in this situation. I saw a round-up of Jews yesterday, led out of their apartment and from the street and carted away to a prison camp. You've been lucky so far, but how long do you think you'll get away with it?"

"Thank you for your concern, Cassie, but I must ask you to leave now."

"But, Luc! You can't just keep the children at home all the time – someone will notice and report you. And even if Simone never leaves the apartment again, one day you will be stopped and asked to identify yourself! For goodness' sake, it even happened to me! And when I didn't have my papers I was arrested on the spot! If it can happen to me it can happen to anyone. Luc, you really must see sense!"

Luc stood up. "I'll show you to the door. Thank you for the gifts for the children – you are very generous."

Simone had been sitting silently, listening intently to what Cassie was saying.

"Luc!" Cassie cried in desperation. "You're from Alsace-Lorraine! That province of France has been directly annexed by Germany. If you were arrested you wouldn't even be considered French anymore, but German. You could be deported to Germany immediately and – and –"

"Will you get out!" Luc snapped in anger and frustration.

"No, Luc!" Simone suddenly cried and held out her hands pleadingly to him. "You need to listen to her! She's speaking the truth! We won't get away with this for much longer, not without help, and Cassie is offering us help. Why turn her away?"

Luc's whole body seemed to sink. He walked slowly over to the sofa beside Simone and sank down on it, burying his face in his hands. Stifled sobs began to escape from him.

"Oh, Luc!" Simone cradled him. "You've been carrying all this on your own. You can't go on much longer with the stress."

Luc looked up and wiped away his tears. His red eyes looked over at Cassie.

"But what can we do?"

"I don't know, Luc. But let's try and come up with something together."

The three sat around the kitchen table drinking coffee.

"The sensible thing would be to get out of Paris," said Cassie.

"But where would we go?" said Simone.

"Down to the South, to Vichy France, or across the border to Switzerland," suggested Cassie.

"It's impossible," said Luc. "We have no papers, we have no passports. We couldn't travel anywhere. We'd never get out of Paris. Besides, Jews are being treated just as badly in Vichy France, and if we ever got to the Swiss border we wouldn't get in. We would be seen as refugees. We would probably be turned back without visas to enter the country. No, the safest thing for us would be to stay here in Paris – *if* we had papers stating we are not Jewish."

"You're right," conceded Cassie. "The priority is to acquire passports."

"For that we would need to send for copies of our birth certificates, and that would expose us as Jewish," said Luc.

"Well, there must be something we can do to get papers that say you're not Jewish," said Cassie.

"How?" said Luc.

They sat in silence for a long while.

Luc finally looked up at Cassie. "Before we left Strasbourg, I was told there was a corrupt official here in Paris, working in the mayor's office, by the name of Duchamps."

"Who did you learn this from?"

"A close friend of mine received a fake marriage certificate from him. It cost a lot of money."

Simone nodded. "That's right. Our friend bribed Duchamps. He said many people had done it."

"Then we must make contact with him," said Cassie.

"It's too risky," said Luc. "We risk exposure. Maybe he's not doing it anymore, not wanting to be discovered by the Nazis."

"My experience is that such people do not change. If he's still in his job then he's still accepting bribes," said Cassie.

"But we can't just go in and meet him. We'd risk too much," said Luc.

"You can't go in, but I can," said Cassie. "Obviously on a pretence. To try and suss him out."

"It's much too dangerous for you," said Luc.

"Well, I can't think of anything else, can you?"

Luc shook his head slowly.

"I'll investigate if he's still there, and if he is – I'll arrange to meet him," said Cassie.

Simone reached forward and grasped her hand. "Be careful."

Cassie nodded and squeezed her hand back. "I will be. And so should you, until we get this sorted out."

When Cassie got home she found the telephone number for Duchamps' office and made an appointment to see him. He did still work in the mayor's office and Cassie found it no problem to arrange to meet him.

As she sat in the drawing room thinking of a plan, the front door opened and a moment later Michelle came in.

"Pardon, Madame, Oberst Bayer is here to see you," she said.

"Show him in."

A moment later Stefan came in, holding a huge box of chocolates.

"For me?" she asked.

"Of course, Cassie. They are liqueurs, very hard to get," he said.

"Not for a man like you, Stefan."

She wondered what on earth he was still doing, calling on her all the time. She had let it be known that she had no interest in him. And yet it seemed he could not stay away. He called on her a lot, always bringing gifts and would spend the time chatting away with her as if they were old friends. She wondered if he was lonely.

He was probably missing home and his family and friends. And of course there was so much hatred towards the occupying army in Paris. But whatever his reasons, she knew she had to continue to indulge him for fear of being deported before she had saved the Labelles.

He sat down beside her and smiled at her. "So what have you been doing all day?"

"Oh, nothing much," she lied. "Shopping, the usual."

"Keep next Thursday night free in your diary, Cassie. I have tickets for you, me and Wally to visit the Chapelle Club."

"Does your hospitality never cease?" she asked.

"Now tell me more stories of your home in Ireland. Did your grandmother, the Countess of Weybridge, visit you much there?"

That evening, as Cassie got ready for bed, the box of chocolates Stefan had given her were open on her dressing table. Wally came over, took one and ate it.

"Where did you manage to get them?" he asked.

"Stefan Bayer brought them today," she said as she continued to remove her make-up.

"Did he? What a kind gesture," said Wally.

"He keeps calling to the house – he's become quite a nuisance," she said.

"I hope you weren't rude to him?"

"No, I managed to be polite."

"Good, make sure you do. I can't tell you how important he is to the bank," said Wally.

"He's invited us to the Chapelle Club on Thursday."

"I can't make it – I'm in Lyons that night," said Wally.

"I'll inform him we can't go in that case."

"No need to do that – you can still go."

She turned around and looked at him. "I don't think it's very appropriate for me to be seen out alone with him," she pointed out.

"Don't be so silly – why would it not be appropriate? He's a friend of ours!"

Cassie fell silent and began to moisturise her face.

"Stefan makes me feel quite uncomfortable, Wally," she said at last. "Not just because of who and what he is, but he keeps calling on me and giving me gifts. I don't want him to get the wrong impression."

Wally didn't answer.

"Wally?" she said and then turned around.

She saw he had fallen asleep on the bed.

CHAPTER 53

On the day Cassie was due to meet Duchamps in the mayor's office, she made sure to dress in her best fur and most expensive dress to impress him. If this man was motivated by money, then she must show she had it.

Duchamps' secretary showed her in.

Cassie walked in quickly and, smiling at him, held out her hand.

"Monsieur Duchamps, so good of you to meet me."

He stood up, stretched his hand across his desk and shook hers. "Please, take a seat."

As Cassie sat down she did a quick analysis of him. He was in his later fifties, slightly overweight, with a friendly smile but dark cunning eyes.

"And how can I help you today, Madame Stanton?"

"Well, I'm trying to arrange a visa for myself to get back to see my family in Ireland on a holiday. There shouldn't be too much trouble. I am a neutral and married to an American."

"Under normal circumstances all you would have to do is get a boat to England, but no chance of that I'm afraid," he said.

She sighed. "I know. What am I to do? I only want to visit, a couple of weeks at most. They worry about me, not having seen me for so long."

"I understand. You could always travel to Switzerland and get a flight from there."

"Yes?"

"But there are hardly any commercial flights. It's too dangerous.

You are taking the risk of being shot down by mistake as an enemy plane."

"Goodness me! I think I'd rather not take such a risk!"

"I think your best option would be to travel down to Spain or Portugal and try to get a ship that's sailing to Ireland," said the man.

Cassie sighed. "What a long way round for such a short trip!"

"I know – it's the inconvenience of war, Madame."

"Very inconvenient, I must say!" Cassie managed to look petulant.

"Hopefully it won't go on for too much longer," said Duchamps.

"Oh, I do hope so, Mr. Duchamps – it's playing havoc with my travel arrangements. So what do I need to go to Spain or Portugal en route to my home?"

"You will need visas to enter Spain and Portugal if you choose to leave from Lisbon. A lot of people are travelling through Lisbon."

Cassie managed to flutter her eyelashes. "Would that be an awful chore to arrange?"

Duchamps smiled at her. "Not in your case, Madame Stanton. It's only an issue for people trying to enter those countries with nowhere to go. You are just a neutral person travelling through en route to your own neutral country. A straightforward situation – alas, one of the very few straightforward ones that come before me every day."

She sat forward and nodded. "Very trying for you, I'm sure. When will the visas be ready?"

"I will need to contact the embassies of Spain and Portugal, do the necessary police check on you and I should have it by next Thursday."

She stood up and shook his hand enthusiastically. "You are the most amazing man!"

"The pleasure is all mine, Madame."

Cassie turned and left his office. Contact had been made. Now she had to put the next part of her plan into action.

Cassie was shown into Duchamps' office. She walked over to his desk, smiling warmly.

"Good to see you again, Monsieur Duchamps," she said, sitting down.

"And you, Madame Stanton. I'm pleased to say that I have all the necessary documentation for your travel arrangements."

Cassie clasped her hands together in delight. "If only everyone in Paris was efficient as you, Monsieur Duchamps!"

"Indeed, I do pride myself on my efficiency," he said, smiling, happy with himself.

"And so you should, you clever man!"

Duchamps handed over the documents. "Your visas allow you entry to Spain and Portugal, so you can travel to Ireland from Lisbon."

She took them and leafed through them. "Was it very difficult for you to arrange?"

"No – as I told you it would be, it was fairly straightforward."

She gazed at him adoringly. "I've always had a soft spot for a capable man."

He put his hands together. "Well, I did try to hurry the process for you somewhat."

"Wonderful!" she said, opening her handbag and putting in the papers. Then she took out five hundred francs and put them on the desk in front of him.

She studied him intently as he looked at the money, first with surprise and then with pleasure. He quickly and silently took the money and put it in a drawer, locking it away. She felt relieved that he had acted the way he did.

"I wonder, while I'm here, if I could discuss another matter with you?" she asked brightly.

"Certainly!" he said happily.

"A friend of mine is looking for some paperwork."

"What kind of paperwork?"

"A marriage certificate."

"But that is simple. Just tell me her name and I'll get you a copy. She was married in Paris, I take it?"

"Well, no, you see, that's the point – she wasn't married at all."

He looked at her, confused. "Then why would she need . . ." He trailed off as he realised what she was saying. "I really don't know what you're talking about." He began to shuffle papers nervously.

She leaned forward to him. "I think you do."

He stopped shuffling the papers, leaned across the desk to her and hissed, "You're taking a stupid risk! I could report you right now and have you carted away."

"For what? I'd only deny I had said anything and say you had taken five hundred francs as a bribe to have my holiday visa speeded up."

He went red in the face.

"Don't mess with me, Monsieur Duchamps," she whispered. "Can you help me or not? As you see from the five hundred francs I gave you for nothing, it will be well worth your while."

"We can't speak here."

"Where then?"

"There's a restaurant near the Sacre Coeur, called Le Petit Café. I'll meet you there tomorrow at one," he said.

"Alright, I'll see you there. Remember, if you tell anyone I'll only deny it, and they will believe me by the time I'm finished, I assure you."

She got up and left.

Cassie sat in the little funicular as it steadily rose up the hill to the Sacre Coeur basilica. When she had first moved to Paris she had climbed the mountain of steps that led up to the basilica. She had been exhausted by the time she reached the top. As her mission that day was too important to arrive exhausted she had opted for the funicular. As the little tram reached the top of the hill she stepped outside and walked across in front of the basilica. There appeared to be hundreds of German soldiers there that day, smiling happily, having their photos taken before the sensational views offered from there across Paris. She quickly made her way behind the church and through the labyrinth of cobbled streets that was Montmartre. Artists were selling their paintings and sketches on the streets: it was still the centre of the artistic community in Paris.

Finally she found the Le Petit Café and entered, bought herself a cup of coffee, found a quiet table at the back of the restaurant and waited.

At exactly one o'clock Duchamps entered the quiet restaurant. As he bought his coffee she studied him and the surroundings to make sure he hadn't brought anybody else with him, but she became confident he was on his own.

Duchamps made his way down to her and joined her at the table.

"I wasn't sure you'd come," she said.

"I don't have much time. What is it you want of me? A marriage certificate? For who and why?"

She steadied herself. "It's not actually a marriage certificate I want."

He looked annoyed. "Stop playing games with me! What is it you want?"

"As I said, I have friends, and they need – they need some false documentation. Birth certificates, passports."

His eyes widened in horror. "How many people?"

"Four."

"*Four*!" he hissed.

"Two adults and two children. They are one family, so that might make it easier."

"It's impossible. Why do they need the false documentation? What have they done that they need to disguise themselves?"

"They haven't *done* anything!" she defended. "They are not criminals if that's what you're afraid of."

He looked at her as realisation dawned. "You're asking me to falsify papers for Jews?"

"You're our only hope." She leaned towards him pleadingly.

"Well, then you have no hope!" He made to stand up.

She leaned across quickly and grasped his arm. "No, please! Here me out!"

Two Nazi officers walked into the restaurant, laughing and joking, and Duchamps quickly sat down again. She released his arm.

"You don't know what you're getting yourself involved in,

Madame Stanton. If the authorities discovered what you are doing it's you who would be arrested, neutral or not, rich American husband or not. Take my advice – go home, and be happy that it's not you that's being targeted."

"I can't do that! I couldn't live with myself if anything happened to them. If you can't help me, then I'll just keep knocking on doors until I find somebody who can," she insisted.

"But you don't know whose doors you are knocking on. You were lucky with me, but maybe the next official will have you arrested on the spot."

"That's a chance I will just have to take."

"Are these people relatives of yours?"

"No. Just friends."

"Look, Madame Stanton, it's not that I'm not sympathetic to your friends' situation. I am. But, to disguise a whole family! I can't risk my own life by doing this."

"But when all this is over, Monsieur Duchamps, and when the questions are asked – what did you do in the war, whose side were you on? What will you say? Who will speak up for you?" she said earnestly. "Just do this one thing, Monsieur Duchamps, and your conscience will be clear. I know you're a good man – I can see it in your face."

"Your flirtation is wasted on me by this stage, Madame Stanton," he sighed.

"I'm asking you, I'm begging you. If you do just this one thing you will be able to explain yourself, live with yourself in the future."

She paused and then played her trump card.

"Whatever it costs, Monsieur Duchamps! Money is no object. Name your price."

He sat, staring at her, and she held her breath.

"It will cost one hundred thousand francs."

With the relief she felt at hearing him agree, she hardly even registered the figure he was quoting.

"Yes, that is fine." Her whole body sank in relief.

"Cash," he said.

"Agreed."

"I will meet you here Friday week, same time. Bring me their photos – all personal information."

He stood and walked out.

She sat there for a while, sipping her coffee, her whole body shaking with relief.

Simone sat on the sofa with her hands clasped together, hardly able to contain herself as Cassie explained about her meeting with Duchamps. Luc stood, hanging on every word.

"But that's wonderful, just wonderful!" exclaimed Simone, closing her eyes. Cassie realised it was the first time she had ever seen Simone look happy.

Luc was just relieved that Duchamps hadn't betrayed them. Even though he knew from his friend that Duchamps was trustworthy.

Simone reached out and grabbed Luc's hand.

"Luc, we could be safe!"

Luc shook his head, bewildered. "Except for the little matter of one hundred thousand francs. We don't have it. We could put together ten thousand francs maybe – but this amount! We're back to where we started."

Cassie sat forward. "I hadn't really thought of the money. I was just too busy trying to get the deal done. Is there anybody you can ask for money?"

Luc shook his head. "No! We don't have close family. And the relatives we have are back in Alsace-Lorraine, if they are still there. We couldn't try to contact them in case it is discovered we are related to them and are Jewish."

Cassie saw their frightened faces and thought hard before speaking. "Don't worry about the money. I'll get it from somewhere."

"How can you get that amount of money?" asked Luc.

"Leave that to me," said Cassie. "I have accounts. I can raise the money."

"Cassie, we can't ask you to do that. You've done too much already," objected Luc.

"I insist," said Cassie.

"No, I won't have you give so much money to him," insisted Luc.

"Luc!" cried Simone. "She's offering to lend us the money. It will solve all our problems. What's wrong with you! It would mean our children will be safe!"

Cassie stood up. "I'd better get going. I need to start raising the money."

Luc walked over to her and embraced her. "I'll pay you back – every franc, I promise."

Cassie nodded and smiled at him. "You'd better start saving then."

On the Thursday evening Wally had gone to business in Lyons and Stefan came and collected Cassie from their house and brought her to the Chapelle Club as arranged. They had a meal and then drank wine, listening to the entertainment on the small stage.

"Can I get you another drink?" asked Stefan.

"No, thank you, I'm not finished this one yet." She raised her half glass of red wine and looked back at the chanteuse who was singing the saddest song in French. A slow mournful song that made Cassie wonder whether she was singing about the loss of her heart or the loss of her country as she looked out at the German soldiers, sleepy from drink at the various tables, holding hands with their French partners.

A girl who was carrying a camera came up to their table.

"Would you like your photo taken, Madame, Monsieur?" she asked with a big smile.

"No!" said Cassie.

"Yes!" said Stefan and he put his arm around Cassie, holding his wineglass in the other.

"Smile!" said the photographer and took their photo. "Give me your address, Monsieur, and I'll post the photo on to you."

Stefan scribbled down his address and gave it to her and she moved on to the next table.

Stefan turned his attention back to Cassie who was gazing again at the chanteuse.

"She's a beautiful singer, don't you think?" he said, raising his wineglass and taking a sip.

"Yes, she is."

"My French isn't so good – what is she singing about?"

"She's singing about a boy she once knew who was taken away from her," answered Cassie, looking sad herself.

"You don't want to be here with me, do you?" said Stefan.

She put down her glass. "Not really."

"Then why did you agree to come?"

"Out of politeness."

"Am I really so terrible?"

"I don't know what you want, Stefan. You hold all the cards here. You know you have the power. You obviously know that I am not particularly friendly with you and, if I am, it's because I have to be because of your position."

"I was hoping – just hoping – that if you spent some time with me, you might actually get to like me."

"But why? Why bother? Why do you care?"

"Because I like you."

"I'm married to Wally, Stefan. And nothing is going to change that."

"I know. But I don't think you're happy in your marriage."

"What makes you say that?"

"Everything, Cassie."

"As I said before, I'm not a good actress in that case."

"Why did you marry him? When you didn't love him?"

"People get married for many reasons. Love is often not the reason."

"I don't like to see you unhappy, Cassie. Why not leave him?"

"Leave him for what? Wally is my life, I don't know any other."

"Does he know how unhappy you are?"

"My happiness has never been a concern of Wally's. I often wonder why he married me. I can't bring him any happiness."

"And why did he marry you then?"

"Because I was a conquest that he felt he had to make. Now he's married to me, I'm sure he wonders what all the fuss was about."

"Can I tell you something?"

"Go ahead."

"I saw your photograph a few years ago in *Tatler* magazine, and you had such an effect on me, I can't explain it. I felt I knew you. I felt we were destined to meet, even though I was only a Bavarian farm boy at the time."

"I think men see me and build me into something they want me to be. It only leads to disappointment."

"I'm not disappointed in any way."

"Well, you should be."

"Why can't you open your heart, take a chance on me?"

"I had my heart broken once and I'll never take a chance on anybody ever again."

"I'm speaking out of turn."

"Yes, you are. I'm married, Stefan, for better or for worse. You should get any silly thoughts of me out of your head. Paris has enough other women, willing and able."

"But they are not you."

"I'm not available, Stefan."

"If I wasn't wearing this uniform, would it make a difference?"

"But you are wearing that uniform, and I despise everything you represent."

"I'm a nice man underneath it."

"Then you wouldn't wear that uniform."

"I have no choice, Cassie. I have to do my duty like everyone else."

"That's for your conscience, not mine," she said, standing up. "I'd like to go home now."

Stefan finished his drink and stood up. "Of course."

"Can I come in for a nightcap?" Stefan asked as the car pulled up in front of Cassie's home.

"I'm quite tired, Stefan," she said.

"I won't stay long – I promise!" he said.

"Just one quick one then."

They got out of the car and walked up to the front door. As

Cassie looked at the Nazi flag on the car, she thought how all their neighbours must now despise them, seeing a high-ranking Nazi officer visiting the house. She took out her key and let them in and they walked into the drawing room. Stefan closed the door as she poured them both a drink.

She walked over to him and handed the glass to him.

"To health and happiness!" he toasted.

"Yes," she said.

"What time is Wally home tomorrow?" he asked.

She shrugged. "I don't know, he didn't say."

She went over and stood with her back to him at the fireplace, placing her glass on the mantelpiece.

She heard Stefan approach and then, to her shock, he put his arms around her.

"Stefan!" she said and quickly turned around to face him.

He immediately put his lips on hers. She was furious and was pushing him away when there was a noise and she saw Michelle had entered the room.

"Oh, pardon, Madame!" apologised Michelle and she quickly left.

Cassie pushed Stefan firmly away.

"How dare you!" she blazed.

"I'm sorry, Cassie, I thought –"

"I know exactly what you thought," she snapped and walked quickly away from him. She lit up a cigarette and sat down. "I think you should leave, Stefan."

"But –"

"Just leave!" she reiterated. "Now!"

He looked at her furious face and then nodded and headed towards the door.

Before leaving he turned and said, "I won't give up on you, Cassie, that I promise you."

A few seconds later she heard the front door close behind him and the car outside pull away. She stubbed out her cigarette and folded her arms. She was furious at what Stefan had done. Furious that Michelle had witnessed it.

She needed to raise the money quickly to secure the Labelles' papers, and then she needed to leave Paris. Whether Wally was coming with her or not. She had had enough. She wanted to go home. And when she thought about it, she hoped Wally wouldn't come with her. She had had enough of this charade of a marriage and her family and friends would have to just suffer the consequences of the fallout of a divorce.

CHAPTER 54

Cassie was in her bedroom the next morning, in her dressing gown. She had hardly slept that night, racking her mind, trying to think of how to raise the money. There wasn't much time. Wally had taken a lot of her jewellery when the occupation started and put it in a security box at the bank for safe keeping. As she looked at the jewellery she had been left with, she doubted it would reach the figure of one hundred thousand francs. And even if it did, she would have to risk selling it on the black market – nor was there really time for all that. She lit a cigarette and looked at her reflection in the mirror as she thought.

There was a knock on the door and Michelle walked in.

"Pardon, Madame, will I run a bath for you?"

Cassie looked at her coolly. "No, it's alright. I'll run my own."

"Are you sure, Madame?"

"Quite sure!" snapped Cassie.

Michelle nodded and left her.

As Cassie sat there she wondered how many times Wally had brought Michelle out on the town when he was supposed to be at business meetings. Michelle who always had to visit her sick aunt a couple of times a week in the evenings. She imagined the two of them seated in the cabarets of Paris, living it up amongst the soldiers enjoying the decadence of Paris.

Cassie got up and walked out of the room and down the stairs. She made her way to Wally's office. She went to where she knew he hid the key to his desk and then sat at the desk and began going through the papers in it. She knew Wally had opened different bank accounts around Paris. She had gone in with him a couple of times to different banks to sign papers. He had told her at the time he had opened joint accounts in both their names for tax reasons. He had told her not to worry about it, that it didn't concern her. But now, as she riffled through his bank statements and books, it very much concerned her.

"How many bank accounts do you have, Wally?" she asked aloud as she found statement after statement.

Finally she found something with both their names on it. She raised the paper and began to read it. She checked the address and remembered it as being one of the banks he had brought her into when they first moved to Paris, to sign documents. It was a bank account in both their names containing one hundred and ten thousand francs.

She clutched the paper happily to herself before tidying away the rest of the statements exactly as she found them. She relocked the desk and then hurried out of the room.

Cassie walked into the bank and waited for one of the desk clerks to be free. She walked up to the desk and sat down.

"*Bonjour, Madame,*" said the female bank clerk.

"*Bonjour.* I have a bank account at this branch and I'd like to withdraw some money, please," she said.

"Certainly. May I have your bank account details, please?"

"Yes." Cassie handed her the statement and her passport.

"Thank you," said the woman, checking the passport. "It is a joint account with your husband."

"That's right," confirmed Cassie.

"And how much would you like to withdraw today?"

"One hundred thousand francs," said Cassie.

The clerk looked up, surprised. "We usually need notice for such a large amount, Madame."

Cassie smiled at her. "Well, I'm giving you notice now! So if you could get me my money?"

The clerk studied the woman opposite her in her expensive furs and dress.

"One moment, please," she said, standing up.

Cassie disguised her nerves. "Is there a problem?"

"If you could wait here," said the woman as she walked off with Cassie's passport.

Cassie watched as the clerk went over to an office door and knocked on it. Cassie took out a cigarette and lit it up, trying to disguise her nerves. How stupid of her to think she would get away with this! They would have to check with such a large amount. How could she possible explain to Wally why she was in a bank taking out a hundred thousand francs without his knowledge or permission?

Cassie saw the clerk come back to the door of the office with an elderly gentleman. The clerk was showing him Cassie's passport and pointing over to Cassie.

Cassie steadied herself as the two walked in her direction.

"Madame Stanton?" said the man.

"Yes?"

"You might remember me. I met you and your husband at a couple of receptions given by the banking federation. Jean Visage?"

Cassie looked at the man and did remember him vaguely.

"Oh, yes, Jean! How are you?" she said, smiling broadly.

"I'm very well. And how is Monsieur Stanton?"

"He's very busy, Jean," Cassie said, raising her eyes to heaven. "Run off his feet with work. He even has me doing his banking for him!"

Jean smiled back at her. "I can imagine he is. He's a very powerful banker."

"So he keeps telling me, Jean. But then I ask him, if he's so powerful, then why doesn't he employ somebody to do his errands for him, instead of sending me!"

Jean laughed loudly. "Well, I suppose there are some errands a man can only trust his wife to do."

"Isn't that the truth! Having said that, I wish running errands for him didn't interfere with my appointments at the hairdresser's! I had to cancel my appointment today to come here."

"Well, we won't detain you much longer." He turned around to the clerk and said, "Well, hurry up, get Madame Stanton her money!"

"Yes, Monsieur!" said the clerk as she raced off.

"And, Madame Stanton, perhaps you would like to come to my office to conclude your transaction? We can count the money out there in private."

He offered her his arm.

She stood up and took it. "How very gallant of you, Jean!"

Half an hour later Cassie walked out of the bank and began to breathe easily again, the hundred thousand francs in her handbag.

CHAPTER 55

Cassie met with Duchamps on the Friday in the same place in Montmartre and discreetly gave him the Labelles' photos and other information.

"It is good they haven't got Jewish names," commented Duchamps.

"And they don't live in a Jewish neighbourhood or have any connections with the Jewish community here. Once they get the papers, they will be safe."

"And what of the money?" asked Duchamps.

"I have already withdrawn it. I will give it to you immediately when you hand me the papers. Shall we meet here again?"

"No, a third time might look suspicious. Ring my secretary next Wednesday and tell her there's a problem with your holiday visa and you need to see me. We can exchange the papers and money in my office, where there is no risk of being seen."

Cassie nodded.

Cassie did as Duchamps ordered and rang his secretary the following Wednesday, requesting an appointment.

"There's a problem with my visa, you see, a spelling wrong. I don't want any hindrance with my travel," she said, putting on an act.

"I can pencil you in for an appointment tomorrow at four?"

"Excellent. I'll see you then," said Cassie and she hung up the telephone.

Cassie had hidden the money in one of her handbags in her dressing room, off the bedroom. She kept dozens of bags there at the bottom of a wardrobe. Wally never even went in there.

She went to lock the bedroom door but, just as she reached it, there was a quick knock and the door opened.

It was Michelle.

"Oh, pardon, Madame!" she said.

Cassie quickly held the door to stop her from entering.

"What is it, Michelle?"

"I just want to check if you are going out today, or if you will require lunch?"

"No, I won't be going out, so I'll have lunch at one," said Cassie.

"Very good, Madame." Michelle retreated.

Cassie closed the door and quickly locked it. She decided she would get rid of Michelle the following week, regardless of any objections Wally might have. Her marriage might be a sham, but she didn't need the constant reminder of the fact with Michelle in the house. Cassie then went to her dressing room, took the bag out and counted the money out on the bed.

Unknown to her, a suspicious Michelle was peeping through the keyhole as she did it.

The morning that Cassie was due to go to Duchamps's office to pay him the money and get the Labelles' papers, Wally was preparing to go to Cherbourg on a business trip for the next couple of days.

"Are you going into the office today?" she asked.

"No, I'm going to work from home and go straight to the station."

"Alright, I'm out shopping today so I'll see when you get back," said Cassie.

She waited until he went down for breakfast before she removed the hundred thousand francs from the bag she had hidden in her wardrobe.

Duchamps' secretary showed Cassie into his office.

"Ah, Monsieur Duchamps, thank you so much for seeing me at

such short notice," said Cassie merrily.

"My secretary said there was a problem with a spelling?" said Duchamps.

"Yes, it may be nothing, but thought I should check with you."

The secretary closed the door and Cassie hurried over to the desk.

"Did you get them?" she asked in a frantic whisper.

Duchamps gestured to her to be silent. "Sit down, Madame, and let me see your passport," he said.

She sat and handed him her passport, realising that they had to go through with the charade, presumably in case the secretary walked in on them for some reason. Duchamps was taking no chances – something she was grateful for.

He began to talk reassuringly about her fictitious spelling problem, meanwhile unlocking his desk drawer, taking out an envelope and sliding it over to her.

She opened the envelope and riffled through the papers inside. Passports, birth certificates, Aryan certification. She breathed a sigh of relief.

As he continued to talk about her passport, she took the envelope with the money in it out of her bag and slid it across to him.

He put it on his lap and opened the envelope. His eyes lit up as he rapidly began to count it.

"Well, thank you, Monsieur," said Cassie. "Thank goodness there is no problem with the passport."

"Everything is in order, Madame," he said meaningfully, before putting the money into his drawer and locking it.

"I won't take up any more of your time, Monsieur," she said, standing up.

He stood and came around the desk to her. Standing quite close he murmured, "I can't warn you enough that nobody must ever find out about this. Not only would the Labelle family be arrested immediately to suffer whatever fate that is unimaginable, but so would you and I. I hope you realise that."

"I fully realise it," Cassie said softly.

Duchamps opened the door and bowed her out.

"Thank you so much for your time, Monsieur Duchamps," she said cheerfully.

"I'm hope you are assured now that there is no problem with your visa, Madame," said Duchamps with a smile.

"Quite assured. The fault was entirely mine – my French spelling is obviously not as good as I thought it was!"

She walked past the secretary's desk with a nod and a smile.

That evening Simone sat staring at the passports and papers on the coffee table in their apartment as Luc examined them.

"They are perfect – they look completely authentic," he said.

"Well, I should hope so! They cost one hundred thousand francs!" said Cassie.

"Oh, Luc!" Simone grabbed her husband's arm and he turned around and started to hug her as she dissolved in tears. "Are we really safe?"

"Yes, thanks to Cassie," he said, looking over at Cassie with tears in his eyes.

He got up and came over to her. She stood and he enveloped her in an embrace.

"We can never repay you for what you have done for us," he whispered.

"Knowing you're safe is all the repayment I ever need," she whispered back.

"I feel as if we have been given a new life. To think that a few papers and passports is the difference between life and . . ." Simone trailed off.

"I think you might look into sending the children to Switzerland as soon as possible, now that they are legitimate to travel," suggested Cassie. "They would be safer there and perhaps you could eventually join them? Do you have any relatives or friends there?"

"Unfortunately, no," said Luc.

"Well, think about it – see if there's any way of sending them there – until the war is over and things get back to normal."

"Will things ever be back to normal, Cassie?" asked Luc. "I think we are deluding ourselves if we think they ever will be."

"It will be one day, Luc, it has to be. The world isn't meant to be like this. Anyway, I'd better be getting back home. Wally will be wondering where I've got to."

Luc nodded and, after Simone embraced Cassie, he walked her to the door.

As he let her out he mouthed, "Thank you," to her.

She squeezed his hand and left.

CHAPTER 56

As Pierre drove the car in through the gate and up the drive to the house, Cassie felt a contentment that she had rarely felt before. The look on the Labelles' faces had made her feel that all the stress she had gone through arranging the papers was worth it.

"Will you be needing me for the rest of the night, Madame?" asked Pierre as she stepped out of the back of the car.

"No, thank you, Pierre. I will see you tomorrow."

"Very good, Madame," said Pierre and he drove the car to the garage to park it for the night.

Cassie let herself in through the front door. Michelle was in the hall.

"Did Monsieur Stanton leave for Cherbourg on time?" Cassie asked, handing Michelle her coat.

"No, he's upstairs . . . Monsieur Stanton is in a very bad mood, Madame."

"Is he?" Cassie sighed, wondering what was wrong with him now.

"Madame, my aunt is not very well this evening . . . will you be needing me for the rest of the evening?"

Cassie viewed her coolly. "No. You can go to her."

Michelle nodded and hurried away to hang up Cassie's coat.

As Cassie opened the bedroom door she could hear rummaging and noise coming from her dressing room. She entered to find Wally ransacking the place.

"What on earth are you doing?" she cried.

He didn't answer her but kept throwing her stuff on to the floor and across the room.

"Wally! What are you doing?"

He stopped and turned to face her and she saw his face was red with rage.

"Where is it?" he demanded.

"Where's what?" she asked.

"My money!"

Her heart started to beat quickly. "I don't know what you're talking about."

"Don't play the innocent with me! What have you done with my money?"

"Wally, will you calm down and explain yourself!"

"No! It's you who need to do the explaining! One hundred thousand francs has been withdrawn from our bank account at the Banque de Lyons. *Where is it?*"

"I don't know anything about your money – it's nothing to do with me!"

He marched over to her, grabbed her arms and shook her.

"*Where is it?*" he shouted at her.

She remained tight-lipped as she pushed him away from her.

"I know one hundred thousand francs was withdrawn from that account and I know you have been storing it here. Michelle told me she saw it."

"The little bitch!" spat Cassie.

He began to open drawers and throw stuff out onto the floor.

"It's not here! You're wasting your time and ruining my clothes!" she said.

"Where have you put it?"

"Why don't you ask your little whore Michelle? She seems to know everything!"

He looked at her in surprise.

"Yes, I know all about you and our French tart of a maid, Wally. No need to hide it from me anymore."

"You've gone mad!" he sneered. "You and your family are all mad! Your stupid parents and your imbecile brother!"

"Maybe you're right, but you've still been screwing the staff, Wally. What does that make you? And I thought you were such a snob. I'm disappointed in you. I thought you would have had better taste."

"Ha! Marriage to you shows how lacking my taste is!"

"If you hate being married to me then divorce me! I've told you I'm willing. Let both of us go free!" she said.

He folded his arms and shook his head, sneering at her. "Is that what all this is about? I should have known you were up to something when you suggested divorce before." Suddenly he screamed at her, *"You're leaving me and you've stolen my money to get away and set up a new life for yourself! You're leaving me, aren't you?"*

"No, Wally, I'm not leaving you, or at least I hadn't planned to up to this point."

"Then why take my money?"

She looked pleadingly at him as she held her hands up. "I can't say!"

"You had better say, or I'll call the police."

"For what? Taking money from a bank account in my own name?"

"I wish I had never married you!"

"Well, it was you who forced me into the marriage, not the other way around! I didn't want to marry you – you forced me into it by blackmailing me, saying that my family would lose Cliffenden."

"Oh, yes, that!" He started to laugh, a hollow nasty sound.

"What's so funny?"

"You see, you think you are so clever, Cassie, but you have no idea of anything. You were never in danger of losing Cliffenden at that time. Your parents had actually managed to turn the fortunes of the place around and you were finally turning a profit. I only said all that in order to have you exactly where I wanted you. If your parents had the brains to hire an independent auditor, they would have discovered that for themselves."

Cassie stared at him, hardly comprehending what he was saying.

She sat down on the bed in shock and said quietly, "You tricked me into marrying you."

"I don't see it like that, but you can see it anyway you want," he said.

"But – but – you ruined everything, for no reason. I could have been happy, and you robbed it from me."

"Happy? Happy doing what? Playing clownish games with Teddy? Seeing who could drink the most, party the longest, play the most outlandish pranks? That's not being happy. I gave you a role in life, a position, I rescued you from that aimless life you had."

As she thought of Bowden, she said, "You don't know anything of my life back then, Wally. Nothing at all. You're a selfish man, Wally."

"I never pretended to be anything else. Now, where have you put my money? When were you planning on doing a moonlight flit? This is your last chance to tell me!" He stood menacingly over her as she sat on the bed.

"I – I won't tell you," she whispered with tears in her eyes.

"In that case I will tear this house apart until I find it!" he said as he went marching to the door.

"That will do you no good. It's no longer here."

"Where's Pierre?"

"Pierre? I presume he's gone home for the night."

"Then I shall tell him to come back," he said, crossing over to the telephone on the side table.

"Pierre? Why do you need him?" demanded Cassie.

"He will be able to tell me your movements for the last week since you withdrew the money."

Cassie began to panic. She tried to keep her composure. "I can't see what that would prove."

"You put that money somewhere, and Pierre will be able to tell me where you've been since Michelle saw the money here."

"What will that prove?"

"I will then ask the police to interview and investigate everybody that you have been with and visited to see if they know what became of my money. I will get to the bottom of this, I promise you."

Cassie panicked as she thought of her movements since she

withdrew the money, about visiting Duchamps and the Labelles. If the police were notified of this and they began to investigate, they would discover what was going on. It would draw their attention to the Labelles and expose them as Jewish with a thorough background search that would prove their new papers were false. Instead of keeping the authorities from the Labelles, she would have led them to their door.

Cassie stood up and raced to Wally, taking the receiver from his hand and slamming it back down on its stand.

"Alright! Alright – I'll tell you," she said.

He watched her as she went and sat down on an armchair. He followed her over and stood looking down at her.

"I'm waiting!" he said.

She bit her lower lip before forcing herself to speak "The money was for the Labelles."

Wally looked at her in confusion. "Luc?"

"Yes, I didn't take the money for myself. I took it for Luc and his family."

"But – why?" Wally shook his head in confusion.

"I discovered something about them, quite by chance, that made me realise they were in danger."

"Cassie – what are you talking about?" he demanded.

"The Labelles are Jewish," whispered Cassie.

Wally's mouth dropped open. "*What?* But that's impossible!"

"They don't come from Paris, and so they came here and re-invented themselves and never told anybody the truth. They've been hiding it."

"But he's put the bank into jeopardy, not admitting this." Wally was stunned.

"He would have been putting his family in far greater jeopardy by saying it," said Cassie.

Wally began to walk up and down, scratching his head, before he turned to her again. "But what has this got to do with you?"

"They had no papers, no identification – they destroyed them all because they identified them as Jewish. I took the hundred thousand francs to bribe an official to create fake papers and passports for them, saying they were Aryans."

"*You did what?*" he yelled at her.

"I had no choice, Wally! I had to! Can't you see?"

"Have you lost your mind? Do you know what you've done?"

"Yes, and I'm very proud of what I've done!"

"Proud of being a fool? Oh Cassie – when are you going to grow up and realise you aren't in Cliffenden anymore? I'm having nothing to do with this!"

"You don't have to, Wally! It's nothing to do with you – you can stay out of it and just pretend you know nothing."

"I'm afraid it's too late for that, Cassie. I have to report this immediately. It's only a matter of time before it comes out anyway and then we will be incriminated. My money buying fake papers for a Jewish employee! I can't even think of the consequences." He crossed over to the telephone.

"What are you doing, Wally?"

"I'm contacting the police to report what has happened," he said.

She looked at him in dismay and quickly rose up and followed him.

"Wally, you can't! You just can't! You will be condemning Luc and Simone and the children to being deported to a life of persecution or worse! They are from Alsace-Lorraine so they are not even considered French by the authorities anymore."

"That is not my problem," he said, picking up the receiver.

She grabbed his arms and looked at him pleadingly. "Wally! Think of me! I will be arrested too! For buying fake papers!"

"You should have thought of that before you got involved in all this. No doubt you'll talk your way out of it – you always do."

"Wally! You can't do this! I'm begging you! If you ever loved me at all, you will not do this!" she pleaded as she gripped both his arms tightly.

"Get out of my sight, Cassie – you disgust me," he said, pushing her away.

He spoke into the receiver. "Can you get me the police, please?"

Cassie stood behind him, shaking in fear as she realised he was going through with it. She thought of Luc and Simone's children.

"Oh, hello, yes," said Wally. "I want to report –"

Cassie lifted up the paperweight on the desk and slammed it into the back of Wally's head.

He stumbled for a second and then collapsed on the floor. Cassie looked at him as he stared up at her in shock.

She went to the telephone and quickly replaced the receiver.

She slowly knelt down beside him and looked at him. He was breathing and staring at her.

"Oh Wally!" she moaned as she lifted his head and cradled it in her lap. "I'm so sorry, Wally!" she whispered and she started to cry.

"Cassie . . ." he whispered.

Cassie sat on the bed, looking down at Wally's lifeless body. She wasn't sure how long she had been sitting there in a trance. She replayed over and over again in her head the minutes and moments that led to her killing him. She hadn't meant to. She had just tried to stop him from calling the police. From what would have been the instant exposure and destruction of the Labelle family.

PART EIGHT

England 1988

CHAPTER 57

The courtroom stayed in absolute silence as Cassie stopped talking.

Joe sighed very loudly as he digested Cassie's story.

"Why didn't you say all this before?" he asked gently.

"Because . . . because I shut it all away. And I didn't think there would be anybody to verify what I said. I don't know what happened to the Labelles. They never came forward to say what happened through the years. They kept their silence, and I thought they had their reasons. Considering the danger they were in during the war, very good reasons. And, besides, I am guilty. I am guilty. I killed him. I killed Wally. I didn't mean to. But I did it. And I've lived with it every second of my life. The guilt is crushing. And when I was finally arrested it was like a weight lifted from my shoulders. Finally . . . *finally* . . . I was facing the justice that I had slipped away from all those years ago."

"And do you now recognise that woman?" he asked, pointing to the same brunette he had indicated earlier.

Cassie looked at her. "I don't recognise her, no. She was just a little girl when I saw her last. But if she is the little girl in this photograph, Daphne Labelle, then yes, I do know her." She gripped the photo he had given to her.

Joe reached out and took the photo from her.

"My lord, this is a photo of Cassie Fullerton Stanton with Daphne Labelle as a child taken in the Labelle's apartment in 1941. I'd like to enter the photo as evidence. Also, we will be calling Daphne Labelle Monville as a witness for the defence to verify Mrs.

Stanton's story. I've finished questioning the witness, my lord."

Sidney stood up. "I have no questions at this time, my lord, but I reserve the right to cross-examine the witness. We need time to consider the new evidence."

Cassie stood in a back room in the court building. She heard the door open and Joe walked in.

"You promised me you wouldn't," she said, staring at him.

"I had no choice, Cassie. When Daphne Labelle came to meet me this morning and explained everything, I had no choice. I was going to put her on the witness box, and it was better for it to come from you first. How are you?"

She shrugged. "I've admitted my guilt. I've given them what they wanted. What they've been chasing for years."

Joe held her by the shoulders. "You admitted you killed Wally. But the circumstance are exceptional."

"It wasn't self-defence. I wasn't in any danger from him."

"But you did it to save four people's lives. And Daphne is saying that too. If it wasn't for you they would have been arrested and killed. You killed in the moment to save the Labelle family from exposure and being arrested. You had no choice!"

"I've always thought I knew best. I always thought, when I was a young woman, that I could manage all situations and manipulate people to get the outcome I wanted. I did it with Wally before I married him. I was tricking him into giving Cliffenden the money by pretending to marry him, and then I was going to run off with Bowden. Look how that backfired on me."

Joe dropped his hands from her shoulders as his own guilt came through about Bowden.

"When I was married to Wally I thought I could save the Labelle family by getting them false papers. And Wally ended up dead from it. I thought I could do anything, and all I did was ruin everything I ever touched."

"Cassie! That isn't true. What you did was courageous and selfless – even heroic. And the killing of Wally was an accident."

Cassie didn't reply.

"She's outside – Daphne," said Joe. "She wants to see you. Are you up to seeing her?"

Cassie bit her lower lip.

"She really wants to see you, Cassie. She owes you her life."

Cassie shook her head. "I can't see her, Joe. Not now, not yet. I used to be afraid of nothing, now I'm afraid of everything."

CHAPTER 58

Daphne was in the stand in court giving her version of the events in Paris.

"The papers that Cassie got for us saved us. After Wally had been murdered it was in all the newspapers how she had killed her husband and taken the hundred thousand francs beforehand. But we knew what the hundred thousand francs were for. Cassie used it to buy our fake papers. Of course my parents couldn't say anything because they would be exposing themselves. So they said nothing. We never knew what became of Cassie, or what happened to her after that night."

"After the war, after the liberation, why didn't your parents come forward and speak the truth and exonerate her?" questioned Joe.

"They were no longer here," said Daphne.

"What happened?"

"I remember, when Cassie brought us the papers, my parents were so thrilled to be safe at last. But Cassie suggested to my parents that now they had our papers, they should try to send me and my brother to Switzerland for safety. And that's what they did. They discovered through contacts that certain Swiss citizens were offering their services as foster parents for refugee children. With our fake papers we got visas to travel to Switzerland and my brother and I were put with foster parents there. My parents were considering applying for entry visas to Switzerland themselves, even though they were nervous of drawing any official attention to themselves."

"And is that what happened?"

"No. A few months later, somebody came into the bank that my father worked for. Somebody from where they originally came from: Alsace-Lorraine. He knew he was Jewish and he reported it to the authorities. They came and arrested my parents during the Drancy Round-up and they were never seen again."

"The papers didn't save them?"

"No, not when they were investigated and the truth was discovered. My brother and I remained in Switzerland for the rest of the war, and then left for Canada, Montreal, to live with an aunt there."

"For people not familiar with the Drancy Round-up, it was the arrest in 1942 of over 13,000 Jews in Paris – men, women and children. More than 4000 children were soon shipped east to Auschwitz where they were immediately murdered in the gas chambers. This would have been the fate of the Labelle children if they had not been sent to safety in Switzerland."

Daphne looked over at Cassie and said, "And it was Cassie's papers that got us to safety. She saved our lives."

Cassie sat transfixed, staring at Daphne, listening to her every word.

She suddenly stood up and uttered, "But it can't be – it just can't be! Simone and Luc were saved, they were saved because I got them fake papers."

"Mrs. Stanton, if you could regain your seat!" said the judge.

"No! No, I will not sit down. Where are Luc and Simone? Where are they?" demanded Cassie.

"I'm – I'm sorry, Cassie," said Daphne.

"They can't be gone! I saved them! It's the only thing that's got me through all these years!"

Joe went quickly over to Cassie. "Cassie, please sit down."

"No! I want to know what happened to Luc and Simone! What you're saying isn't true, Daphne! The papers were full proof they weren't Jewish. I got them from an official, all stamped and everything!"

"Mrs. Stanton, please sit down!" demanded the judge.

"Luc and Simone . . ." Cassie said again.

"Cassie . . ." whispered Joe. All he could do was stare at her in her despair, unable to reach out to her.

"I'm calling for a recess. Mr. Grady, I suggest you try and control your client!" said the judge.

Joe opened the door of the room and came in to find Cassie staring into space.

"Cassie –" he began.

"You shouldn't have done all this!" she said to him angrily. "You shouldn't have come back in to my life. You should have left me to another barrister who would have left me to my fate. You have taken everything away from me!"

"Cassie, everything was being taken from you anyway. I've given you a chance."

"You haven't! It was the only thing that kept me going, that the Labelles had been saved. It made everything else worthwhile. Even killing Wally, it was somehow excusable because of why I did it. Now they're dead, and what was it all for? I didn't save them. I just prolonged their suffering."

"But you saved their children. You heard Daphne say – they could never have left Paris for Switzerland if it wasn't for you."

"Just get out, Joe, leave me alone. You don't know what you've taken from me," she said and she turned furiously away from him.

Joe was summing up in front of the court. He looked at Cassie who was staring straight ahead, ignoring him.

He walked up and down the courtroom.

"Yes, Cassie Fullerton Stanton killed her husband. We've heard it from her own mouth in her own words. But we have now also heard everything else as well. These were exceptional circumstances and very dangerous times. She took Wally Stanton's life – unintentionally – to save four others, the Labelle family. We've heard that from Daphne Labelle. I must tell you that Cassie Fullerton did not tell me, her barrister, all this. The first I learned of it was from Daphne Labelle when she approached me. If Daphne hadn't come forward, then my client would never have spoken about this. She hasn't spoken about it in nearly fifty years. What else could she have done when Wally Stanton picked up that telephone to the Gestapo to expose the Labelle family as Jews? All she was doing was trying to stop that call being made to save that family. And if she hadn't? Well, we've already learned of Luc and Simone Labelles' fate. The same would have happened to their children, on that night, if Wally Stanton had not been stopped from making that call. Imagine Cassie Fullerton's situation at the time, when she realised she had killed her husband. She couldn't have told the truth to the authorities as she would have exposed the Labelles to their fate. So she went into hiding. And then the legend of Cassie Fullerton emerged, the decadent lifestyle, the lovers, the reckless aristocrat, the Nazi sympathiser. Before she knew it she had been tried by the media and the public as the wicked woman. And all the time we didn't know the truth behind the headlines. But now we do. Cassie Fullerton isn't a wicked woman. She's a heroine. She deserves our applause."

Joe sat down to a silent courtroom.

CHAPTER 59

"I have listened and studied the evidence brought before the court," said the judge. "Owing to the circumstances surrounding this crime, I am rejecting the extradition request for Cassandra Fullerton Stanton. Mrs. Stanton, you are free to go."

Cassie sat stock still, unable to grasp what the judge had said. It was only when there were people standing and applauding in the public gallery that reality began to hit her.

Joe was standing in front of her. He was smiling from ear to ear.

"Come on, Cassie, you're free to go. Let's go home," he said.

Joe quickly led Cassie through the press pack that were waiting outside the courthouse for them.

"Cassie, how does it feel to be free?" called one journalist.

"Cassie, how did you escape from Paris after you killed him?" roared another journalist.

"We've no comment to make, other than we are very pleased with today's result," said Joe as he ushered her into the back of the waiting car and it sped off.

"I don't understand," said Cassie. "They are not going to extradite me to stand trial?"

Joe took her hand and held it tightly.

"Everyone now knows why you did what you did, Cassie. The judge freed you. You're free. You don't have to hide or run anymore. You can go back to being Cassie Fullerton, with nothing to be ashamed of, and everything to be proud of."

Joe wasn't sure how to handle Cassie when they got back to the penthouse. She seemed in a state of shock. He wasn't sure if she was still angry with him for calling her to the stand or introducing Daphne Labelle's evidence into the court.

She sat down on the couch, turned to him and said, "Well, are those bottles of champagnes in your kitchen for display purposes only?"

"Sorry?"

"I think we have some celebrating to do, don't you?"

"Well, if you're in the mood for celebrating, then I think we should hit the town!"

"I don't think so," she demurred.

"Of course we should! I'll book us a restaurant."

"No, Joe, I really don't think I can face going out."

He came over and sat beside her. "You need to realise you are a free woman. You don't have to hide anymore."

"It's going to be hard to change the habits of a lifetime," she said.

"Well, you can try and start tonight by going out properly with me and celebrating your freedom in style. The Cassie Fullerton I used to know would be out every night, if the opportunity arose."

"But she doesn't exist anymore," said Cassie.

"I'm sure she does somewhere buried deep inside you!" he said and looked at her mockingly. "Perhaps Miss Cassie doesn't want to be seen out in the company of her former footman? It's not the company she should be keeping?"

"Don't be silly!" She managed to laugh.

"Excellent! That's settled then. I'll book the restaurant."

"Good evening, Mr. Grady, good evening, Ms Fullerton," said the doorman at Claridges as he opened the door for them.

"Good evening," Cassie nodded and smiled at him as they walked past. She winked at Joe. "I take it he recognises my photo from the newspapers and he doesn't remember me from my time when I used to come here all the time as a young girl."

"I think you might be right – he doesn't look as if he was even born when you were here last. Either that or he's Dorian Gray!"

As Cassie walked through the foyer she stopped and looked around.

She remembered constantly skipping through that foyer as a young girl when she was a socialite. It hadn't changed hardly at all – unlike her.

"I never thought I'd be here again," she said. "Never thought I'd be able to come here again. They were such good times I had here."

Joe just smiled at her and directed her to the restaurant. The head waiter greeted them and showed them to their table. Joe had requested a quiet corner table so they wouldn't be disturbed. It was just as well he had, as everyone was staring at Cassie she walked through and whispering to each other.

They sat down at the table and both ordered a steak dinner in wine sauce. The waiter opened a bottle of champagne and poured them each a glass.

"Now, isn't this a much better place to have that champagne than in my apartment?"

"Yes," she agreed. "If people could stop looking at me!"

"Come on, Cassie. People used to do that to you all the time when you were young. It should be like second nature to you."

"Back then, people used to look for the right reasons – now they are looking for the wrong ones!"

Joe viewed a woman warily as she got up from her table and made her way over to them.

"Yes, can I help you?" he asked coolly.

"I'm sorry to disturb you, but I wondered could I have Cassie's autograph?"

"Oh!" Cassie said, surprised, as the woman thrust a menu and a pen at her.

"Yes, I guess so." She scribbled her name across the menu.

"And if you could just date it as well, please. The day you were exonerated!"

"Of course," smiled Cassie and did as she was bid before handing back the signed menu.

"Can I just say, I think what you did was marvellous!" said the woman before going back to her table.

Cassie was astonished. "I think I'm going to find it hard to get used to praise," she said, "after all the dreadful things that were written about me over the years and during the trial."

"Now that everyone knows the truth, you should take the praise. You deserve it."

"The person who deserves the praise is you. For persevering even when I was totally uncooperative. I'd say I was the most difficult client you've ever had!"

"You would have some stiff competition there, but you would certainly be a contender!" he said and they both laughed. "Here's to you!"

They raised their champagne glasses and clinked.

"I still can't believe that I'm sitting in Claridges with Miss Cassie!" said Joe. "I would never have believed it in my wildest dreams when I was back at Cliffenden. Your world seemed so distant from mine. Even though we lived in the same house."

"The world has changed, Joe, and we've changed along with it," said Cassie.

"So what are your plans now?" asked Joe.

"I really hadn't thought! I thought I'd be in a prison for the rest of my life. I suppose I'll start thinking about that tomorrow."

"Well, just so you know, my office has been inundated with enquires about you all day."

"What kind of enquiries?" She looked alarmed.

"A lot of television shows and newspapers and magazines want to interview you," said Joe.

"Goodness me!"

"A couple of publishers want to approach you about your autobiography."

"Good heavens!"

"Also your cousin, The Earl of Weybridge, gave a statement to the press saying he was delighted with the outcome of the trial, you were a credit to the family and that you would be coming to stay with him for the foreseeable future!"

"Well, he's changed sides very quickly!"

"He also contacted my office and said he wouldn't take no for answer," said Joe.

"I don't know what to say about all this!" Cassie was shocked.

"Also Daphne Labelle really wants to see you and she would like you to come and stay with her in Canada. She says she considers you family."

Cassie eyes started to fill with tears and she quickly willed them away.

"I know I need and want to see her, but I'm going to have to prepare myself. I'm still getting over the shock of what happened to Luc and Simone."

"Of course." He nodded in sympathy and then he smiled and said, "So you have plenty of options to choose from."

"I'll have to think about all this. I haven't been Cassie Fullerton for a very long time. I've been Sarah King. I've now been Sarah King for twice as long as I was Cassie Fullerton. I think I might even be quite happy being Sarah King by this stage. I think I might be my happiest just going back to my little hotel in Morecambe Bay and running it quietly and anonymously as I have for the last forty-plus years."

"Well, that is your choice," he said, wondering how anonymous she could ever hope to be again.

After dinner Joe leaned forward to her. "And now I really need to ask you something and I really hope you'll tell me."

"What is it?"

"I'm burning with curiosity about the final piece of your story, the final piece of the jigsaw."

"Which is?" She raised an eyebrow curiously.

"How did you manage to escape from Paris that night after Wally was killed? How did you get by all the road blocks and Gestapo and travel bans and restrictions that were in France during the occupation when everyone was looking for you?"

"I might be jeopardising my book deal if I tell you," she teased.

"You can trust me – I'm your lawyer. Anything you tell me has to remain confidential!"

She took a sip of her champagne as the memories came flooding back to her.

PART NINE

France 1940s

CHAPTER 60

Cassie stared down at Wally's dead body lying out on their bedroom floor after she had killed him.

"I had no choice . . . I had no choice," she kept repeating to herself. "I had to save those children . . . oh, Wally, why couldn't you have listened to me?"

But she had committed murder, regardless of the circumstances.

She seemed to be locked in a private world with no sound as she continued to stare at Wally.

But suddenly noise began to re-merge. Cars driving by, laughter from a house nearby, somebody singing somewhere in the distance. The outside world began to come back into her sphere. And then she was overcome with terror. About what would happen to her. She would be arrested by the Nazis.

She would be stripped of all her rights. She would be killed.

Suddenly the doorbell rang, screaming through the silence of the house, jolting her into reality. She stood up and went to the door. She wasn't sure if Michelle had left, or if she was still in the house. Had she heard what had happened? Had she already telephoned for the police? Was that them at the door waiting to arrest her? She looked down at her blood-splattered dress, went to the wardrobe, grabbed a coat and put it on, buttoning it up the front.

She quickly left the room and walked down the stairs.

"Michelle?" she called loudly.

But there was no answer.

"*Michelle!*" she all but screamed.

411

But there was still no answer and Cassie realised she had probably left after she had said she was going and hadn't been in the house when the murder took place.

The doorbell rang again and again.

Whoever was there must have heard her calling Michelle. Not to open the door might arouse suspicion later.

Cassie crossed over to the door and opened it.

There stood Stefan Bayer.

She froze.

"Ah, Cassie, I was just about to leave," he said, smiling at her. "I thought there was nobody home."

She stared at him, not knowing what to say. She knew her fate would be sealed by the next thing she did and said.

"I'm sorry, I thought Michelle was still here and was answering the door . . . She's gone though . . . I was upstairs . . ."

"Ahh, I see," he said, smiling at her. "May I come in?"

She stared at him for a few moments as he hovered there.

She hesitated and then said, "Yes, of course."

She stepped out of his way and he walked into the hallway.

"Is Wally home?" he asked as he walked into the drawing room.

"Eh, no – he was, but he's left. He's gone away on business to – to –" She couldn't think.

"To Cherbourg?" he answered.

"Yes, to Cherbourg – how did you know?"

Stefan smiled at her. "I was in a meeting with him yesterday and he told me he was planning on going."

"Oh – I see," she said.

"He got off safely?"

"Yes – he won't be back for a couple of days."

As Cassie sat down on a couch she tried not to let him see the panic that she was feeling. She had to pretend everything was normal while she thought how to deal with this.

She looked at him curiously. "If you knew Wally wasn't here then why did you call?"

He smiled. "I thought you might be lonely, so I thought I'd look in on you."

"That's very thoughtful of you, but as you can see I'm fine."

He studied her. "Are you sure? You don't look alright. You're very pale."

"Do I?" she managed to give a little laugh. "I'm fine, Stefan."

"Are you cold?"

"No."

"Then why are you wearing your coat?"

"Oh, I – I just got in before you. I didn't have a chance to take my coat off."

He looked at her quizzically. "Oh, I see."

As she thought of Wally's dead body upstairs, she realised she needed to act more normally.

She stood up and said cheerily. "I'm just going to hang up my coat, Stefan, and freshen up. Help yourself to a drink." She gestured towards the drinks cabinet.

She walked out the room, up the stairs and into the bedroom, locking the door behind her. She stared down at Wally's body, not believing what had occurred. She threw off her coat, stripped off the dress she was wearing in the dressing room and hid it, then changed into another. Then she sat down on the bed, thinking. She had to get Stefan out of the house as quickly as possible and then she needed to get far away from here. If it was discovered what she had done she would be executed without even a fair trial. She needed to get away, but how could she?

As soon as Wally's body was discovered there would be road blocks all around Paris and through France searching for her. France was now a military zone and she would be discovered in no time.

She left the room, still thinking, and returned downstairs to Stefan.

"I poured you a drink," he said, handing her a glass of wine.

She realised her hands were shaking when she reached out for it. She took a large gulp.

"You look as if you needed that," he said.

He filled her glass again and sat down on the sofa beside her.

"I really wanted to apologise for my behaviour last time I was here," he said. "My poor excuse at a pass at you."

"That wasn't a poor excuse – that was a full-blown attempt," she said.

"Well, I apologise."

They sat in silence for a while.

"Stefan – I don't think I'm in the mood for company tonight. Would you mind terribly if I asked you to go?"

His expression turned to a mixture of disappointment and anger. "I see . . . I'd hoped to take you out tonight and show you the delights of Paris."

"I think you've shown me enough of the delights of Paris in my husband's absence, don't you?"

"A husband who doesn't make you happy and doesn't appreciate you. A husband who makes you unhappy. I just want to bring some happiness into your life."

She finished her glass of wine. "I think it's too late for that."

"It's not too late for anything. Anything is possible. When a farm boy like me has become an oberst and one of the most important men in Paris. When a farm boy like me is sitting here with a celebrated lady like you – holding her hand." He reached forward, took her hand and started to stroke it.

She stared at him, trying to comprehend everything that was happening.

"Just because I was unhappy in my marriage with Wally doesn't mean I'm going to jump into bed with you!"

"Was?"

"Sorry?"

"You said 'was' . . ?"

"Figure of speech."

His expression became serious. "Or was it?"

She felt her heart flutter with nerves. "What do you mean?"

"You marriage is over, Cassie – even you describe it in past tense. Come with me tonight, let me offer you Paris on a plate. Anything you want, I will make sure you have."

She sat thinking and then said, "But I've seen everything there is to see in Paris, Stefan – you can't show me anything I haven't seen already. Besides, I've been seen too much out with you in Paris already – people are talking, and there isn't even anything to talk about."

"Let them talk!"

"You, as a Nazi officer in Paris, do not have a reputation to maintain. I do."

"So then – we'll just stay here," he suggested as he put his arms around her.

"Under my husband's roof? I do have some scruples, Monsieur," she said.

He suddenly stood up, annoyed. "Alright, Cassie Fullerton, enough is enough! You obviously have no interest in me whatsoever. I have been wasting my time with you. I thought we had a connection – I was obviously wrong. I'll go now and leave you alone."

He began to walk towards the door.

"Wait!" she called after him.

He stopped, turned and looked at her.

She walked towards him and took his hand.

"Let's get out of here," she said.

He looked surprised. "Where to?"

"I can't be seen in Paris with you, not if we are to become – lovers."

He leaned forward and kissed her passionately.

"I knew it!" he whispered. "I knew you would be mine."

"Not here, not in Paris."

He looked at her, confused. "Where then?"

"Biarritz," she said.

"*Biarritz!*"

"Don't sound so surprised! You once invited me there, don't you remember? In fact, you promised to take me there sometime!"

"But – it's hours away."

"Well, Wally isn't back until Friday – we've plenty of time."

He looked into her blue eyes and then started laughing. "Very well – why not? If you want to go to Biarritz – then to Biarritz we shall go!"

She pulled away from him and gave him a flirtatious look. "How will we get there?"

"I'll arrange for a plane to take us." He went to the telephone, picked up the receiver and said, "I'll make the arrangements."

"I'll go pack my suitcase," she said.

Upstairs in her room she locked the door behind her and, leaning against it, started to breathe in a panicked fashion. She took deep breaths, trying to calm herself down. Then she rushed across to where Wally's body was on the ground and, grabbing him under the arms, with great difficulty pulled him into the bathroom, leaving him on the floor there. She locked the bathroom door and, opening the window, threw the key out into the garden.

Then she went to the wardrobe, grabbed a small suitcase and started to pack. She grabbed some clothes and put them in, then what jewellery Wally hadn't put away in the bank and all the money that was there. Then she turned, left the room and walked down the stairs. She saw Stefan waiting for her, smiling, at the bottom of the stairs.

"It's all arranged," he said, taking her suitcase.

They went outside and she locked the door. Then she smiled at him and took his arm as they walked down to the car.

Stefan's chauffeur stood to attention, then opened the back door of the car and they sat in.

As they went down the drive, Cassie looked back at the house one last time before turning and smiling at Stefan.

CHAPTER 61

The Germans had taken control of Beauvais Airport when they had taken over Paris and, as Stefan's car pulled up at the airport, Cassie saw it was now used mainly as a military airport. Before going there they had stopped off at Stefan's apartment on the Avenue Foch where he had packed a bag.

As they walked through the airport Cassie saw the Luftwaffe pilots as they were preparing for their night's work ahead. They would soon be flying from Beauvais across the Channel to bomb London and other cities in Britain.

"Is everything alright? You seem very nervous?" asked Stefan.

"Why wouldn't I be? It's not every day I run off with a Nazi officer to have an affair," she said.

He smiled at her. "You won't be disappointed, I promise you."

"Good evening, Oberst Bayer," said an officer.

"Is my plane ready?" asked Stefan.

"Of course – please follow me," he said.

They followed him out to the airstrip to a small passenger plane.

"Everything in order for tonight's raid?" asked Stefan.

"Certainly, sir – we are just checking everything before we begin the attack."

Cassie thought of all the people in London that these planes would soon rain down bombs on.

She could not get the image of Wally's dead body out of her head. If Stefan knew what she had done, he would not be escorting her to Biarritz for a weekend of fun, but to the nearest interrogation centre.

"Now, my darling Cassie, are you ready?" he asked as she stood transfixed, looking at the plane.

She quickly broke out of her trance and smiled at him. "Of course."

She walked up the steps to the plane and he followed her.

Inside, the small plane was furnished luxuriously.

The pilot came in with a female member of the Luftwaffe.

"Good evening, Captain, are we all set for a comfortable flight?" asked Stefan.

"Yes, Oberst, calm weather conditions – we should have a smooth flight," said the captain.

"Excellent – then our bombers should have an easy journey to Britain as well," said Stefan.

Cassie was tempted to ask him if he knew the consequences of what that "smooth flight" to Britain would be. But she knew she had to watch every word she said. If she put a foot wrong, he might become suspicious.

As the propellers of the plane began to rotate she fastened her seat belt and the plane started to journey down the runway and took off into the skies. She began to breathe a little easier as the plane flew over the Eiffel Tower and she watched Paris disappear into the distance from her window.

The female officer had come out of the cockpit, holding a bottle of champagne. She popped the champagne and filled the two glasses she had put on the table between Stefan and Cassie. She also set out pâté and caviar.

"You think of everything, Stefan," said Cassie as she lifted her glass and took a sip.

"Will there be anything else, Oberst?" asked the officer.

"No, you may leave us."

The officer returned to the cockpit and closed the door.

Stefan raised his glass and chinked it against Cassie's.

"I wish you a wonderful weekend," he toasted.

She smiled and leaned towards him. "So tell me, Stefan – how did a farm boy from Bavaria reach the heights of being one of the most important men in Paris, with private planes at his beck and call?"

"Well," said Stefan, "that is actually a very interesting story . . ."

Cassie glanced out the window and saw the twinkling lights of Biarritz glisten as the plane began to descend. The bottle of champagne had been drunk, nearly all by Stefan as Cassie had listened to every detail of his life, acting suitably impressed and amazed when the need arose.

"Are you enjoying yourself, Cassie?" asked Stefan.

"Stefan, I can honestly say, I have never been seduced in such circumstances ever before."

The car pulled up outside the Hôtel du Palais in Biarritz and the driver got out and, opening the door for Stefan and Cassie, saluted.

As Cassie looked up at the majestic building, her mind was still whirling with stress but her face looked calm as if she were enjoying herself. She remembered the many games of charades she had played at Cliffenden – did she ever think she would be playing such a real-life game of charades?

A hotel porter came hurrying to take their luggage.

They entered the hotel foyer.

"Welcome, Oberst Bayer, a pleasure to have you stay with us," greeted the hotel manager.

"Is my suite ready?" asked Stefan.

"Waiting for you," said the manager. "If you could follow me?"

As Cassie stepped into the lift, she thought it odd that she hadn't been addressed once. But then she realised that to the staff she was quite invisible. To them she was just another woman who was a German officer's entertainment for the weekend. She felt they probably hated her, thinking she was a collaborator, a whore. Under normal circumstances she would have been furious, outraged. But now she was just grateful that she was invisible to them. She needed to be invisible after what she had done.

Stefan put his arm around her waist as they left the lift and the hotel manager showed them into a suite.

Champagne, fruit and chocolates awaited them.

"Will, there be anything else, Oberst?" asked the manager.

"No, you may leave us." Stefan waved a hand in the air and the manager exited, closing the door behind him.

Cassie looked around the grand suite. She went over to the French windows, opened them and walked out onto the balcony looking out at the sea and Biarritz under the stars. Down in the streets below, she saw many German soldiers who rather than patrolling looked to be drunk and enjoying themselves. She knew Biarritz was another vacation destination for the soldiers before they were sent off to the front. From what she could see many were in the company of French women, laughing and joking. Stefan came out onto the balcony and stood behind her. He put his arms around her and kissed her neck.

"I can't believe we're here," he whispered. "Alone at last."

She turned around and kissed him before gently pushing him away and walking back into the room. She took her suitcase and handbag and went into the dressing room with them.

He followed her in, took her hand and drew her back out into the main room.

"Leave that," he said and kissed her again. Then he lifted the champagne bottle from the ice bucket.

"Wait," she urged, taking the bottle off him and putting it back.

"What's the matter?"

"I didn't want to come to Biarritz just to stay in a hotel room with you the whole time. I came to Biarritz so I could enjoy it with you. I don't know what the other women are like that you take away on trips, but I'd like to be wined and dined a little beforehand."

"I'll order room service," he said, going to pick up the telephone.

"No, Stefan. We are going out to see Biarritz – the champagne can wait till later."

He smiled at her. "Whatever you want."

"I'll just fetch my handbag from the dressing room," she smiled.

Walking through the streets of Biarritz that night, Cassie was mesmerised by the place which seemed to be as busy as any holiday destination she had ever been in.

Stefan had already drunk the most part of a bottle of champagne on the flight there, and she aimed to make sure his inebriation went further. She led him from bar to restaurant drinking wine, all the time appearing to be fascinated with the details of his life, all the time making sure she kept her large handbag held tightly.

"And when you reached Berlin, what happened then?" she asked, gazing at him adoringly across a table at a restaurant, and she filled his wineglass again.

"Well, I was asked to meet the Führer. I was understandably very nervous to meet the man himself."

"I can imagine! Is he as charismatic in real life as they say?"

"Yes, I believe he is." Stefan nodded in admiration.

She felt like throwing the glass of wine into his face but just smiled.

Stefan enjoyed being seen with Cassie. As they walked through the streets of Biarritz and into the hotels and restaurants, he noticed the admiring looks she was getting. This wasn't the usual kind of woman the Germans were going out with in France. He knew he had reached the top.

She held his arm tightly as they approached the famous casino.

"Oh, Stefan, let's go into the casino – I adore casinos!" said Cassie.

"Yes, I quite like them myself," said Stefan.

There was a German officer standing on duty at the entrance of the hotel.

"Good evening, Oberst Bayer," said the officer, recognising Bayer straight away.

"Good evening," nodded Stefan as he led Cassie through the main doors.

She checked her coat in and then, clutching her handbag close with one arm, slipped the other through Stefan's.

"Lead on!" she said, smiling, and he grinned back at her.

They walked between the playing tables and roulette tables, watching the games being played.

"Are you interested in joining a game of baccarat, sir?" asked a croupier. "There's room for one more."

Stafan shook his head and waved his hand.

"Oh, Stefan, do!" pleaded Cassie. "I'd love to see you play. I'm sure you're an excellent card player."

"Maybe a quick game then," said Stefan as he sat in the empty chair and took out his wallet.

Cassie stood behind him, smiling, as she draped her arm across his shoulders and ordered him a double whiskey.

As the game wore on, Stefan was losing heavily and was not in a good mood.

"Your luck will change, I just know it," Cassie whispered into his ear and ordered another double whiskey from the waiter.

She knew Stefan was a man who hated to lose and, as she watched the intensity in his eyes as he concentrated on the game, she discreetly took her hand from his shoulder and backed away from the table. She kept slowly backing into the crowd who were milling around and then turned and calmly walked through the building to the foyer. There she checked her coat out and slipped it on.

The officer who had greeted them was still at the door and smiled at her. "Leaving so soon, Madame?"

"Eh, yes," she smiled.

"The Oberst is not leaving with you?"

"No, he's engrossed in a game of baccarat." She turned her charm on him. "To be honest, gambling always bores me, so I'm heading back to the hotel."

"Have a nice night, Madame," he smiled.

"Thank you," Cassie said.

She walked down the steps and across the street where she got into the first taxi.

The taxi driver looked in the mirror and was surprised to see a woman sitting there. All his customers were German soldiers.

"Can you take me to Hendeye?" she said.

He nodded, started the car and began to drive slowly down the street which was full of people strolling along.

"If you can go as quickly as you can, please," she said anxiously as she obscured her face from the passing crowds.

"Alright, alright!" he said as he slowly manoeuvred the car through the crowd.

"How far is it?"

"Eleven kilometres. It won't take too long once I hit the open road," he said.

She opened her bag, took out her cigarette case and anxiously lit a cigarette.

At last they were driving along country roads. Cassie became increasingly nervous. Apart from her fears that she might be pursued, her handbag contained a large amount of money and jewellery. She hoped that would not arouse suspicion if the police checked her bag. If it did, should she attempt to bribe them or would that be too dangerous?

"You had better have all your paperwork in place, if you aim to pass over the border," said the driver.

She said nothing but dragged on her cigarette.

"When the Germans invaded, the border was teeming with people trying to get to the other side," he said. "Most weren't accepted . . . they were turned back."

"Just hurry, please," she said as she looked nervously behind to see if there were any cars following them. But the road was deserted.

It seemed like an eternity until they reached Hendeye and drove up to the border control.

"Thank you," said Cassie as she paid the driver.

She got out of the car.

"Good luck, Madame!" he called after her.

Stefan angrily got up from the baccarat table, having lost another hand, and looked around for Cassie. As he walked quickly around the tables, he could see no sign of her. After a good while he became concerned and walked to the front entrance where the officer who had greeted them was still present.

"Officer, the woman I came in with, have you seen her?" asked Stefan.

"Yes, Oberst, she left some time ago."

Stefan looked at him, shocked. "Where did she go to, do you know?"

"She said she was going back to the hotel, as she didn't like gambling."

"But it was she who encouraged me to play!" Stefan was angry. "Call me a taxi!"

"Certainly, sir," said the officer as he ran out on to the pavement and whistled.

A taxi driving down the street pulled over.

The officer opened the back door for Stefan to get in.

"Hotel du Palais," ordered Stefan.

As the taxi drove through the streets, the taxi driver glanced in his mirror and saw Stefan was a high-ranking officer.

"Are you enjoying your stay in Biarritz, Monsieur?" asked the taxi driver.

"I hope to," said Stefan, looking out the window.

"Some gambling in the casino?" said the taxi driver.

Stefan nodded.

"Did you win, Monsieur?"

"No." Stefan's mind was racing as to why Cassie left without telling him she was going back to the hotel. Why would she have done such a thing? Why not tell him she was leaving and he could leave too? What was she up to?

"Ah, forget about gambling, Monsieur! There are some wonderful nightclubs in this city. That's the way to relax! You're sure to meet a beautiful woman there who will keep you company. There are many beautiful women in Biarritz. Not just French but foreigners too . . . I just gave a lift to a very beautiful woman. She seemed English, but she can't be – if she was she would have left France by now . . . perhaps she's American. Too bad she was leaving town."

"Where was she going?" asked Stefan urgently.

"Hendeye, across the border," said the taxi driver.

As Cassie approached the border crossing she could see it was a bridge. On the French side was a large barrier across the road and a building to the right. There were French police and German soldiers patrolling. There were also a number of people who seemed to be just waiting there. She wondered if they were waiting for people to cross over from Spain or had been refused entry to the other side.

She walked as confidently as possible and ignored the looks of the soldiers and police as she walked past them. She went into the small building. There was a queue of people there and she joined them. Some of them seemed to be locals who were just passing back and forth over the border.

Eventually she was nearly at the top of the queue. There was a man in front of her with two small children. The little girl smiled at her and Cassie smiled back. She reminded her of the Labelle daughter. As she thought of the Labelles safe in Paris, she reminded herself of why she was here, why she had gone through all this.

The policeman was examining the man's papers and passport.

"You have no visa," said the official to the man. "Access denied."

"But – but my wife is waiting for us just across the border," said the man.

"That is not my concern. You cannot leave the country without the necessary papers," said the official abruptly.

"But we can't go back. We have no home anymore – we have to get to the other side."

"Access denied," snapped the official.

"You have our passports, is that not enough?" pleaded the man.

"You don't have permission to enter Spain! No visa – no entry! Now step aside for the next person!" insisted the official.

As the man led his two frightened children back out of the building, Cassie wondered what had brought them there. What their story was.

She stepped up confidently to the official.

"Hello!" she said, smiling at him.

He looked at her coldly. "Papers."

She riffled through her handbag and handed over her passport. She hoped her nervousness didn't show.

"Irish?" he said.

"That's right. I'm travelling home to Ireland through Spain and Portugal," she said.

"Transit visa?" said the man.

She handed him over the visas she had received from Duchamps when she was pretending that was her business with him.

The official studied the visas and then looked up at her.

She smiled at him. "Very long way round to get home unfortunately! And I have to book a passage on a ship – I hope it doesn't get torpedoed or something!"

He studied her. "Where is your luggage?"

Cassie hadn't anticipated that question.

"My husband went ahead of me – he has our luggage – he's waiting the other side of the border for me," she said with a smile, praying the official wouldn't ask for further details.

"Access granted! Have a safe onward trip," he said, handing her back her papers and passport before calling "Next!"

Her heart pounding, she walked on past the official and out through a door where a policeman and two armed German soldiers stood guard.

She smiled at them and walked past them through another door that allowed her onto the bridge. The bridge seemed to go on forever in front of her, and yet she knew it wasn't that far. She fought the desire to run to the other side. Instead she walked calmly across. As she walked she thought of Cliffenden. Of the comfort of home and her family. She would be there soon. As she approached the end of the bridge, there were Spanish officials there. Seeing her come, they raised the barricade and she walked towards it.

"*Cassie!*"

The shout came from behind her. She recognised Stefan's voice and didn't look back. She kept on walking.

"*Halt!*" shouted another voice from behind her.

She was within reach of the barricade and she kept going, increasing her pace. She quickly walked under the barricade and into Spain. The Spanish officials there looked at her passport, quickly stamped her visa and then urged her on. It was only then that she turned around and saw Stefan standing on the other side of the bridge at the barrier for the French border. He was standing beside a soldier who had trained his gun on her.

She stood and stared at Stefan and then raised her hand and waved sadly at him.

He raised his hand and waved back.

Cassie then turned and quickly walked away from the border.

CHAPTER 62

Stefan sat at his office at Gestapo Headquarters in Paris, thinking about Cassie. What on earth had happened? What was she playing at? They went to Biarritz to consummate their relationship and have a good time and then she had just disappeared off into the night, without a word of explanation. And crossed over the border to Spain. He couldn't get the vision of her walking across the bridge at Hendeye out of his mind. What about Wally? Did he know she had gone to Spain? His mind was mired in confusion.

One of his officers knocked on the door and entered.

Stefan spun around on swivel-chair and looked at him. "Yes?"

"The latest round-up of Jews this morning went without any obstruction," said the officer.

Stefan nodded. "Anything else?"

"There's been a murder in Neuilly. The American banker Wally Stanton had been found in his house."

Stefan sat abruptly up. "What? Wally is dead?"

"Yes, the maid discovered the body in the house this morning. The wife has gone missing. She wasn't in the house and they found a dress of hers splattered with his blood. Stanton's body had been pulled into the bathroom and locked there."

Stefan stared at the officer in shock.

"The police have launched a massive manhunt for her. Nobody knows where she is, but she won't get far. The whole of Paris is looking for her. I'll keep you informed of developments.

The officer saluted and then left the office.

Stefan sat back in his chair, trying to comprehend the details. And suddenly everything made sense to him. Her strange behaviour and then her suggestion to go to Biarritz. She had killed Wally and had planned her escape. She had used him in order to get away. He had provided her with an escape route. He had given her a top-level and quick escort to the border and out of their jurisdiction. He realised he could never tell anybody what had happened. He would be guilty of escorting a murderess to safety under the Reich's nose. He shuddered as he thought of what the consequences for him would be.

Cassie Fullerton had outsmarted him.

CHAPTER 63

Cassie sat at a table outside a restaurant in Lisbon under the sun. She looked across the giant square that was beside the sea as thoughts of the last few weeks went through her mind. Wally was dead and she had escaped. She knew what she had done, but when she thought of the Labelles she realised she'd had no option. The Labelles would have faced death if she hadn't acted the way she had. Not that that lessened her feelings of guilt. She would get home. She would deal with it all when she got home to Cliffenden. She would deal with everything then in the safety of her home with her family. It had taken a while to travel across Spain to get to Lisbon and she had been resting for the past few days but that day she would see about booking a passage on a ship for Britain or Ireland, whichever was leaving first.

She could hear a British couple talking at a neighbouring table. Apparently they had just arrived in Lisbon from England and she wondered what had brought them there. They paid their bill and left. She noticed they had left a newspaper on their table and, seeing it was a copy of *The Times*, she went and got it and sat back in her chair to read what was going on at home. It had been so long since she had read an English newspaper. She saw the newspaper was several days old and guessed they must have brought it from London with them. She looked at the front page which was all about the war, the blitz on London, rationing, fighting in North Africa. She looked through the pages and saw it was nearly entirely taken up with the war.

She stopped suddenly when she saw a photograph of herself on an inside page under the headline **Police in Paris Seek Wife in Murder of American Banker.**

She quickly read on.

Police in Paris were last night searching for the wife of American banker, Wally Stanton, who was found bludgeoned to death in their home in Neuilly. Stanton's wife, socialite Cassie Stanton, is believed to have fled the scene after murdering her husband and hiding the body in the couple's bathroom. The body was discovered by the couple's maid the next day.

Cassie Fullerton Stanton, an Irish aristocrat, is a well-known figure on the London social scene, as well as being a niece of the Earl of Weybridge. The Fullerton family at their magnificent stately home of Cliffenden in the South of Ireland have refused to comment.

The American Embassy in France has put pressure on the occupation administration and the government in Vichy to apprehend the suspect at the earliest opportunity. American authorities have also contacted the British and Irish governments to look out for the suspect should she try to re-enter Britain or Ireland and to issue an immediate arrest warrant for her. The suspect faces the death penalty for the murder, which police say was committed in cold blood . . .

Cassie quickly folded the newspaper and put it under her arm. She stared out at the square in panic. She looked around and saw nobody was looking at her as they chatted away in this oasis away from the war. She reached for her sunglasses and put them on. Paying the bill, she rose and walked away from the restaurant, clutching the handbag that she had brought from Paris which still contained what money and jewels she had taken from the house. As she walked across the square, she realised she could not go home. She knew now there was no escaping what she had done.

She would never be able to return home and see her family or Cliffenden again. She would have to live her life on the run. She quickly walked away from the square and into one of the streets that led away from it which was thronged with people. As she walked down the streets, she disappeared into the crowd.

PART TEN

England 1988

CHAPTER 64

Joe sat listening in amazement as Cassie concluded her story in the restaurant at Claridges. By then the restaurant had emptied out and they were the last ones remaining.

"So you got escorted out of Paris to the border by a top official under their noses," he said.

"Yes. By the time Wally's murder was discovered the next day, I was safely in Spain. I had at the time fully intended to go back to Ireland. But then when I saw that the authorities in Britain and Ireland were looking for me . . . I couldn't explain to them what had happened because I would have been putting the Labelles in danger. The case was too high-profile, I realised. So I left Lisbon and stayed for the rest of the war in a little town by the sea in Portugal, living very simply. I used to go into Lisbon and pick up the newspapers left by British and Americans passing through – and then one day I read in the obituaries that Teddy had been killed. Everything changed for me then. I was so lost. I didn't think there was any reason to come and explain things anyway. I could never have gone back to Cliffenden – too many memories of Teddy."

"And what of your parents? Lady Dorothy and Howard?"

"I felt I had already brought enough disgrace on them. Could you imagine if they had to witness a trial? And back then I would have been hanged. As bad as everything was for them with Teddy gone and me a wanted woman, they could have never have survived that. I did send them a letter once, just letting them know I was alright and had started a new life."

435

"I see," sighed Joe. "And how did you get back to England?"

"After the war finished Europe was teeming with millions of refugees being displaced. It was easy to get lost in the crowd as I travelled back to England. It was easy for me to creep back in. I called myself Sarah King and made my way to that little sleepy village in the far north of England and said all my papers had been lost in the war and applied for a new national insurance number. I had one item of jewellery left and sold it and bought a rundown hotel. And that's where I lived, year in, year out. After a while I think I even stopped thinking I was Cassie Fullerton. It was far easier just being Sarah King, running a quiet but respectable boarding establishment with a sea view."

It was night-time and Cassie was due to leave Joe's penthouse the next day. As they sat in the living room he felt sad that she wouldn't be there anymore. But now she needed to get on with her life and he had done as much as he could do for her.

"I'll never be able to thank you enough for all you did for me," said Cassie as she sat on the sofa across from him.

"I was only too delighted to help," said Joe. Then he grinned at her, raising an eyebrow. "So the Earl of Weybridge had a change of heart?"

Cassie laughed. "He certainly did! He absolutely insists I stay with him for a while. I know he lambasted me to the press, but he didn't know the facts. I guess it's a case of forgive and forget. We were quite close when we were young. I've been without family for so long, I'd love to see him again."

"Good, I'm glad. I remember him when he was a young earl staying at Cliffenden – he was always very charming," he said.

"He probably thinks me staying at his stately house will be good for the tourist-attraction value as well, but that is probably just the cynic in me!" she said with a laugh. "And then I probably will go home to Morecambe Bay and think about everything. What about you, Joe?"

"What about me?" he asked, surprised.

"What are you going to do now?"

"Me? There's nothing for me to do. Just get on with my life as normal."

"Don't you think you should take some time out from your 'normal life'?"

"I don't know what you mean."

"Joe, it seems to me that your family is falling apart. I was talking to your son George the night you went out walking for hours, and don't you think it's high time you put your own house in order instead of rushing around settling everybody else's?"

"There's nothing wrong with my family, Cassie," said Joe, offended.

"I'm not saying there is. You have a wonderful son, and I'm sure a wonderful daughter, and from what I see of her a beautiful and very spirited wife."

"I know all that," said Joe.

"But do you? Do you really? Because I think they have drifted away from you and you're about to lose them for good, Joe."

"I can't do anything more than I've done for them," he said.

She arched an eyebrow cynically. "Can't you really? You need to get to know them, Joe. They've grown up, they've changed and you haven't been part of that. It's not too late – you can still change that."

"I don't know how to change anything."

"One small step at a time, Joe."

"I – I can't be something I'm not! I can't suddenly become all touchy-feely."

"They don't want you to be something you're not. They just want you. And Ann needs you, Joe."

"Ann doesn't need me, or anyone. She's perfectly contented with her life, believe me."

"She didn't look like that to me."

"You only met her briefly and you don't know anything about her!"

"You've given me a lot of advice, Joe. Now I'm trying to give you some. Will you listen to me?"

"I think it's too late for us anyway. We were always a mismatch."

"Opposites attract!"

"We're too opposite." Joe didn't speak for a while, then said, "My wife is seeing somebody else, Cassie."

"Oh, I see," said Cassie, frowning. "Is it serious?"

"I don't know anything about it."

"So you will divorce?"

"No, I don't think so. She hasn't mentioned that."

"But do you want a divorce from her?"

"No, of course not!"

"Then you need to do something about it, Joe. You need to fight for her and your family. I've seen you in action – nobody can fight like you – start fighting for them before it's too late. You don't want to end up like me, on your own. I'd give anything to have what you have. But life took me in a completely different direction."

Joe nodded and was lost in thought.

"I remember, when I started working at Cliffenden, Teddy called me one of your waifs and strays."

"Did he?"

"Yes, Mr. Bruton and your mother didn't want to keep me at all. They wanted a trained footman from Dublin, but you insisted that I stay on in Cliffenden. And Teddy said you were always picking up waifs and strays. He was right. The Labelles were more waifs and strays you came to rescue. Perhaps Bowden Grey was too?"

"Bowden?" she repeated his name.

"Do you ever think of Bowden Grey?" he asked.

"Bowden . . . that's a name I haven't heard in a very long time."

"But do you? Do you think of him?"

"Of course I do. How could I not? He was the love of my life. I often think of what could have been with him. But he had other ideas. I thought we were so close, we had telepathy. But we didn't. When he ran out on me that time, I thought I'd never recover. To just run out without a word or an explanation, that wasn't my Bowden. So I obviously never really knew him. I never really got over his desertion. I simply could not believe it."

Joe stared at her while his body filled with nerves. He couldn't ever remember being so nervous. He got up and walked out of the room.

She watched him curiously, wondering what he was doing. He came back a few minutes later and sat back on the couch opposite her. He was holding an envelope and she could see that his hands were shaking.

"I think you had better read this," he said and held out the envelope to her.

She looked down at the envelope and reached out and took it. She saw it was a very old envelope with just '*Cassie*' written across the front.

"What is this?" she asked.

"Just read it, please," he said.

She opened the envelope and unfolded the letter inside and began to read.

He watched her face as she read, watched as it became shadowed with confusion. She continued to stare at the letter.

She held the letter out to him. "What's this?"

"It's a letter from Bowden."

"I can see that . . . but I don't understand . . ."

"Bowden gave it to me to give to you the weekend he left. The weekend of your engagement party to Wally."

She gazed at the letter and read it again.

"But I never saw this letter before," she said.

"I know – I didn't give it to you."

"But why didn't you give it to me?" She was desperately trying to understand.

His eyes filled with tears. "Because I didn't want you to read it."

Her fine features creased in confusion, waiting for an explanation.

"I didn't give it to you, because I didn't want you to go with him. I didn't want you to elope with him."

"But *why*?"

"Because I didn't think you knew what you were doing. I thought you could never adapt to a life with him where there was no money and comfort and security."

"But – but that wasn't your decision!"

"I know . . . it wasn't the only reason. Wally had taken me aside and said that if you married him that he would take me to live in his house and I'd become your butler."

"What?"

"I did it out of selfish reasons as much as any. I thought it would be a good opportunity for me and that you would have a life of luxury with Wally. I didn't know what would happen. I didn't know that Wally was tricking me and had no intention of making me his butler. I didn't know just how unhappy you would be with Wally and what that would lead to."

Cassie stared down at the letter. "But, all this time, I didn't know why Bowden did what he did. Why he had abandoned me. He hadn't abandoned me – he thought I had abandoned him . . ."

"I've no excuse, Cassie. If I could turn back time . . . but I can't. And I didn't just destroy your relationship with Bowden, I destroyed your life."

Cassie stared up at him and saw he was rubbing tears from his eyes with the palms of his hands.

"But you destroyed your own life too, living with this all these years," she said.

"I thought I knew best," he said. "But I knew nothing. And I betrayed you and Bowden. I betrayed the trust you had put in me. Your happiness depended on me acting as your messenger, and I deliberately betrayed that. I was stupid."

"We were the stupid ones, putting the responsibility of our future happiness on such young and inexperienced shoulders," she whispered as she stared down at the letter.

"I'm so sorry, Cassie."

"It could have been all so different. We could have been happy. He didn't abandon me, he loved me . . ."

She stood up, still holding the letter and walked over to the wall of windows. She looked out at the London skyline under the night sky.

He watched her in silence.

She put her hand to her mouth and closed her eyes as the tears began to silently fall down her face. Suddenly she was crying and then sobbing as she bent over and crumpled Bowden's letter in her hands.

"Cassie!" he said, jumping up and rushing over to her.

And he saw all the pain stored up for decades written across her face. She reached out for him with a hand on his shoulder and then fell into his arms as her tears flowed freely.

CHAPTER 65

Joe sat on the train, looking out at the countryside that was basking in autumn sunshine. It had been a couple of weeks since Cassie had left his apartment and he hadn't heard anything from her since. He hadn't expected to. He never expected to hear anything from her again. And it wasn't just because of the revelation of how he had hidden Bowden's letter. He felt that it was just Cassie. She just slipped away and didn't look back. It was her nature and it had been her life. The night he had revealed the existence of Bowden's letter, she didn't say any more about it. She had just continued to cry for what seemed like an eternity. Joe reckoned she had been storing all that emotion up for so many years, and when she finally let go it didn't easily stop. He wasn't sure if he would have felt better if she had got angry and furious at him and blamed him for ruining her life. It might have been hard to listen to, but it might have lifted his guilt. But she hadn't. She didn't seem to blame him at all; she seemed to blame herself for creating the situation in the first place. Maybe life had taught her not to blame individuals that happened to be caught up in situations outside their control.

The next day, he had seen her to the train station. They had said a quick goodbye.

"Thank you for everything," she had said. "You'll never know how much I appreciate everything you did for me."

The way she had said it nearly made him think she was thanking him for his friendship to her when he worked as a footman, and not just as a barrister.

"Your train is about to leave," he had said to her. "You'll miss it."

"Oh, I'd better rush!" she had said and made a face. "From what I remember of the Earl of Weybridge, he hated being kept waiting." She had leaned forward and kissed him on the cheek. "Goodbye, Joe."

Then she had rushed over to the train, carrying her suitcase. She stepped up and into the train, then turned around and gave him a fleeting smile and a wave. And then she was gone.

Now two weeks later he was making his own train journey.

The taxi pulled up outside his home in Cambridge. He paid the taxi driver and climbed up the steps, letting himself in. He could hear music coming from out the back and, still carrying his suitcase, made his way down the hall carefully. He wasn't sure what he would be interrupting. He stopped at the patio windows and saw Ann on her own, sitting out sunbathing in what was turning out to be an Indian summer. He was relieved to see she was on her own. He walked through and put his suitcase down on the patio.

"Joe!" she said, seeing him. "I wasn't expecting you! You didn't say you were coming!"

"I didn't realise I needed an invitation to come home?"

"A bit of notice would have been nice!"

"Or *did* I need to give notice to come home?"

She looked down at his suitcase. "What are you doing here?"

"I've taken some time off," he said.

She looked at him blankly. "I see you won your case."

"Yes, a favourable result."

"I'm sure Cassie Fullerton is delighted?"

"Not quite as delighted as you might expect. But at least it's all behind her now."

"Hmmm, is she still at the penthouse?"

"No, of course not. She's gone to stay with her cousin."

"I see. Let's hope she doesn't end up killing him!"

"Ann!"

"Just saying!" She viewed him suspiciously. "So why are you here, Joe?"

"I wanted to see you."

"That makes a change. Well, you've caught me at a bad time. I'm packed with social occasions this week. I've got the golf club dance on tonight."

"I see," he said, looking disappointed.

She noticed his disappointment. "You – you could always come with me? But I know how you hate those dos."

"No, I'd like to go. It would be nice to go and see everyone again."

"You'll only be complaining ten minutes in the door," she warned.

"No, I won't, I promise."

She looked down at his suitcase and then at him. "I suppose I could always give it a miss tonight."

"Whatever you want, I'm happy with."

She looked at him, perplexed. "Could the real Joe Grady please come forth?"

He started laughing. "I am the real Joe Grady! Did you not know that I have a hidden very flexible side to me."

"Well, no, I didn't! It's so well hidden that I've never seen it!"

"Maybe you were looking in the wrong places," he said.

"Maybe I wasn't looking at all," she said. "Well, you had better unpack that suitcase. I hate creased clothes."

"You know – so do I. That is one thing at least we have in common."

She raised her eyes to heaven as she got to her feet.

"Come on," she said and led him inside.

EPILOGUE

Ireland 1988

CHAPTER 66

In the weeks that followed Joe was busy with his daughter Pamela's wedding. Luckily Ann took the whole event in charge and all he had to do was be present as the decisions were being made and agree to them. As he had suspected, he never heard from Cassie after the trial. He hoped she would be alright. In a way she had rescued him just as much as he had rescued her. Ann had been right when she had said Cassie could be a catalyst to their marriage. She had been, but in a positive way. Cassie had made him see what was worth fighting for and he had rescued his relationship with his family just in the nick of time. He remembered Cassie's words to him, wishing she'd had what he had. And his thoughts drifted to Bowden. What had become of him? What kind of life did he have? Had Bowden gone on to find happiness or had Joe's action so many years ago set him on a course for destruction as it had Cassie. He needed to find out.

And so he began to try and trace him. As Bowden was such an uncommon name he thought it would be easy to trace. He decided the easiest way would be through telephone directories. Bowden had apparently left for America and so Joe checked phone directories in the major cities there, but could find no listing. He then turned to the UK directories but could find no Bowden Grey. Getting more desperate, he decided to try Irish phone directories and to his surprise found Bowden Grey listed as living in Dunmore in Ireland. He recognised the address as being Bowden's family home.

Joe was amazed and figured that, after some years adventuring, Bowden must have returned home, either to mind his parents when they were getting older or take over the farm once they passed away. He wondered whether he had ever married. Perhaps he had come back to wait for Cassie, living his life in the hope she would one day come back to Cliffenden.

Joe turned the car into the gateways of Cliffenden and began to drive up the long avenue. Ann sat in the seat beside him and George was in the back seat. It was a week after their daughter had been married.

"Imagine that Pamela and Tom are enjoying the sunshine in the Seychelles, while we have come here!" said Ann as she looked out at the snow-covered ground. "We could have gone to the Seychelles as well."

"And joined them on their honeymoon?" Joe was incredulous.

"Well, somewhere else equally hot then. I could do with a sun break after all the fuss of the wedding," said Ann.

"Mum, you know we've come here for a reason," said George. "To see where Dad is from – it's like a pilgrimage."

"Well, I wish we came on the pilgrimage in the summer – at least it would be warmer," said Ann.

The stately house came into view and Joe slowed down the car as he stared at the building. It was the exact same as when he had worked there in the 1930s, even though it had now been converted into a hotel.

"It's the exact same," said Joe.

"And your father isn't actually from Cliffenden, George – he's from a cottage down in the village – he merely worked here for a few years."

"I know all that," said George who was staring at the building, intrigued, as Joe pulled up outside it.

Joe stepped out of the car and stared up at the building as all his memories of the place came flooding back.

"Pretty impressive," said George as he stood beside him.

A porter came out of the front door and over to the car.

"Welcome to the Cliffenden House Hotel," he said. "May I take your luggage?"

George went and took his parents' luggage out of the back of the car and gave it to him, while retaining his own bags, while Joe stood transfixed by the building.

"Will we go and book in? It's too freezing cold to be standing around here," said Ann.

"Of course," said Joe and they followed George and the porter inside. Ann slipped her arm through Joe's as they walked up the steps and inside the building.

The old hallway of Cliffenden had now been turned into the hotel foyer, but Joe stared in disbelief as hardly anything had been changed since the days of the Fullertons. There was a reception now built in under the stairs, but everything else seemed the same. The same interiors had been maintained. The same paintings on the walls. As Ann and George booked in at Reception, Joe wandered over to what had been the drawing room and went inside.

The drawing room was now the hotel bar. Elegant tables and chairs were now placed throughout the room, some occupied with hotel guests enjoying a drink. As he walked through the room, he saw that the wallpaper and curtains were still in the same style as when it had been a private family house. And the patio windows still ran down the opposite wall, giving that marvellous view past the cliffs to the sea.

As Joe looked at the bar running down one wall, being attended to by a barman, he was amused to think how Teddy would love to have a permanent bar and barman in his drawing room catering to his every need.

He turned and walked back into the foyer and looked into what had been the dining room next door. This had now been converted into the hotel restaurant and staff were busy preparing the room for the evening meals. Joe resisted the urge to join in and start polishing the silver like he had so many times in there.

"Joe!" he heard from the foyer as Ann called him and he returned to join her and George.

"We're all booked in," said Ann.

"If you follow me I'll show you to your rooms," said the porter.

Joe walked up the staircase with George and Ann as the porter led the way.

On the first floor the porter stopped and opened a door.

"This is your room, sir," he said to George.

Joe followed Geroge in and looked around.

"This was Master Teddy's room," Joe said to George. "Cassie's brother. He was quite a character. I used to bring him breakfast here every morning, which included a half teapot of gin."

"Really?" George laughed at the thought of it.

"We'll meet you down in the lobby in half an hour, George, and we can get some lunch," said Ann who was waiting at the door.

But Joe was going around the room inspecting everything.

"Joe, the porter is waiting!" said Ann, jolting him back to the present day.

"Yes, sorry," said Joe, leaving the room and following them down the corridor where the porter opened another door and led them in.

"Well, this is nice!" said Ann as she looked around the grand room.

"So it should be – it was Lady Dorothy and Mr. Howard's room," said Joe.

"Really? Well, at least it isn't Miss Cassie's room!" said Ann.

"Anything else, sir?" asked the porter.

"No, that's all, thank you," said Joe and he took out his wallet and tipped the porter.

The porter looked down at the tip and smiled disbelievingly. "Thank you, sir!"

"That was a bit overgenerous," commented Ann once the porter had left.

"Of course," said Joe, smiling. "I used to be him, remember. I used to do his job here."

"I doubt anyone tipped you back then like that!"

"I remember each and every guest who came here. The ones who were nice to me and the ones who weren't. It makes all the difference," said Joe.

After lunch Ann and George went to the swimming pool and spa that the stables at the back of the house had been converted into, leaving Joe to explore the building at his leisure. The staff looked at him curiously as he went around inspecting every nook and cranny. He ventured up into the attic rooms that had all been converted into hotel bedrooms. He found his way into his old bedroom and then down the backstairs that led down to the kitchens in the basement. The kitchens had now been converted into a modern hotel kitchen where chefs were busy working away, preparing the food for the evening.

"Can I help you, sir?" asked one of the chefs.

"No, carry on!" said Joe as he looked at the spot where Mrs. Crowther had been in permanent residence drinking her sherry, and the alcove where he and Kathy had played draughts at night.

Then he went up the stairs that led back to the foyer.

The door to the library was closed.

As he paused there the receptionist passed by.

"That's the library, sir," she said. "The morning papers are in there if you want to take a read."

He nodded and walked into the library.

It took his breath away. The room was completely undisturbed from how he remembered it. It was empty and he walked around and stared up at the large black-and-white photograph that was hanging on a wall. It showed the Fullerton family in their heyday. It was taken on the front steps of the house. Lady Dorothy and Howard were standing on the steps, and Cassie and Teddy were seated on the steps in front of them. It was a joyous family photograph and just as he remembered them. Teddy was pulling a face and had his arm around Cassie. Cassie was laughing. Joe wondered what Teddy had said to her to make her laugh so.

A waitress came in and saw him.

"Can I get you tea or coffee, sir?" she asked.

"No, I'm fine, thank you," he said, staring at the photo.

"That's the family who used to live here," said the waitress.

"I know," said Joe, his eyes not leaving the photo.

It was late afternoon by the time Joe had finished exploring

Cliffenden. He walked out of the front door and down to his car. He stepped in, started it up, turned the car around and drove down the avenue. When he reached the gateway he turned and headed towards the Greys' house, Bowden's home.

He knew what he had to do now. He hadn't just come to Cliffenden to revisit his old memories. He had come here on a mission.

As he made the journey, he thought back to the times he had made that journey delivering letters and messages between the two young lovers. And the final letter to Cassie. As he approached the Greys' house, he hoped that house too would be the same as it had been and untouched by time, in much the same way Cliffenden had.

He reached the driveway, drove in and stopped the car.

He got out and looked up at the building. It looked more or less as he remembered. It always had a rundown look to it, and had deteriorated some more. He steadied himself as he approached the front door, preparing himself for meeting Bowden again. Preparing himself for how he would explain what he had done back then. Perhaps Bowden wouldn't be as understanding as Cassie. But this was Joe's chance to put it right. To put Cassie and Bowden back in contact. Let Bowden know that Cassie had not rejected him and had loved him through the years with undiminished feeling. He knocked loudly on the door. When there was no answer he knocked again. There was no car in the drive and Joe wondered if Bowden was down in the village. He wandered over to the drawing-room window and looked in. The room was completely empty – no furniture whatsoever. As Joe looked through the other windows he saw the whole house seemed to be stripped of furniture.

"Can I help you?" came a voice.

Turning around, Joe saw a man in his forties there. "Yes, I'm looking for Bowden Grey. I believe he owns this house, or did?"

"Yes, he did, but he died – must be – three years ago," said the man.

Joe's heart sank. "I see."

"I bought the farm when it came up for sale."

Joe nodded sadly. "He didn't have any children, I take it?"

"No, never married it seems. He was very quiet to be honest, kept himself to himself."

"Yes, that's how remember him."

"You were a friend of his?" asked the man.

"No, I just knew him through a friend. We were talking about him recently and I thought I'd look him up as I was in the area."

As Joe sat into his car he took a final look at the Greys' house. Then he started the engine and drove away.

This was one situation that Joe could not mend, he realised. He had missed his opportunity to explain to Bowden what he had done and Cassie's true feelings for him. Bowden had lived there all those years thinking Cassie had deserted him and, like Cassie, seemed to have never found happiness with anybody else.

It was just as Cassie tried to explain to everybody when she was young: they were meant for each other.

Joe reached the gates of the hotel, turned in and continued up the avenue to Cliffenden.